The Connolly
Affair
"The First Dance"

A Novel
-By-

Brett Scott Ermilio

To my love,
To my everything,
I dedicate this book to you,
With all my loving heart.
I love you, Ashley Dawn Ermilio

ACKNOWLEDGEMENTS

I am thankful for the following people and their support:
First and foremost, my love, my wife. She enables everything that I am.
To my children, Phoenix, Bailey, Tyler and Ella—you are my little dreamers.
To my mother who is my constant editor and greatest supporter. Thank you,
Mom! You are amazing!
To Sue Aeling, the best mother-in-law in the world! Thank you for your help!
To Jacquelyn, an amazing editor who brought *The Connolly Affair* to life.
To Taylor, who gave me great advice and brought it all together.
To Michael Feldman and his constant support.
To Kaitlyn Johnson, thank you for your support.
To my sister, Shere, my rock who is always there.
To Mariah Smith, thank you for your artistic talents.

Introduction
Introduction

He is a good husband—great even. Aiden Scott Connolly: a caring man. I remember the moment I fell in love with him. We worked together in a restaurant. We were younger then. I was working to make a few extra bucks to help pay for college while I was a senior in high school. He was my assistant manager. I knew Aiden from our school days, growing up in the same town. But he was a couple of years older than me.

I remember looking outside and noticing something odd. Jennifer, an older server at the diner, and I saw a disheveled man step off a public bus. He was alone and swinging a red and white cane by his feet. With each sway of the cane, the older man was searching for his next step.

The auburn brittle leaves danced across the street as the old man's cane struck the pavement. We found ourselves watching with curiosity. He staggered and hesitated, causing him to freeze. A look of confusion overtook him.

It was this pause that caused Aiden to react. We didn't even know Aiden was behind us, but he must have seen the same thing we did. The blind man, for whatever reason, seemed lost. As if without a thought, the instincts of the *just* man made him leap into action like a small town superhero.

That's the moment it happened—twenty yards away, without a word, without a touch—I fell in love. I had never been so certain of anything. My kind man. Aiden Connolly, helping a lost blind man find his way. It was such a simple act—a generous one any man could do. But there was a purity to it—a selflessness that made it undeniably human and authentic.

And when Aiden returned from delivering the elderly man to his destination, I looked upon Aiden differently from that day forward. So much wonder and amazement happened in between that day and the day I broke my vows. I had an affair, betraying my Aiden, my loving, kind husband. So many memories, so many sacred treasures to protect.

See, everything new became old. Everything special became ordinary. I'd love to blame him for my betrayals, but mirrors are all too honest. There is no way around it. I made this choice.

But even so, it is hard to fathom happiness, evaporating like a water droplet on a blistering hot day. That's what happened. Our spark is gone; our flame has dulled.

Arguments have sprung up. We have been heading down a dark tunnel with no end in sight. We are no longer who we once were. Things just aren't the same anymore.

And there it was. I had an honest and kind husband. I had two amazing children. I was a partner at my law firm. And in a single moment, I risked it all.

One

One

"Nicki…Nicki…are you awake?"

I find myself daydreaming at work more and more. I always used to make fun of romance novels. I had friends who swore by them and each time they brought it up, I'd shoot them down.

"They're smut—they're ridiculous," I'd joke and make fun of all my best friends. Now, I find myself engaged in book after book, thirsting for the sex and intrigue like a carnal college boy. Is it the randomness of the encounters? The desire to be bad? The feeling of doing something against the grain for once in my life? I don't know. But I'm in! I love them now. I'm a fan—a *big* fan. Nicki Connolly buys the best and worst of romance novels and will do so until the end of time.

But right now, the echoes of my name are drawing me back from the strapping Kentucky farm boy that Veronica Palsey had just met. She was leading the strapping young man to the barn at night just as I ran into my meeting. Certainly, Veronica was about to be had by the young farm hand—a tall brooding man much younger than her. Before I could even read the words on the page, as I walked into my meeting, I could hear the moans of ecstasy. I could feel his rough hands running along my arms, slowly undressing me. The anticipation of reading this next chapter has my normally sharp mind drifting into the abyss of sex and romance.

"So…?" Charles Rapture, the distinguished head partner at the law firm (in which I am privileged enough to sit in the inner circle of), poses. His voice carries a slight strain and an underlying annoyance; the impatience of a powerful man who has little nerves for delays.

"I was just thinking." I collect myself and begin, attempting to save face for zoning out like a school girl in math class. "In order for us to maximize the exposure in the Ramsey Class Action, we should find as many experts the defendants have used in the past and steal them away. There's an intriguing man by the name of Schecter I think could be of value."

With my one sweeping thought, I killed it. I went from wishing I was the random traveler in the heartland being taken by a young man in one singular, random, extraordinary sex act, to pulling out my newest and best legal tactic for my billion-dollar lawsuit. Heading a lawsuit for my firm of such magnitude squarely puts my name and reputation under the microscope. There is little tolerance for a woman to be swimming in the depths of the *man ocean* and daydream even for the slightest moment. I have to be on my game twenty-four-seven. But there is a poetry to my momentary lapse. I dreamt of the farm boy and, at the same time, drew rave reviews at my meeting. The contradiction was priceless.

"Well done. What sort of budget are we talking about?" James Bonner quizzes.

It's no surprise. He pulls in half a million a year at minimum and drives a seven-year-old Cadillac. I don't have anything against Cadys or against being frugal, for the matter. But, when I became the first partner at the firm of Rapture and Myers, I was told to ditch my beautiful, little, red Jetta and go more *presentable*. Apparently, a red Jetta represented some sort of weakness. It screamed vagina to them. But a seven-year-old beat-up Cadillac, somehow, some way, represented a strong, sturdy penis. I'll never get men and their cars. But, either way, I drive an Excursion now, so I guess I have the biggest dick of all the partners, not that I'm bragging. It does double as a soccer mom transport and shuttling us around, so everything worked out in the end.

"I can swing some of the travel budget in, since we no longer have to depose Dr. Waltrop in Canada," I run off with certainty, offering my Plan B.

"Why is that?" Charles asks with curiosity.

"He's dead," Bob Myers states with delight. Bob is a shark. He is the man you never want to rear-end; the man a policeman will never write a ticket for. Bob is a *made* man in this world. He is a traveler with many connections and no limitations. Although he's nearly sixty-five, Robert Franklin Myers has never lived harder or better. Young women, amazing vacations, and celebrity friends—he literally is the Hugh Hefner of the legal field. If I were a man, I'd probably want to be Bob Myers.

"Do I need to express the importance of this case?" Charles Rapture levels out to me. Of course, he didn't need to. I am a partner. And if this were James Bonner's case or Lincoln Thomas, the other partner, nobody would emphasize the importance. Lincoln is the first African-American partner at the firm. He doesn't say much at the meetings, but when he does, it usually means something. I like Lincoln. He is my favorite of the inner circle at Rapture and Myers.

"I do and I will follow through," I reply with the utmost confidence. My voice doesn't waver, but in my mind, I know there is much at play and even more I do not control in the Ramsey case. I act like I've been sitting at the grown-ups table all my life when, in reality, I just got my promotion to partner a year ago. It's almost completely in part because I landed the Ramsey Case. The case is worth tens of millions, if not more, and the publicity could multiply our exposure ten-fold. There are many lawyers who have worked as hard and won as many cases. Some have been with the company longer and achieved more prominence. But my one big case dwarfs their many logged hours. This case is a monster. It's a career-maker or breaker. I'm one step away from having everything I've ever wanted at a law firm; all the years I've been in to prepare for this moment. But in a flash, it could all be taken away. How I do love the rush of it all, though. The pressure at times is unpalatable. It's fantastic.

We wrap up the partner's meeting with some more details and I walk the halls back to my beautiful corner office. The view is to die for. Overlooking West Los Angeles and getting a glimpse of the ocean on a clear day is simply awesome. It's breathtaking and always seems to cool my senses. It's my zen.

Moments after I enter my office, Angela pounces. My trusted assistant, who goes to great lengths to maintain my sanity, is always a sight for sore eyes. I'd be completely lost without her.

"You have lunch with Aiden, today," Angela lists off to remind me.

Once upon a time, centuries ago, lunch with my nearly perfect husband, Aiden, alone, would have been such a treat. My level of excitement would have been epic. Now the blood barely shifts with the mention of his name. I find myself indifferent at times.

"Thank you, Angela." I settle myself and catch a glimpse of my current guilty pleasure—my one escape from reality—my romance novel. Angela disappears out of the room just as quickly as she had snuck in. And just as I'm about to reach for my book, there's a soft knock at my office door.

Lincoln is standing at my doorway.

"Yes, Lincoln," I welcome him and abandon my forbidden novel for a moment.

A visit from Lincoln isn't unheard of. He is the only partner I have any kind of personal connection with. Maybe it's a minority thing—a woman in a man's game and he's a black man in a white collar world. Either way, he's a very good man and my sounding board.

"Have a moment?" he asks.

Really, I don't. I'm going to run late to my monthly lunch date with Aiden. But for Lincoln, I'll make the time. He is a wealth of knowledge and always delivers gems.

"Yes, of course, Link. Come in."

Lincoln makes his way into the office and we settle down on my two leather sofa chairs.

"Anything to drink?" I offer, eluding to my minibar. I'm not a frequenter of alcohol in the afternoon, but all partners get top-end offices. No expense spared with fine oak furnishings, leather chairs, a glass minibar, and antique Tiffany lamps that provide gentle but beautiful lighting.

We grab a seat and I flip on the lamp, allowing the natural light from my large floor-to-ceiling windows to act as a subtle compliment to this conversation.

"I like you, Connolly," Lincoln begins.

I feel as though this conversation is a warning—right away, making me nervous. I've been in this office less than a year and I already get the feeling I should keep some moving boxes in the closet

"This case is what will solidify you to the partners or will turn them away. I know them. They like wins. This is your first big at-bat in the spotlight. How you handle this could dictate your future with the company." Lincoln gets right to the point. I'd expect nothing less from him and appreciate the candor.

"I understand," I reply. But really, I don't. How could they promote me to partner and then just get rid of me? Or demote me over one case?

"They wanted the Ramsey Class Action. That is, in part, how you were promoted. They knew you were talking to Freese and Jones. And they didn't want to risk losing the Ramsey endgame. I believe you are deserving of your partnership: I brought you to the table long ago. But know your future here is tied to this case. All the eyes in the room will be on you."

And there it was. Lincoln laid out the terms of my case, a case that's gone on for nearly two years now. But with trial quickly approaching in the spring, everything is coming to a head. Clearly, my future is dependent on this case whether it is fair or not.

Lincoln left me in the dust with that conversation, but I had to hear it. I would rather know what I'm up against than guess. That is why I like Lincoln so much. He tells me how it is.

I race in my Excursion to my lunch date. Surprisingly, I show up on time. I'm first to the table. Somehow, someway, I beat Aiden there. Alone at the quaint table for two, I pull out my guilty pleasure. Sipping water, I fall right back to where I left off earlier.

Veronica Palsey slowly makes her way to the barn. The moonlight provides enough light to guide her steps, each one made with the knowledge that something unknown waits for her. Her hair glimmers in the moonlight. A few steps from the mouth of the barn, Veronica freezes. Her conscious attempts to communicate with her during this momentary pause. She has a life—a different kind of life. "What should I do? What am I doing?" *Veronica can't get away from her own Jimminey Crickett. And then it happens. She steps forward, a small step at first, then another. Like a snowball rolling downhill, Veronica's steps broaden and she crosses the threshold into the barn. A single lamp has been lit, illuminating the young farm boy standing there. He has a glimmer of a smile, a twinkle in his eye. He is gorgeous and any doubts are immediately lifted upon her seeing his face.*

"Nicki." Aiden's voice snaps me out of the barn and I quickly glance up and slam the book shut.

"Yes, dear."

I stand up and we kiss. He smiles at me, his eyes flashing down at my guilty pleasure.

"It makes the time go by faster," I offer, making an excuse.

He smirks and nods, giving me my privacy. It's easier for him to just let me go on with the books then potentially ask if there may be a reason why I've been so drawn to reading them.

"How are things?" My husband asks, as if he's barely seen me all week. It's an interesting way to begin a conversation with the person you sleep next to every night. That is what we have become in many ways—two ships passing in the night. We share a moment or two and then off and away we go to our own manifests.

"Good. Intense. Work is...well, you know," I elude, knowing my husband doesn't want to hear the daily grind at the law office. He is a contractor. A man who built his own company and, when I stayed home with the girls, made us a nice living. Now, with my career taking leaps and bounds, he has reduced his work load and has become a casual contractor. He oversees jobs and occasionally does some hands-on work. More than not, he tends to the daily challenges of our two daughters. God bless him for that. They can both be a handful; the best and worst of what Mother Nature has to offer. But, I love my two little bugs.

"Yeah. I hear ya," is the only response Aiden can give. He has become bored of my work speak and I barely got through the first sentence. It's partially my fault. I really didn't give him a good opening line. But then again, what would be the point. He has no interest in it anyway.

Our lunch continues as it began. Two ships passing by. Then, it is over.

I arrive back at the office to a lot of excitement. There is a strange buzz circling around—an energy that is infecting the halls of the normally docile office to the point of drawing me over into the conference room. The first look I get is from Lincoln and it is full of concern. It's a strange glare, considering the positive energy circling all around.

Bob, Charles, and James are all hovering over someone—something. As they applaud and step back, I see with my own eyes their new toy. Taylor Diamond. Taylor is an incredibly aggressive young attorney with a long list of clients and an even longer list of successes. He looks like he just fell out of a Yale fraternity magazine; the ideal stunner of a man. His face maintains the perfect jaw structure, his blue eyes and perfect wavy, black hair only further compliment his broad shoulders and, near perfect, six-foot physique. *Oh, my God. He's incredible.* For a moment, I forget that I am a partner in my law firm and not a school girl, staring at the shockingly handsome, cool senior at Liberty High.

Taylor slowly stands up, his body and height safely rising above and encompassing my own shadow. He even smiles like an all-star. It's all too much and I fall victim again, disappearing into his blue eyes. I quickly recover as his hand was left extended for a good three seconds before my brown eyes could even recognize his hand existed.

"Oh, sorry," I reply, shaking it. I awkwardly clasp my other hand on top of his as if I were an eighty-year-old man, consoling a youngster. *What the hell is wrong with you, Nicki? Pull it together!*

"Nice to meet you. I'm Taylor Diamond." He smiles and seems kind. He isn't cocky. "I've actually heard a lot about you, Nicki. You're an amazing attorney. I'm very excited to be here," Taylor's words roll of his tongue with ease and are like a secret potion, drawing me further and further into everything that is him.

"I didn't know we were bringing anyone on board." I return to reality and realize that the man-club just made a decision without even conferring with me. *Wow.* The beautiful male-legal-model just lit a fire under me, and I turn my focus from his perfect, tight, round ass to the fact that I may be out on my, above average, rear if my case goes the wrong way. Could Mr. Diamond potentially be my replacement? It's not like the Yankees are going to sign a big, free agent to just let him sit on the bench. You sign a big name because you want them to be a primetime player. Now I was staring at the man who could potentially replace me, and what is worse, he is incredibly handsome and nice. Shit. I'm totally screwed.

Now I know why Lincoln came to me. Now I know why he gave me *the look* when I entered the conference room. With Taylor's contract signed—the ink dried—I was now going to have to up my game. If my class action lawsuit didn't carry a massive amount of weight before, it sure did now. Things couldn't be worse.

"Nicki, we are going to have Taylor jump on the Ramsey case with you. He is going to sit second chair and I think you will find he is going to be a huge asset," Charles declares.

"You're getting an ace in the hole!" Bob chimes in.

Double-shit. I'm royally screwed.

Taylor turns and stares right at me. I'm not sure if I am a small fish in the pond and he is the giant awesome looking shark that is just about to devour me, or if I am just crazy paranoid. Either way—game on.

Two

I am moments from finishing packing up. It's 6:15pm and I'm already late. The time flashes over and over again in my mind as a constant taunt. My husband will have words for me. I feel as though I'm letting my daughters down the most, though. Lacy and Ariel are the innocent bystanders to my hustle and bustle life. I am moments from leaving—seconds. I place my guilty pleasure inside my satchel. I throw my light black suit jacket over my body. I shut my most favorite auburn colored Tiffany lamp off; the red, brown, green, and yellow glass look like plates taken off the ceiling of a cathedral. It is officially the last step in me leaving. Darkness has now fully encompassed my office with the exception of the light from the Bank of America sign next door, penetrating my floor-to-ceiling windows. And if this was it . . . if this was the only reason I was late, I could hold my head up high, and look my husband directly into his eyes.

I go to leave when suddenly, I look up, and he appears. Taylor Diamond. He is leaning against my door frame. I'm not sure how long he has been standing there, a second . . . two perhaps—maybe thirty. He has a strange glow about him. His cheeks are ever so slightly raised, giving the impression of a smile. But I can't tell if he is happy or has a look of knowing something I don't know. Maybe he was promised my office if I fail and is laying out his new redecorating plans in his mind. This sort of smile is driving me mad. It doesn't help that his smirk, if that's what it is, is attached to this face and head of hair. Jesus, he probably will never lose one strand for the rest of his life. It is a perfect thick tone. How did this movie star end up in my doorway?

For a moment or two, I look back at him. The two of us share an electric stare. Our eyes connect. The light from outside perfectly streams across his face as if he *is* the movie star in the room and this was *his* staring scene. The light dances off his perfect face and beautiful blue eyes. *Dammit, those eyes!*

"I wanted to catch you before you left," the soft spoken Taylor sparks the start of a conversation. I have no idea which direction it may go.

Thank God he spoke first, I was losing my shit.

"Okay," I reply. "You caught me." The words fumble out of my mouth as if I was playing coy in a romance novel of my own. I'm going to need a copyeditor in my brain before I speak to Mr. Diamond from here on out.

"I am fond of your skills. You have done great corporate law work for quite some time," Taylor begins.

Compliments. What does he want? I think to myself.

"Ya know, we met once before," Taylor drops a bombshell on me.

When?! Where?! I rack my brain for answers. I know I would have remembered his face. At worst, I would have remembered his eyes. Jesus. Those eyes cut through all my walls as if they never existed. He is gorgeous— probably kills in jury trials, too.

Taylor waits and just stares at me. This conversation isn't going as well as I would have hoped for.

"I was hoping I could catch you for a few minutes and you could go over the Ramsey Class Action."

Taylor wanted some late night coaching. Veronica Palsey would definitely look at this situation far differently than Nicki Connolly. Here I stand, a thirty-nine-year-old mother of two, staring into the eyes of a thirty-four-year-old heartthrob. He wants to "study"—to stay late after school. The way he is looking at me, his gaze, says anything other than work, but I'm not exactly sure. I don't think I've ever felt so incompetent. I have always been able to read people. It is a gift that helps me greatly when I depose a witness and appear before a jury. I am *always* on my game, focused. *Seriously, does the light from outside have to shine directly on his face and highlight his incredible, sea-blue eyes?!*

"I don't think now is the best time," I finally say something sensible.

"Do you have somewhere else to be?" Taylor pokes. Maybe he doesn't know I have a family. Maybe he wants to test my commitment to my job. Perhaps he is a mole placed by Charles, who lacks confidence in the firm's biggest case in over a decade. I can't read this dude and it's absolutely killing me right now.

"I am late," is all I say. *Dammit!* I didn't even mention my kids . . . my husband. He totally left the door open and I backed away. Why?

"All right, all right," he kindly replies. "I can walk you down to your car. I'm going to head out also," Taylor offers. His words are sincere. It's totally annoying how sincere he is. I wish he was cocky. I wish he was crude or rude. I don't like how much awesomeness he exudes all at once. *Seriously, give me something to hang my hat on here.* Give me a reason not to want to constantly stare at your face. And that's nothing compared to his body, but I'm not even going to start in on that.

"Thanks," is all I say. I make the slow steps toward him. I feel like I'm walking up to the stage of the Academy Awards. Each one of my steps, being judged by someone. I don't think my feet have ever felt heavier, at least not since I took my high-speed Zumba class right after an insane cardio-trampoline class. That was truly a long three days of recovery. And up until that day, my feet have never felt so heavy, or as worthless as they do now.

"You all right?" Taylor asks with a half-cocked smile.

He notices me walking like the Tin Man and probably thinks I have something shoved up my rear. *Pull it together, Nick! Pull it together!* I remind myself again and again, and then slowly loosen up my strides and ease my steps.

"I'm fine. Thank you. I had a crazy palates class yesterday," is the only excuse I can muster. I haven't done palates in weeks—maybe months. I don't remember anymore. The days have melted into one another and the weeks have followed. Time, which used to have so much meaning to me as a child, now seems to be an endless cycle of stuff that repeats and repeats like *Groundhog Day.*

We walk, side by side, over to the elevator. There isn't a word spoken as we make our way down the hall. I feel his eyes glance over at me. I'm not sure of the look on his face because I cannot bring myself to do the same. I feel as if I catch his prefect blues, it could lead me down a tragic road I'm not ready to head. *Stay focused, Nick! Don't fall down.* Suddenly, I'm practicing how to walk properly. I don't think I have ever had so much focus on taking steps—*right then left, right then left.*

We both make it to the elevator and I turn right into him. We slightly bump into one another, my clumsiness naturally surfacing at the worst of times.

"Sorry," I counter my error.

"It's fine," Taylor once again lets me off the hook.

I take my elevator card out and swipe it. The doors close and the excruciating two minutes begin. I look up, to the side, bite my lip, anything and everything to push time forward. But it does little to help. Time has virtually stopped."Aren't you curious?" Taylor drops this loaded question. I am once again thrown back on my mental heels. *What did he mean by that?*

"What's that?" I reply with curiosity. I'm drawn in by Taylor in a way I have not felt in some time. Standing in the elevator, his perfect smell infiltrates my nasal cavity.

Damn it, he even smells amazing. Isimiaki, perhaps? A sweet scent, but he's such a man, he pulls it off with ease. He's turned this grown woman into a teenager again. The butterflies rage inside me, but I think it best not to acknowledge they exist. At least, for now.

"The conference in Chicago," Taylor illuminates the mystery. "Seven years ago. It wasn't a huge gathering, but it was a long seminar."

"Corporate law." I smile, knowing exactly what he is talking about. The memory shoots back to me, a borderline horrifying experience from my past. It wasn't scary horrifying, just embarrassing horrifying.

"That's right. Corporate law and the ever-changing landscape occurring around the world. It was priceless and inspiring," he jabs.

"I introduced the key note speaker as a man." I chuckle, the memory engrained in my brain forever.

"Yes, you did." He smiles with great amusement.

"I did have a good speech though," I poke back.

"Yes, you did." Taylor tilts his head and grins, his eyes and smile empowering me. He is looking at me as if I inspired him. I feel as though he just injected me with confidence and got my adrenaline flowing with his one half-cocked smile. We are stuck in a trance, engaged in an unbreakable moment.

Thank goodness for the elevator doors. Their screeching breaks our trance and I smile inside, stepping out of the elevator.

"It was nice to meet you, Mr. Diamond," I state with professional sincerity.

"Likewise, Mrs. Connolly," he says with perfection.

We part as we exit the elevator. *Don't look back, Nicki. Don't look back.* I can tell myself a million times, but I feel like a child staring at a candy bowl. Of course, they aren't allowed to reach for candy, but they do. And just as the child reaches for candy, I look back. Taylor is walking away, heading over to a classic Mercedes Roadster. What a crazy coincidence. The car my father loved more than life itself, a refurbished perfect beauty, sitting right in the parking garage where I work. Taylor smoothly steps into his classic convertible—a cherry one at that—a sight to behold for any car lover. I certainly am not one of them, but I do have an appreciation for this one in particular. It has perfectly polished chrome and white trimmed hubcaps with red lining, which could make any girl weak in the knees. This car is beautiful.

I reach to open my gas guzzler and, the door smacks me right in my lip, causing my satchel to fly off my arm on to the ground. After the punch from my metal door, I peek up to make sure I wasn't spotted being a total idiot. Taylor's smooth ride is long gone, humming out of the garage. Me, I'm the moron left with a fat lip. I reach down, pick up my bag, and lick my new wound, a split bloody lip. Punishment from the marriage Gods above, perhaps? A warning of sorts? I believe in these things, premonitions, fate—all of it. I am a Scorpio, so my passion for life is constant and driving. Right now, my passion is starting to drive me insane.

Taylor Diamond. The name washes through my mind over and over again. His smile. His scent. His way. It's all so intoxicating. I drive in the darkness, unaware of the world around me. It's as if I'm on autopilot, the car somehow driving itself home as I ponder carnal thought after thought about a man I barely know, a man who I met just a few hours before under unexpected circumstances. *It's a trap*, I tell myself. I must override my loins and hope good sense wins out. This man could be my replacement at some point. And with that, a new idea sparks my mind.

I arrive at home, late. I know what is coming, the look of disappointment from my loving husband. After all, his lone goal is just to have me present, something I have failed miserably at recently. During my star-struck year of legal practice, time has bent into a meaning I never knew possible. I have risen to the top—the cream of the crop— and all my hard work is paying off. My ambition has driven me through two births and a long career delay. And still . . . I have risen. I can't help but find conflict between my accomplishments and my guilt for not being home more for my family. It isn't fair. Why are women always expected to be home? I am ambitious. My husband should find that quality attractive. At this point, I'd settle for Aiden to find it accepting.

"Hello!" I shout with glee as I open the door, hoping to start things off right this evening.

Nothing. The dining room is a ghost town. Instead of a tumbleweed rolling by, I could swear I see a small lint ball tumble into the dark corner of the room. Atop the dining room table, awaiting me is a box of cold pizza. Aiden must have taken the easy way out tonight with the girls. Makes sense, since Lacy and Ariel had soccer practices today.

The pizza box is lifted up just slightly so I can see there a few slices left for me. The plates have been cleared, with one single paper plate remaining. Three drink glasses are spread about the table, all empty. Three. Just three. It's a stark reminder that the fourth person was absent, as if they didn't even exist. That would be me.

"Hello?" I shout to the top of our two-story home.

"Up here, Mom!" the giggling collective voices of Lacy and Ariel shout down.

I make my way upstairs and hear the constant chorus of my two young girls laughing. They sound as if they are having the time of their lives. I can see their faces in my mind before I even get to their bedroom. I know that laughter well, the uncontrollable giggling. You can't help but smile yourself when you hear it. I miss this. I don't get this as much anymore.

I arrive at my bedroom and there they are, my husband playing Twister with our two girls. They are all in contorted, hilarious positions and I can't resist a smile myself.

"Hey, babe," Aiden greets me causally and kindly. Aiden isn't the most flexible of men. He is an old school, blue collar man. He played football in high school, once upon a time. I saw him as a senior, when I cheered for him. I was a sophomore at the time. Six feet one inch, strong, fairly tone with a little belly, skin tanned from the sun's rays and dirty-blond hair. His eyes are light brown; a man who would blend into a crowd, and happily at that.

Lacy spins and tries to move, but when she does, my whole intertwined family comes crashing down to the ground with an eruption of insane joy and laughter.

Aiden relents, gets up, and kisses me on the cheek. "How was your day?" he asks. We met for lunch but it was so *blah*. And now he asks the general textbook question?

"Okay," I reply with little to add. What could I add? If I told him a total hottie just entered my life, and that I've literally been fixated on him about every minute for the last six hours, the conversation would probably head into a different direction. So *okay* works a heck of a lot better in this situation. It's annoying that I'm even thinking about Taylor Diamond at this point. He may be pining for my job as we speak. But, something about him has me hooked. I wish I could put my finger on it. I don't get this way about random men. I'm not that kind of girl. But there is *something.*

"Your lip," he points out.

Yes, my lip, I think to myself. The same lip you should have seen when I first entered the room. The one you didn't kiss. Is it too much for a wife to want her husband to kiss her *hello* and *goodbye* on the lips? I got a cheek peck as if we were old friends saying *howdy.* This isn't the 1950s. I'm not Joan Clever. Maybe my mental rant is uncalled for. Maybe my good husband does enough. And maybe it's my issues—not his. But I want more from him. Inside, I'm begging him to give me more. I want some passion—any passion. We have love—mutual love and appreciation for one another as human beings. But I want to feel with him as I feel when I read about Veronica Palsey.

After we put our two darling children to bed, I take a nice warm shower. The days usually run off me in here. The water purifies my body and recalibrates my mind for the next day ahead. But, not tonight. A smile haunts me; his deep blue eyes and half-cocked smile seeps through my soul and penetrates the highest walls I possess.

I towel off and place my robe on. After a quick floss and the brushing of my teeth, I enter our bedroom where my husband awaits in just his boxers. I feel relaxed but am quickly ambushed with a rogue wave of flatulence. *Ugh. Marriage.* I shake it off and move on. The TV is on, and since it's been three weeks since we had sex, there is a fifty-fifty chance I may get some. I had shaved my legs and groomed my vag, just in case.

As I get into bed, Aiden smiles. I know that sinister grin. He is staring at me. With my chest still glistening from my shower and the tops of my breasts bustling out of my robe, my husband is hooked like a hapless fish in a lake. Aiden turns the light off by the bed and mutes the television. He moves in for the kill. A kiss and a handful of my right breast. It's always my right breast first because it's slightly bigger than the left. Thus begins the playbook my husband has mentally put together on how to give Nicki Connolly an orgasm.

See, my husband knows my spots. He has paid attention to what works and what doesn't over the years. He is an A+ student in bed. He knows how to get me to the BIG "O". It's not that he isn't good. It's just the same playbook again and again. That is where he fails. He gets a *D* for originality, like an amateur cook following to the strictest of recipes. Once in a while he adds a little salt, (finger bang), or a little pepper, (doggie style), but generally, he sticks to the same routine.

THE PLAYBOOK TO NICKI'S BIG "O"

Step 1: Begin with breast examination. *This is more for him than me, but I'm game if done right.*
Step 2: Engage in kissing—slow at first—then passionate. This includes sucking on my ear lobes (not inside, wet willy style though). This makes me crazy and he knows it.
Step 3: Here's where Aiden can go wild card on me. Once a month, he fingers me. It must be a mood thing or a hand cramping issue. He does work with tools all day being in construction, so maybe his fingers are tired. But either way, missionary is soon to follow.
Step 4: With Missionary engaged, he goes through a various run of speed drills and build-ups. It's like he's an athlete practicing stamina. But it works for me most of the time.

> A) A subsection to Step 4 is that we continue kissing and engage in some petting during the missionary step.

Step 5: Once exhausted or depleted, Aiden pulls me on top, like a boat capsizing over. Okay, now it's my turn to go to work.
Step 6: Tuned up and ready to go, I try to find my rhythm on the horse . . . *so to speak.* Me on top can be pretty interesting. Using a series of buttons on my body, like a pilot guiding a plane, Aiden hits my spots at different times. He starts at the small of my back to rev my engine up. Some pressing near my tail bone really gets me rolling. His hands move to my breasts again; a second examination. Then to my inner thighs for a blast off, and the Big "O" is usually achieved. He is good at holding out until I finish; a man that always holds the door open for me.

Step 7: The afterglow and a mental high-five. Operation Joint Orgasms: Successful.

End of Playbook.

Three

Aiden fades to the sheep and I can't quite follow yet. Time for a night cap and some cold pizza. I use a glass of chardonnay to cool my jets and a thought strikes me—my contract. What's my exposure at my firm if something goes wrong? Could I be replaced just like *that*? What exactly is in my partnership agreement? Of course I went through it as well as my own attorney, but I can't help the ill feeling I'm having. A small byline in the contract suddenly comes to mind; a piece of information that could ruffle my feathers further. I head to the office downstairs and go through my file cabinet. I pull out my contract and bore into it. As I move on to my second glass of wine, I come across a clause at the end.

If the two managing partners, Charles Rapture and William Myers, decide in the first twenty-four months of Partnership that the newly appointed Partner has failed to live up to the standards by which a Partner is judged, as defined in Appendix 12A, then the managing partners have the right to demote or terminate newly appointed partner at their own discretion.

Holy shit. Nice miss, Nicki. Obviously, the clause is performance related. I know for a fact that my performance will always be on par, but with this huge case, I can't help the paranoia seeping in. *I have to find out more about Taylor!* Glass number three and I'm starting to head toward super tipsy. A Google search is in order.

I head to our study where my husband and I frequent, when we need to disappear into our work. He has the left side of the room and the right side is mine. Really, we are starting to overflow in the house and probably will need a second study in the future, but with my husband's business pulling back, the workload seems to be balancing more in my direction.

I fire up my laptop. I am going to creep like crazy on Taylor and find out whatever the Web has to offer! Facebook—bring it on. Twitter—where you at Mr. Diamond? Heck, I'll even look way back to Myspace if I have to! Either way, I'm finding something out on this guy right now. Because nothing goes better with being mildly drunk from Chardonnay than stalking a dude I totally want to ride. *Shit.* I didn't mean that. I sort of didn't. *Focus, Nicki!!!*

Google search engaged!

Holy Crap! There's a lot of info on this guy and his father. **Wealthy Trust Fund Kid Makes Good.** Another headline reads: **Diamond Industries Continues to Flourish.** *Jesus,* he's loaded. That certainly explains the mint condition, classic Roadster he's driving. And shit, I'd have a million dollar smile too if I was worth millions!

I dive into an article. I scan with my blurry chardonnay-filled goggles. Father passed away not too long ago. Looks like a great childhood. Parents taught him the realities of life; lots of charity work, etcetera. Became a public defender. Represented those in need. *Is this guy a saint or a lawyer?* Family is the most important thing in life.

He reads like an angel. What am I up against here? He's younger, more successful, wealthy, traveled, well-accomplished, strong family name, and looks like a Greek god. And here I am, a thirty-something late-bloomer, entrenched in a man's club. *Shit, I'm screwed.*

It's not even a fair fight. And now he's handcuffing my case. Time to shut it *OFF!* I "x" out the screen. If I research him anymore, I'm going to visit my two best friends: Ben and Jerry. Oh, man, this is gonna be hard. I'm a girl from the outskirts of Barstow, California. He was born with a silver spoon in his mouth. At best, my spoon was wooden when I was born, and probably broken at that. I've been called white trash. Yes, it was long ago, and a far cry from the attorney I've become, the partner I am, but I know who I am. I'm regular. Not chosen, like him. He seems like royalty and I'm *bust-my-ass* regular. I love a good fight, but right now, I'm fighting to just stay awake. My eyes are shutting down the show for the day. Tonight's battle is done. I cave, knowing I will need to regroup and strategize tomorrow. Good night, world.

———————

The alarm buzzes. *Oh, sweet Chardonnay.* My head is killing me, but I have to work up the strength and a brave face. I drag myself to the bathroom mirror.

Holy shit, I look like crap. With a quick wash of my hair, brush of my teeth, I grab my make-up and head downstairs in my robe. I feed the kids cereal and make sure they have everything they need for the day. Next, I apply my make-up as they finish up. I hug them as they run out the door and make sure to kiss Aiden *on the lips* before wishing them all a good day. Now it's my turn. I quickly get dressed, grab my things, and head out the door, as well.

In the car, on the way to work, I drink some coffee and drive through the autumn breeze. *How beautiful.* It's an unseasonably cold fall and the California trees are responding; rare SoCal beauty as the leaves turn auburn. Aiden and I moved to Thousand Oaks years ago and bought our first house. It's a wonderful town, and the trees are only reminding me that we made a great decision planting our roots here.

I reach the office and Taylor Diamond's affect is obvious. Every secretary on our two floors is doing a flyby on Taylor's office. A few freshly baked goods even made their way onto his desk. They all seem to be pinning for his assistant gig, a position yet to be filled. Girl after girl smiles and shoots looks at Taylor as if he were a 24 karat diamond himself. *Pun intended.*

I try to bury myself in my case files. Then, just as I start to focus, Charles appears at my office door. Taylor last night and Charles today. Where the heck is my fantastic assistant, Angela? My office door has suddenly become as loose as a swinging one in an old West saloon.

"How is the Ramsey case going?" Charles strangely begins. He is not a man to mince words or waste time, but I feel as though he is fishing. My paranoia continues to grow.

"We've got our ducks in a row. Maybe just a deposition or two more, and a few of the experts that the Harper and Penn Firm have used before. Just like I mentioned before," I clearly lay it out to him. I've got little to explain, but this is his company. I just want room to breathe and work. And right now, Charles is standing a little too close for my toes liking.

"Yes, the law offices of Harper and Penn. A mighty strong firm. Their pockets are much deeper than ours. Big clients…billion-dollar clients at that. It would be a big win for us," Charles crows to me as if I didn't already know all of this. *I've been at this for years now, Charlie. You don't think I know who and what Harper and Penn is all about?*

"It *will be* a big win, sir. They made people sick, and they will pay. I've been on this case for over four years, when we started with just one client. Two court delays and a ton of filings and depositions. I've lived this. I'm on it No stone unturned. I'm near the goal line and I'm going into the end zone standing," I fire off in man-speak. I am confident. I know we have a great case. *It's the biggest case of my life, for more reasons than you know, Charles Rutledge.*

"Listen, I want to make something clear—," Charles begins in, what is destined to be, a sentence I'm not going to like hear to its end.

"—we love your talent, Nicki. We've supported it. And we do have faith in you . . . ," *Just not enough to brief me on the Diamond hire.*

"When you've asked for more funds to cover research and depositions, we have been there to do so," Charles continues.

I subtly nod, agreeing with Charles. His speech is odd, almost ill-timed. Where is he going with this and why?

"We have discussed all options of this case with you…and without you." *Bam!* That one hurt. *Without.* What the fuck?

"The firm is interested in a big settlement. We do not want a protracted trial which will certainly lead to a win for us and then a subsequent appeal. It all becomes quite messy. Make sure this case is settled. That is *the* goal of this firm. That is the strategy we will employ," Charles makes the declaration, and I am floored in shock.

Huh! Did he just tell me what to do with my case without any input from me?

"All right." Charles rises to his feet, seemingly satisfied. I must have accidentally been nodding still, because he seems to think I'm perfectly okay with his newly formed edict. He turns and then pauses, glancing back at me for some reassurance. My stark silence is probably making him second guess my position on the matter.

"Are we on the same page?" he speaks to me not as a partner, but as a dictator declares to a weak general.

Screw off, dickhole, is what I want to tell him. My lips quiver with shock and dismay, both fighting to blurt out some anger-driven response. I feel like going on a tirade and asking who he thinks he is. I can definitely take my case elsewhere, but there are vested interests that go beyond this firm, and switching horses at this stage is impossible. The Ramsay suit isn't just with me; it's with the firm as well. And we are *way* too deep in to screw anything up. There are literally a thousand reasons for me to be pissed off right now, but until I can fully wrap my head around what is happening around me, I concede.

"Sure," the subservient answer of a *good girl* slips out of my fuming lips. I hate myself right now for eating shit on this.

"Good." The cocky, old, legal vet smiles and glides toward my office door.

I am glad his back is to me because I can't help but fire daggers out of my eyes at this little snow job he just pulled off.

"Oh." Charles pauses at my doorway. "And we are gearing up for quite the Christmas party this year!" he announces with delight.

It's the middle of October, buddy—chill out! I shout inwardly. I fight back the anger and display my worst fake smile. It's the same smile I give my mother-in-law, Helen, when she criticizes my Thanksgiving cooking.

He finally leaves and I shake my head in disbelief. *Dammit! Dammit!* I'm so annoyed. *Grrrr.* What the heck is happening in this place right now? I feel as though I'm in a bad dream. First, there is the new super-hot guy that may be taking my job. Then, these crazy case demands and Lincoln's cryptic warning all slamming into each other. As I ponder all forty thoughts at once, my trusted assistant, Angela, finally appears. She is carrying two cups of Starbucks coffee which I sorely need one of *immediately.* Aiden gets crappy, cheap coffee that tastes like dirt and I can't stand it. I barely drank any on the way in.

"Welcome back!" I sarcastically blurt out as if I were a volcano about to explode.

Angela freezes, immediately recognizing my a-hole tone. She clearly has no idea what she is walking into.

"Sorry. What's up?" I drop down from a 9 to a 3 as she places my beautiful, newborn Starbucks baby into my hands.

"Mr. Diamond will be ready for you in conference room B in five minutes," Angela states and then nearly gasps with pent up excitement. She clearly is taken by the new hot mystery man.

"Oh, will he?" I fire back, raising my right eyebrow. Everyone seems to be leading me around like I'm some sort of puppy in this office. I'm quite certain I've earned more respect than this.

"Yeah," Angela once again seems to recognize my strange tone and treads on egg shells. "I think he said he was sorry for being late. He made it sound like you set it up," Angela is careful with her wording and takes a small step back. I could swear she is searching the room with her eyes for cameras. Definitely my fault. She must think menopause is right around the corner for me.

"I'm sorry. That's right. I had forgotten," I try to recover. Poor Angela. She is my rock in the office. I always try to make sure I don't direct my anger upon the one who takes care of me the most. I decide to change my tune and get a little giddy as my first sips of coffee immediately help me find my inner chi.

"What do you girls call him?" I ask with a devious smile. I know all too well that the moment Taylor Diamond stepped into our offices; the peanut gallery of assistants already had a nickname well-devised.

"It's early," Angela looks behind her making sure no one is approaching.

I patiently wait, knowing she is about to spill the beans. I may be a partner, be we are friends and this is what we do best.

"Okay," she excitedly relents like she has no intention of keeping the secret.

"Twenty-four Karat Diamond." She smiles. She has a glow about her as if she just pitched the next big Hollywood blockbuster, and is awaiting my reaction.

I ponder for a moment and then smile. "I like it." Of course I do. I already had it planted in thoughts of my own. Good to know I'm on the same page as the peanut gallery.

Angela starts to turn to leave the room, but something is burning inside of me. I feel like I want to talk about Taylor. I need someone to talk to about the thoughts swirling in my mind. Just a general conversation to bounce things off of someone. I'm so curious what others think of him. It's more about the professional aspect, but a little *girl talk* about *Mr. Twenty-Four Karat* wouldn't hurt either.

"Angie?" I call out and she stops at the office doorway, her head tilting curiously back.

"What's up, boss?" she asks.

What a loaded question. I have far too many thoughts, trying to get out at once, to properly and safely articulate them to her. Taylor Diamond: the man of the hour at Rapture and Myers. I want to ask Angela what people are saying about him. I want to ask what everyone has heard. I want to know the gossip. I feel like a school girl, trying to search out facts about a silly crush I have. And as I ponder the many questions barreling into one another, inside my head, I feel my face flushing. Before I can even speak, a single rational thought dulls all the rest. *What of your reputation?* If there was even a leak of information that I was remotely attracted to him, a married woman with two daughters, it could ruin the reputation I've worked tooth and nail to earn. I do want to know more than just the filth. I want to know more professionally about him. But the two ideals could converge and make me look bad. So, whether it is professional or personal information, I shy away from both at the mere appearance of looking bad.

"Conference room B you said?" I submit a question I already know the answer to in order to save myself from myself.

"You should head over now," Angela offers with a silent wink and smirk. Her tone is so playful, as if daring me.

I shrug off Angela's intriguing tone and grab my file box. I make my way to the drawn shades of conference room B. Normally, the vertical shades are left open to the, nearly, all-glass encased room. But now, the ceiling's high shades are drawn and the lights are off, only the light of day sneaking in from the far window where the high curtains hang on either side but often are never drawn shut. The blinds inside are swaying ever so slightly, gaining a trickle of separation. A shadowed figure is moving around inside. I look around, but the offices are quiet, and people are working . . . too busy to be spying on me, at least. I turn my attention back to the glass and peer through the tiny spaces in the blinds. That is when I see him. He appears to have just pulled up his pants over his boxers, but I was a moment too late for that show. All of a sudden, I've become a peeping tom, creeping on the *Twenty-four Karat Diamond*. I get a glimpse of his perfect washboard abs. It's as if he were a model that had been photo-shopped. But he wasn't touched up or handled with oils. No, his abs rippled without even knowing they were being gazed upon. His arms were so tone. It seemed every inch of him had a muscle that perfectly bulged—from his shoulder blades down to the V-line leading just below his waistline, where his pants hung south of his baby-blue boxers. He was a Greek god, chiseled ever so perfectly. I couldn't have imagined such a man standing before me. And even though glass separates us and my view is partially obstructed, I see everything I need to. His body is forever engrained in my memory. Holy cow. This is far more than I expected to see of him this morning.

His hand, all of a sudden, reaches down below the table, and the top of his back is momentarily visible. There's a tattoo on his back, just above his right shoulder.

A hawk with its wings spread. And on his right bicep, I see a tattoo there as well. It's an angle with the letters MD. His head pops up and his eyes flash right at me. *Oh, my God!* I am frozen . . . breathless. I can't move or even flinch. I pray he has no idea I'm here. However, I want to see more—*I must see more.* I can't help but wonder *has he known all along . . . that I've been watching him?* How embarrassing. *Jesus, Nicki.* I feel like a deer caught in headlights on a dark, rural road.

Four

I regroup and move slowly to the door as if I had been walking that way the entire time. I will attempt to remain inconspicuous. Just as I go to push the door forward, I nearly face plant into the glass. *Pull the door, stupid.* I take a deep breath and shuffle the slipping box in my arms. *Who the hell changes in the conference room?* I hold the file box firm to my hip and pull the door back toward me. As I step into the dark room, he is there, smiling—a vision of perfection. That freakin' smile. It kills me. It's so innocent, but with his looks, you know it can't be.

"I'm sorry I was late today. I hope I didn't keep you waiting," Taylor softly apologizes.

His voice is like a knife, cutting through warm butter, so smooth and soft. He's youthful but has an old spirit. I wonder if he ever gets nervous or blushes.

"I wasn't sure if someone was in here. I thought I saw something moving in the dark…" I look for Taylor to chime in and explain. More than anything, I want him to tell me if he saw me creeping on him.

"I went to try out the gym downstairs this morning and lost track of time. Then, I lost track of my clothes. I shut the curtains, which took me five minutes to figure out, by the way. And then I locked the door . . . or at least, I thought I did. I told Angela I needed fifteen minutes to change before she sent you over," Taylor explains. I'm honestly having a difficult time following because his mannerisms are so amazing. His honesty about the vertical blinds was so adorable. His smile never seemed to waver, and his cheeks slightly blushed. Maybe Mr. Diamond can be embarrassed. Maybe he is human after all. And *fifteen minutes?* I'm not sure if I should scold Angela for putting me in this line of fire, or thank her for the peep show. Either way, instead of being the wide-eyed, embarrassed cougar, I feel as though Taylor and I connected. And, I guess *cougar* is strong-worded. I'm only four and a half years his elder. If I was a man and he was a woman, he'd probably be too old for me. But, back to Taylor.

He is perfectly flawed: forgetting where his clothes were, having difficulty with the blinds, not knowing how to lock a door, which in fact, doesn't lock. It broke last year during a divorce mediation; the wife lost her mind and literally ripped the doorknob off when her husband showed pictures of her having an affair. Ah, the Franklins were an interesting pair, to say the least. I digress.

Beautifully flawed and human, two personality traits that make him unbearably cute.

"Oh," I pretend to be caught off-guard. "I knew I saw someone shuffling about," my voice strains high and I speak with a near-perfect British accent. What the frick is the matter with me and when did the Queen of England possess my soul?

"Do you go?" Taylor poses; a strange reply. Was that an offer to join him? Was it an opening to meet up?

"Of course. It's a great stress reliever," I chime in with, but in actuality, the best stress reliever is sex. The gym, though, is a solid, but distant, second.

"I go every morning. I feel like it clears my mind. First time I left my change of clothes at home, though. I'm lucky I had a spare set. I didn't get to try the gym out yesterday," he continues to rattle off the reasons why he was nearly undressed in front of me.

I couldn't care less the why. I am happy it happened. His way . . . the ease of his words . . . his sensual lips . . . drive me insane. It's all I can do not to fall victim to Taylor Diamond's incredible blue eyes, but his voice draws my own eyes to him. His essence penetrates every inch of my being. I smile at him, but feel as though my grin is going crooked. It definitely feels like an abnormal smile. Of course, I exaggerate all this in my mind. I am still married and still professional. But these flirtatious thoughts are a nice distraction from an otherwise stressful, boring existence.

He smiles back, half-amused.

Snap out of it, Nicki! Thank goodness for my conscious. I have no idea how long I've been smiling at him. I must look like a freak. I'm no better than all the office assistants hounding over the Twenty-four Karat Man.

"The file?" Taylor asks.

"Yes. The file. I brought all the files from the Ramsey case and now I'm going to set them down on the conference table," I do the play-by-play of my life and set the box down on the table. I'm so embarrassing.

"What were you smiling at?" Taylor asks. Surely he is a man that knows that girlish stare. I'm sure he saw me outside too. I am just another girl, awestruck by this gorgeous creature. I start to feel small then, suddenly, my legal senses jump in.

"A story. My oldest daughter, Lacy, she had told me a funny story this morning." *Phew! Disaster averted.* I reach into the box and pull out a handful of files.

"What was it?" Taylor asks with his complete attention hanging on my words. He isn't trying to be sly or catch me in my obvious lie. I sold it pretty well. He is legitimately interested. *Damn.* Another sexy quality. And *shit.* Now I need to expound upon my ridiculous lie with a funny story.

"Well, it's really not that impressive," I state with obvious intentions of skirting the story entirely.

"It's all right. I love children; they are truly amazing."

Double shit. This guy is infallible!

"Okay. It's more of an inside thing, but I'll give it a go."

Taylor sits down at the opposite end of the conference table. He has a million-dollar smile on, waiting like a kid watching a magician who's about to pull a rabbit out of the hat.

"Lacy, my oldest, asked me if she could play with some of the boys down the street. I told to her she couldn't, that those boys are too rough. Lacy thought for a moment and asked, 'If I find a smooth one, can I play with him?'"

He smiles, seemingly amused. It is a true story, but Lacy asked me that nearly four years ago.

"That's great. Family is everything," Taylor states with conviction and has an intense seriousness behind his eyes. I don't know him all that well, but it is the first intense look he gave me, and the authenticity is chilling. He clearly values the relationship of family and complimented me in turn. It's strange to hear Taylor so intensely project that as I sit before him. Is this a message to me? Did he know I've been mentally swamped by his being, daydreaming about him far too much since the moment we met?

I mentally move on. I turn to my files and before I can even get a word out Taylor speaks.

"I read them," he states.

"Which file?" I ask.

"All of them."

"All of them?" I again ask. How could he have read a thousand documents?

"I was up late. Another reason why I got a late jump today. I read through the entire case."

I stare at Taylor and cross my arms, attempting to read his tells.

"I would hate to play you in poker," I jest with a playful smirk on my face.

"I don't gamble," Taylor says with a spark in his eye, a gleam of sincerity. It's almost interesting watching him speak. When he shares something close to him, a value like about the importance of family, I feel as though a different man is exposed. His smile and quiet confidence provide walls as high as the Great Walls themselves.

"Why don't you? Are you afraid to lose?" I come right after Taylor, hoping to shake him up a bit. Why not? I feel like I've been on my heels for the last twenty-four hours. It was time for me to go on the offense.

"Afraid? Me?" he stabs back. Clearly, I have touched a slight nerve.

"How many loses have you had?" My barrage can only weaken his high walls.

He smiles and jerks his head back a little. Perhaps I have dented his perfectly sculpted armor. Either way, after a glance to the ground, Taylor looks back up, his face tilting just slightly to the side. I enjoy the look he's giving me. This is the first time I feel his eyes surveying every inch of my body. I'd feel self-conscious about this, but I've shaken him up just a bit. I sit down and smile as I cross my legs. My lips are pouty and confident. He sits at the other end of the table. Our stare feels as though it will last forever; the seconds feeling like minutes. He slightly licks his lips, the first sign his mouth has dried. I did get him. I got through the perfect, high walls. I may not stay inside long, but I managed to get there. Maybe now he will think about *me* for a while.

"They all said you were good," a compliment flung to distract me, I think.

"I am," I shoot back. I feel as though I've turned the tables a bit. "Everybody loses sometime," I teach the younger man a lesson. I like this spot. I like the control.

"This is true," he agrees. There is a moment . . . a single moment of silence. I feel like we are fencing, taking a slow circle around one another, waiting for our next verbal strike.

"We all deal with losses at some point in our lives," he profoundly states with that sparkle again. It is clearly an open doorway into something much more. He probably has lost someone close to him. I know about his father from my Chardonnay research. I hope I didn't go too far and bring this conversation down. "But it's those losses," he continues after a dramatically long pause, "...it's those losses that teach us what the wins are all about. How can we know and understand joy, if we first do not experience pain and loss?" And now my younger foe is teaching me a lesson.

"Touché, Taylor Diamond," I stick a fork in the conversation, choosing to move on. "You went over every single file in one night?" I ask with an unconvinced playful grin. I return back to where we started, knowing full well I can't let him get away with this.

"Were you really smiling about Lacy's story before or just smiling at me?" *Whoa!* He just called me out and inside, I shrivel into a small ball, my face turning red. I may have broken through some of his walls, but he clearly still has the upper hand. I gulp, an abnormal nervousness for me, as I have become lost in a room with Taylor Diamond.

"Maybe," I playfully smile back, returning his invitation. I feel as though I'm falling deeper into some sort of emotional quicksand, which my brain has become powerless against.

"It all took place just outside of Barstow, in the desert community of Ramsey," I dive into the case head first. As I speak, I almost feel as though he is right beside me, like it's the heat of his breath that is cascading against my skin. And his eyes . . . his eyes are bearing down upon me as I review the case. He remains silent, listening intently to every word. He is so distracting, but I keep my head in the work and stay focused.

"They were poisoned through the air," I continue. I go on to explain some of the gut-wrenching details; a small desert town, breathing in toxins, year after year, during the fall and winter months as the Santa Ana winds changed. The poisons were pushed right into the small valley of said town. Doctors, environmentalists, and even an injunction to shut down the factory were facilitated to force them to alter their production methods. All this from one factory producing a popular brand of hot salsa. It took years of people coming down with what they thought was a hybrid of the stomach flu to figure out a pattern. And when a thirteen-year-old showed kidney damage consistent with that of a sixty-year-old, the Ramsey Class Action Lawsuit was born. The case is sad and tragic. Whenever I think about it, I feel my stomach turn. For nearly three hours, I review the details, catching Taylor up on all he has missed. I leave out my conversation with Charles and his settlement demands. My clients want court. They want to embarrass the big company that has poisoned them. And in many ways, the company knew it but covered it up. I have been pining to find a *smoking gun* in the case. Thus far, I have the people and their medical records. It is enough, but I want more. The people of Ramsey want Belton Food Corporation to suffer, making their guts turn for a while. Taylor takes sporadically jots notes down. After I lay out the case, my mind returns back to him. His smell, despite sitting nearly ten full yards away from me, is intoxicating. He stares at me and I realize he knows so much more about me than I do him.

"What next?" Taylor looks up and smiles.

Damn it—*why does he have to be so hot?!* I look at his smile and all I can think of is him taking me. *I want him! Jesus, Nicki . . . snap out of it!*

"All right." I abruptly begin packing up my things.

"Did you want to review strategies?" he asks.

"I-I…yes…we will," I fumble along. Right now, the vision of his perfectly cut abs haunts me. I have to get out of this room.

"Ok, then." Taylor seems all too amused watching me struggle.

"I have to run—later, though!" I proclaim, snatching up all my files and shoving them into the box in no particular order.

"Just call me direct. I don't have an assistant yet. But my calendar is pretty open; I'm all yours." His words are innocent in nature, but right now, they are only piling on to my uncontrollable urges and I let out an internal gasp. My heart beats faster, and my breath quickens.

"Tomorrow," nearly breathless, I offer. "Angela will give you the details." I grab my box and rush to the door of the room, nearly sprinting away. I feel a swell of inner emotion causing my anxiety to soar. It's pushing me to rush home. I have to have a release before I lose my mind. What the hell has Taylor Diamond done to me?! Is this some kind of *love at first sight* nonsense? I've never acted this way. It's totally unprofessional. Maybe I have a chemical imbalance. This goes beyond anything I've experienced before.

My mind has never been so consumed by one person. I feel fixated on him. Why? What has he done to earn this attention? Yes, he's hot. Yes, he's seemingly rich. And yes, he looks like he just fell out of a *Men's Fitness Magazine*. Err…I'm not sure where I'm going with this but I'm not stating my case well.

I'm a firm believer of *chemistry* when it comes to people; pheromones to be exact. It's the essence of a person that is released; an unseen amount of energy that floats through the air. You can't help but being drawn by it . . . by that person. And right now, I'm drawn to Taylor Diamond. His pheromones call to me every time I am near him. I *need* to have him. I *need* to feel him inside me, just once. I *need* to break this trance. I'm going to have him right now. Well, the only way I can right now.

With that, I head out of the conference room, sprinting by Angela and head into my office with the file box in my hands. "I'm leaving for lunch," I declare, grabbing my purse.

"How was the one-on-one meeting?" Angela, who was right on my heels, asks like a school girl dying for information.

"Just catching him up on the case," I state with great poise. No one can know the feelings brewing inside me . . . not even Angela. No one at this office can know about my school girl crush.

"All right. Did you see anything interesting?" Angela deviously asks. She sent me over there early fully knowing Taylor could be changing when I arrived.

"Nope," I casually return. I fumble for my keys in a rush as if one of my children just got rushed to the hospital.

"You all right?"

"Oh, yeah. Just *really* hungry," I reply. Before I can even blink, I'm in my car and pulling into my driveway.

Five

The house is quiet. My husband is on a job fifty miles away today and the kids are at school. I'll grab a glass of Chardonnay and sip, savoring the silence. I close my eyes and replay staring at the closed vertical blinds, guarding conference room B.

I see Taylor's body as he places a white collared shirt around his shoulders. The ripples in his abdominal cage make me crazy; the muscles are so finely cut. I long to place my hands along his core . . . along each one of his tight firm sides.

I glide smoothly into my bathroom as if I'm walking on air. The image of Taylor, bending down—his shoulders, the tattoos—I see them clear as day. He looks up, staring right at me. Our eyes connect. We freeze. A glass wall and vertical blinds are all that stand between the longing . . . between the uncontrollable forces drawing us closer together.

I'm lighting candles as the bathtub fills up. Vanilla relaxation crystals and some fine vanilla bath soap I got for Christmas three years prior, finally makes their inaugural appearance in my tub. Another sip of Chardonnay, and I set the glass down. I fall back into my fantasy.

I see his penetrating eyes. We are waiting, neither of us wanting to make the first move. I cannot bring myself to initiate anything, but then, his finger rises and he waves me forward. He wants me in that dark room.

I slowly step forward, very small steps. Our eyes remain engaged as we pass each small, hanging vertical blind. Nothing is going to keep us apart. But I go oh-so-slowly. I want to tease him. He knows I want him, but I want him to suffer just a bit, waiting for me. I want him to erupt inside with anticipation just like I am. And as I reach the door, I pause, seductively looking up and smiling at him. Again, I want control, and I want him to think this may not happen.

We exchange a mischievous smile through a small crack in the blinds, and I enter the room slowly, closing the door behind me. We stare at one another from one end of the table to the other. Only tiny bit of light from the drawn shades are able to penetrate the room through the cracks, leaving it dark but visible. With his dress shirt unbuttoned, Taylor stands facing me. My eyes helplessly drift down from his beautiful blues, past his perfect nose, southbound to his strong chin and continuing past his neck to his hairless chest. What perfection. I continue to pan my eyes down and come to his six, rippling abdominal muscles. Then my eyes float to his baby blue boxers, poking up just above his beltless black suit pants. The curves of his pelvic muscles, running down into his boxers are like a runway, begging me to land upon it.

Again, we just stare at one another seductively; silent foreplay. I feel a rush of heat beginning to build inside me. We take steps toward one another and now we are nose to nose. Our lips are just a breath away, and I'm dying to pull him closer. Then, his face slowly inches forward; his hand gently patrolling the outside of my black sports jacket. He guides it off my shoulders and as it slips down to my forearms, I feel the warmth of his breath on my neck. I swallow, my breathing getting rapid, the moment slowly building. Then, button by button, he so carefully undoes my white blouse. We stare intensely at one another—both of us wanting the other. The looks are animalistic, and the passion is tantamount to a volcano building toward eruption. He fingers gently remove my blouse, his touch sending chills up my spine. Now my white, laced bra is exposed. He then reaches down to my legs, running his fingers up, pushing against the pleats of my black skirt. He peels back my stockings, carefully running them down my legs while I moan. He reaches my feet and removes my shoes one at a time, and then, the stockings. He rushes his hands back up the sides of my calves, past my knees, along my thighs, and up under my skirt to my hips, exposing my white laced panties. My mouth quivers as his hands move up to my hips. I want so badly to take him, to throw him on the table, and ride him. But he is meticulous and patient, so I wait.

He pulls down on my skirt, leaving just my white laced panties on. My breath quickens as it hits the floor. He stands back up and before he can do anything, I take his opened, white collar shirt and run it off his toned, firm shoulders. I almost lift up onto my tippy-toes as I reach and clear his broad shoulders and arms, letting the shirt fall to the floor. My hands move right to his pants, slowly unbuttoning them and then work at his zipper. My fingers trace along the side of his abs and down to his hips. I take my time freeing him of his pants before my hands make their way to his rock hard ass.

I repeat the action, this time with the removal of his boxers, leaving his entire perfectly toned body visible by the shadows of the day. Everywhere I look, there is a curve. There isn't even an ounce of extra weight that I can find with my probing hands. I reach down and I go for it. I find his penis, taking it into the palm of my right hand. I seem to catch him off guard, but as I run my fingers from the base of his penis to the tip, he closes his eyes and his head dips back in elation. I sense his pleasure; his silent looks and increased breathing tell me all I need to know. I massage his well-endowed, firm member, enjoying the effect it's having on him. The fact that he is manscaped is just a bonus. With his mind and body occupied, my mouth touches down on his chest, skirting feather-like kisses across his heated skin. As if unable to take any more, his head bows and he slowly steps forward, pushing my body back to the

*table. My grip is released; using my hands to sustain my
balance as my ass softly gets pressed up against the table.
He whooshes the office chair away for more space and then
turns me around. I feel as though he may bend me over the
table and have at me. I want him to. But, not yet. He
prolongs my agony by running his hands from my thighs,
up my sides, and then to my chest. My fingers are clenching
the table's edge, readying myself for anything while
wanting Taylor to do everything to me.*

*His fingers run along the sides of my breasts, and
then his lips land on the back of my neck. One singular,
sensual kiss sends chills rushing down my spine, to the tips
of my toes. His fingers, like the smoothness of a thief,
unlock my bra in one motion. His hands run down to my
white laced panties and he pulls them to the ground. Before
I even know what's happening, I'm turned back around to
face him again. He lifts my naked body up into the air and
gently lies me down on the table. He pushes up on me and
lays my head back, making sure it lands as softly as a
feather.*

I submerge into my tub—eyes closed—completely
enveloped in my perfect fantasy. I take the shower head
and point it right at my spot, letting the pulsating water
tease me. My legs rise up out of the soap-filled tub and I
plant my feet on its wall, near the ledge, for leverage. I am
primed and ready to go.

*His mouth is pressed against my left inner thigh. I
lean back and my chest bows up in anticipation. Each time
he presses his lips against my thigh, his mouth edges closer
and closer to my throbbing spot. And then, Oh, God. His
tongue darts out, flicking the edges of my opening. He
slowly licks around my hood, playing with the outer rim,
driving me insane.*

*I run my right hand up my chest, pressing my palm
up against my breast, caressing my nipple. My left hand
grazes the side of my face, ever so gently, as I run my*

fingers up through my hair. The anticipation and the build-up make me want to yank my hair out of my head, my writhing growing and growing.

"Oh, ah," *I moan in ecstasy as Taylor's tongue penetrates my pussy lips and then continues to gently lick.* "Yes," *my breathless voice leaks out. Taylor goes deeper until he is firmly planted inside, his tongue surveying every inch of my insides. It's as if he knows exactly where I like to be touched and keeps hitting the spot again relentlessly!* "Oh, God!"

The energy builds inside me, and my arms fly around the back of his head, burying him deeper inside of me, if that's even possible. I want to explode. My breathing quickens, my lungs reaching full capacity.

The tub is frothing with warm, soapy water as I writhe uncontrollably. My index and middle fingers rub my firm, engorged clit. My eyes shut so tightly; my thoughts so far away from me. I'm swept up in my dream, like a leaf in a wind storm. I reach over and grab my strategically placed Rabbit Pearl.

My voice heightens to an octave unfamiliar to me. *But I have to try to remain quiet; at any moment, we could be found. The light from the hall could encroach into the room, finding my sprawled out, naked body being had for all to see.*

Abruptly, he pulls back and brings my body forward. Within a second, he's inside of me. "Oh fuck!" *I crow in enjoyment.* Finally—penetration; it's absolutely amazing. It's slow and steady, a rhythmic build perfect to my liking. He pushes deeper *inside, making me accommodate his size relentlessly. His thrusts are soft and consistent. I want it harder, though. I can't wait any more. I reach to clasp his back, latching on.* Harder now, *I mentally project. I want him to leave nothing left of me. I dig my nails into his back and he grunts and moans. He, too, is in the throes of passions. My fingers drag across his back as he thrusts harder and deeper. I've dug into my thoroughbred and he is responding.*

Our sounds start to sync up as he thrusts again and again. I shriek, the pleasure almost too much for me to handle; an unstoppable flow of energy cresting inside me.

I place my hands around his perfectly apple-shaped ass and squeeze for my life. I pull him harder into me; I want it. I can barely breathe; his entire being fills up inside me. "YES! YES! YES!" We yell in unison, both of us on the doorstep of simultaneous orgasms.

"Ah!*" The pressure erupts, and I explode in joy; an infusion of tingling energy flows everywhere throughout my body. My breathing comes to a near hold as I come around him. The release is epic, like warm butter seeping out from my insides.*

"Oh!*" I gasp, my voice no longer loud but breathy.*

"*Oh,*" escapes my lips again as I struggle to breathe; my body frozen. Finally, I am able to let go and exhale, a long, satisfyingly, relaxing breath out. "*Oh, yes,*" I breathe in deeply.

My eyes slowly open and I survey my steamy bathroom. The mirrors are clouded as a deep fog has set in the room. My face is flushed, and I feel as though I just ran the most amazing mile ever. The tingling and chills that had consumed my being are slowly leaving my body.

"Mom?" the quizzical tone comes through my bathroom door of what sounds like my oldest, Lacy.

Oh, shit! I gasp in my head.

Six

"Mom, you okay?" Lacy repeats.

"Yes, honey. I'm fine."

Lacy tries to open the door, but it's locked.

"I'm in the tub, honey," I alert, hoping this will send her away or prompt a question through the door. I need time to cool down with my cheeks being flushed. The door jiggles and like a highly trained cat burglar, my oldest breaks into the bathroom. I realize the rabbit is above the water, in my right hand, and I quickly drown it. In my haste, it turns on and bubbles start firing up like a sub about to resurface.

"What's that?" Lacy tilts her head with a curious look upon on her face.

"My stomach's upset." I sink further into my candle lit bath.

"I thought you were hurt. I could have sworn I heard screaming," Lacy looks around suspiciously.

Oh, no! What if I shouted his name in the throes of passion? A memory search turns up nothing and I shrink at the prospect of this possible embarrassment.

"It was the TV. Before I got in the tub, it was way too loud . . . so I turned it off." My excuse may not pass the smell test to most, but I'm hoping my oldest will buy it.

"It sounded like someone was getting murdered in here."

"Yeah, crazy show, right? It's all gone now," I wrap up my excuse with a bow and close the mystery. It's so ironic. I've never done anything wrong in my life. I never got detention—not once. I never stole from anyone or anything—not even a penny. I never cheated on any of my three boyfriends—not even Paul Bernstein in the sixth grade. I met Aiden in high school and we've made it all the way. There was a break during my college years, an opportunity for us to see the world. He dropped out of junior college and went into construction. I came back from grad school and fate brought us together at Maloney's, a West Los Angeles bar. Two kids later and here we are. And now, I'm lying to my oldest. I have a dirty taste in my mouth, but it's offset by a thrilling feeling of sexual relief; the kind of release I have not experienced in a very long time, if at all.

Lacy stares at me. I'm unsure if she has bought any of it. Her eyes flash around the room once again as if she's Sherlock Holmes, piecing together a crime. I am the suspect as she surveys my expression closely.

"You do look sick. Your cheeks are so red," she hypothesizes.

"Yes. What can I help you with, honey?" I move Lacy along.

After a moment of hesitation, she sighs dramatically. "Ariel won't stop taking my hair ties!" she proclaims.

I let out a breath of air full of relief. This emergency will be easy to handle. And although I didn't get to relish in my afterglow, I do take a great deal of solace in the fact that my stress levels and desires have both been sufficiently quelled.

———————

I head downstairs with my robe on and a towel wrapped around my head. I find Aiden flipping through the mail.

"What are you doing home?" he asks, seemingly surprised and confused to see me. His surprise seems legitimate (Aiden isn't that good of an actor). So I, quite possibly, escaped with the narrowest of margins. I cower at the thought of Aiden hearing me screaming in ecstasy when he is standing one floor below me.

"I wasn't feeling well earlier. I just . . . I needed some down time," I explain.

"I'm sure. With the case and your family stuff—you have a lot going on," Aiden kindly and agreeably comforts me.

"So, a half day for the kids? I didn't even realize." I feel as though the 'Mother of the Year Award' is further away than ever.

"Yup. I'm not sure why, although parent-teacher conferences are coming up. And we need to settle on Halloween costumes," Aiden dictates to me the most current family manifesto as I sit clueless, consumed by: work, my case, my family, and now, Taylor Diamond. Fortunately for me, my little fantasy session has, for the meantime, put to bed my urges, and one of my distractions, just as I had hoped. It also was pretty freakin' amazing, so even though I'm playing hooky from work, I feel like ten million bucks inside. Yoga's got nothing on a phenomenal masturbation session.

"Okay. Let's talk about it." I sit beside the kitchen island on one of the two stools. Our kitchen was upgraded, thanks to Aiden's awesome handy work, almost three years ago. We gutted the old dining room, blew out a wall, and created an open concept kitchen complete with new appliances, furnishings, and a table. We were doing well financially, so we spent a lot of what we had saved. But now, between the firm being down the last few years and Aiden taking on less jobs to play "Mr. Mom", money is, once again, getting tight.

"Actually, I told the girls we'd head over to the park. They're all caught up on homework." Aiden has it all planned . . . all laid out, and I'm the passenger along for the ride.

"I'll come." I jump, desperately needing to feel like a mother at this moment.

"You don't have to. You can just relax, if you want. We won't be long," he offers me a way out. I'm not sure if he doesn't want me around or if he is genuinely concerned about me being overworked.

"I want to. We'll make it a family outing!"

"Sounds good." He smiles in a welcoming fashion.

We take my Excursion and head to the park. Upon getting there, the kids spring out in excitement, rushing to go find playmates. Aiden and I casually stroll over to the center vestibule where a few parents have congregated. A beautiful blonde whips her head around and I see that it's Jessica Norwalk. She does a triple-take upon seeing me, going from happy . . . to surprised . . . to dramatically surprised.

"Hey!" she yells at me. Jessica is gorgeous. She is my *pretty* friend. In fact, I've known her since grade school, when we had our ups and downs together. Both girls of the California desert, we managed to make our way to Thousand Oaks, an oasis about seventy miles northwest of our childhood stomping ground.

In high school, Jessica and I were inseparable. She has always been gorgeous while I was the late bloomer. I never felt carried along though. We are girlfriends and have always shared everything. We even, knowingly, shared Gunner Pritchat during those years. We quickly conspired to turn the table on him. It was the last time Gunner pulled that, and all it took was some healthy globs of Icy Hot in his jock to get the point across. *That was one funny football practice.* And that's when we became infamous; part outcasts, part *"we don't give a shit"* girls. But, we always got good grades and *always* had each other's back. Even now, during her separation from her husband John. Except, I feel as though I've let her down a little. I'm so wrapped up in my own shit.

"I didn't expect to see you here!" She jumps up.

"What's up?!" I excitedly holler and we hug.

"I haven't seen you in forever," she points out the obvious. I take it as a tiny jab, but I deserve it.

"I'm sorry, Jess." I wince.

"Tara and I are doing lunch tomorrow. I know you don't have a lot of time, but can you try to stop by?"

Wow . . . that one hurt. My best two friends in the world are meeting for lunch and I didn't even know it.

"Definitely! Text me where and when; I'm there," I proclaim without even conferring with Angela. I shoot Angela a text immediately to let her know, in case she needs a head start shuffling my schedule around.

I hear something and snap my head towards the playground. I see Haley hanging upside down off the monkey bars. My mouth drops and Jessica reacts to my face and whips her head around.

"Haley, get down!" Jessica smiles and flees to get her daughter Haley who is the same age as Ariel. I drop down a peg more. My guilt now is circulating over not being an effective mom and how, apparently, I've sucked as a friend. I let out a sigh and turn to Aiden.

"I've been awful, haven't I?" I ask but it's more of a confession.

"You've been pretty busy," he kindly replies. He could have verbally beaten me down a bit here but chooses not to. He is indifferent in many ways. I think Aiden enjoys his solitude from me, which also makes me feel bad. He's never too high or too low.

The kids play as the sun dips down. We head home shortly after.

The routine: dinner, showers, reading to the kids, and my two angels are down for bed. Aiden is glued to the television, and I choose to fall back into Veronica Palsey's sexual romps across the heartland. Then, bed for me as well.

Seven

Seven

I kiss the girls and Aiden gives me a *peck* before they're off for their day. I grab my gym bag, having a suddenly renewed focus to hit the gym. It's not out of character for me. I used to regularly hit the World Fitness Gym at the base of our office building two to three times a week. It's included in my benefits, so why not? But lately, like everything else, my mind-cleansing work-out routines have fallen by the wayside as life steamrolls over me. Suffocated is the best word I'd use to describe how I feel inside; suffocated and all too routine.

As I drive to the gym, a tiny thought keeps creeping in my head. I deny its existence but it's definitely there. *Will Taylor be at the gym?* I'm not going for him; *at least I tell myself that.* I'm not going to catch a glimpse of him or showboat, giving him a little of myself for his own private *highlight reel.* I befriend denial.

I enter the gym and my eyes search. I pan across the half-filled, bustling, early morning crew and fail to see Taylor. There is a little let down inside me, the realization that part of my inspiration is simply to be near him. This school girl was hoping to run into her crush—as wrong as that seems. But, I suppress the wrong and welcome the excitement of it all, even if it is all in my head.

First things first—stretch. I'm able to get a little privacy in the yoga room, which is vacant, and try to collect my thoughts. My mind drifts into simple questions. *Am I fooling myself? Should I appreciate my husband more for what he does?* Aiden and I haven't been the same in a while. We talked about going to a marriage counselor in passing. Or, at least, I asked if we could. He is private and quiet. He wasn't interested. So now, I feel the effect of passion infused inside me; a feeling I long for and have not recognized in a long while.

Taylor Diamond. A few shared looks and a chemical urge, driving me toward him, which I cannot explain. This is all just fantasy, tales being spun in my head to provide a distraction from my stressful life. After all, everyone needs to dream. Everyone needs fantasies to escape the realities of the daily grind. The realities of life that feel like quicksand at times and make the calendar roll forward from season to season; life passing us by. I feel as though I'm on the carrousel going round and round, unable to stop. *And,* I want to. I want to break free of this mundane life. I want to be saved from it.

A shadow casts over me. My stomach churns with excitement and my hopeful eyes pan up. It's Tabatha, a pretty, blonde, chatty, office assistant. She works for Bob Myers, naturally. He has a propensity for blondes.

"Hey, Mrs. Connolly!" she welcomes, seemingly excited and surprised to see me.

"Hi, Tabatha. And please, call me Nicki. It's a gym," I make it clear that a formal designation outside our law office isn't necessary. And Mrs. Connolly, to me, only adds years to my age with just the mere sound of it. I'm hoping to do some age reduction now not advance my years.

"I didn't know you hit the gym in the morning," Tabatha innocently states, but my ears sense a condescending tone. I ignore my conscious, taking her words at face value.

"Yeah. I used to be a regular. Gotta get back into the groove," I push the conversation along by hopping up to my feet.

I enter the gym and get on an elliptical to get my blood flowing. Like a lost puppy, Tabatha follows me. "Did you see the new guy?" she excitedly gossips.

I already know who she's talking about. *And, did I see him?!* He screwed my brains out in an amazing fantasy I was fighting back to replay over and over again in my head.

"I saw him. We're going to be working together," I casually state; a nice flop sweat starting to form on my skin.

"You're working with 24 Karat?!" Tabatha shouts, completely giddy.

"Yes." I smirk, my best effort not to be equally joyful.

"He's hot."

"I guess." I pretend to be distracted.

"You guess? I know you're married, but you're definitely not dead!"

"I guess he's cute," I casually relent.

"He's gorgeous!" Tabatha continues. "What I wouldn't give for a crack at that!" Tabatha runs a bit harder on the treadmill next to me, getting a little worked up.

She finally begins to focus on her workout, so I slip away quietly, deciding to go work on my abs. Lying on a mat, I start alternating crunches, lifting my head slightly toward one knee and then the other. I continue to work my oblique when another shadow is cast upon me. *Here we go again.* Half annoyed, I stop and look up only to find Taylor Diamond. His hair is wet and he has a towel wrapped around his waist. His thin, white T-shirt clings to his chiseled body, making it almost see-through. Apparently, he'd been in the pool all along. Looks like I'll need to keep a spare bathing suit in my gym bag.

"Expecting someone else?" Taylor jokes, tilting his head. I roll up quickly to my feet.

"Hello, Mr. Diamond." I smirk, giving nothing more away to him.

"Glad to see you're feeling better, Ms. Connolly," he playfully grins and nods respectively, moving on. Every time I see him, he looks like a different version of the most perfect dark-haired, blue-eyed movie star.

Feeling satisfied with my workout, I head to the woman's locker room. As I shower, flashes of Taylor's face dance in my head. Mr. Diamond stepping out of a pool, water falling slowly down his body, would surely be a sight to behold. I'm dreaming of that million-dollar smile at the moment and how his eyes always seem to penetrate every part of me. I feel so weak around him yet, so internally charged. As I drift in and out of my shower, a familiar voice breaks my moment of Zen, yet again.

"Hey!" Tabatha shouts in excitement as she enters the shower stall adjacent to me. The showers at the gym are very nice. The floors and walls are tiled with beautiful faux stone. The shower heads are strong with excellent spray action. I remember being able to lose myself in these showers in the past. The only drawback is that every two shower stalls have lower divides—about neck level—so women can chat. Longer divides, on either side, keep things private and allow women to have discussions if they choose to. Normally, there are numerous open showers, so women space out. Right now, I wish that was Tabitha's case.

"Hi," I offer back.

"Oh, my God, these shower heads are great. I wish I had this kind of power at home," she jokes.

I smile off her humor and continue to wash, water drenching my face. I open my rain-soaked eyes to Tabatha leaning over the edge of our divide, almost on her tippy-toes to survey my body.

"Jesus, your body is amazing," she raves. I'm uncomfortable and flattered all at once. She returns back to showering, her twenty-five-year-old body making me envious at first glance. I'm humble about my looks. Being a late bloomer, you're forced to be. Years of torment will do that to you.

I don't focus on my body as much anymore. I stare in the mirror, like everyone else does, but with so many distractions of late, I look a lot less. I come from a conservative family anyhow; naked bodies were not visible, and information wasn't really shared. It was my best friend, Jessica who taught me about blow jobs. What a surprise that was for me in the ninth grade! I still remember how she described it as licking a lollipop and sucking on an ice cream bar. My first reaction was, *well, why don't I just lick the lollipop and eat the ice cream? It seems like they'd both taste a heck of a lot better anyways.* Not only did my friends offer instructions, they supplied me with visuals from various outlets. Shortly after, an older boy named Aiden Connolly asked me out. So, while I can be sexual, I have felt lacking, for a long time, in that department. I have only had one true lover in my life and it is an intimidating thought to think about having any others. I have never felt sexually empowered at any moment in my life. The closest time would have to be just eighteen measly hours prior, by myself, in a bathroom.

I make my way to the office, feeling refreshed. Placing my things down, I find a hot Starbucks coffee cup on my desk. I start flipping through a few files on my desk when Angela gently knocks and enters.

"You okay?" Angela tentatively asks.

"I'm good. All better, thanks."

"I got the text. Lunch with Ms. Norwalk is in for today. You did want to head out to the desert this afternoon. Is that still on?" she queries.

"Yes. See if Taylor can tag along. It's time he heads out there, so he can see what this is really all about," I explain.

"Okay. You got it, boss." Angela bounces toward my office door. She then turns around swiftly. "And you have the Lowry mediation in conference room B in one hour," she adds.

"Thanks, Angie!" I smile.

Ugh . . . the Lowry case—what a mess. Twelve years of marriage, two affairs, spying on one another, and now . . . divorce. The accusations alone can make your skin crawl. And I am the one that has to sit through, at least, an hour long torture session as they replay their worst highlights again and again. This is our third mediation and our final swing to avoid heading into court.

After re-reading my Lowry notes and studying up, I step out of my office with my black briefcase and slowly walk the halls to conference room B. I crack random smiles as I make my way over there; the highlight reel running in my head, showing flashes of me being taken to task by Taylor.

I move into the room, almost giddy, when I'm struck by the angry glares of four faces that are in no mood to laugh.

Eight

The Lowry's. They are the reason divorce scares the hell out of me. I've seen it all. I've handled divorce law for a while, but went to corporate after too many sad stories. I still offer my services as a mediator in the field, which helps keep the lights on. But the Lowry Case could be the one that gets me to remove my name off the divorce mediation list forever.

Two wealthy spouses (as I don't do pro-bono in this field any more); the money makes everything worse. The wealthy are far more fascinating with their calculated blow by blow of a marriage imploding before my eyes. It's a war waged where both participants have stopped caring about the damage they will inflict. They have become more obsessed with winning and that is what drives their anger.

Roger Lowry: a powerful businessman. He is second generation money, but displays first generation ego. You know the kind of man that finds success for the first time, and flaunts it as if he had never had a hundred in his pocket. His vacation pictures are posted all over the Cyber sphere; first-class all the way. If he gets a pedicure done, expect a sarcastic tweet. He is a man with a big mouth and an even bigger ego when it comes to the world at large. A Florida native, his family participation in sketchy deals all through the Caribbean, including his own, have made them rich and made this case far more difficult to decipher than anything I've ever been a part of.

Shelly Lowry is a decedent from the Jamison entourage, an influential family from Texas with big oil dollars. She was the former beauty queen, a busty blonde who won 'All-County' in a beauty contest and finished second for the designation of 'Miss Texas', years back.

They seemed like a perfect match on paper. But paper doesn't buy happiness and, in this case, neither does over five hundred million dollars in assets.

They have two kids to deal with. That is the icing on this twisted cake. Shelly wants to move back to her home in Dallas, Texas, while Roger's affairs are now anchored in Los Angeles; his business dealings take him all over. But their multi-million dollar mansion resides in Los Angeles, just one of five family properties scattered about the United States alone.

Within moments of me sitting, it begins. The lawyers toss exposing questions like grenades at their enemy on the opposite side of the table. The facts and accusations are a dizzying barrage of stones hurled back and forth. Mr. Lowry, as always, sits quietly as his attorney does battle for him. It's Shelly that jumps out of her seat, hollering and boiling over. It's a regular blitz of activity; the two sides attacking at a feverish pace.

I try to quell the noise and keep perspective, but I do recognize some facts—some of the cold details of a marriage gone stale—and . . . in some ways, I relate.

"Listen!" I interrupt Mr. Lowry's attorney as he displays photos of Mrs. Lowry with the pool man. *Oh, so cliché.* And equally cliché are the photos Mrs. Lowry hurls across the table of her soon-to-be ex-husband, squeezing the naked, perfectly fit, and rock-hard ass cheeks of his beautiful twenty-two-year-old assistant. In a small way, the mirror is too close to my face, so I interrupt and take control of the room. "This is it," I begin with a stern voice and determined tone. "This is the end of the road. I've sat through blood baths—brutal, verbal blood baths. I've seen the broken hearts of countless children, caught in these sideshows. I understand there are dual prenups at play. But, you both cheated. Forget the acts; the warm bodies you used to escape. You strayed long ago with your hearts. Your children have felt it somehow—someway—already. I can make a list, based on your arguments . . . based on fairness. And you will want to go with that list because I know enough to make it. Or, you can wait for Judge Lattimore to make that list for you both. I can *guarantee* he won't care about what you want nearly as much as I will. I'm going to step out of the room now. Please confer with your attorneys.

I get up and exit the room. I let out a deep breath of air, standing just outside the door. In some ways, I feel as though this could be a glance into my future. My brain has been so disconnected from my heart lately that I don't know where exactly I am at. Suddenly, I feel two wayward eyes fixated on me.

"Nice speech," Mr. Everywhere, Taylor Diamond, says with a smirk.

"It's exhausting. Too many arguments; too many hours. Why can't they just agree to disagree and just end it?" I shake my head.

"Because they love each other," Taylor, simplistically, replies.

"That's love?!" I scoff.

"It's years of pent up frustration and anger. They feel they failed, and they blame themselves and each other. Only two people can get to this point if they loved . . . if they loved each other with tremendous force, at one point. Nobody said love had to last forever. That's just our Disney fantasies."

"Happily ever after," I smile, adding to his thoughts.

"There are two absolutes about matters of the heart. There are always winners and there are always losers." Taylor states with intense blue eyes.

"And where is it you fall?" I ask with a smirk.

Taylor offers me an amused smile. Then the door to the conference room opens.

Shelly Lowry steps out. "Oh, excuse me. We were all done in *there*..." Shelly's voice trails as her eyes fixate on Taylor. "Mr. Diamond," she says with surprise and a complete resurrection of her Southern Drawl. It's as if seeing him has flipped a switch, bringing the old Texas school girl right out of her.

"Good to see you, Ms. Lowry," Taylor says with a running smile.

"Like I was saying, we're ready to talk in there. I just needed to freshen up a bit," Shelly reiterates to me, but her eyes can't seem to help but shoot repeated glances over at Taylor as if he were a movie star. She makes her way by us, giving him a seductive glance on her way down the hall.

I turn back to Taylor with a surprised look of my own. "She is clearly impressed with you," I joke, fishing for answers like a girlfriend probing her boyfriend.

"Familiar circles; long, long ago," he puts a quick cryptic end to that line of inquiry. "What time did you want to head out this afternoon?" he asks quickly before I can spend any real time thinking about how he and Shelly know each other. For a moment, I have to recalibrate my brain and figure out what he is asking me. "To the desert," he adds, as if sensing my hesitation and confusion.

"Of course. About 1:30. I'll meet you here," I reply.

"Then, it's a date," Taylor's final words as he parts. A weakness strikes my knees and I let out a tiny breath of air; his words hitting me.

Shelly Lowry sidles in beside me, a devious grin on her face. "Taylor Diamond," she begins, "Well done, Ms. Connolly. Well done, indeed," she compliments me.

"Oh, no," I kindly deny. "We're just working together," I point out our professional relationship.

"I've seen that look before, darlin'. He wants you. That boy is smitten with you, and Taylor Diamond doesn't get smitten often. I was parsley on the side of the plate, a moment ago, and I'm never parsley," Shelly paints an agonizing picture of forbidden potential.

"I-I…" the words are lost in my brain, unsure of how to respond.

"I'm quite certain you'll enjoy. Most eligible bachelor around, that one," she finishes with a hint of jealousy. Taylor wasn't giving this nearly divorced cougar a second glance. She leans in close to my ear, "It's something you'll never forget," her breathy voice declares. Shelly heads back inside the room, and I'm left to dissect that statement. Was it a warning? Was it a push forward? I can't grasp what she means.

Could she be right? Is Taylor Diamond crushing on me? That would be the day! And . . . I'm not sure how I feel about that. Obviously, I'd feel great! But I'm not sure beyond that.

No, he can't. He can't be. That's crazy. *Or, is it?* Doesn't matter. Focus, Nicki. Work, work, work. I take in a deep breath and head back into conference room B to close the mediation of the Lowry's once and for all.

Lunch. After a morning workout, I'm starving and can't wait to catch up with my bestic, Jessica, and our mutual bestie, Tara Jones.

I got a text; we're meeting at Antonio's, near my office in West Los Angeles. I didn't even ask for an easy journey to lunch. I would have driven to the Valley, if I had to. I have been the bad friend, and this gathering is long overdue. But, that's how Jessica is. She may come off as bitchy at times, but she just has a strong personality. She's tough. She also has my back twenty-four seven.

I arrive five minutes early and find Jessica and Tara seated outside on the patio, enjoying this pleasant fall day. Both are donned in sunglasses and casual attire. They are laughing, talking, and sipping from their drinks already. I'm on time but feel late to the party. And, I can't help but feel replaced by a new version of me.

Tara Jones is awesome; don't get me wrong. She is a good friend and a newer addition to our trio, which once, not too long ago, was just a duo. Tara, Jess, and I all used to hang out at the playground together with our kids. My youngest, Ariel, Jessica's daughter, Hayley, and Tara's oldest, Ben, are all the same age. It was nice; coffee in one hand and babies in the other, we'd keep each other occupied and sane. Tara went on to have two more kids and is still married, while Jess just has the one and is months away from closing out her divorce.

I reach the table and an appletini is dropped in my hand by the waiter, Mario.

"Our go-to drink." I smile, holding it up in a "cheers" gesture.

"Right on cue," Jessica jokes. I'm there for a split second before I fall right back into the groove of the *girl time* I've so badly missed.

"Who is it?" Tara prompts Jessica.

"Oh, please," she passes off with a slightly guilty tell.

"It's a man," I step right in, knowing the conversation as if I had been there all along. I smile wryly and sip my appletini, excitedly awaiting Jessica's response.

"It's two men," she starts with her own devious grin.

"Ha! I have to live vicariously through you, now—it's official! You *and* Veronica Palsey," Tara announces with an uncomfortably high volume. Good thing we're outside; this lunch is bound to get rowdy. My friends also enjoy reading about the exploits of Veronica Palsey. We're all drawn in by the fantasy.

We digest an amusing avalanche of Jessica's love life; her two hunky love interests as she happily moves on from her former life with her ex-husband. And after having a couple drinks to wash down her fantastic passion-filled tales, all eyes turn to me.

"We see Aiden at school and the park," Tara starts. She's needling for information, I think. Something tells me she may sense that all isn't perfect in Connolly paradise.

"How *is* everything?" Jessica, with a devilish grin, digs in. I feel as though I'm being tag-teamed. My girls sense some blood in the water and circle like sharks. I can't blame them; I would have done the same thing, but I don't like being in the hot seat and suddenly, I'm at a loss for words again.

"Um . . . well . . . I . . . uh . . . err…" I ramble and stutter along, not quite certain how to explain my dull marriage and new wandering eye.

"Oh my!" Tara gets excited, widening her eyes in anticipation, I guess.

"Do you have a side piece?" Jessica jumps in with the same enthusiasm as Tara.

"No wonder she's been so busy!" Tara jokes, the women's thirst for drama unquenchable.

I stare at their sinisterly excited faces and know there is only one way out—the truth.

"No, no. No affair." I smirk as they almost look disappointed hearing the truth. The news of an affair would have made their day just a bit juicier and more delectable.

"But…" Jessica confidently probes with a suspicious squint as if she knows there is more to the story. Everyone is an investigative reporter around me these days.

"I am working with an accomplished lawyer who's a little younger than us," I professionally begin.

"Is he hot?" Tara pounces, not letting me skirt around anything.

"Well…handsome, yeah. Okay, he's pretty damn hot," I cave and giggle.

"Have you fantasized about him?" Jessica plunges in for the kill. Naturally, the next best thing to learning I'm having crazy, adulteress sex would be to find out I've been fantasizing about it. All of a sudden, I've become their guilty pleasure, giving our Veronica Palsey book club the backseat. Jessica and Tara started it and of course now I'm getting just as obsessed with romance novels as they are. But the words on the pages, even the most eloquently stated ones, pale in comparison to the zeal at which my two friends are barreling down upon me. I seem to have evolved into their real-life version of Veronica Palsey. The way their eyes are scanning my face and body, like they are searching for confirmation, tells me that much.

"I love Aiden," I declare with a mischievous smirk.

"How many times?" Jessica playfully fires back, not letting me off the hook so easily.

"A few small daydreams here and there. What girl hasn't?" I try to be casual about it.

"There's more," Jessica relentlessly charges forward.

"And one real good fantasy," I give, exposing the one guilty pleasure I participated in.

"How good?" she asks quickly. Tara leans halfway over the table, sipping her appletini, but I can tell she's all ears.

Jessica's questions are bordering on harassment to this point, but I give her one last nugget. "Enough to allow me to move on," I concisely close the pages to my book on my friends. We sit back and enjoy the soft breeze, the seventy degree weather, and our appletinis. I enjoy my time with the girls, knowing I have a business date with Taylor just minutes away. I am intrigued as to what will come next.

Nine

Nine

"I can drive," Taylor kindly offers. I would love to take a ride in his classic Mercedes Roadster. We would fly through the desert with the top down, and it would be all too easy . . . all too much like a dream. But, right now, I need to stay entrenched in reality.

"I got it," I assert, remaining in control of the trip and wanting to make certain I keep my eye on the ball.

My Excursion makes its way from the 405 freeway north to the 101 east and, after a few more freeway exchanges, we finally reach the 15 and head east across the Southern California Desert. The traffic happens to be relatively light; the afternoon journey providing minimal obstacles as we head across the normally congested roads.

Some classic rock to keep the mood light and upbeat; I won't get too distracted with bands like Boston and Journey playing. Taylor is quiet for the beginning of the trip. It is uncharacteristic for both of us. I've never been in the same vicinity as him and not had some sort of verbal exchange.

"I like your whip," Taylor comments as he looks my car over, with a big smile on his face, breaking the relatively silent ride. I scoff at his use of *whip.*

"You down with the new slang of the day?" I joke with Taylor.

I get a smirk. "This is a nice car, though. Well done," he reiterates. I'm quite sure he is sincere, but he could afford a souped up Lincoln Navigator that's twice the price of my big girl. But, I'll take the pat on the back.

"It has to survive my two daughters on occasion. It used to be an everyday thing with the kids, but as I got busier, Aiden had to take over," I casually inform.

Taylor gives me a look of confusion. It takes me a second before I realize that I've never verbally introduced Aiden's name in a conversation with Taylor. It is a subconscious error, but one that was most likely done with bad intentions.

"My husband," I clarify.

"Ah, yes. I figured. Someone has to be there for the kids on a regular basis when you work the long days and travel. I envy parents. A dubious task: raising children. They're born into this world so vulnerable. They are so susceptible to anything and everything," he ponders the challenges of raising children aloud.

"It is. There always seems to be a difficult choice waiting beyond the bend," I enlighten the childless man. At least I assume, from my one night of creeping on the internet, he doesn't have kids.

"It is thankless while, at the same time, rewarding. An oxymoronic journey of epic proportions," Taylor shares his personal insight on the matter, his eyes once again shimmering when he speaks from his inner self. It is an interesting occurrence to see the man, who is seemingly made of armor, display random pieces of himself, so often masked by cloaks of sarcasm and that billion dollar smile.

"Have you ever thought about having children?" I curiously ask, hoping to get more.

"Not today. And not tomorrow. Beyond that, I don't like to plan too far ahead," he replies, but his answer is evasive.

"I don't buy it," I call bullshit. Taylor gives me a surprised smile, the clear reaction of a man not used to being spoken to that way.

"Children require attention I am unable to provide." The calculated, cold response rings of truth far more than his claim to live one day at a time.

"Unable or unwilling?" I find it impossible not to mince words with him, something inside me charging fearlessly ahead deeper into the conversation.

"Are you always this blunt?"

"Do you want me to stop asking you questions?" I quip.

"No. Ask whatever you want. I like your ambition," he compliments.

"My ambition." I laugh, amused that he recognizes an attribute few in my life consider a positive.

"Is that funny?"

"It's not an attribute I've found others believe to be of value in women," I plainly state.

"I value it. Otherwise, what's the point of it all?" Taylor and I definitely meet at the same crossroads on ambition. "And I think it's an attribute that is very sexy in a woman, with all due respect," an aggressive compliment made with a gentleman's tongue. *Taylor Diamond, you can't be this perfect.*

"Where'd you grow up?" he changes direction. I can't tell if we're on a first date or he's making casual conversation. Taylor is a difficult man to read, although, I'm not an expert in that field, by any means.

"Out here, in the desert. People don't have much out here. But they got what they got." I explain with few details, attempting to remain on par with his modus operandi.

"A home is a special place. It's a place for family— to feel safe. As long as you have a happy home, you are rich," Taylor again spreads his philosophy with ease, like a well-versed politician.

"So, wealthy is in the eye of the beholder?" I jab back. I'm cresting toward upper-middle class and I still feel as though we struggle. I don't know a world like Taylor's, where money has virtually become just an object, as opposed to the chain and shackles of life that constantly binds your every action. "I'd have you ask people out here in the desert what they think of that hypothesis." I put some of my own personal color on the discussion.

"What amount of money will make the Lowry's happy?" the lawyer inside Taylor comes out to play, waging a healthy debate on the subject.

"Point well taken. But with money being the primary source of stress and discontent in marriages, how can you ignore that it plays a huge role?" I fire back. Financial inequality is a subject I am more well-versed in than he.

"And this fact was extracted from what publication?"

"I think Cosmo, so you know it's serious." I smile with the delivery of my paper-thin resource.

"Yes. Then, by all means, proceed."

"Well . . . that was pretty much it," I feebly rest my case.

"A Cosmo Magazine article, *possibly,* and some life experience? Well, that is a mountain for me to climb, but I would say only this, that although monetary issues can be a concern and a hot-button in many marriages, it will always be friendship that binds people for life. Marriage goes against animalistic urges; the passion that blazes inside people. It is an institution literally built to restrict the evolvement and active exchange of passion from person to person. It can be a difficult concept to grasp. Men have always been hunters and women aren't too far behind," he states with confidence.

"And all this from the man who touts family as such an important entity?" I fire back with curiosity.

Taylor smiles and glances away, looking out at the desert. I can't tell if I've insulted him or out-flanked him. I wait a moment, and then he speaks. "Family is *very* important. I always say, *never forget where you came from.*

You only have one bloodline. I'm humbled by it. Have you done an ancestry search?"

"No." I can't tell if that was the smoothest gear-switch ever or if he is heading on a tangent.

"Pretty interesting. My family was traced all the way back to Ancient Rome. But much of the time, my family lived in Liverpool and greater London after that. It's extraordinary to look behind you every once in a while. You can see those footsteps, the path they forged to make your path possible," Taylor goes on. It is an interesting lesson. I couldn't tell you who came before me in my family. Even my great grandparents are a bit sketchy. But all the way back to Rome?

"Like the real Ancient Rome?" I ask with disbelief and a serious lack of historical moxy.

"Way back. Yes."

"What was your relative, a great warrior or something?" I ask, assuming this so-called ancient relative was a master swordsman or a heroic warmonger. I am searching for a story that will knock my socks off. Either way, I'm skeptical, to say the least.

"He was a shoe maker," Taylor states with serious simplistic enlightenment. "Just a shoe maker."

"Interesting. So, an entrepreneur way back then," I mildly joke, but Taylor's family history reveal is palatable and he has managed to draw me in. I believe him.

"Something like that. It's funny; he kept very good records, this simple man. He had a family and if he was a great warrior, I doubt my family would exist today. The toll, the deaths, great warriors fall to great glory but, all too often, it is the fallen souls who fail to exit beyond their legend. If my relative fought in the army way back when, if he drew a sword instead of making a shoe, who knows if I'd be here. So, here I am…a decedent of a Roman shoe maker." He smiles.

Taylor is a dynamic man. He talks to me as if we are old friends and I'm suddenly trapped between my fantasies and being a peer. Either way—I'm married—a fact I feel the constant need to remind myself about, when I'm around Mr. Diamond.

Ambition, wealth, incredible looks, depth, that billion dollar smile, and those eyes—those damn blue eyes. His "*E-Harmony*" resume would be off the charts! We rest our minds and mouths on Taylor's deep thoughts with a few moments of silence.

Our arrival in Ramsey is quiet. Our only scheduled stop is at my cousins, Rebecca's, house. The entire Class Action lawsuit was born here. Both Rebecca and her daughter, Casey, are sick. Casey has kidney and lung damage. She used to go running every day, play with her friends. She was a normal kid that seasonally dominated on the soccer field. Becca always sent me videos of Casey before she got sick. Being the same age, Becca and I have always been close. We were both desert rats. You gotta stick together out there; it can be a hard, lost place.

As we pull up to Rebecca's small home, I find it difficult to channel the strength to enter inside. An old, broken down pick-up sits on concrete blocks, on the dirt driveway, just to the side of the house. I turn my luxury cruiser off. My Excursion is worth more than all of Rebecca's worldly possessions, which often has me feeling a little guilty. Why do I have so much, and *still* we argue about money, while Rebecca has so little?

Taylor is about to get out of the car when he sees me hesitate. "You're close?" Taylor dissects, as if he knows my relationship with Rebecca goes beyond a lawyer and client.

"She's my cousin. Yeah. We've always been real close," I say with an impassioned, soft tone.

"The case is good. We're gonna win. Don't worry," Taylor tries to calm my nerves. But it goes beyond the case.

"I know. It's just hard knowing this could have been me. We started in the same place and I could have very easily ended up here."

"You can't apologize for success," Taylor declares, an issue he knows all too well.

"What about luck? What of luck and fate?" I propose to Taylor, hoping he will share more insight with me, as I continue to stall.

"Fate is a fickle word. Luck is for suckers. People struggle and words like *fate* and *luck* create excuses where voids are left to be filled." Taylor's harsh words are a declaration of success and ambition. He may be generous and giving, but the last thing Taylor will feel is guilt over wealth. That much is clear.

"Okay. Let's do this." I gain the courage to exit my SUV and head to the front door.

Taylor quietly surveys the area. Toys on the yard, dirt, weeds, chipped paint. He seems to be focusing on everything: toys in the yard, dirt, weeds, chipped paint, staring at them as if they were clues to a crime.

"What are you doing?"

"I'm watching," he causally states. I pass it off as nothing, "Nicki!" Rebecca whips the door open in excitement. Her face is pale but contains numerous freckles, spotted from years in the hot sun. She is thin too; life, taking a toll on her, giving her the appearance of a forty-five year old woman, not thirty-nine. Once beautiful, she is now a beaten woman. As always though, Rebecca still carries a wonderful spirit about her. That is something that can never be stolen from her.

I hug Becca with all my might. "I'm so happy to see you!" I blurt out. It is a business trip, but I'm happy to be here on any account.

We soak each other in for a moment, and then I realize my manners as Rebecca almost gawks at Taylor, clearly impressed with his looks.

"Oh! My manners! This is Mr. Diamond," I introduce.

Taylor smiles and nods to Rebecca. "Hello, Ms. Braxton." He did study the files; I never told him Rebecca's last name.

"I'm charmed." She smiles, seemingly still enamored with Taylor's sharp, impressive appearance. Taylor turns and starts to roam the living room on his own.

"How are you guys holding up?" I ask, knowing the answer before I even pose the question. It's not like it's white noise, but my eyes flash to Taylor as Rebecca speaks. He is closely surveying the room just as he did outside. He examines the pictures on the wall, like he's soaking in the details as if they were of his own family. Rebecca uses words like *hard* and *scared* and things discussed again and again. Her life has been tough . . . her road hard. Nothing has changed for her, so I listen, but I don't hear every word coming out of her mouth. Taylor's peculiar tour around the room has me captivated.

"Is she here?" Taylor interrupts Rebecca mid-sentence. "I'm sorry to interrupt. I just really want to see her." Taylor shows great sincerity as always. His interest, and the concern on his face, fills the room with emotion that Rebecca also can't help but respond to.

"Of course, Mr. Diamond," she happily welcomes.

"Please, call me Taylor."

"Then, you best call me, Rebecca, because you're working with my girl, which means you're one of the family now." Rebecca, as always, happily welcomes others into her inner circle. She would literally give the shirt off her back to help a homeless man tomorrow, and yet, she has nothing and owes everyone.

We walk down the hall with Taylor dragging behind, still looking closely at the various historical images lining the Braxton Family walls.

Rebecca comes to a door and pauses. She turns back to Taylor and me. "I don't care that I need dialysis or that my lungs have been chewed to the point where walking thirty yards is a challenge. *This* is what kills me. Behind this door. This kills me," Becca finishes her lead-in before opening the door to the playroom in the back of the house.

Casey sits on a couch in the playroom with an oxygen tank beside her, pumping fresh air into her damaged lungs. A sweet-looking blonde haired girl, with soft, white skin and beautiful, brown eyes make it hard to digest that she is so sick.

"Hey, Case," Rebecca begins with introductions, but gets no further when Casey jumps up off the couch.

"Auntie, Nick!" Casey shouts with joy. She rushes to me, her oxygen tank, on wheels, dragging a few feet as she squeezes my waist with one of the greatest hugs of my life. "Mommy said you were getting close to making me better!" Casey proclaims with excitement. I flash a concerned look at Rebecca, her need for optimism and hope surpassing reality. I feel as though I'm caught in the eye of a storm. It's a feeling I'm well versed in when I visit them. No one should represent a relative, especially one in a situation like this. It tears me apart. But, this goes beyond just Rebecca and Casey, even though I wouldn't have been in Ramsey otherwise. There are many more who have been poisoned; more sad stories. Casey is the youngest to be affected in this way, and I sob inside, remembering the young girl, dashing about, just years before. She has been condemned to the life of a seventy-year-old, two-pack-a-day smoker—a crime she never committed in her innocent life. I love her too much for this. My cousin's baby; it's just not fair.

I have tears in my eyes as I turn to see Taylor. He's staring right at us, tears in his eyes as well. It's as if my pain has become his pain as he empathizes with my family's plight.

I kiss Casey on the head and introduce her to Taylor. The three of us talk. Casey's stories are grounded to endless optimism and funny incidents inside her home. We talk for about ten minutes before she needs to sit back down and relax from all the excitement.

Rebecca leads Taylor and me outside to talk more, leaving Casey to her cartoons. She takes out an E-cig; she used to be a smoker. It's been a very contentious part of the case, up to this point. Desert rats like to smoke. I don't know why, but when I was young, I did too. Given the census of smokers, I know it will be hell discussing the facts of the case. The defense already attempted to have the class action thrown out, citing smoking as a major cause for much of the lung problems. But, there's the abundance of kidney issues that has been left unexplained. "These aren't bad." Rebecca inhales the vapor smoke and blows it out as she leans against her old, broken-down pick-up.

"How's Ben?" I ask, knowing the answer could be rough.

"You know," she bravely states. "He's stressed . . . frustrated. Hours were cut at the shop," Rebecca follows up. Her husband, Ben, works as a mechanic. The pick-up on cement blocks is his latest toy in attempts to make a few extra bucks. But, rebuilding an engine costs money. Buying tires costs money. It looks as if he has a way to go with this project. "It's the desert, babe," Rebecca sums it all up in one harsh phrase. And that *is* the desert—extreme and harsh. You are on your own, living on a barren island, subjected to the same challenges as snakes and lizards. There is no *easy* out here—at least—not the majority of it.

We talk about the case, the timetable. *Soon,* I tell her. But in all honesty, the answers are largely unknown. However, Rebecca and her family are desperate for money, much like how the desert sands of Death Valley thirsts for water. And as much as the Braxton's need the money,

Rebecca wants their day in court. She wants them to know what Casey looks like; to feel her pain . . . hear her words.

Taylor heads back over to my car, giving Rebecca and me one last moment alone. I take out my check book and write a check for $4,000. I tell her it is an advance on her case, something the firm does. She would never take money directly from me, but that's what I'm doing. I'm trying to keep her afloat as long as possible. Aiden will kill me, but she is family and I *need* to help her.

Taylor and I get back in my Excursion and drive. Thoughts of what we just witnessed swim in *both* of our heads, I'm sure. It's rough to hear, even harder to see. It is quiet until Taylor gently places his left hand upon my right hand on the steering wheel. His fingers become my fingers. Our hands become one. I freeze.

Ten

We need to shoot across the desert before sundown to avoid the daily grind of LA's rush hour traffic. But his hand is upon mine. Traffic to hell, what is he doing?

I pull up to a stop sign. There are no cars behind or ahead. So, I wait for an answer. I turn my head slightly and look over at Taylor, our eyes matching up. We are synced up like a perfectly playing record. My heart is racing and I feel as though his beats are my beats. This moment—the pause—seems to last so long. It's as if our spirits touch, sharing an original moment only we can speak of. It's a silent secret of endless bounds, a confession between us. It can mean everything and nothing at all in one crushing stare.

"I want you to go somewhere," his soft voice beckons me, challenging feelings of optimism, intrigue, and excitement.

"Where?" my near breathless voice asks. I'm compelled to adhere to his every command.

"We're close. We're very close," his lips so gently move as he speaks, as if carrying the motion of the afternoon along in his words. It's impossible not be swept up by the depth of his empathy. I haven't shared with anyone in so long; feelings and emotions. I want to share something with someone—I need to. We are extremely attracted to one another. It is fast and furious. But chemical attractions are compelling and, by those standards, we are a nuclear duo right now.

"Okay," I respond in kind. It is a simple *yes* to be led on whatever adventure is to come. I'm intrigued beyond words at what Taylor Diamond has up his sleeve.

I drive. He directs me for twenty miles through the heart of the California Desert. "Turn here," he confidently prompts. We are close. His voice tells the story of someone excited and anxious to arrive. It isn't just me that is hopeful of something. Taylor Diamond is invested in some way, shape or form with me. He has emotional investment. I may be blind to some things, but I feel it inside me like I've never felt anything before. I know I want to believe that. It's been so long since I have felt *wanted*. And for some reason, when he looks at me, he looks deep inside and touches something no one else can find. It's weird and sounds stranger as I try to work it out in my head.

"What is it?" I ask with curiosity.

"Not yet," he denies me, teasing me with the unknown.

"What does it look like?" I ask like a child begging for answers, any sort of clue to help me figure out the mystery.

"I want you to see it with your own two eyes. I don't want to ruin it with words," Taylor poetically states, raising the stakes of what I am about to see. I drive a few more miles as the sun slowly descends behind the tallest mountain bordering the massive desert valley. Darkness is slowly starting to encroach upon the desert cacti.

"Here!" He points with urgency.

I turn down a small dirt road, my eyes panning around for answers. A sign reads: *Fossil Falls*. It's a state park of some kind, and I find a place to park. I stare through the dashboard, my eyes looking in awe at the structures before me; thousands upon thousands of fossilized black rocks. They stand tall and short. They look magnificent, their smooth, black coating, glistening off the sun's final rays of the day. The rock formations stretch as far as the eye can see.

We exit my Excursion as I continue to stare, captivated at the gravity of what I'm looking at. All this time . . . I grew up in the desert and never knew of such a place. And grant it, I was young, and traveling an hour to see rocks isn't exactly what a teenager does for shits and giggles. But this is a site to behold.

Created from ancient, cinder cone volcanoes, random black, shiny lava formations dried and became this peaceful entrapment of nature. It is chaos transformed into an unspoken, silent beauty.

Alone at Fossil Falls, we stroll through the structures as if we were at a park, each of us weaving our own path by the formations. As we pass a divide, our eyes meet up and we continue on. Another barrier comes between us on our lazy stroll and once again, our eyes meet up beyond the structure. We are two teenagers participating in a cat and mouse game of budding feelings. It feels perfectly childlike and wonderful.

I know why Taylor likes this place. It's quiet, beautiful, and untouched. It is mysterious and priceless all in one, two of Taylor's more shimmering qualities. To see it, to stand amongst the island of cooled lava rock, surrounded by vast desert, is truly an experience I'll never forget.

We walk further into the black rock forest and enter a deep decent into a shadowed, twenty-foot, carved out ravine. We are still alone amongst the monuments, carefully making our way down into the ravine. My heart is racing. I joked about this being a first date, but what a feeling I have now. In the ravine, I'm surrounded by smoothed, black, cold lava. I'm struck by the beauty and solitude of it all. In the context of who I am with, and where I am, this is overwhelming all my better judgments and sensibilities. Everything has been put aside for this amazing moment in time. I run my hands along the cold, black walls, a stark contrast to the hot desert ground it is surrounded by. It is a physical memory I want forever. The touch of the rock is almost like glazed, smooth marble, worn by water over thousands of years.

I continue to the other side of the ravine. I turn and see Taylor at the other end. We are now bookmarking the nearly twenty yards of space in the small valley. We stare at one another, both remaining silent. The moment is taking on a life of its own. Anything could happen down here and no one would know. It's just me, Taylor, a setting sun, an acre of cold fossilized ancient remains, and the silence. Barely, the whistle of the wind is present in the sacred moment we are sharing. It's captivating, as if we are being transported to another world. We just look at one another, two adults surrounded by fossilized rock with a darkening, beautiful, blue sky above.

"You like it here?" my voice echoes as if I were in a cave.

"When I need to think, I come here."

"This isn't your *go-to* on dates is it?" I joke with a half-cocked smile. The move into our personal lives is risky. The words fall quickly out of my mouth and I barely have time to analyze them. I'm not certain I want to head down this road. I mean—*I do!* But . . . I also don't.

"No. No dates," Taylor responds with a relaxed, cool smile.

"It's pretty amazing." I run my hand along the smooth wall, once again, to support my excitement. It's comfortable talking about the scenic beauty, an easy tangent from where I was heading.

"It is. Sometimes people come by, but not too often. And almost never at night," Taylor kicks the door open to our seclusion. Is it some sort of invitation? Is he testing my interest, gaging me like an animal?

"You have a strange way about you." I make my own judgments and decide to test Taylor.

"How so?"

"You look at me like you know me."

I feel Taylor's piercing eyes constantly upon me, soaking in every inch of me despite staring directly into my eyes. "Do you want me to change?" He fires another challenge back at me. I try to extract information, emotion from him. I want to know more about him. I want to know how he feels. But he is outflanking me at every turn, throwing it back toward me. And before I know it, with each question, with each response, we are slowly moving closer to one another. It's not conscious, at first. We just are taking small steps, so it's easier to hear one another. We are drawn to one another like flies to a light. Entranced, we continue to move toward one another as the conversation continues.

"No. But you know I can't change who I am," I begin to speak in codes, believing we both are on the same level, moving emotionally closer and closer together.

"Who asked you to change?" Taylor answers with a question.

"Not many people run into a burning house," my coded words are meant to protect me, to maintain a shield around my truths. Right now, I am uncertain how deep I am swimming or how much further I'm willing to go.

"Maybe I'm a firefighter," Taylor offers.

"You don't know me well enough yet to put out all my fires," my subconscious launches a defense challenging what is happening; my own mind waging an internal power struggle.

"I'll learn," Taylor poignantly replies. Our feet continue to move closer to one another.

"This case is everything to me. It's my family," I desperately plea. The words are not for Taylor to hear, they are for me to hear; an attempt to convince myself to walk away.

"It should. It should mean all of that to you," Taylor agrees with me and I am being uncontrollably pulled closer and closer to him.

"We're using a lot of words—but there is no direction. We are in a fog." I point out the cloak and dagger game of communication we are playing.

"Sometimes it's better not to plan." Taylor and I arrive at one another.

"I have a lot to lose with *everything*," I relate to Taylor, my internal fear over the unknown over where we were heading.

"Who said you have to risk anything?" Taylor whispers with a breathy sultry sexiness that has my knees weakening.

"I am. Just by being here. By standing here. By being here with you," I make it clear the risk I'm taking by even having fantasies and feelings for Taylor.

"Nothing bad will happen to you," he states with a comforting certainty. "This is where you are safe," he guarantees valiantly.

"Then why am I so terrified?" My voice too trails, our lips moving closer, just inches apart from one another.

"Are you afraid or are you excited?" Taylor poses.

"Both," my breath nearly gone from my lungs.

"You're safe," Taylor once gain promises.

"How many women have you brought here?" I ask under my breath with a smirk on my face, once again posing the familiar question to Taylor.

"None," he states with complete honesty, staring into my eyes.

With our lips just an inch away, I'm shaking, the excitement boiling over inside of me. The butterflies are swirling all around inside my stomach as my lips quiver. My heart is racing as nothing separates us but the warm breaths coming from our mouth. I close my eyes fully immersing myself into the unknown.

"I see someone!!!" A young boy screams from above, Taylor and I jumping back away as if we were caught red-handed.

I need to catch my breath. If I had asthma, I'd need Abuteral STAT. I take deep breaths in and swallow, my throat parched from my nerves in overdrive. Taylor has a boyish smile he flashes at me. Not embarrassment, not regret, but a sweet smile of excitement. He too was lost in the moment, and happily at that.

"There are other people here!" The ten year old boy has a flashlight on him and other footsteps approach, that of a family. The parents and two other children join the young boy. And with their entrance, we make a quiet exit.

We're in my Excursion, heading back toward Los Angeles. It is silent at first, our series of indirect questions and responses sucking the air out of our lungs. Our lips were less than an inch apart. I could taste his breath on my tongue, the warm air that trickled out of his mouth. I'd feel uncomfortable normally, but our dialogue has somehow left me invigorated. The anticipation of *something* has got me spinning.

"Did you enjoy it?" Taylor grins, breaking the ice.

"It was amazing. Thank you for bringing me there," I spread sincere gratitude and appreciation upon Taylor.

"It was *nearly* perfect," Taylor alludes to what *almost* was. I can't believe I did that or . . . almost did. I wonder if his eyes were closed. I wonder what would have happened next.

"It was just what I needed," I follow up.

"You should come out with me," he bluntly states. I'm not certain if this is a date request or where he is heading. I can't just live another life. I'm a wife . . . a mother.

"Errr…umm…" I have no idea how to react. I ramble in my head, with indecision, while all that trickles out of my mouth are noises of uncertainty and complex confusion.

"Some of the assistants are grabbing a drink. I told them I'd join," Taylor innocently offers.

Ah, far less complicated than I thought. But I feel sucker-punched in the gut now. I want the date offer back. I may have been indecisive, but now I want that decision to fall back to me. Just Taylor and me. I want that chance again, even as my Jiminy Cricket battles me, inside my head, with flashing red lights, stop signs, and angry grumblings. But, my conscious is tuned out by the symphony of chance, possibility, and passion. It is drowned out by a cacophony of soaring emotions, bursting to come out of me. I love feeling this way. I miss this feeling. I feel like a little girl, living out a mad crush. I feel alive.

"Hmm. I'm not sure I have..." I begin with intentions of backing out of any evening shenanigans.

"Take a leap of faith." There he goes again; the coded messages. The words with so many meanings, my mind and heart are challenged. And I *love* a good challenge.

"Faith, huh?" I smile.

"Faith and some vodka never hurt anyone," Taylor smiles.

We arrive at Jacob's Bar, under the veil of darkness, concealed as travel partners. It is quaint and lively. It's also a block from the offices, so when the assistants head off for drinks, they go here. Angela has always invited me and, when they first started going out, a few attorneys and I joined them. But, people leave—they move on—and I was left, standing alone with the assistants. I don't know why that deterred me from going, but it did. Now, that I'm a partner, I've been so busy. My hair hasn't come down in a long time. But, Taylor Diamond has, successfully, cast his spell upon me—once again, and I feel obligated to join in.

We weave through a mellow happy hour crowd, amidst the dark atmosphere of the bar. The lively environment, headlined by fun, energetic classic rock, blasting through the speakers, sets the perfect mood. Seated at a booth are Angela, Tabatha, and Ronald Thomas.

Ronald is a legal administrative assistant, the office researcher and a damn good one. He's also hilarious; the life of any party. He carries his flamboyant homosexuality as a badge of honor on his dark, black skin. And any party isn't a party without him. Ronald's skin is dark or as he puts it: *Africa Black*. He is a true joy to hang out with, but I'd rather not see our best researcher at the moment. He is straightforward as a spear, when he speaks. He is not afraid to speak his mind and any expression ending with *caution to the wind* is one Ronald Thomas is not familiar with. He knows I'm married and although he is drinking, I'm nervous he'll see right through me. Taylor's made to play poker while I wear my "tells like an eight-year-old" face.

"Hey, you two!" A surprised and excited Angela welcomes Taylor and me. She comes over and gives me a *buzzed* hug.

With a few empty glasses, the assistants have a head start on us and I could use some old fashion liquid courage to help settle me down.

"We just came back from Ramsey," I quickly establish our alibi prior to any accusations flying around the room.

Ronald sips his drink with a devious smile on his face.

"You wish," I hurl at Ronald, a playful pre-emptive strike, making sure he doesn't jump to conclusions about Taylor and me—at least, not yet.

"I sure do, honey!" Ronald slides his way out of the booth and gleefully approaches Taylor.

"Mr. Diamond, you are a sight."

"This is Ronald Thomas, an exceptional researcher in our office," I take care of the introductions.

"And, he's probably wishing you were gay, right about now!" Angela jokes, noticing Ronald's clear interest in Taylor's physique.

"You must be an angel because you look like you just fell from Heaven! Oh, my!" Ronald jokes, as he always does, with his boisterous self.

"Don't worry, he bites—but he's very good at his job," I add, attempting to keep the conversation in a safe place. I find myself deflecting from Taylor, trying to keep the spotlight off of him.

"And, right now, Mr. Diamond, he's researching you!" Tabatha jokes. Angela, Tabatha, and Ronald burst into laughter. They clearly have had *a lot* to drink.

Taylor and I share a smile, amused.

"It's a pleasure to meet you, Ronald." Taylor extends his hand.

Ronald turns away from Taylor and toward us, sporting a playful grin. "Pleasure's all mine!" He fans himself, as he shakes Taylor's hand.

"I'm gonna grab a drink. I got this round, guys," Taylor kindly offers.

"Long Island! White Russian! Blue Lagoon!" The drink orders come flying out from the peanut gallery. Then, he turns to me.

"I don't know," I bashfully attempt to resist.

"One. Just one," his simple plea.

"Come on, you hard ass!" Ronald yells. "And, I mean that literally; I can bounce quarters off that thing!" he jokes, checking out my rear.

"You know you want to!" Angela eggs me on, too.

"Just do it!" Tabatha shouts randomly, eyeing Taylor from top to bottom, as if he was a meal and she was starving for some food.

Taylor, once again, smiles at me; his head tilting, his eyebrows rising, begging me to drink.

"Grey Goose and lime, on the rocks," I say with class. A subtle nod and he is off. I sit down at the table with the gang, who stare at me as if I have three heads. They are looking for answers; it's clear they think something may be up.

"You are *so* freakin' lucky!" Tabatha crows.

"How do you restrain yourself, girl?!" Ronald jumps in.

"I mean, Aiden is super nice, Nick…but, holy shit!" Angela hollers. All three of them laugh and chuckle at their drunken comments, amusing themselves. Inside, I let out a huge sigh of relief. They aren't *on* to me, they're jealous of me. I am so relieved.

Taylor arrives back at the table, as everyone around me continues to laugh and joke. He sits across from me, each of us bookmarking the half circle booth. Their words are empty as my eyes pan back and forth across at Taylor, hoping his eyes meet up with mine. Back and forth, drink after drink, but our eyes never connect. In fact, he is too entrenched in conversations around the table, and charming the pants off of everyone else. He pays little attention to me. And before I know it, I have one, two, and then three drinks in me.

A glance at my phone and I see a text from Aiden: *What time are you coming home?* The text was from an hour ago. *Shit.*

I slowly nod and sneak away from the table. I am hoping no one is going to miss me, as I have mentally turned the page on this night. I walk toward a crowd of people, circling the bar. I try to make my way through, so I can use the bathroom, before I head out. I make it inside and wonder where I am. Physically, I know. I'm in the bathroom at Jacob's Bar. But mentally, where the hell am I? It's getting late. The girls are probably in bed. And I'm peeing in a bathroom, buzzed off my ass, for the second time today. This is all so I can hang around the dreamy Taylor Diamond? A dark cloud of guilt makes its way overhead. I finish up in the bathroom, and I am faced with the same sea of people as before. I want to sneak out. No goodbyes. No hugs. No kisses. No awkwardness. I just want to leave.

The people traffic makes it difficult. And all of a sudden, a hand grabs my hand. I whip my head around and see Taylor. My feet are anchored to the sticky floor. My breathing seizes. The world has, once again, stopped. Taylor and I have entered that special bubble we created. Our hands are clasped together. His fingers feel strong but soft. I close my eyes and then open them again, just to make sure this is real. I shoot a look over just ten yards away, where three chatty office assistants would just love to see our hands together. We are camouflaged by a few bar tables and the crowd of people. But at any moment, a single eye can sift through the thin layer of protection and find us, touching, our hands together, our clear interest in one another, there for all to see. Then it would all be over.

I can't, the words echo in my head but fail to reach my lips.

All we can do is stare at one another. His eyes haven't found me for nearly two hours, sitting just a few feet away. Now, they can't seem to turn away.

My phone vibrates in my pocket. I close my eyes, once again. I have two distinct paths . . . two distinct choices. I don't know what to do. Where do I go from here?

Eleven

Eleven

I strike the bathroom door with my palm, barely able to keep my balance as our passionate kiss overwhelms all my senses. Our faces, our mouths, our lips, are pressed up so fiercely against one another; we are fused like two pieces of metal.

Our hands are used as guides to keep our balance as we crash into the women's lavatory at Jacob's Bar.

I hear a lone woman finish washing her hands, and then she heads out. Taylor and I step back from one another, heavily breathing. He slowly reaches the doorknob and locks it. It didn't matter either way to me. I just want him inside of me.

He takes small, slow steps towards me. I wait by the sink, my hands clasping the edges of the black, ceramic tiling. I tilt my head down, my best seductive glare, oozing off of me. I lean just a little back on the counter top, giving him a clear roadmap to my body's primary desire. He sidles up in front of me, and my legs open, stretching the material of my skirt. My inner thighs give him a clear, directional guide. He steps into me, his hand running up my legs, *all* the way up my thighs. His fingertips reach the crest of my spot and slowly, he reaches higher to pull my panties down. Our eyes never break apart. Our intense stare is a preview of things to come. It would take a bomb to break our mutual impassioned trance.

He takes my panties down to my ankles. He pulls them over one foot, then another. I reach out and unbuckle his belt, not too fast; I want to tease him just a little. Then my hands make their way right to his zipper. I slowly unzip his pants and run fingers under his boxers and grab his hard dick in my hand. I gently massage it and his head bends back. I can tell he is going insane inside.

He picks me up onto the counter, the perfect height for what is about to transpire. His hands run up my thighs, this time pushing my skirt all the way up to my waist. I pull his pants and boxers down, both sliding to his ankles. And, as if we were perfectly in sync, I pull him forward as he steps toward me. I guide him inside of me and feel myself stretch to accommodate his size. It is amazing.

Oh! Ah! We both exude sounds of ecstasy as he thrusts again and again. Our mouths reacquaint themselves and we passionately kiss. My hands quickly fly down to my sides, holding the edge of the black countertop. He thrusts again and again, penetrating deeper and deeper inside me. My fingers clinch harder, barely able to keep my body in place.

He raises his hands against my cheeks as we kiss. His right hand runs up through my hair as we go faster and faster.

My head leans back as I tilt my entire body backwards, being taken like never before.

Oh, my God! Screams of joy, in my head, as I gladly take in all that Taylor Diamond has to offer.

His breathing is heavy as his head tilts back, he too enjoying every second of our afterhours session.

"*Harder,*" my breathless lungs muster any and all air to make one simple command of him. And he obliges. He goes harder, our muted grunts and sounds of sex start to fill the bathroom walls.

He charges ahead again and again. I don't usually come like this; not in this position. I can't, that I know of. But, right now, I feel as though I'm about to explode.

Yes. Yes. Again my muted voice slips out words.

A strange sound is brewing by the door. People sound as if they are grumbling and talking just a few feet away. Do they hear us? Are we that noisy?

I don't care but their grumbling gets louder and louder.

Taylor's rhythm continues and I feel as though I'm going to rip the entire countertop off as I hold on for dear life.

"Yes! Yes! Yes!"

And then...

I whip up in bed, covered in sweat. I'm out of breath, and it takes a moment for me to get my bearings down. I pan my eyes around my own bedroom, the last place I expected to be. Lying next to me, asleep, snoring with the rage of a bear is Aiden. He is out cold, oblivious to my current state.

"Jesus," I mumble to myself, still half out of breath. I run my hands through my damp hair. It was all a fantastic fantasy. Another amazing dream.

Damn.

It was hard to pull away from Taylor at the bar, but I had no choice. There was nowhere to go. No good out. With our co-workers a few yards away and a husband calling me to find my whereabouts, this was not the time; this was not the place.

I re-route my brain away from the fantastic dream and slowly recalibrate myself to my daily surroundings.

I take a walk and head downstairs to grab a drink. I need a drink. Not of alcohol. *Too much of that.* I need to dial it back a bit and have some milk.

My mind flashes back to the moment—the moment when he grabbed my hand in the bar. As I sit on a bar stool at my kitchen island, sipping my milk, I ponder that moment. Our hands were clasped. We were together. We took a huge step. I took a big step. I wanted his hand in my hand. I wanted that moment so badly.

I close my eyes and wish I could split myself in half. I want to live two lives. I have a great deal of frustration that has built up in my home, but I wish I could walk two paths simultaneously. I love my husband. I love my kids. But, I have never felt more alive than when walking by the side of Taylor Diamond. I've never felt more excitement than when he held my hand. I've never wanted to be somewhere else so badly. I want so much more.

Another sip of my milk and I see the faces of my girls: Lacy and Ariel; my wonders of the world. I see their smiles. I see how amazing they are and how much I miss them. I feel like they've grown each time I see them. How can a mother not see their child grow? If she spends a hundred hours a week at her job, that's how.

And, so there are two worlds; two distinct directions I may travel. I'm at a crossroads in my life but I also feel as though I've created the choice. I can walk away from Taylor at any time. I can try to ignore the feelings, heating up inside me like a volcano daring to erupt. I can try to do all those things, but it would be futile. I cannot deny it all. I can't just sweep feelings under the carpet like a Stepford Wife and live life the way I *should.* I've always lived life that way. I've always been so good. And now, I can't help but have so many bad thoughts. So many *wonderfully bad* thoughts.

I walk through the house, looking at what I have helped build. Many days, happy *and* sad, I've argued in this house. I've loved in this house. I've raised two wonderful daughters in this house. Now, I've dreamed of having a wonderful affair in this house. I've fantasized about another man. Why can't we live two lives?

I want to do the right thing, but my insides won't let me. I'm being driven by something so strong inside me, it's frightening. I can't help it. I yearn for it. I want to share more sacred moments with Taylor I need to.

I walk upstairs and am met by Ariel, standing at the top of them. "Baby, why are you up? It's so late," I ask.

"I can't sleep. My head hurts," Ariel quietly pleads with me for some help.

"Come." I place my arm around my little girl and take her back to her bedroom. I lead her back into bed and spend twenty glorious minutes as Mommy. Just Mommy. Not Nicki Connolly. Not a partner at the law firm of Ferguson and Myers. Not as a *potential* adulterer. I am simply Mommy. That's a role I truly love and will never give up.

I run my fingers through Ariel's hair and help her relax. Slowly but surely, she succumbs to the night and exhaustion and is taken away by The Sandman.

———————

After the usual morning routine of getting my family off to their respective places for the day, I grab my gym bag and head out.

My drive is quiet and uneventful. I feel emotionally paralyzed. The more I'm away from Taylor, the greater the mental debate rages on. The moment I am in his presence, the debate is ended. Two paths. I'm walking two lines. But I know inside, you can't ride two horses with one ass. Something will have to give. For now, I happily delay and arrive at the gym; time to work out. If I happen to stargaze at Taylor Diamond, then so be it.

As soon as I enter the gym, I'm looking for him; not being obvious, but more informally searching around. My eyes scan the entire gym. Today, I brought a bathing suit. I want to get into the heated pool and swim some laps. If Taylor is there, then he is there. If he is not, then he is not. I need the laps. I need the solitude. I want to swim away my mind and just give myself a break.

I get into the pool. An older woman and man are near the far edge, doing some water aerobics. I swim lap after lap. I swim for an hour, and then a warm shower. No stalkers this morning; Tabatha is nowhere to be seen. I try to wash my congested thoughts away. All of this is therapeutic and wonderful.

After getting cleaned up, I make a quiet walk to my office. Angela is away from her desk, but I see her Starbucks on the table. I happily enter my office and find my morning Joe ready for me. Starbucks, after a drinking night and a good swim is wonderful medicine.

Angela enters after me and delivers my schedule. My mind is somewhere in space as I operate on autopilot today. As she directs me on my packed day, I wonder if a strange, dark and handsome man will walk through my door. Will Taylor Diamond make a random appearance? What does he have to say about everything? With just one look, I'd know what he is thinking. With one look, I would have some clue as to what is happening.

Angela's words are unable to penetrate my wandering mind, but I digest enough of the gist to move forward. My day is stockpiled with billable hours that don't surround the Ramsey Case; some off-site work, some in my office. The day whips by without me being able to catch even a glimpse of the elusive Taylor Diamond. I can replay my favorite moments of yesterday again and again, but I'm dying to see him. I want to know how he is going to look at me. I want to know what he is going to think of me.

Today turns into tomorrow and my routine continues. Nothing new; nothing out of the ordinary. I hit the gym and stay on the inside. I run, I do abs. No sign of Taylor. Nothing. Not a scent of his presence.

Up to the office and another full-slate of billable hours. I even do a *fly-by* of Taylor's office and he is nowhere to be found. The office is dark. Still, there is no assistant at the desk before his door. I can't ask around. I can't let anyone know I'm looking for him. I know we're working together, but I can't bring myself to text or call. I don't have anything new to discuss on the case, and I'm not his girlfriend. I don't have the right to keep tabs on him. He is a professional, just like me, and has things to do. *Ugh.* Where is he?

I arrive home after two days of nothing. Sure, I logged some good hours for the firm and did my job, but I really liked my new distraction. Life seems so plain without him. Upon entering my front door, I am met with a very annoyed husband.

"How could you?" he barks with fortitude. Oh, *shit*, he must know something. How? When? I can't put the pieces of the puzzle back together fast enough. I am a deer in headlights and don't know how to reply.

"Not even a word? Nothing to say for yourself?" Aiden again charges forward into the conversation with words anchored by conviction. He is upset. His anger is rarely displayed, but right now, he is downright pissed. He is biting his upper lip. His face is red, filled with fury. He looks as though he wants to unleash hell upon me, but it is not in his way. He is not a passionate soul. He is balanced and reserved. And right now, his reservations are fighting with his anger in an epic internal struggle of his own.

"I don't know what you mean?" I play dumb. It's the only angle I can figure. I want to see exactly what Aiden's evidence is. It's lawyer 101, don't say anything you don't need to say. So, I wait patiently through my nerves, allowing Aiden to sift through his anger and spell out in detail what he is so angry about.

"You said you wouldn't," he utters with sorrow-filled frustration.

I am perplexed, unable to properly dissect where we are heading. Is this about Taylor? Now I am uncertain if I got caught with something. But, I remind myself I've done nothing wrong. I have the guilt of an adulterer, but not the true experience to speak of. My mind has wandered but my body is still intact. I quickly recover and step forward with a clear conscious to enter this confusing line of questioning.

"I'm really confused here, Aid. What exactly are you upset about?" Now I firmly place the ball back in his court, no longer afraid of what he might ask me. There is nothing he can ask me that I can't honestly answer. I will not incriminate myself.

"You gave your cousin more money. You promised last time that it was the last time, that you wouldn't write any more big checks to her," Aiden pleads like a man that is financially stressed and concerned.

Oh. I'm relieved inside. *Shit.* He is right, but I couldn't help myself. I have to be there for Becca. She is my blood. She is my family. She has nothing and is teetering on the brink of hell. Her medical bills are enormous and unpayable. She can't work. Her husband is losing hours at his job. They are sinking faster than the Titanic and I am the only one that can help them. They need a lifeline and I couldn't live with myself if I didn't provide one.

"I know I did," I begin in a conciliatory tone.

Aiden just stands with his hands on his hips, an angry father, looking disgruntled. It's true I've made more money than him the last few years and I do feel entitled to help my family, but it should be a shared decision. I did commit to him that I wasn't going to write any more checks. I've given Rebecca over thirty thousand dollars over a two year period now. We have overextended ourselves for their family, while placing undue stress and pressure on our own. I get that. But if Aiden saw Casey as much as I have, his heart would melt just as mine has.

"I'm sorry, Aiden. They're just so desperate," I continue, attempting to appeal to Aiden's better senses.

"Our savings is almost gone. This case of yours, my reduced hours, we're starting to run on fumes. We're almost out of money, Nick. Gone. Done," Aiden lays things out pretty clearly.

"I hear you. We're going to get it back. We'll get it all back ten-fold. We are going to be okay," I attempt to relax Aiden's senses, but in reality, it's the same lie that Rebecca delivered to Casey about doctor's making her better and the case coming to a close. It is a carrot. I'm trying to extend a false olive branch, which under other circumstances, could be seen as being overly optimistic. But unfortunately, I know it's a lie. I have no guarantees on that return. I could punt the case. We could go to court, which could extend matters for years with appeals. I am not only a part of breaking us emotionally, now Aiden has called me out on breaking us financially. I feel terrible any which way I look at it.

"You always do this, Nick. You do what you want. You get to go *your* way. When you wanted to get back into law, I supported you. When you had a bigger role at the firm, I supported you. When you were made partner, I completely submarined my business to support you. I've been there for you every step of the way. I've tried. But you are sucking the life out of us, one day at a time. Our girls need things, too. They deserve things. And you are taking away from them. I have no say. That's why I'm angry," Aiden asserts.

Aiden makes excellent points. And I know he is right. We are giving away what we have. But we also live in a home that is valued at far more than my cousin will ever make. We have things. We have great things. So although Aiden is right, I'm still torn.

"I had to," I state with simplicity.

Aiden shakes his head and runs his hands through his air, no great comeback prepared for such a simple excuse.

"Whatever." He turns and walks away, the trail of frustration a stiff scent that I'm left pondering.

Aiden is about to leave the room when he stops and turns.

"I went to the girls' teachers' conferences today. They're both doing great. I tried you at the office but Angela said you were with a client. I hope it was a good client." Aiden's final words sting as he leaves the room and lets me swim in my own pool of self-guilt.

I take a deep breath and sink into my emotional abyss. *What next?* My phone vibrates and I look down and see an update from Angela.

Meeting set up tomorrow for Ramsey Mediation: 10AM; their offices.

I let out a *sigh* of frustration. And the beat goes on.

Twelve

After a quiet night of silence between Aiden and me, we commence the morning routine. Barely a look or a glance from Aiden. He is still seething inside, I know it. I try to not commit myself one way or the other to guilt or righteousness. I leave it all alone. I have a big day and other fish to fry.

Once they leave the house, my mind wanders to the Ramsey Case. I begin to stress over the mediation with Harper and Penn. A very large intimidating law firm, I've already met with them before, but never on *their* turf. Each phone conversation with the big boys over there has made me want to deal with them less and less. They are smug and deal from high walls, showing little empathy or care for what lies below the clouds. They are on another stratosphere with their clients. Now, I have been invited into their den for the very first time. It's usually Angela and me. Angie comes for support. But this time, I am heading in alone. It is me against the lions.

Before I head into a tense situation, I like to practice talking. I speak to myself in front of the mirror, in the shower, anywhere and everywhere, so I can practice my speeches, ensure my answers are perfect and just right.

As the water from our showerhead washes over me, I play both sides in the negotiation. I prepare for what they will say to me. The questions will fire out about smokers, about climate, about the land before people moved there. I prepare for their line of prestigious attorneys to fire query after query upon me, slinging them like catapults launching fire-torched rocks. That is their true strength in mediation. Their case is weak. They don't have a great defense. But the onus is on me. I have to prove my case, beyond a reasonable doubt to extract money out of a billion dollar company, protected by a platinum-walled group of attorneys. They are impenetrable and never lose.

As I talk it out, an annoying thought keeps crossing my brain again and again. *I should text him.* Taylor should be there. He is on the case now and would provide me some extra ammunition. Even though he is new to the dance, it would help my standing. I don't have the courage to call him, but I should text him. But I can't. I figure I will head in alone and see what this charade is about. I can always fill him in, back at the office. I'm bound to see him there today, unless he is out of town. With no assistant and no knowledge of his schedule, it's difficult for me to know anything about his whereabouts. But I *can* ask. I could ask the high-level assistants. I *could* ask Charles Rapture. If Bob Meyers is in, I *can* approach him. They would surly know where Taylor has gone. We generally have to file our whereabouts and log our hours with their assistants, so surely they would know. But I can't. I can't ask them. I don't want anyone to know I want to see Taylor. Sure, I have the perfect alibi. *It's for the case.* But inside, I know it's not. That feeling is what prevents me from being logical. So, I'll go to the mediation on my own.

———————

I pull up underneath the twenty-story building in Beverly Hills, with anxiety beginning to boil inside me. I feel I'm on enemy turf before I even exit the car. It is valet parking in their garage. The normally cold walls of a parking garage have been replaced by marble plated columns and a beautiful glass door entryway on the first level. It's only the visible one of the garage and I'm quite certain the valet boys are used to parking the cars in the catacombs of cold cement. What a level this is though. What an opening act.

Two armed guards stand by the glass doors as I hand my Excursion over to the valet. At least it's not my beat up, old Jetta. The Excursion doesn't quite fit in amongst the sea of BMWs, Mercedes, and drop dead gorgeous sports cars, but it will do.

I walk past the security guards and am escorted though a metal detector. This place is no joke. The floors are all marble. The cost of them must be extraordinary. The detail in the black marble walls, combined with the black and white marble flooring, is only further made impressive by more marble columns inside the lobby. A few pieces of art on the wall, encased in glass, with security systems attached, stand out to me. One looks like a Picasso, another looks like Monet's Impressionism. I am not an art connoisseur, whatsoever, but I took Art History back in college and recognize the handprints of some of the greats. This art is *definitely* expensive. I couldn't afford one for my living room, above the mantle, let alone one that I could stash in the lobby of an office building.

A very attractive blonde woman sits at the reception desk. She looks as though she just fell out of a Playboy catalog. Sure, she is dressed in a business suit, but with her collar slightly opened, giving a gaze at her very well-endowed breast. I feel as though she would have cleavage for days, if she just removed one more button. Of course, that is the allure. She probably makes men's minds aimlessly wander about before they even step into the elevator.

I might as well be in Ancient Rome right now with the perfection displayed in this lobby. I step into the luxurious, wide-spaced elevator. The opposite side is glass, open to looking out at greater Los Angeles with a taste of the Pacific Ocean in the distance. *Holy Shit*, they are richer than I thought. This place screams intimidation. I'm totally screwed. It was a mistake to come alone. And moreover, I probably should have insisted they come to our conference room, like our first meeting.

The elevator ride isn't long up to the twentieth floor penthouse, my destination. I gaze out at the calm and peaceful city. I can only shake my head at the tremendous chaos swirling around it.

Thanksgiving is close, then Christmas. Our big court date is coming in April, so everything is coming together. I know Rebecca and the people of Ramsey want to push for more than a settlement. I'll have to set up a meeting with the town next week and head back out there to let them know what transpired today.

The elevator *dings* and I'm here. The sleek silver doors open, and I am nearly hit in the face with the firm's assistant, behind a half-circular, black marble desk and the huge platinum lettering that reads: Harper and Penn.

No doubt I'm in the right place. I take a step forward and hear some bustle around me. The assistant has a head set on and a lavish suit. She is a sexy brunette, much like the blonde downstairs, looking as if she came out of the same catalog. These women are impressive, and again, are a distraction for most, I'm sure. But, not me. Not now.

I approach the secretary. "I'm Nicki Connolly from Rapture and Myers," I clearly announce my presence.

"They are all waiting for you right down the hall, in the conference room on the left. Would you like a beverage?" she offers. And before I know it, a very handsome man is standing just a few feet away from me, wearing a very expensive suit. All of the people here look as though they model for Abercrombie and Fitch.

"I will escort you to the conference room, Ms. Connolly," the beautiful, male assistant kindly states.

"Nothing for me, thanks," I turn down the drink offer and step toward the gentleman escort.

"Follow me," he states with a cocksure smile. The people here don't seem to have a care in the world.

I follow him through a series of halls. The black carpeting is complemented by the perfectly painted white walls. More paintings (these without security systems), line the walls as we walk. There are a few cut-outs in the walls that feature glass-encased sculptures. The sculptures are from ancient Rome and Greece. They may be copies or they may be originals; I wouldn't know the difference.

I am escorted to a glass box. The conference room sits exposed, surrounded by a giant library of books and research tables. The glass box is sound proof and sits in the center of the giant room with its own set of lights inside. I get to be a rat in a cage.

I feel as though this is the definition of intimidation. Seven men—many of them, old enough to be my father—rise to their feet as I enter the glass box; all conversations, coming to a halt. The door is closed by the Abercrombie model behind me, and I am officially in their den. The lights above make me feel as though I'm in an interrogation room and the fine upstanding wealthy aristocrats of Harper and Penn are the detectives waiting to pounce.

I am alone on my side of the glass table. The chairs are padded but all glass, matching the motif of the conference room. My side of the table has a single bottle of water. I'm confused because I didn't ask for any.

"Hello again, Ms. Connolly," Albert Penn, the son of Randolph Penn greets me. Albert is older; nearly sixty, and his father, long gone, started this firm many moons ago. It was originally an East Coast firm, based out of New York. The firm expanded to the West Coast in the 1990s when Albert officially took over. Both are highly respected and normally represent billion dollar companies. *Must be nice for them.*

I nod to Albert, and his contingent of legal henchman all nod, silently welcoming me. I feel as though I'm in Japan nodding again and again to the six other men. After introductions are done, I have a seat.

"All right, let's get this show on the road," I start, pulling out my files to begin discussing whatever it is I'm here for.

"We were going to wait for your colleague," Albert states as he and his team shuffle through some papers.

My colleague? I ask myself in confusion. Then, a hand hits my shoulder. "I'm right here," the cool, calm, collected voice of Taylor Diamond settles the room completely.

I close my eyes, thankful and embarrassed. I'm so happy he is here, but I'm also embarrassed I didn't even tell him about the meeting. Angela must have clued him in.

Taylor takes a seat next to me, and I get a smile and wink.

"It's nice to see you," I say with a grin.

"The feeling is mutual," as always, Taylor is dynamically cryptic.

"I called you here, Ms. Connolly, to discuss a few items. We are prepared to make a settlement offer. In addition to that, we are willing to look at the medical files of those in the greatest of need and make considerations to aid them immediately," Albert Penn begins. It's quite a meeting already. I've said but a few words and they are going to make me an offer to settle and possibly pay for medical costs in advance? That is insane. They are essentially admitting guilt. I look around the room and see no one typing . . . no one taking notes.

"This is off the record?" I plainly ask.

"It is a casual meeting. We're just talking here," Albert plays games with me.

"There are seven of you, sitting before me, in suits that cost a combined fifteen thousand dollars. Mr. Penn, there is nothing casual about me sitting here right now," I fire back with some piss and vinegar. I want to make sure we won't be bullied, nor will we thank our lucky stars for some low-ball offer and the commitment to paying some medical bills. But beyond my pissing contest, I am doing cartwheels in my mind over the fact that I'm getting a settlement offer. Finally, something is being offered! Even if we are just talking in a glass box, it's a great start. The medical concerns are just a bonus.

"We would need to see some of the more severe medical records. If there are any additional records you haven't filed, it would help us to understand what your clients need," Albert again leads with options in my favor. This meeting is definitely going the right way.

And then there is Taylor. He is right beside me and I am overjoyed he is sitting here. I want to look him in the eye to see what his stare tells me, but my mind is elsewhere, too focused on the war being waged on an entirely glass table inside of an entirely glass box.

"My clients don't want to settle. They have said they want their day in court," I explain, throwing a giant monkey wrench in their plans. Playing hard to get is a power move by me. I want them to shuffle in their chairs a bit.

Albert Penn throws a brief look over Taylor's way, as if seeing if he has something to say on the matter. It's an odd expression. I look over at Taylor and see a blank one on his face. He is staring forward at the line of elder legal minds.

"This is the position of your firm and your clients?" Albert asks with great confusion. He believes we will take the crumbs from the big boy table, I bet. We are a smaller firm and I represent poor desert rats. The high society men of Harper and Penn are well aware of that.

"These people are suffering every day, Mr. Penn. They have children who are suffering. This is all directly due to Beltran Food Corporation and the toxins you have spewed into the air, and possibly, the ground. Now, I understand they have made changes to their processing plant in Ramsey and the air pollution is no longer an issue, but the damage is done for many of them. The changes in the plant—alone—highlight the mistakes that were being made. That plant has adversely affected ninety living souls and ten deceased ones. That's one hundred people that have medical proof of the airborne toxins. This personal injury class action law suit is not going to end because you slide a piece of paper across the desk with a large figure on it, Mr. Penn. This is going to end when you give the people of Ramsey what they deserve." I lay out a lengthy assertive notation on my position and that of my clients. I can swing an iron hammer just as well as anyone.

"And what of the government reports of nuclear waste being buried nearby Ramsey?" Albert Penn slides a document across the table to us. "We are filing this today." His Trump Card. Reasonable doubt. "And, we have already cited that the plant was within code standards in the past. The fact that extreme wind currents *possibly* carried toxins in the air that *could* have affected the residents of Ramsey is a long leap from proof and absolute guilt. I think you will be hard-pressed to survive the reasonable conclusions that our experts will make against yours. I understand you have spoken to experts we used in the past. I like that strategy. But, when push comes to shove, this case is going to drag on for a decade, darling. There isn't much you can do about that," Albert Penn states with certainty. His threat is just that, a threat. But, the manipulated facts and façade they may put on is something that I have been dealing with for a few years. The length of a trial and appeal processes could be a few more years. Ten is pushing it. The document unearthed by Harper and Penn, being filed in court, is a potential nuclear bomb to my case. It's information that was not made public, and is another reason someone could lay even an ounce of doubt on our case. I try to act as if the new piece of information doesn't even matter, but I nervously scatter my brain for a thought. I think we have both thrown our dicks on the table now, and it's time to reason.

Before I can say a word... "Darling?" Taylor chuckles and shakes his head. Taylor's tone is condescending. He seems annoyed by Albert Penn disrespectfully throwing his weight around. "The Roby trials, which you are referring to in this document, provide that barrels of nuclear waste are properly disposed of in the ground by surrounding areas of Ramsey. Although there was a leak found fifteen years ago in a single barrel, it was determined human error was the cause, and no ill effects ever arose from the leak. Certainly, you can hypothesize and attempt to throw a Hail Mary pass here, but the fact of the matter is, unless you have dug a lot of deep holes in the desert and have proof of any leaks, I'd have to say this report is a bunch of..." Taylor sarcastically turns to me for a split second, "...and pardon me, darling, when I say this," then he shoots back at Albert Penn, "...bullshit."

Boom! That's my boy! I am entranced, watching Taylor thunder away. But, I have little time to celebrate. I whip my satisfied eyes back over at Albert who shuffles uncomfortably in his chair.

There is a moment of silence as Albert and his two senior lawyers, sitting beside him, confer. One of the men writes something down on a piece of paper. Albert turns back to us.

"We can spend hours dancing. Let's cut to the chase. I am going to give you a number; a fair offer. I suggest you speak to your clients. A non-disclosure will be attached to any agreement and it will remain sealed—no public release—no press.

I take the piece of paper and place it in my pocket, not even looking at it. It's a show of power. They will not impress me with numbers on a piece of paper.

"Okay," Albert concedes and rises to his feet.

"Thank you for having us," I say with subdued delight and optimism. As much as I know the small desert community of Ramsey, California wants a hanging, I need closure. Not because of my firm's pressure, not because of Aiden, not because of my cousin, but it's because of Taylor. The longer this case goes on, the more I am likely to fall deeper and deeper into Taylor's world. For me, that's a scary proposition; good and bad.

Just as we were escorted in, Mr. Abercrombie escorts Taylor and me out. He takes us back to the front and over to the elevators. The Harper and Penn sign seems far less intimidating now. We stand side by side, neither of us looking at the other. The elevator doors open and we slide inside.

The secretary is smirking at us as we stand beside one another. Her smile is for Taylor, as her eyes pan to him. The steel doors slowly start to close and a smile emerges on my face, causing the beautiful woman's to dissipate. The doors close shut and Taylor and I are finally alone again.

Thirteen

Thirteen

The elevator starts to drop, silence inside as Santa Monica is the backdrop behind us. It is a clear day and the Pacific Ocean is perfectly visible in the skyline.

I see his reflection outlined in the steel doors, his face is fogged by the steel, but I see him. And, *he* is looking at *me*. The two of us are staring at one another, but neither of us makes a sound.

I turn my face slightly, but refuse to look directly into his deep-blue eyes.

"Thank you, for that." I am very appreciative for Taylor's help. I still don't want to look him in the eyes, though. I am so curious where he is right now. Is he upset at me? Does he think I led him on? His presence couldn't have hurt in the meeting. A strong reputation like Taylor's travels just as strategically as a great speech. And he didn't disappoint in the office. He stepped on Harper and Penn, Attorneys at Law, like they were the shit underneath his shoe. He spoke like he owned them. He silenced their aggressive charge. He was a great partner today.

Ten . . . nine . . . eight, we dip floor by floor, and then it happens. His hand finds my hand, once again. No eye contact, just the distorted glare from the steel doors before us. Our hands easily fuse together again like a magnet on a metallic surface.

Three . . . two . . . one; there's a *ding,* and our hands simultaneously release. We have made a pact now. In the shadows, we can connect. In the cover of dark is our opportunity; our opportunity to escape this world together. It is there where we can try to live free, like our bodies deserve.

The steel cage opens and we step out of the elevator, like the professionals we are. We have no expressions on our faces and we pass by the blonde receptionist without a glance. We move past security and exit to the valet. There is no one at the station at the moment. Taylor turns to me. I feel his eyes on me. I'm apprehensive about looking, but I easily give in.

"Wanna go for a ride?" he asks with boyish charm.

The valet comes running over. "Sorry for the wait," he apologizes. "One or two tickets?" the valet asks. Taylor looks at me and smiles. His baby blues have a boyish glimmer as if the world is our oyster. Anything is possible.

"Well, what will it be, Ms. Connolly?" Taylor asks with quiet confidence.

"Just one," I have an open afternoon. Why not enjoy a ride.

Taylor subtly nods and hands his ticket over to the valet. He charges off for the car, leaving us.

"Where are we going?" I ask with curiosity.

"A ride with a view," he suavely replies.

I nod with a smile attached, amused, yet again, by Taylor's charm.

His Roadster pulls up. I see him slip the valet a twenty as he passes by. The valet opens my door and glances at the twenty with an excited subdued smile. "Thank you, both," the valet says with great sincerity and appreciation attached.

"It's all her. She's inspiring," Taylor compliments me, as if I had done something right and he gets into his classic Mercedes. I get in on my side and the valet closes the door. Seat belts are fastened and we are off.

The top goes down and Dave Matthews Band is playing through the speakers. "Two Step" roars as we speed off. With the top pulled back, I feel invigorated as the air crashes into my face. I am feeling alive. I feel like a modern day villager, being swept up by a prince. Before I know it, we've made our way to the Pacific Coast Highway.

"You want lunch in San Diego or Santa Barbara?" he ever-so-casually poses as he glances over.

What amazing options. Each are about a hundred and forty miles away; San Diego to the south and Santa Barbara to the north. The choices are dubious and I go with an old favorite of mine—Santa Barbara.

"I love Isla Vista," I tell Taylor.

"Santa Barbara it is." Taylor agreeably nods and we head north.

Isla Vista is a college town in Santa Barbara. I did my undergraduate degree there and graduated a proud Gaucho before heading north to Stanford for law. I'm very familiar with the area.

The car flies up PCH. We pass Oxnard and continue north. The ocean is pacing us to the west. It's a clear, crisp day. The sun is shining and with the Roadster's top down, I'm enjoying every moment. It's been too long since I've driven by the ocean. It's been too long since I've felt this way. I feel as though I have roamed the desert for centuries, searching for water and I have, just now, finally found it. And I can't get enough. Music, wind, and a scenic view. No talking, to spoil our time. The further north we go, the better the ocean view. *I so miss this.*

We arrive in Santa Barbara and Taylor drives into the downtown area; an old world alive with kitschy shops and a sweet solace. The old architecture downtown is a hark back to the old Spanish buildings reminiscent in the southwest. The historic adobes stand with white painted sides, red borders and red roof tops. The Spanish Colonial and Mission Revival styles reflect the era as many of the structures were built in the early 1900s; a perfect physical memory caught in time.

We hit the streets by foot and few words. Our hands, once again, find one another and we stroll, like a couple, amongst the strangers of Santa Barbara. We exchange a few smiles, each of us seemingly surprised we made it this far. I'm two hours from my house, in Thousand Oaks, but I might as well be on another spiritually enlightened planet.

I feel safe, happy and alive. A fog has been lifted, and I'm breathing freely and clearly. I don't remember this feeling, but there's no doubting it now—I'm on a date. Casual people are around us, scattered about, as if everybody is adhering to a personal space policy. An old couple is strolling down Main Street on one sidewalk and, across the street, a young, budding couple is laughing and chatting as they walk the boulevard hand-in-hand. Two men in suits and sunglasses look as though they just completed a business transaction, and are walking toward us about a half a block away. The streets are relatively quiet. A few stray thick ominous clouds have moved overhead, beginning a game of peekaboo with the sun. It is a perfect afternoon as a soft breeze starts.

As Taylor and I walk, I receive a text: *How is the meeting? Is it over yet?* Angela, always supportive, is watching over me like an older sister.

I text back: *Running late. Cancel my afternoon appointment. All good, though.*

And now I've lied to Angela. But I don't care. I've rarely lived my dreams during my life. It was a fight tooth and nail for me to go back into law. I remember it like yesterday. Aiden's disappointed glare. It was silent and we didn't talk for almost a month. I mean, we talked, but we didn't *talk.* It was all superficial. Aiden hated me for a long time. Maybe he still does. I'm almost certain he resents me for going back to law. I feel it every day. He hides things well, but a woman knows. Aiden doesn't know that I see it, but I do . . . every tall tale sign: his crumbling lip, eyes that peer away with momentary annoyance, jaw tightening, clinching of fingers, subtle shakes of his head, and so on. A silent divide like a Great Wall has been established.

"How about here?" Taylor breaks me from my troubles and brings me right back to our private oasis. It's a quaint Mexican restaurant he's referring to. The sign reads: Gerardo's. I've seen it and I remember it's very nice inside; far too expensive for my frugal college days back as a UCSB Gaucho. I haven't been back here in a long time. I miss this place. It's peaceful, quiet, historical, and beautiful. The atmosphere is infallible.

We enter Gerardo's. We are immediately smacked in the face with the perfect Mexican ambiance. Music played in the backdrop through wall speakers spreading Latin flavor throughout the dimly lit restaurant. Natural light is used inexplicably well as the glass restaurant front allows it to leak perfectly inside. Hanging antique chandelier lamps, on a low dim, provide lighting accent for each individual circular table in the restaurant. Small, stout, red bottles with lit candles mark the center of each table. The walls are decorated with paintings and old, Mexican antique paraphernalia. The historical value around us sets the mood and environment perfectly; it is, unarguably, amazingly romantic.

A kind senorita greets us by the podium up front.

"Hola!" she says with exuberance.

"Dos, por favor," Taylor smoothly slips into Spanish with a perfect accent. This well-traveled man looks and sounds every part he plays.

"Right this way," the senorita articulates with a thick Mexican accent, grabbing two lunch menus and leading us, with a smile, to our seats.

Within seconds of being seated, a man in a waiter's uniform delivers chips and salsa from the back. There are three choices of salsa: pico de gallo, salsa verde, and a red salsa. I notice two waitresses in the corner, curiously looking in our direction. One of them runs to the back, disappearing behind a curtain leading to the kitchen.

"You have been here before?" I curiously ask.

Before Taylor can answer, an old Mexican chef makes his way to our table. He has a big belly, a chef's hat, and a large, white apron.

"Hello, Mr. Diamond!" he happily greets and clasps Taylor's extended hand.

"Hello, Gerardo," Taylor returns, the two men reacquainting themselves.

I have a smile on my face in almost disbelief of Taylor. He must truly know everyone.

"Gerardo, this is my good friend, Nicki," Taylor introduces me.

"Ah, senorita, muy bonita, gracias for visiting mi restaurante." Gerardo, in a kind tone, graciously welcomes me. He takes my right hand and kisses the back of it.

"Thank you," I respond, overwhelmed by my royal treatment.

"I have muy especial food for you today," Gerardo brags to us.

"Thank you, Gerardo." Taylor offers an appreciative smile. Gerardo happily stampers away back to the kitchen from which he came. "I've been here a time or two," Taylor jokes with a half-cocked smile.

"Yeah, I bet," I laugh and then he follows suit.

A waitress drops off two large margaritas and we are officially taken away into a romantic lunch, which qualifies well beyond any first date I ever had.

We drink, smiling at one another. Taylor looks proud of himself, like he knows he has set the perfect mood. It's a lovely place and we are treated like royalty. They rush an amazing Mexican egg roll appetizer over and homemade guacamole spinach wraps. Baked enchiladas with refried beans, rice, sour cream, and a small specially-made corn ball make for an exquisitely perfect lunch.

We mainly smile at one another and remain silent.

"What's the smile for?" he asks with a debonair grin.

"You. Just…all of it," I say a lot while saying nothing, a game Taylor has perfected.

"Gerardo is an old friend of my father's. Would you like to hear the story?" Taylor changes the subject.

"Of course." I do want to know. I want to know anything and everything about him.

"Whenever we came to our villa in Santa Barbara, we ate at a small restaurant called Tito's. Tito was a hard man and he treated his employees poorly. The food was wonderful, due to their head chef, Gerardo. But one day, things weren't so great in the restaurant. Tito slapped his wife when my father was present. My father confronted Tito and was thrown out of the restaurant shortly after. My father always had bodyguards, so if he didn't want to leave, he wouldn't have. But, satisfied all was taken care of after Tito's wife left, my father obliged. He was always a complicated man. But, he did have a sense of right and wrong outside the business world. And seeing Tito treat his head chef so poorly, all the time, and then slap his own wife, it was all too much for my father. So, he purchased a small location on Main Street, here in Santa Barbara, the exact place we are sitting right now, made his way into Tito's restaurant and marched right past him, into the back kitchen. Tito was stunned and then shouted. My father walked up to Gerardo and handed him a set of keys and the deed. He told Gerardo he was an excellent chef and wished him luck with his new restaurant. Gerardo is a good man with a big family. I was always happy my father did that. And, he did that in front of me on purpose. He brought me into Tito's to show me what he was doing. He shared with me his power and compassion all at once." Taylor sips his drink and his eyes pan away. The subject of his father is clearly a close and personal one to him.

"What happened to Tito's?" I ask, following up with curiosity.

"It closed down and Tito died soon after," Taylor abruptly finishes reminiscing, making me feel as though there is more to the story.

"That's a pretty incredible story." I am happy Taylor shared so much with me. I feel excited that it was not cryptic, but instead, he spoke to me about something very personal.

"Yeah," he solemnly replies. He clearly doesn't share information with most, as displayed by him shifting just a little uncomfortably in his chair. He looks back up at me. "What is it?"

"What?" I ask, confused.

"The number in your pocket," he points out. He is referring to the number that Albert Penn slid across the table to me. I still hadn't checked.

"Oh, shit! I totally forgot." I cringe in near embarrassment and transfer to excitement.

I pull out the paper and read the number. *$100,000,000.* I stare, things getting real. The number is big and exciting. *Wow!*

I hand the piece of paper over to Taylor. He looks at the number and then flashes his eyes back up, nodding, showing little emotion either way.

"It's a good offer," he states.

"It was my target," I share. It all seems so random. "And with a medical kicker," I continue.

"It's a good offer," he repeats. Taylor crumbles up the piece of paper. "Wanna get out of here?" he asks, wanting to move the date forward.

"Yeah, definitely." I smile, excited to turn the page and see what will happen next.

We step outside the restaurant and the world has changed. Dark clouds have impeded our perfect afternoon overhead. The wind has picked up. A storm is near and heading our way. Main Street is near empty, all except the two men in suits and sunglasses. They are across the street, a few store fronts down sitting on a street bench. If I didn't know better by their angled heads, I'd say they were staring right at us. One man is tall with silver hair, the other short and balding. Both men look strong under their suits; their broad shoulders a dead giveaway. I study them now. Something is not right about them.

"Come on," Taylor pulls me along and we head in the opposite direction down Main Street, back to his car. I glance back a few moments later and they are gone. *Strange.*

We hop back into Taylor's Roadster and I find myself curiously looking in the side mirror. There are no cars behind us but suddenly, I taste paranoia. Is someone spying on me? Is it the Harper-Penn people wanting to collect dirt on my behalf to try and weaken my personal position in the case? I was warned about this. Big cases like this spur strange occurrences. Private detectives make their money off of class action cases and insurance claims. These guys didn't look like PI's, though. They looked serious. Still, there is no one in the rear view mirror as I internally obsess.

"Is it all right if we stop by my place? It's on the way. I need to feed and let Charlie out before the storm comes," Taylor asks innocently.

"Sure," I say without a thought. I really am more interested in figuring out if someone is spying on me, so I'm temporarily distracted.

The drive back down Pacific Coast Highway is relaxing. On the way up, my blood was raging with excitement. Now, things are calm. I feel as though I am somehow on par with Taylor. He isn't a dream any more. He is a man before me.

Radiohead's "Fake Plastic Trees" is playing, further mellowing our mood. Gerardo's amazing Mexican cuisine has set in and I relax, enjoying the ocean out on the passenger's side window this time. I stare at the deep, dark, puffy clouds that fill the sky as far as the eye can see. Rogue lightning strikes fire down from the clouds, chasing us down the coast from a great distance. It's only three o'clock, but it feels as though darkness is coming early tonight.

I am curious about a number of things as we drive. I wonder how my girls are doing. Our moments together aren't nearly the same as they once were. I miss their daily arguments over mundane things. I wonder how Ramsey will take the offer. Surely, they will decline and drive for court. I am hoping I can send a counter they can live with and conclude this case; one that has taken the life out of me. I wonder why Taylor is here with me; a *royal* trip to Santa Barbara that makes me feel like we could walk through any door, any place in the world, and if I'm by his side, I'd be greeted with open arms. And I finally wonder where Taylor disappeared to the last three days. I'm beginning to grow attached to him. It's too easy. Strangely, I know so little about him. Maybe that's the allure—to keep things just far enough away, so it doesn't get too real.

"Are you all right?" Taylor softly asks.

"Yes. Sorry…of course. I just have a lot on my mind," I reply as I fall into a bit of a mood for no reason. I have a lot to think about and it seems the long melodic drive with the oncoming storm has brought the best out of my complicated mind, making my thoughts sorted.

"We don't need to stop by my place," Taylor kindly offers a way out. "Charlie can wait an extra hour, if need be."

"No, no. I'm fine. I want to meet Charlie," I rebound to let him know my qualms are not with him and the sweet afternoon we have shared.

"You're a complicated soul, Ms. Connolly," Taylor suggests.

"Aren't all women?" I jest back, the two of us getting back into rhythm.

"No, no. Definitely not. And I know you know that," Taylor calls bullshit on me this time. I smile.

"I like that you're complicated," Taylor begins. "Too many times, people site complications as *issues.* They want easy. Life is hard. Easy is a dime a dozen. Easy is boring. But complicated challenges your mind . . . your inner self. I like your complications, Nicki," he lays out an extremely complex compliment. I'd need about an hour of deep thought to extract all the meaning from his admissions. I choose to play the cards at face value and reply.

"You do have a way with words, Mr. Diamond." I smirk.

He smiles. I've given him exactly what he wanted; someone he sees as an intellectually driven equal. I have Taylor by a few years, but he is an old soul. He is a quiet man with endless depth and complication who has *lived* life far more than most. Maybe this is all more than I thought. Perhaps his feelings are evolving with mine.

"Charlie. He's a…?" I ask, wondering what sort of creature Charlie is.

"A yellow lab…and, a she," Taylor informs me. "Estella usually stays in my Malibu home, but she has family in town. So I've been spending some extra time with Charlie, my sweet girl," he adds, providing me some possibilities on his whereabouts the last couple of days.

"Your Malibu home?"

"I have a few," Taylor seems to try and not sound conceded when alluding to his many homes. "But to me, home is home. One home would be better than many," he expresses some distaste for his wealth and upbringing.

"You've lived well," I half ask and state at the same time.

"Yes. Very. But detached. Very detached."

We rest our conversation on that note and successfully beat the storm to Malibu. As the world grows darker, the 4pm hour comes upon us. More lightning strikes occur over the ocean and sounds of thunder fill the air. The smell of imminent rain is followed by a few rain drops. The clouds are bursting at the seams and about to break.

We pull up to Taylor's private Malibu Beach house. He enters a code on a large black covered gate and it opens. I feel as though I'm with a movie star as he enters behind the opening gate. The home is large, but not a palace. It rests between a lot of palm trees and shrubs on either side to conceal its privacy. I step out of the car and the moist air is even more prevalent. *It smells refreshing.*

We make our way down the finely, cobbled driveway to a grey stone walkway. Beautiful, vibrant, red roses and yellow flowers line the walkway with solar powered lights built into the ground beneath my feet. The porch is empty but is the perfect area for decoration. It's clear Taylor doesn't spend time out front.

He opens the door and is immediately greeted by an excited Charlie. The beautiful yellow Lab jumps up on his hind legs and greets her master with great joy.

"Hey, girl," he happily engages his best friend. It's a sweet sight and I find myself smiling inside. My face succumbs and a smile emerges there as well.

I move through the home, giving myself a tour of the downstairs. The house is well decorated, clean, and refined. Fixtures are all matching. The kitchen is mostly white with splashes of red for added color. Hanging lamps drop from the ceiling about the black countertop, acting as a breakfast bar extension with accompanying high black backed bar chairs with steel legs. The living room is modern with a huge flat screen TV, black leather couches, black fixtures, and white walls. Charlie's black, large, plush bed sits in a corner by an oversized, black, leather recliner with her name etched in white stitches on it.

The flooring is all black as well; a fine ceramic tiling floor with a hint of sparkles mixed into them. It is all modern and it is perfect and spotless.

"Doesn't look like a bachelor pad," I joke.

"I didn't decorate, although, I do have my fingerprints on the TV, the Bose sound system, and my recliner. Oh, and Charlie's downstairs bed," Taylor enlightens me as he grabs the leash and heads out back with Charlie. "We'll be right back. Make yourself at home," he offers, giving me the "guest treatment," before heading outside. I continue to visually inspect.

The back walls, bordering Taylor's home, are completely glass. It's an amazing vision to behold. The open downstairs floor plan leads perfectly to the insane ocean view. The home is just high enough on a burn to look down upon the cold, refreshing, poetic waters of the Pacific.

Taylor walks Charlie around the beach and I look out toward the magnificent deck, attached to the rear sliding glass doors. It has nice patio furniture, a barbeque pit built into the deck, more solar lighting, crafted into the deck itself, and a beautiful, black iron rod railing wrapped with white, strung lights, marking it. Much like the inside, it is modern, hip, finely crafted, and clean.

I step out onto the deck. I am frightened . . . *so* frightened. I can see myself here. This is where I *could* be. It feels right and a swell of anxiety rushes through my body. The sky opens up and rain pours down upon me.

Run, Nicki! My final warning from my internal conscious. With the swell of energy, I can't help but take off and I run in the opposite direction of Taylor and Charlie. I toss my heels and run as fast and far as I can, along the wet sand. Lightning strikes fire down above the ocean and the dark, grumbling sky yields no ground, pummeling me with rain drops.

I run nearly a quarter of a mile away and stop, exhausted from my rainy run in the wet beach sand. I want to cry, overwhelmed with too many emotions, but I can't. My heartbeats thump loudly; the excitement overbearing.

I slow my senses, staring at the chaotic waves, watching the lightning shoot down from the sky, feeling the rain drops wash the doubt off my body. I gather myself and hear distant barking in the rain. Charlie rushes up to me and gives me kisses.

I look up and see an equally drenched Taylor Diamond, standing twenty yards away. *Shit,* he's so gorgeous. Even the rain doesn't faze Taylor, who still sports a smile for me. I think he's happy I didn't run any further.

"So what now?" he shouts over the rain.

"I…I…" I honestly have no idea how to answer, so I stop trying. I walk through the pouring rain back toward him. The world has grown dark. The lightning strikes, providing the only illumination around. Thunder rolls above as I step right up to his rain soaked body and without hesitation lunge forward into his arms; the two of us, passionately kissing and embracing each other.

Our tongues crash into one another, surveying the inner sanctum of the other's mouth. With our faces pressed up against each other, the passion, built up inside of us, explodes into one amazing, long kiss. His hands wrap around my back, and then one releases and finds the side of my face, gently caressing it. My arms are wrapped around the back of Taylor's neck as I stand on my tippy toes. One of my hands slips to the side of his face. We are a beacon of light amongst the chaos swirling around us.

My hand slides off his face to his chest, as we slowly back away, our eyes fixated upon one another.

I was breathless before, from my run. Now, this time, from an amazing life-changing kiss.

"This is dangerous," he says.

I hope it's not a negative toward us and our kiss. I immediately become paranoid, my face dropping with concern.

"I don't care," I put my foot down without regard.

He smiles again—that crazy-hot, damn smile.

"What's so funny?" I ask.

"I was talking about the lighting," Taylor replies and we both have a laugh.

Charlie barks, breaking our *couples'* gaze.

"All right, let's go inside. But only because Charlie wants to," I smirk with my playful reply.

"Okay," he agrees with a dreamy wet smile.

He takes my hand and we walk to his beach house with an excited Charlie running out in front of us.

I've never lied, cheated, or stolen. And now, Taylor Diamond has become my perfect lie. I am, for the first time, a cheater. I don't know what will come next. I'm riding a wave of passion, of life, of invigoration, and I hope it never ends. I hope this feeling lasts forever.

With our hands clinched together, we head inside amidst the raging storm around us, soaking wet, needing to get out of our clothes.

Fourteen

Fourteen

Taylor drives me back to the office building at Harper and Penn, where my car is parked. We are both still wet from the storm and have towels in the car to help dry ourselves off. I would have loved to stay in his Malibu home a bit longer, but the excitement we shared is enough for one day. And I am already late. We are both left with glossy-eyed smiles to take as our parting gifts for the afternoon.

Taylor stops at a red light and glances down at his phone. He has a text and it seems to be perplexing him, causing his eyebrows to furrow. An annoyed expression leaks through his normal poker face. His phone attention reminds me to check mine, which had been turned to silent during our lunch rendezvous.

I missed a call from Aiden. He texted, as well: *I need to stay at the site late. Janice is over with the girls.*

I text Aiden back that I'm on my way, even though I'm still a few minutes out from my car.

"Is it Aiden?" Taylor casually asks.

"He's working late today," I confirm his suspicions. I have so many thoughts and toss Taylor a loaded question in exchange for his hint of jealousy. "What's next for us?"

Taylor nods, the question is not easy for either of us to answer with any sort of accuracy. He knows things have changed. This isn't a fantasy of mine this time. We committed to something, something just for us.

"We go forward," he states with utter simplicity and a twinkle of hope from his eyes.

I nod, accepting the unknown.

"I'll be away for a bit—a week maybe. I have to fly out tonight," Taylor begins, breaking the bad news. He refers to his phone as the culprit. My excitement over the afternoon is quelled a bit with this revelation. "I'm sorry," he apologizes.

"Is it for the firm?" I ask, my jealous nature peeking out and taking a spin.

"It is. Tokyo and possibly Sydney, after," he alerts me to his itinerary, a global man with global clients. Work hasn't been a topic of conversation in our short time together. I have no idea where he will be at any given time. His travels are a mystery to me, and he has no assistant for me to poke and prod at.

"Have a safe flight," I wish him as we arrive at the Harper-Penn office building, where our morning began.

"I know," he comfortingly states as if he can sense my disappointment.

"What?" I play dumb, wanting to draw more out of him.

"This means something to me. It means a lot," Taylor states, and places his hand upon mine.

"How many girls did you take to Fossil Falls?" I ask just one more time with a smile on my face, playing with Taylor for the final time before we part.

"Only one. Only you," he states with certainty and sincerity. He pulls my hand to his lips, gently kissing it.

"Thank you," I reply. "Thank you for everything." My gratitude goes beyond just a few words. I have felt feelings foreign to me. The lunch, the day, the kiss, it is all a fairy tale of emotion. Even if that is all it was meant to be, it was something amazing; something I'll never forget. What a week I've had.

"No, Nicki, thank you." Taylor's smile starts to flee as he knows he is about to drive away.

I slowly start to pull my hand away from his to get out of the car but he clasps my hand, holding on just for a few more moments. His eyes are burying into my soul as I stare back at him. One more breathless moment. One more last long stare of epic proportions.

I get out of the Roadster; eyes from inside the lobby and the valet upon us. We are once again in the light of day and we quietly bury our mutual secret, for now.

After the valet gets my car, I'm driving home on the 101 freeway. I am moving slowly, stuck in the muddy rush hour traffic, day-dreaming amidst the rain and sea of cars. That kiss in the pouring rain, it was everything I hoped it would be. It was magical, a romantic fantasy I'm, all of a sudden, living out. And I want more.

It takes nearly ninety minutes for me to get home, but it might as well have been five minutes. Time flew as I watched my kiss happen over and over again in my mind. I can still taste him on my lips, smell his sweet scent.

Our neighborhood *go-to* babysitter, Janice, is in the living room, watching TV as I enter the house. She's sixteen and very reliable.

"Thanks, Janice," I greet her.

"No problem, Mrs. C." Janice pops up off the couch as she finishes sending a text. I give her a twenty for her time.

"Kids ate already. Just doing homework in their rooms," Janice gives me the run-down as she quickly heads to the front door.

"Thanks, again!" I shout as she leaves.

"Mommy!" Ariel and Casey come charging down the stairs to greet me.

It's strange. I'm so excited to see them and normally guilt would creep in. But it's not. I'm mentally having my cake and eating it. A rogue thought—a small thought, passing by, slips into my brain—*life without Aiden is a possibility.* It's a nasty, cruel thought and maybe I'm just whipped up in the emotional frenzy of Taylor

Diamond, but it is just one thought, and it is justified—we aren't happy.

I squeeze my girls tightly. "Mom, come see my Halloween costume!" Ariel shouts.

"Yeah, Mom! Me too!" Lacy agreeably yells.

They try on their costumes. Ariel is dressed as a fairy and Lacy is the candy corn princess. They pose and I get some good pictures and bonding time with my girls. Ariel disappears to go shower and Lacy approaches me in a curious manner. Something seems to be on her mind.

"Come here, baby," I prompt Lacy over to the end of her bed, where I was perched for their Halloween fashion show. Lacy comes over and sits down next to me. "What's up?" I ask her.

"Why have you and daddy been fighting so much lately?" Lacy comes right at me with a heartbreaking question no parent wants to answer. Her big brown eyes are looking up at me as a child in the middle of two parents drifting apart. And, it's true; Aiden and I are drifting apart. Clearly, we are.

"Sometimes adults have disagreements, baby. But it doesn't mean we don't love each other and it doesn't mean anything is wrong. It's like you and Ariel. You guys argue over things," I point out, hoping to relate this as softly as I can to something Lacy can understand. It's also a lie cloaked to be a soft landing excuse. Aiden and I are arguing more and we have grown apart . . . way apart.

"Like when Ariel steals my brush and steals my hair clips and steals my make-up and steals my..." Lacy starts to name the many things that her sister does to bother her.

"Yes, yes," I interrupt her with a smile. She smiles back.

"You understand?" I ask her.

"Yeah, I do." She leans in and I hug her. I pat Lacy on the back, feeling badly about Aiden and my issues leaking down to the kids. After Ariel gets out of the shower, Lacy jumps in. I get them reading and into bed.

Then it's my turn. I take a nice, hot shower while the girls watch a little television just prior to them falling asleep. It's a Friday, so they have a green light to do so, and an extended curfew. The warm water, running down my face only brings me back to Taylor. That was a hell of a kiss.

Finished, I step out of the shower and place my robe on. I stare into the mirror, looking dead at my reflection. I smile, accepting who and what I am, knowing I am not a bad person.

I turn and open up the bathroom door and catch Aiden, heading by me into the bathroom. "Hey, babe," he says with a cold tongue, no warmth or excitement to speak of.

"Hey, how was your day?" I ask as he disappears into the bathroom and fires on the water for himself.

"Long," is all I get. I'm sure Aiden is still sore over my financial support of Rebecca's family.

I nod. I'm not too interested in making up with Aiden. My family means more to me than money I can make up. I get the practicality of saving money and not giving it away, but family is family. Rebecca and Casey are desperate. I tried to get them to move out here, but Rebecca refused. She is living in *her* home. And home is home.

Wanna go shopping? I awake to a text from Jessica. *Heck yeah!* I reply. *Sitter?* I follow up with Jessica. *Got one already.* Jessica states, fully prepared.

After Aiden showered, he alerted me he had to work Saturday. It's fortunate I didn't have a client or a need to head to Ramsey just yet. I fire off a text to Angela to set up a meeting in Ramsey, at the high school, for Tuesday evening to discuss the case. That's the roughest part. Setting up meetings with the people from Ramsey usually has to happen at night, when they are out of work. I'd do a Saturday meeting, but with so little notice, that won't work. And I can't wait a full week with the offer. So, Tuesday night it is. And to be honest, my schedule is fairly open.

Great! Jessica texts back.

Aiden tosses on his work outfit, an old pair of blue jeans and a beat-up white t-shirt. "I'm gonna hang out with Jess for a few today," I let him know.

"Norwalk?" he asks, like he's unsure which Jess it is. I don't get the question, since I'd never call anyone else Jess.

"Yeah, what other Jessica do I know?" I light-heartedly quiz Aiden with some morning sarcasm.

"I don't know who you know, Nick," Aiden shoots back with traces of cynicism. "Don't make it too long. Like you've said, you haven't spent much time with the girls." Aiden's words are meant to hurt. He says them in a blithe matter-of-fact tone to make the sting worse. Any show of emotion or passion is beyond his now more robotic subdued way.

"You got it, Dad," I try to keep my sarcasm light just after two direct hits by Aiden. If he says one more thing I'm going World War III on his ass.

Deep breaths, Nicki. Deep breaths.

Aiden quickly leaves for work, and I make a brilliant pancake and egg breakfast for my girls. Lacy and Ariel always enjoy hanging out with Jessica's daughter, Tara, so heading over there is a big upside for them.

I head to Jessica's and it's off to shopping. Normally, a mall trip is in order, but ever since Jessica got separated and she inherited over a million dollars from her mother passing, her financial taste has grown. Lately, Jess has higher-priced fashion desires. She loves to dress up and look sexy. Jessica has always been beautiful. She used to wear second-hand clothing. But, just after high school, Jessica's father was hit by a drunk driver. They lost her father and inherited a lot of money. She never told me how much, but her mother was able to not work and transplant herself out of the desert and into Westlake, California. That's initially why Jessica moved to Thousand Oaks. Being just a few miles from her mother made both of their lives easier. Now Jessica likes to shop on Rodeo Drive and check out the high-end clothes there. Me, I could always shop anywhere. I've always been simple in that way. I do go to Macy's for my work suits, but that's about it.

The skies have cleared from yesterday's hard hitting storm. Crisp and clear seventy degree weather is perfect for walking Rodeo and doing some fine window shopping.

"I'm glad that case could be coming to a close," Jessica comments, continuing a conversation we started in the car on the way over.

"Definitely," I say. "How's it going with the two men?" I flash Jessica a sinister grin.

"It's all just casual." She flashes a devious grin of her own. I giggle with her, the two of us reverting back to our high school gossip days.

We enter a sheik lingerie store and immediately my eyes pop out of my head. I'm far more conservative than my sexy blonde friend. Jessica turns to me and smiles.

Can you handle this?" she asks with a big grin knowing I'm not the first to go to a Victoria's Secret. But this place is quadruple Victoria's prices, so I'm way out of my depth.

I play along for the fun ride. "I'm fine." My adult-self takes over and assures my shy-self that all will be well.

We walk through the store, parting. Jess goes straight to matching sets of bras and panties. Her eyes are fixated on an extremely sexy, black-laced thong and bra set, holding them up before her eyes. She is entranced by the undergarments. I stroll by nightgowns and bathrobes, starting out light.

"I love this!" Jessica announces with a sales rep by her side. I look over and focus on an even smaller, more revealing, black-laced thong with accompanying bra. It is perfect for Jessica. Her God-given body has always been made to sin, but she's never been a sinner. She had a rep in high school mainly because of her looks and one boy, Tommy Fulton, who talked a lot of crap about her. Typical story. A hot girl who turns down the starting varsity pitcher is bound to get shit. She was only a sophomore and he was a senior. So, it made big news and he spun it as a one-night stand and that he blew her off. She didn't care. She never cared. A rep was a rep. Jessica didn't concern herself with it and if people thought she was a whore, whatever. They didn't know her. Of course, now, juggling two men at once, post her failed marriage, is a whole other story. I definitely plan on hearing more about that.

Jessica returns from the changing room and heads to the register. Shortly after, she comes dancing over to me with a big grin as if she just got a Christmas present.

"I got you something," she giggles as we leave.

"You got me something?"

"I got you something." She widens her eyes. "Sexy underwear and matching top. It's deep purple. Very hot and very lacey." Jessica can hardly contain her excitement.

"How do you know it will fit?" I ask, looking for an out.

"Nick, your body is the same size as mine. It's always been. We traveled from a four to an eight and back to a four again. You've always had the right curves and a great body. You got it going on, girl." Jessica laughs and rambunctiously smacks me on the rear. That's Jessica for you.

"Thanks," I shyly reply.

"Let's eat. I'm starving," she shifts gears.

"Sounds good to me." I'm also game for a bite to eat.

"Hmmm…where to go," Jessica ponders. My eyes trail off at our surroundings and catch a familiar object, a classic Mercedes Roadster, *exactly* like Taylor's.

I take a step forward, away from Jessica, attempting to see a license plate or any distinguishing mark. But the car is too far away and turns down a street out of my sight.

Was that Taylor? He was supposed to be gone already. I fill with self-doubt and concern. *Is he lying to me?* I wish the negative thoughts would go away. They mar my good time.

"Nick? Nick!" Jessica struggles to pull me out of my trance.

"Yes?" I reply.

"So, which one?" Jessica looks for me to answer a question I never even heard.

"Let's go with your gut," I generically reply, having no idea what I'm potentially agreeing to.

"Sushi it is!" Jessica proclaims.

Phew! Glad it wasn't Mongolian barbeque or greasy burgers. Sushi works great for me.

―――――――

We are sitting at the Soh Sushi Bar, sipping warm Saki and chomping on a variety platter we opted to share.

"And that's it? Nothing more with either guy?" I continue to probe Jessica over her two male suitors.

"That's it. But let's talk about you," Jessica digs in, sensing something, I'm sure.

"What do you mean?" I say with girlish embarrassment, feeling the heat hit my cheeks.

"I know you. I know that sparkle in your eyes. I know something's up. What is it?" Jessica insists.

"Okay," I relent, wanting so badly to share my crush with somebody else. And there is no better person to do it with. "It's just a silly crush; a new guy from work," I make it far more simple than it is, not only trying to devalue it for Jessica, but for myself as well.

"Hmmm." Jessica stares at me like a fortune teller, sensing the story goes far deeper than I have led on.

"Oh, honey, I know there's more," Jessica relishes the roles of detective and gently pushes for more.

"I don't know. He just makes me feel . . . I don't know," I want to plead the fifth, but that's not going to fly with Jessica.

"You really like him!" Jessica pounces.

"It's…weird, I guess." Not exactly the words of Hemingway, but I, all of a sudden, feel like a suspect in a crime investigation, under the hot lamps.

"Have you guys kanoodled?" Jessica uses her favorite word to substitute for sex.

"No!" I loudly whisper to remain inconspicuous as if others are listening.

"But you did something. Nicole Dawn Connolly, you did something!" Jessica stabs with near certainty.

"Yes. A thousand times in my mind and a hundred different ways," I begin.

"But…?"

"A kiss. Just a kiss," I give in like a criminal beaten down. A weight of secrecy is lifted; I'm no longer a prisoner of the biggest secret of my life.

"You naughty girl," Jessica says before downing her Saki. "I think we're gonna need a refill of this." She holds her empty glass up, jiggling it for emphasis.

"Yeah," I dully agree. Doubt and guilt, unwanted bedfellows, drift around my mind like a thick fog encasing my happiness, confining it to a small place in my head. "I have to use the bathroom," I announce before stepping away from the hot seat and strolling aimlessly around this foreign sushi place. I walk down a hall that leads to a couple of locked doors that must be closets or a back door.

I turn and see what looks like the silver-haired man from the streets of Santa Barbara, wearing a polo shirt, baseball cap, and sunglasses, making it difficult to tell. But my heart skips a beat and I'm frozen, unable to move or speak. I think this is the man. I'm almost certain of it.

"Dead end," his dark, raspy voice uncoils words as if he were a villain.

"Wha-what?" I shudder, with a breathless disjointed word, leaking out of my frightened mouth.

"Never know when you're gonna make a wrong turn," the silver-haired villain states.

The door behind me is busted open and I jump. An employee brings in a garbage can from the alley behind us. I look back and the silver-haired man is gone.

Fifteen

I get the girls after shopping. Once we get home, they race upstairs to their electronic holes and quietly disappear.

I have a small bag I bring upstairs with me and lock my bedroom door. I open up the bag and find the deep purple underwear set Jessica got for me. After successfully stonewalling her advances for more information on Taylor, I successfully escaped without exposing too much of the *new* feelings swirling inside me.

I undress and take out the pair of laced panties and bra, laying them on the bed. *They are beautiful and sexy.* It's ironic; Aiden has never been a fan of purple anything. It's silly, but he is a Green Bay Packers fan—diehard, at that. And I guess with their rival team, The Vikings, donning purple, this has, somehow, led Aiden down the irrational path of hating all things purple. I'm not a football fan at all, so the colors and teams mean little to me. But, he is a *huge* fan of black panties. I guess I should have swapped out with Jessica.

Wow! I stare down at the $199.99 price tag in awe. That much for so little—literally! The set will provide barely any coverage on my body. Curious, I decide to find out how they look.

I slip on the panties, pulling them up. They arch just slightly up toward my hips, a nice snug backing, cut off near the bottom of my butt. It is perfect, hugging my curves just the right way. I'm thankful Jess didn't buy me anal floss. I've had enough of those come and go. I stand in front of my body-length mirror and pose, turning to the left, then to the right. These are sexy. I hold my breasts in my arms as I turn. I throw a few pouty, longing looks at the mirror as if I am a naughty underwear model. Then I burst into laughter, not for a second feeling myself.

Next, is the bra; I want to see how the matching set looks. The underwear is perfect as Jessica said. She should get a job as a personal shopper.

As I stare back into the mirror, I see myself and smile. I feel sexy, special. Everything is just perfect; the way my curves look and the way the lingerie clings perfectly to my body. I don't often look at myself—not like this. I see myself as a woman. I see myself as something to behold. I see *Nicki.* And I enjoy the view. So I allow my mind to wander. And then I see Taylor, fully clothed, wrapping his arms around me from behind. He's wet from a storm and kisses my neck. He can't resist the sexy panties. They draw him in. I see him caressing my skin, searching endlessly to make me feel pleasure of any kind. His gentle kisses are broken up by subtle warm breaths felt against my neck and collar bones. He probes me with his mouth.

Slam. The front door jars me out of my beautiful moment.

"I'm home!" Aiden's voice is distant. I move quickly to undress and hide the panties deep in my underwear drawer and toss on sweats and a sports bra with just as much haste.

The door knob is jimmied. "Nicki, you in there?" Aiden asks. His voice sounds confused, probably because the bedroom door is never locked with him outside of it.

I grab a yoga mat from under the bed, toss it on the ground, and walk casually to the door and unlock it. "Oh, sorry," I say.

Aiden looks over my crazy put together outfit of random sweat pants and a sports bra that don't match. "Why was the door locked?"

I casually turn around, step onto the yoga mat and begin stretching.

"Just wanted to get a little yoga in," I say nonchalantly.

"Okay. Whatever floats your boat," Aiden sarcastically adds, with the roll of his eyes.

I grimace, not so he can see, though. His lack of support over anything I do kills me inside. There is a resentment building in me, as well. I feel as though it's an arms race of frustration and we'll see whose will build the most.

"I gotta shower. Muddy out there today," Aiden's voice trails as he disappears into the bathroom.

I hadn't thought about it before, but they never work in the rain. Last night at the site would have been a rarity. They must be behind to be that desperate. Judging by Aiden's demeanor of late, and high level of grumpiness, I'd say about two or three weeks behind.

———————

Sunday and Monday were slow days, especially with Taylor gone. I wanted to text him. But for now, I do not. I spend Sunday with my girls, enjoying my limited time with them. The park, board games and ice cream. All good things. Tuesday arrives.

"Hey, boss," Angela starts as she walks into my office.

"What's up, Ang?" I ask as I prepare my files and pitch for Ramsey, scheduled tonight in the desert.

"Rapture and Myers," Angie says.

"Myers is here?" I ask, surprised.

"Yeah, I guess." She looks concerned. I can't tell why.

"What?"

"Is everything okay?" Angie asks with a hint of uncertainty.

"Of course, why?" I don't know where this could be heading.

"You seem different lately; up and down." Angie knows me better than Aiden. She lives with my moods. I trust her with my life, but I haven't confided to her about my issues with Aiden or things with Taylor. It's just too close to work. I need everything separated right now. It's all too much.

"I'll fill you in when we head out to the desert," I tell Angie to put her off. In reality, I haven't decided if I'm going to. But, it puts it all to rest.

I gather myself and head over to see Charles Rapture and Bob Myers in Charlie's office. I'm not sure why they are bringing me in, but the impromptu meeting is very unusual. Charles is so calculating . . . so prepared. This all seems random and strange.

I approach the door and Charles and Bob are standing outside his office, his assistant nowhere to be seen. Upon seeing me, both men smile and become excited. "Nicki!" Charles welcomes me as if I just won him the Super Bowl.

"There's my girl!" Bob chimes in with his happy *hello.*

"Hey." I'm dumbfounded about this overwhelming response. It's as if they are about to hoist me on their shoulders and I have no idea why.

"Nicki, I know you have a planned meeting tonight, but we want to take you to lunch, first." Charles lays out a nice afternoon plan. I'm not sure where lunch is going to head. Suddenly I'm having a *Jerry McGuire* moment. *What do these two old dogs have up their sleeves now?*

Bob brought his midnight blue Rolls Royce in today and we all pile into the beautiful car. The two partners sit up front and I'm alone in the back, feeling as though I'm about to get *whacked.* My mind keeps bouncing back and forth, unsure of what exactly is happening.

We take a very short ride down the street to Le Fritz, a close by French restaurant. It's expensive and clear I'm definitely not getting the pink slip in this scenario. Context gives me optimism, but about what? I can't figure what's going on.

"This place is aces," Charles boasts.

"And they make a killer martini," Bob chimes in.

The normally reserved pair never get this excited and chatty, except for once a year, when they kick back a few too many at the annual Christmas party.

We walk through the doors and appetizers are already on the table. Gourmet humus and some mini crab crescent roll creations, with spinach, highlight the beautiful appetizers. Cheese and fruit plates are also on the table with a basket of French bread. A bottle of champagne is rushed over within seconds of me sitting at the table and of course, Bob's dirty martini. It's a whirlwind of activity.

"What gives?" I crack, as the waiter pours three glasses of champagne.

"Well, Bob and I are very impressed with you, Nicki. We're so happy and thrilled over the offer you received for the Ramsey suit."

And there it is. I've been ambushed by the two bosses. They think a check is in the mail when it isn't even close to being cut. I know my cousin speaks for many of the residents. They don't have the same desire to settle quietly as Charles and Bob, who are seeing dollar signs fall from the sky.

"Yes. Well, I'll take it to the people." I try and level off their excitement a little with the bitter taste of uncertainty.

"I'm sure they'll jump," Bob jumps in.

"They were pretty set on court—"

"—Court?! What are they, nuts?" Charles interrupts me and shakes his head. "These people are poor. They have nothing. Each of them would receive a substantial amount of money and medical benefits," Charles rips off the terms as if he sat before Albert Penn, in the chair beside me.

"I didn't even get a chance to speak with you yet. Did Penn fax over terms? He wanted this off the record." I am still confused and begin probing for more answers.

"Well, now it's on the record." Charles lays his solid foot down.

"I don't know if they will settle," I deliver the realistic news, again, trying to defuse Charles and Bob's premature jubilation.

"Then it's your job to make them, Nicki," Bob follows up.

"Do you know why we made you partner?" Charles's question is a potential trap. It's always best to avoid giving information. Only answer the basic and most minimal facts. If you exaggerate or lie, you will need to make that false information work and lies always grow. If you say what you think someone wants you to say, you could walk into a trap and incriminate yourself. I have no idea what these two old men want, but many answers are going to be short with no elaboration.

"No. I don't," I offer. I will let Charles tell me.

"We promoted you because you always got things done. You're an excellent attorney and provided an original point of view. We need you to get *this* done." Charles and Bob have made it clear, settle and settle as soon as possible.

"You know I will try," I tell them, the decision not resting in my hands alone.

"Don't try, darlin', just do," Bob says as he nearly finishes what's left of his martini.

"All right," my reply is simple and I am definitely *yessing* them. This lunch has the unmistakable resonance of tortious interference. The stench is thick and my anger elevated. Forces are working around me. Where there's smoke, there's fire. I just have to find which building is burning around me before I take any action.

I want to fire back about their *out* clause in my contract. The fact that the partnership isn't tenured for another year makes me believe my position at the firm is directly tied to my Ramsey result. It's all too much and I switch quickly to small talk, taking the high-road. I ask about their families, life, and successfully steer off Ramsey for the remainder of our appetizer samplers and drinks.

Once I'm back at the office, I grab Angela and escape the confined air of West Los Angeles and Rapture and Myers. We are a little early, but I gotta get out of the city. I drive, heading to the desert, leaving well before any rush hour could set in.

"You're going fast today," Angela states curiously.

"Can I talk to you about something?"

"Of course," she agreeably replies, shifting in her seat to face me more, as if she's sensing a juicy scoop coming from me.

"You know Aiden and I aren't in the best of places," I start.

"Divorce?" she guesses.

"No. Not…I don't know," I fumble with the *D* word, unsure if I even want to touch such a hot button right now.

"Sorry. Go ahead. I'll shut up." Angela peers in.

"I have a crush," I start soft-gauging Angela's response.

"Who is he?" she replies with great interest.

"It's Taylor," I say out loud, the words flowing easier each time I announce it.

"Well, who doesn't?" Angela points out the obvious, as everyone in the office has a little crush on *Mr. Twenty-four Karat*. I remain silent, not knowing the exact words. And then as if a light bulb turns on, Angela's eyes widen. "You and him?" she asks with a devilish grin.

It's a secret I would keep. It's one I *should* keep. But Angela is my *everything girl* and I need someone on my team with this. Jessica is my bff and can give me guidance, but Angela can protect me. She can help me like no one else can.

I let a smile creep out and her jaw drops to the floor of the car.

"Holy shit!" she yells. "Holy shitballs!" she yells again.

"I know," I try to calm her excitement and shock.

"This is huge! I mean, he is sooo hot! I mean, no offense to Aiden, but, holy shitballs!" Angela is like a spouting volcano, firing words out uncontrollably as if she were about to burst.

"It's early. We've just talked a lot." I try to suppress her exuberance.

"Wait, you haven't...?" She makes a nearly closed fist with her left hand and inserts her index finger from the right hand to simulate sex.

"Angie!" I playfully smack her and immediately blush up.

"Is it big? How big?" Angie is nearly on my lap, wanting details.

"Whoa, man! Ease off the throttle, girl," I joke.

Angie sits with a smile, calming down. "I bet it's big," she mumbles and giggles like a school girl.

"No sex. No visual on his manhood," I lay out with hand gestures settling the conversation down.

"Well, what then?" Angela is begging for any dirt, for once, someone's trying to live vicariously through me.

"We kissed," I confirm the truth.

"You kissed! Holy shit, this is huge!" Angie again erupts. I shake my head with an exhausted amused grin. "How was it?" she quickly fires back.

"Okay, it was..." I hold off a second and glance at her begging eyes. *Oh, what the hell!* "It was *freakin'* amazing!" I pronounce with vigor.

"I knew it!" she screams. I am overwhelmed by her misguided support, not sure what to say. "Where? How? Was it in the office, after hours?" she rattles off another barrage of questions.

"No! Never in the office! It was on the beach, in the pouring rain. Lightning was everywhere. It was like a perfect fairytale," I reminisce with a sweet smile on my face; a satisfying memory of epic proportions.

"Oh, my God." Angie stares at me as if an alien is seated by my side.

"What? What is it?" I ask.

"You really like him." She hits the nail on the head, seeing through it all. I do. I have strong feelings for the mysterious creature. I can't help it.

"I don't know him very well. But, what I do know—I just can't help myself. I do. I really like him." My confession sends Angela into a rare quiet moment of pause.

"You do what you think is best. I always have your back," Angie finally says; my loyal assistant to the end.

"Thanks, Ang. I just don't know, ya know? It's hard. This is a big deal."

"I can't imagine. Aiden's been a little bit of a prick lately. He'll call just to see where you're at, sometimes. He keeps tabs, like he owns you. He is acting weird."

Angela's admission is something new and my brows furrow, annoyed. "He's keeping tabs on me?"

"Yeah. Over the last year. Especially the last month or two. He tells me not to bother you, if you're in a meeting."

"You probably talk to him more than I do." *That stubborn man.* "I just think we are on different tracks right now." I show my hand, annoyed by it all.

"You gotta promise me one thing though, Nicki," Angie starts, staring seriously at me.

"Okay. What's that?"

"Tell me how big it is when you find out!" She bursts into laughter.

I blush, giggle and shake my head. "Angela Jean Potter, you are bad!"

Sixteen

Sixteen

We are driving through the streets of Ramsey as the sun disappears from the sky and darkness takes over.

I am thinking of you right now. I glance down at my phone and see the text from Taylor. I pull up to the school where we are holding the meeting. It's going down inside the gymnasium. Not wanting an inquisition or audience participation, I try not to react in front of Angela.

"This place is sad." Angie looks around at the poor destitute desert town.

"It can be a rough life," I reply. I see her staring with a sad face at the barren land consumed by the sun and dry climate. Weeds, trash, and a lifeless world reside around us. Even in the darkening skies, the desert can show its harshest colors.

I miss your lips. I quickly reply back to Taylor and conceal my phone. I want to know so badly where he is, what city he is in. I want to know if that was him I saw the other day, in his Roadster, on Rodeo Drive. I want to know so much more about him, but I constantly remind myself to pace my urges; subdue my desire to devour information all at once. I haven't been courted or felt like this—*if this is what THIS actually is*—in so long. I honestly don't know what to say or do.

"We're doing it in the gymnasium?" Angela asks to confirm, breaking my distracting thoughts.

"Yeah, should be about a hundred to a hundred and fifty people Rebecca said," I acknowledge the set-up to Angela.

"You think they'll be happy?" she asks with a hopeful tone.

I want to touch you. Taylor's next text sends my mind into a tizzy, and chills run throughout my body.

"Nick?" Angie asks, as I'm distracted again, this time, staring at my phone. I am so obvious at this point, falling deeper into this conversation.

"What?" I reply out of sorts.

"You think they'll be happy or pissed?" she repeats and adds a little more context this time to her question.

"I don't know. It's a good start. A fair offer. You wanna get up and greet everyone that gets here early and just be a presence in there? I'm just gonna make a few notes for my speech to them," I lie. The only writing I'm going to be doing is with my fingers, pounding letters on my phone to send text messages back and forth with Taylor.

"Yeah. No problem." Angie grabs a small box of materials to bring with her and exits the car. She walks into the gymnasium. Once I see the door closed, I dive back into my phone.

I sit back in my seat readying for something exciting. Every experience with Taylor seems like a new one, whether real or fantasy. I value the quiet atmosphere of my vehicle, the bubble for which I can envision Taylor's deep blue eyes as he texts me. I want to close my eyes in peace and see him standing before me, imagine feeling his body the way my hands did on the beach just four days ago. It was quick and passionate, but I remember his touch and smell well.

I open my eyes and text back. *I want to feel you.* I pause for a moment and then go for it. *I want to feel ALL of you.* I hit send and a giddy nervous smile emerges on my face. My breath quickens as the excitement of it is too much to bear. I am hoping I didn't go too far. I've taken the kind of leaps and bounds with Taylor that I never have in my entire life. In fact, I've never had an intimate text moment. No sexting ever. My husband is stone cold, to-the-point with his texting.

I anxiously wait, my breath short and holding now. *What if he doesn't reply? What if I've gone too far too fast? What game are we playing?* I question myself over and over again as anxiety starts to build inside me. Then, it appears.

Where would you touch me? His text is clearly aggressive and exactly what I wanted to see. I swallow nervously. I'm a fusion of intense sexual energy and breathless exhilaration.

First, your face. I love your face. Then my hands would wander. They would travel slowly south. I'd unbutton your shirt, while staring into your blue eyes. I hit the send button and anxiously wait. The smile on my face is big, an uncontrollably ear-to-ear grin. My chest slowly heaves, the excitement churning inside me.

I'd stare right back at you and caress your face, waiting until you could remove my shirt.

I lick my lips and feel passion burning inside me. My body is heating up, following the pacing of my sexting. I glance up and wonder if anyone can see me. Satisfied I'm in the clear, I dive back down into my phone and pound away.

What would you do after I remove your shirt? I can't help myself. I am entranced by the mere chance that this could happen. It's so strange. I'm out-of-body whenever I'm engaged in any sort of communication with Taylor. He can be a thousand miles away and my imagination is enough. What a hold he has on me. I hope he feels an ounce of the passion I have brewing inside.

I wait to see more, and then the words appear.

I would slowly unbutton your shirt, staring back into your eyes. Then, my mouth would dive forward to your clavicle, and begin to probe your naked skin.

Holy shit, I'm so turned on right now, it's filling me with energy like I've never felt. A fantasy is a fantasy. I've had a few. But a fantasy takes only one person. This is two people initiating an invitation . . . an invitation to so much more. This is no longer fantasy—it's real. I text back.

I'd run my hand though your hair, enjoying every one of your kisses. Then, I'd let my hands search for your belt buckle. I'd unfasten it smoothly, but quickly. I'd follow up with your zipper, carefully pulling it down. And then I'd slide my hand into your boxers and take a hold of you, caressing you over and over again.

My blood is near boiling. After texting him that, I sit back with a satisfied victorious grin. I shift in my seat, completely worked up now. If Taylor was within fifty miles of me, I'd probably rush to rip his clothes off and take him wherever he stood. To hell with it all—I want him. I can't stop myself. Taylor shoots back a text. I stare down at my phone, my vision just making it past my slowly heaving chest.

I'd reach up your legs and under your skirt. I'd let my fingers float to your panties and slowly pull them down. I'd know I'm moments away from being inside you. I'd have to kiss you, because I need to enter you in some way. I need to penetrate you, somehow.

Taylor's words prompt me to run my hand along my breast and down to my leg. My hand dips to between my thighs and I press against myself, pushing so gently on that perfect spot. I am so hot, I forget it is my turn to text when Taylor takes initiative and shoots me another reply.

I can't wait anymore. I tear off your panties and pick you up slamming your back up against the wall. Your legs wrap around my waist as I slowly enter you. I'd pump myself into you, gently, again and again. I feel like an animal that has been caged and needs to explode. I want you so badly, right now, Nicki.

I am breathless and awed reading his text. My excitement is at critical levels of built-up energy. If I was a nuclear power plant, an alarm would be sounding, because I'd be about to blow. My body and mind have one singular goal right now: Taylor Diamond.

Knock-knock.

I'm startled and jump out of my trance, like a shocked child who just got caught trying to steal money from their parent's wallet.

"Nicki? You in there?" Angela asks through a thick layer of fogged up glass that makes it impossible for anyone to see inside my car.

I can barely see Angela through the cloudy glass. It looks as if I have been in a sauna. "Yes, yes. Sorry." I lower my driver's side window.

"Hey, what are you doing in there?" she asks, looking around at the windows. "Looks like you and a guy just went at it for an hour! And your cheeks are flush!" Angela jokes, thoroughly amusing herself.

"Just practicing the speech. Intense, ya know?"

"Okay. There are a lot of people there. They all came early. Seem real excited."

"That's great. I'll get my things together and head inside."

"Okay. Enjoy your *practicing*," Angela jokes and giggles. She turns and heads back inside the gym.

I let out a breath of air and fondly look back down at my phone. My face is a little sad, having to break away from our connection. I can't touch Taylor, but, in a strange way, I felt him and it felt so good.

Angela almost caught us ☺, I text back to Taylor. It's the beginning of the end of our text session. *I wish you were here,* I send back.

Satisfied I've wrapped things up with Taylor, my mind starts to refocus. It's time to put my game face on. As wonderful as it was sexting with Taylor, I have something

154

extremely important to deal with and that fact smacks me directly in the face now.

I miss you. I'll be back soon, Taylor texts back.

I smile. Then, I erase our thread, ridding my phone of any evidence which could incriminate me.

I gather my things and march into the gymnasium, where the anxious and excited residents await. I step inside and there is an immediate reaction. They start to applaud and the applause moves to a cheer. I'm not sure what I've done to deserve such a response, but I shyly smile, humbled by their praise.

"There's an offer!" a random man shouts.

"How much?" a female voice yells.

"How much do we each get?" another voice echoes similar sentiment.

How much they ask. Well, that's where things get complicated. The firm is owed expenses. In fact, I have a scheduled trip coming up to meet with a few additional experts. It's literally the day after Halloween. They wanted to meet the day of, but that's not going to happen. I couldn't' do that to my girls. I'm hoping Taylor is back in time for that trip, but I honestly don't know anything. The money. The firm gets a cut. That cut is substantial. It will be thirty-three percent. Then money is dispersed amongst the class action participants by percentage, those most affected getting a greater percent of the money than those with minor complications. There are also medical bills that will be paid off the top, as well. The formula can be very complex. Whatever number I quote is not going to end in a simple math equation.

"Hello, everyone. I know you're anxious about the first offer. Let me emphasize that the offer is not binding. We can counter, we can reject, or we can accept."

"Or we can drag them through the mud, in court!" Rebecca shouts, getting a lot of support and applause from her fellow Ramsey residents. Angela shoots an ominous look at me. She knows we are in a mob mentality world. Just the flow of the crowd, up and down, depending on the majority, is fairly striking. "Right, Nicki?" Rebecca pulls me into answering the option of forging ahead to court, no matter what.

"Yeah, or that," I quietly agree.

I take a deep breath and begin, revealing the many, many details Ramsey has in store for them. It's not just about the money. It's also about medical care payments . . . future medical needs. There are a lot of details to discuss, and I don't have all the answers just yet. I go over as many unknowns I can think of: the estimated amounts distributed and the health insurance. I talk about the request to see additional medical records, and the offer to begin helping those in need now. I talk for nearly an hour and field a barrage of questions over each point from the confused residents. Many of them are limited in their education.

A lot of chatter emanates through the crowd, seated in the bleachers of the gymnasium. I can see families disagreeing, some are excited, and others confused. I need to help them.

"Nothing has to be decided today. We're not going to move mountains tonight." I try to calm their nerves and excitement.

"We should vote!" a voice yells. Many agree.

"What do you think, Rebecca?" another voice beckons Rebecca to give her opinion. Rebecca is where this case began and has often been the residential point-person for this case.

Rebecca hears more and more people calling for her and stands up, walking up next to me. I am uncertain what she is going to do and I give her a perplexed look. "I'm going to speak," she alerts me.

"Okay," I agreeably step aside. Angela and I shrug in confusion.

"Hi, everyone," Rebecca starts. Numerous cheers and *hellos* rain down upon Rebecca, welcoming her to the stage. "I'm Rebecca Braxton, for anyone that doesn't know, but I think I know you all. They are offering insurance and a lot of money. So that's all good. But can they just buy us off? Is this offer all we're worth?"

I just want to crawl up and die as Rebecca does a hard sell to push us deeper toward a court appearance. I hear the echoing sentiment of Charles Rapture and Bob Myers in my head. The strain of this case doesn't get any easier as it goes on. The case has been rough all-around and I want there to be an end in sight. But, Rebecca is steadfast and she wants blood and headlines. She wants the Beltan Food Corporation to pay. And as Rebecca speaks, many of Ramsey's residents are nodding and agreeing. The mob has spoken. Rebecca finishes her speech and there is a lot of chatter and discussion in the stands.

"Rebecca, this is a good offer," I begin.

"Ya know, I thought all I wanted was for them to pay for our bills, my time out of work, what they've taken away. But now, I want them to *really pay.* Not out of revenge, but out of right. There must be a right and wrong. And they know they're wrong. They already wanna settle." Rebecca has a good point, but it's not that simple. Nothing is ever that simple.

"Yes, but they have evidence of other tampering in the ground. This case could go on for years. They can file more extensions and appeals. This is what they do. I just—"

"—you just gotta have a little faith, cousin. Maybe we'll accept an offer at some point, but not this one." She is clear with her intentions. And Rebecca influences the mob—she controls them.

I nod, understanding.

After a *no* vote and the town unable to construct details on a counter, I am left going back to Los Angeles empty-handed. Angela and I leave the gym with our tails between our legs. We walk back over to my car, in the dark of night, and I notice a folded paper on my windshield. I open it up and it reads: *Meet me at Ben's Bar—alone—8pm sharp.*

"What is it?" Angela asks me.

"I don't know. But we got another stop to make."

Seventeen

Seventeen

We park down the street from Ben's Bar. There is little activity surrounding the dive bar, which is centrally located on the main strip of town. The area is a collective ghost town of businesses come and gone. Numerous store fronts are vacant with *For Rent* signs in their windows. A couple of the locations are selling all together, hoping to get anything for their depressed properties.

"What now?" she asks me, as we stare out the car windows at the bar. The time on the car clock reads 7:28.

"I'll go in first—alone. You come in second, and just sit at the bar and drink. Don't pay me any attention. I'm supposed to be alone. Try and get a glance of something." I lay out my very weak unstructured plan.

"This is great! So exciting." Angela seems jazzed by the thrill of it all. I'm nervous. This can be a dangerous game and I feel blind following an anonymous letter into a strange bar.

I get out of the car and make the walk over. I look around, seeing if any stray eyes are glaring at me. I can't be sure, in the dark of night, if I see anyone in the cars outside. I can't see well and don't want to be too obvious.

I casually head into the bar and see a number of people in the sparsely crowded drinking hole. Customers are sitting in small groups. The place has a distinct musty beer and cigarette scent. I feel as though the bar has its own tropical climate. There are no martinis or foo foo drinks going out on this night. It's a lot of beer and some shots of tequila. This is the bar of lost hope and I've entered as a foreigner.

As I make my way to a small table, a few sets of creepy eyes make their way toward me like fly to honey. I

159

stick out like a sore thumb in my matching pant suit. I look nothing like a rugged factory worker or a man without a job, drinking their sorrows away. I don't look like a trashy woman, overdressing to impress with her leather-bound, tanned skin, numerous tattoos and random glitter lotion to enhance their cleavage sparkle. I quietly sit and wait. I look around but see nothing.

"Hey, hon," a kind waitress approaches me.

"Hi. Um…got a drink menu?" I almost hesitate to ask, knowing the answer before she can return my request.

The waitress chuckles, seemingly amused. "In chalk, behind the bar, darlin'. I'll be back." The waitress, with her boobs pressed up as high as possible, underneath her black tank top, turns and walks off. Her jeans are a size too small and hug her sides so tightly, her thong peeks out with each step. She could pull her tank top lower, but I'm guessing the tips are better with the cleavage and thong making regular appearances before the male dominated crowd.

I look around and still nothing. I check my cell and the time reads: 7:32.

Angela enters the bar and spots me. She looks away and then back at me just long enough to wink. Note to self: *Don't bring Angela on future covert operations.* She sits at the bar and is able to make immediate conversation with the men around her. Why not? She is new, cute, and in her twenties. She is like a princess in this desert town and Angela's bubbly, easy-going personality only attract more men around her.

"Oh, honey, looks like it's been decided for ya. Here ya go." The waitress sets down a cocktail napkin and drink. The drink is a beer in a large plastic cup. I guess I should be happy it wasn't in a glass, given the location. Before I can ask the waitress who sent the drink, she dashes off to make conversation with regulars. I've been there before. I get it.

I look down and see faint writing in black ink, below my plastic beer cup. It reads: *Women's bathroom-now!* I stand up, looking around. I see nothing. Angela is distracted at the bar and drawing numerous suitors. I have to go there and see what this is about. I must know. I take a deep breath and bring my purse with me to the bathroom. I reach into my purse and grab my mace. I clinch it firmly in my fingers, readying for anything.

I approach the bathrooms in a dark corner of the bar. Down the dark hall are two doors. One is labeled *Gents* and the other *Ladies*. I push the ladies restroom door open slowly, peeking inside. Inside this bathroom is the health department's worst nightmare. A roach scatters under a corroded dirty floor tile, causing my skin to crawl. The glass above the rust-stained sink is cracked, and I cringe at the prospect of looking behind the graffiti-stained doors.

"Give me your phone number," the muffled male voice asks.

"Can I see you?"

"Last chance," the voice repeats.

I inform him of my number and a small, plastic bag is shoved out. I look down and see a flash drive inside the bag. I quickly bend down and pick it up.

"I will contact you. My name will always be *hunted*, all lower case letters. Understood?" The voice is specific and short. The paranoia is clearly getting the best of him, and suddenly, I feel as though I'm in a cloak and dagger situation.

"When will you contact me?" my next question is stated softly. I'm clearly walking on egg shells here.

"How far are you willing to go with this?" the mysterious voice beckons me.

"All the way," I say without hesitation.

I wait, a moment of silence. Nothing is happening. I look in between the crack of the bathroom stall and see the clothes on a body moving around. Then, it's gone. A

creaking window is opened above the bathroom stall and I
see the feet of the man, scurrying out.

Shit. I'm struck with a decision and barely hesitate.
I open up the stall and look up at the small window. I
secure the plastic bag in my pocket and step up onto the
dirty toilet. I use the stall to get up to the window and pull
myself up through the small opening, just as the man did. I
struggle, pulling myself through and fall awkwardly to the
ground. I hit wet dirt and am immediately disgusted. I sit
up and gather myself, looking around. I see the mystery
man jogging toward the end of the alley. I'm sitting dead
center in the alley, with little chance of catching the man.

I'm suddenly the star of the show, spotlights shining
upon me from behind. I turn and look back and see the
headlights of a screeching sedan heading right toward me.
My mouth hangs open, momentary shock weighing me to
the ground.

"Run!" the mystery man shouts from the other end
of the street. He quickly disappears after he clears the end
of the alley, turning the corner for his getaway.

I sense the danger of a car, bearing down upon me,
and rush up to my feet. I kick off my heels and run down
the alley, taking my chances barefoot. I run in the same
direction as the man. The dark sedan races toward me, its
engine getting louder and louder, closing in on my location.

I whip around the corner of the alley and clear back
out to a street, more in the open under the light of street
lamps. I keep going as I hear the car come to an abrupt halt
on the dirt just at the edge of the alley. The sedan seems
satisfied to hide there and waits.

I look to my right and try to find a door to enter. I
keep glancing behind me, trying to make sure no one is
following me. The sound of a car door opening and closing
from behind me scares the heck out of me. I look
feverously for a door to duck into. I pass by two closed-
down store fronts and finally come across an open business,

a Mexican restaurant and cantina. I step inside, breathless. I get a few strange looks as I make my way inside: dirtied, barefoot, and looking like a hot mess. I gather myself and think quickly.

The manager, a portly, dark-skinned, middle-aged man, approaches and I pull my wallet out. I flash my ID badge from work. I never have to use it for security, but it was created for that purpose.

"I'm with," I signal the manager closer to me. He obliges, leans in and I continue. "I'm with the Health Department," I whisper. The manager looks me up and down both concerned and confused. "My heels broke. Very annoying, being a woman. I just need to see your kitchen and I'll be out of your way. A woman said they saw a rat in there," I say quietly to keep things easy.

"Sure, sure. No rats here," the manager adamantly defends. I follow him to the kitchen, glancing behind me. We step through a door, just as I hear the door by the entrance open again. I don't look back but continue on. We enter the kitchen where the cooks are hustling to finish dinner service. "Look. Clean," he says with a thick, Mexican accent.

"Looks good to me. I'll close this complaint. Is that the back door?" I point to a sign reading EXIT by the dish station.

"Yes."

"I'll let myself out through the back door. Keep up the good work." I quickly exit the restaurant. I enter another dark alley in between the two buildings. I look left and then right, trying to get my bearings and figure out how to get back to the bar. Now, I just want to grab Angela and rush home. I want to see what's on the flash drive. I want to get out safely.

The dark sedan passes by one end of the street and stops just before it clears the alley. I press myself up against the wall, hoping they didn't see me. I wait; the car not moving. Then it backs up to get a better look down the alley, I think. I try to blend into the wall the best I can. It's dark, so I have a chance. The car pulls away and continues on. I can breathe again. I shake my head and walk toward the other end.

I breach the alley and immediately walk into the silver-haired man. I'm frozen. My mouth hangs open, unable to speak or move. A small grin overcomes his face. The streets are empty and I feel scared for my life. "Where is he?" the silver-haired man asks. His eyes are grey, matching his short, finely cut hair. He's over six feet tall and looks like a giant right now without my shoes on.

"Who?" my carefully crafted legal response.

"You know who." The man looks down at me with a glazed smile and I feel threatened. I am paralyzed, unable to talk or move. I stare up at the man, wondering who he is. His confident smile gives the impression he is untouchable or, at least, he feels that way. This man seems to have no fear. He looks like a sociopath—a killer for hire. My mind wanders into the abyss of the worst-case scenarios. "How are your girls, Nicki?" His voice sends chills, racing from my head to the tips of my toes. The content itself is a horrifying turn. He knows me. He knows of my children. Who is this man?

"Who are you?" I fire out, growing upset with his intimate knowledge of my personal life.

"It's not who I am that matters. It's what you're going to do that will make all the difference in your little world. Are we clear?" The man softly grabs my shoulders just to get his point across. His point is well-received. But, I have something for him. I snap my mace out and spray wildly. It's as if I'm protecting myself from a wild bear. I continue as he yells in pain. But his pain is mixed with anger and a deep growl infects his yelling as he lowers his voice.

I take off; his yells and screams quickly dissipating to nothing. I look behind me as I run and the silver-haired man is gone without a trace. I look up and the bar is a few feet from me. I breathe a sigh of relief and step back inside: barefoot, dirtied, and disheveled.

Angie has a small crowd of fans when I approach her. "We gotta go," I alert her.

She is sipping on, what looks like, a Long Island Iced Tea when she turns and looks at me, her eyes bulging out. "What happened to you?"

"Long story. We gotta go—fast!"

Angela nods, getting up amidst a sea of moans and groans and heads out with me. We stop outside and I grab her arm, looking both ways. I try to see and listen, trying to sense if there is anything or anyone that will get in the way of us getting to my car. I'm worried we could get run down at any moment.

"What's going on?" a concerned Angela asks.

"Let's go." I give the *all-clear* to cross the street. We are half-way across when headlights fire upon us from down the street. It's the dark sedan. "Run!" I shout to Angela. We race across the street as the car screeches and heads quickly toward us.

"Oh, my God!" Angela yells. We clear the street as the sedan whizzes by dangerously close to my Excursion. The sedan keeps going and disappears down the street.

"What the heck was that?" she asks. I can see that she is clearly scared, never mind confused.

"I need to get to a computer."

Eighteen

I brought Angela home and one thing she kept saying, on the way back to Los Angeles, rang true again and again—*you should call the cops.* It's definitely on the table. This was scary. This is something that is far out of my control. Who were these men? They followed Taylor and me. They followed me. They were there in Ramsey, asking about the mystery man. I just don't get it. The pieces don't fit together. I have to figure this out. Maybe my lap top will help.

I am so late getting home. I texted Aiden it would be like 9pm but it's almost 11pm. Being that he is an early bird, he probably doesn't even know I'm not home yet. Another indication we are circling the drain.

I go straight to my downstairs office. The house is as silent as a church mouse. I take the baggie and pull the flash drive out. I plug it right into my computer without a thought or concern. I'm anxious and want to see what this is all about.

One file pops. One singular file is all I have for my effort. *This better be good!* I just dumped a $75 pair of shoes for this and beat-up my $150 work suit. I pull up the one file and anxiously wait for it to open. It's a single page with the top reading: *Confidential*. The word runs clear across the top of the entire page. The memo appears to be an inner-office memo sent via special courier. I've seen them before on rare occasion.

CONFIDENTIAL CONFIDENTIAL
CONFIDENTIAL CONFIDENTIAL

We are immediately to seize using C-Standard rated chemicals
in processing any and all food. It is clear that contaminants are causing extraneous issues. We are employing B-Standard
rated chemicals for the time being and will wait to see if the processing improves or we must return to A-Standard. If A-Standard is again necessary, we will need to layoff two hundred workers to counter the costs. The reasons for changes are
listed in the Calixo Report, showing the chemical issues. Tests are showing contaminants "may" be airborne and possibly disturbing ground water. This is an Executive Order. Comply immediately.
Yours,
R.D.

SHRED SHRED SHRED SHRED SHRED SHRED SHRED SHRED SHRED

"Holy shit," the words slip out of my mouth with excitement. My smoking gun! If this mystery man can corroborate the existence of this memo and where he got it, it's game over. At worst, this is a phenomenal bargaining chip I can shove up Albert Penn's ass and his smug group of elitists. I have to be contacted by this man. I have no way to get in touch with him myself. So I move my focus to the existence of this man, R.D. It's strange because I don't recognize those initials of any high executive. I go through my paperwork and pull out my roster of Beltan Food Corp and their key players. When I look through, I only see the president, Victor Harris. Who else, other than Victor, could send an *Executive Order*? In fact, only one board member even has those initials, a Richard Drew. But he is head of advertising, so that makes no sense. I'm going to need more help on this one. I know where to go. First, it's bed time. Then, in the morning, I'm getting to the office early.

―――――――――

After a terrible night of sleep, I get into work. Nothing from Taylor and I refuse to chase my favorite ghost. If he is on the other side of the world, it's better he does his thing. When he comes back, we will have a lot to discuss.

I rush into the office and look for Ronald. Ronald is an excellent researcher but also has a close friend that could be of big use to me. He used to date a private investigator, not too long ago, and I heard he was one of the best around.

It doesn't take long. I find Ronald in our small library room doing some work. He is all alone. The library room, as we call it, is a fourteen by fourteen room, filled with books and two computers for online research. The room is more for studying and thinking, although the books are of great use to some who wish to hold knowledge in their hands as opposed to pushing buttons to find answers. With so much available online these days, this room isn't used as much as it used to be.

"What case is that?" I ask.

"Nicki-baby! Good to see you!" Ronald blurts out, excited to see me.

"I need a favor," I start.

"Don't we all, honey. In fact, where's that hot party favor you usually travel with?"

"Taylor?" I ask.

"You send shivers down my spine every time you mention his name to me," Ronald jokes. He's in a playful mood.

"You're too funny," I jest.

"Seriously though, honey, what can I get you? If you need it, Ronny can get it." Ronald is always the sweetheart. He'd go the extra mile for anyone.

"Your ex, Philip. The detective."

"You need a good dick," he jokes with a playfully evil grin.

"Yes, I do," I reply with a smirk. "You guys still talk?"

"Honey, we do more than talk. Ronny never has exes, just more options."

"So, you'll make the call?"

Ronny picks up his phone. "Texting as we speak."

"You're the best," I compliment.

"Nick?" he calls to me with a concerned tone.

"Yeah?"

"Everything all right? Is this serious?"

"All good. Just need some stuff done for the Ramsey case. It may help put everything to rest," I state with an ounce of confidence, I hope.

I am sitting in my office alone, staring out my window toward the late morning skyline. There is a lot of activity in the office as men in white outfits from a security company are scuffling about. I have no idea what they are doing as I remain off in my own world. There is so much to think about. It is a rare opportunity of self-reflection. As I wonder who and where I am, at this point in my life, my phone vibrates on the table. I pick up the phone and see a text.

I got you, girl. Meet at his office, 1245 4th Street, Downtown, high noon. Ronald's text gives me some optimism.

Thanks, Ronny! You're amazing! Ronald comes though again.

I gather my things and head to the parking garage. I stop just as I enter the underground dark unit. It is so silent, it's eerie. I hold my breath, wanting to listen for anything or anyone. *I have a bad feeling.*

Multiple white vans marked *CRANE SECURITY*, are parked in a loading zone, providing the perfect coverage for someone after me. They must be the team of men upstairs riffling through our offices. I look around and slowly make my way to my car.

With each step I take, I pause, a slight hesitation of uncertainty. I feel stalked and unnerved. Things are escalating and so is my anxiety. White noise of traffic and life from the streets surrounding our building is all that infiltrates the cold dark walls I'm trapped inside. I hold my breath, the feeling getting stronger. Then, distant footsteps.

They are from somewhere inside the garage, a gentle echo giving me little to go on. The location is skewed by the echo, but I feel as though my time is short. My heart starts to race, knowing another encounter with the silver-haired man would not be a pleasant one for me. My car is not too far, parked in its usually assigned spot. A partnership *at least* got me that. As the footsteps get louder, I rush to my car. I struggle with the keys, naturally finding Aiden's spare car key first. I flip around my ring of fifteen keys and finally find mine. The footsteps are gone as I rush to hit the unlock button and my keys slip though my nervous hands, falling to the ground. It's like a bad horror movie in the making. I quickly kneel down and grab them and as I rise, I feel a shadow cast over me. I can barely move. Is this it? I close my eyes as if praying to a God I have little relationship with would help. I open my eyes and look up.

I expect the devil himself, with his silver hair and danger-soaked smirk. Instead, I find the perfect smile. I gasp with excitement and lunge forward into Taylor's arms in elation.

"Oh, thank God it's you!" I squeeze him tightly. He must think I've gone mad. I momentarily forget where I am and then gather myself, stepping back from him, looking around to make sure no one saw my display.

"Sorry," I apologize to Taylor.

"I was going to surprise you. My trip got cut short," he says with a thankful grin as he surveys my state of mind closely with concern.

"You did," I joke again, my voice filled with relief.

"Are you okay?" he asks.

"Jump in. I gotta catch you up. We have a date downtown with a P.I."

"I'll drive us," Taylor offers to drive my car. I nod, thankful to have him by my side. I toss him the keys and we are off.

My mind is a mess. But I do the best recap I can of the two male stalkers and my Ramsey meeting. Catching Taylor up is crucial. He is my new partner in this case and so much more outside. It's a very strange tenuous web I'm weaving and I just need to keep focusing on a singular message: one step at a time. It's a critical reminder as things have changed so much in less than two weeks.

"I missed you," his sincere, beautiful words flow right to my heart. I turn my exhausted head and look at him with a dopey smile. I'm so smitten with him. And when he looks at me, he displays a similar grin, showing he is smitten as well. That draws me great comfort and happiness. I settle down.

"These men. What did they look like?" Taylor starts to probe the facts set before us.

"It was weird. They were just there in Santa Barbara. I saw the one man in a restaurant with Jessica right after I thought I saw you go speeding by on Rodeo, the afternoon you were supposed to be gone. And then, they popped up in Ramsey, at least the one man I saw. That silver-haired freak. He always has this weird smirk on his face. It's as if he grimaces all day long only to post a small evil smile just for me." I stop talking and look at Taylor. I sound insane.

"Are you all right?" he gives me a quick glance, his brows furrowed.

"Physically. Of course. He barely touched me. Mentally, probably not," I respond with honest sarcasm.

"What do you mean he barely touched you?" Taylor is upset, the first time I've seen some anger behind his blue eyes.

"Oh, my goodness! I forgot to tell you. I maced him in the face! Like all over. He put his hands on my shoulders and made a threat of sorts. I had forgotten the strange threat. But I know it's all about this case," I ramble along the details as they come to me.

"What do you mean a threat?"

"About my girls. He knew I had two daughters," I explain.

"And he said that to you?!" his voice rises. I can see he is getting more upset. Since we aren't really *together,* he is completely on the outside. He is somewhat helpless and I can see that bothers him.

"There is more to this than we know, Taylor. There is so much more." I look at him. He is seething as he drives. Many thoughts are running through his brain and I wish I could read his mind now more than ever.

"He can't put his hands on you and he has no right to threaten your girls," Taylor speaks with venom and the sound of vengeance in his voice.

"I was going to call the police," I begin to speak.

"You have to."

"Maybe that's what the extra security is at the office?" I hypothesize.

"What extra security?" he asks.

"The two white vans parked in our garage. There were bunches of guys upstairs working on things in the office. No idea what."

Taylor shakes his head, the avalanche of information affecting him far more than I've ever seen. The normally cool, calm, controlled man is definitely ruffled. Perhaps I should share in his emotions. I feel numb for the most part, focused on the task at hand. But Taylor's anger over my girls being mentioned by the silver-haired man gives me great pause. I definitely should do something about this vail threat. But what would I say?

"You have to tell the police," Taylor repeats.

"I'm just not sure what to say," I reply.

"I'll make a call. I know a detective in the LAPD. That man is not going to threaten your family. He is not going to get near your family," he states with absolute conviction, again spewing anger.

"Thank you. I appreciate that. I just wish we knew who he was."

"I'll take care of this," Taylor reiterates.

A moment of silence goes by as he digests all the information. "I missed you too. I'm really happy you're back," I remind Taylor exactly how I feel.

He breaks his frustrated trance and cracks his typical smile. He looks at me longingly and takes his right hand and places it upon my hand. We interlock our fingers together like old lovers. One kiss has gone a long way. It may be a way of showing his feelings toward me or it may just be a way of him of showing support for me, to settle me down. Either way, our hands fit together like a perfect puzzle. The rest of the ride is quiet as we exchange each other's presence as opposed to filling the air with more stress and difficult decisions.

We arrive in Downtown Los Angeles on 4th street. Downtown LA is best described as a beat-up inner city with splashes of reemergence. There are classic old buildings built back in the sixties and seventies, as well as some new upgrades and development going on highlighted by Staples Center and the Convention Center. But down by 4th street, there is far less intrigue and far more visible struggle. Vagrants are commonplace, sprinkled in alleys and on street corners. It's a different kind of poor. It's a land of unknowns, living with no hope.

We park in front of the building with a white sign in the window reading: *DETECTIVE PHIL.* I guess it's a play on Dr. Phil, but a strange way to announce yourself. This is definitely not the location of a high-end talented detective, but the man's reputation goes further than his storefront.

"This is the place?" Taylor asks with surprise.

"Yeah. I guess," is the only response I can muster. I too am not impressed by this destitute street and location for a detective. But, let's hope this is just Phil keeping a *low profile.*

We make our way up a short set of creaking, cracked stairs. Taylor and I are both a little hesitant as we make our way up, but I have no choice. I need Detective Phil. We enter through a door marked *Office.* We get inside and see a small room with a woman chomping on gum and sitting before a computer. Her hair is big, firetruck-red, and curly. It's also clear that she did not shy away from make-up this morning. Her big lips are reminiscent of a transvestite, but her cleavage screams all woman. She is curvaceous and shows it; a tight skirt is wrapped around her waist and legs. But her red, frilled blouse beats her skirt, when it comes to tightness. Her black bra, below her blouse, is crafted just to give a look of trashiness. I wouldn't be surprised if she worked the streets at some point in her life. Taylor and I freeze, not sure if we're in the right place.

The woman looks up and places glasses on her face. "What you two's want?" Her accent is reminiscent of the deep-south, perhaps Alabama. But she also has a trashy feel. It is clear she is not well-refined, to say the least.

"Is this the private investigator's office?" I ask, clearly confused by my surroundings.

"Well, it ain't Disneyland, sweetheart." The desk clerk is full of piss and vinegar.

"Is Phil here?" I move along with the conversation hoping to get to my ultimate goal.

"He's with somebody. Have a seat." The woman extends her hand in a direction of two chairs that look as if they had been lifted right out of a first grade elementary school class.

Taylor and I shrug and have a seat. We sit side by side, our eyes roaming around the cracked painted off-white walls of a building that is more likely to be condemned than remodeled in the short term. A single door which reads: *Detective Phil* is the only part of the small office we haven't seen.

"I'm supposed to offer you's some coffee or water," the strange secretary says, before she goes back to burying her nose in her computer. Taylor and I look at the odd red headed woman and then at one another, confused. I think we both were expecting more to her statement. She looks up and sees us just looking at her. "Oh, my manners!" She states, realizing she didn't finish her thought before, I think.

"It's all right," I reply, attempting to be as casual as possible. And anyway, I've never wanted to be waited on hand-and-foot. I've been the waitress, the one chained to servitude. I've been on the other side of the coin and despite wearing a decent looking business suit, I am as easy-going and low-maintenance as it gets.

"Ya know, you're perdy," the woman glances up and compliments.

"Thanks," I humbly reply, unsure of making any sort of conversation. The whole situation seems awkward. "I was talking to him. But you got your thing too. My bell just doesn't sway that way, honey."

"Thanks," Taylor shoots a quick grin over at me, amused the woman called him pretty. I subtly shake my head at him, the two of us thoroughly entertained by this woman and we share in our silence, reading each other's faces. It's nonverbal communication that comes with time normally. For Taylor and me, we've graduated pretty quickly to sharing such a moment together.

"Like I was sayin'," the secretary begins, getting back to a thought she started minutes before. "We got some coffee and tea and maybe some water, if you like. It's right there in the bathroom." She points to her right where a small closet-looking door resides. "You's can go in there and help yourselves, if you please. I haven't figured out the coffee maker myself. Although, you two look like Starbucks folks, just like me, so I'm doubting you will touch that thing," she relates herself to us.

"Oh, no, thank you," I kindly reply, still grinning and still amused by this character.

She looks right at Taylor, changing her smile to a more aggressive glow. "I'll run to Starbucks for you, honey," she says to him.

"No. But, thank you. I appreciate the offer." He smiles.

"Oh, my manners again! You two are together, aren't ya?" she asks.

"Um…uh…ummm," I half shake my head *no* and stammer along with no clear answer in sight.

"We always like to work closely together," Taylor states the situation perfectly. Not a denial but at the same time, pairing us side-by-side in such a way that can only bring happiness to me. He sure knows his way around words.

"Oh, yeah. I can tell. True love birds, the two of you." She chomps her gum and points at us with her pen, analyzing us with her creepy eyes.

The office door quickly swings open and Detective Phil appears. He sees us sitting in the chairs and whips his head back to his assistant.

"Teresa, you properly offer these folks some drinks or snacks?"

"Oh, shoot. I forgot about the peanuts," she replies.

"That's all right. Next time. Okay?" Phil lets her off the hook easy.

"You got it boss-man," Teresa says and goes back to her gum and her work.

Phil turns to us with a welcoming smile. "I'm Detective Phil. Come on in." He holds his hand out, welcoming us into his office. At about five feet eight inches tall, Phil is a little on the short side. He's dressed in a collared shirt and snug-fitting, blue jeans. He also has on a gold Rolex watch. It could be a fake, but looks real on the surface, *not that I would know much better.* He has a five-o'clock shadow going, but is pretty handsome. His wavy, black hair, kind demeanor, and fit physique explains why Ronald and he were a couple. Unlike Ronald, you'd have no idea Phil was gay. In fact, if I saw him on the street, I'd assume otherwise. But I have little experience and absolutely zero *gaydar* to speak of.

"Welcome. My apologies. I'm in transition right now," Phil makes excuses for his office's appearance. The inside of his office is a little different. Leather chairs, a solid oak, finely-finished desk, sports paraphernalia on the walls, and an old grandfather clock make this a far better looking furnished office than the four walls the furnishings reside inside of. Standing nearly seven feet tall and two feet wide, the grandfather clock clearly stands out as the office's prize piece. Its beveled glass and beautiful polished brass dial features stand out. A rotating moon dial and decorative corner spandrels pop to the eye, and the classic, raised brass Roman numerals stand out, as the classy piece shines in the room. Polished brass lyre pendulum and weight shells hang, making this exquisite antique a strange bedfellow to the rest of this office.

"That's a Hermle," Taylor points out, staring at the antique clock. He has a confident and impressed grin on his face.

Phil smiles and nods, equally impressed by Taylor's knowledge. "That's right. You have fine taste."

"What is a Hermle?" I ask in confusion.

"The clock." Phil points out. "It was a gift from a high-end client long ago. It's worth over five thousand dollars," he proudly states.

"Probably closer to ten," Taylor confidently grins.

"Probably," Phil agrees with a smirk.

"It looks impressive," I add, not really into material things but definitely impressed with the clock's beauty.

"I'm sorry for the office and Teresa. She's sorta new." Phil waves his hand around for emphasis.

"I heard that!" Teresa shouts from the other room.

Phil leans forward to whisper. "She's my brother's wife's sister. So…yeah." He rolls his eyes and sits back at his desk. "I've had some bad luck in recent months, but I'm on the way back."

"Ronald said you are a great detective," I point out.

"Ronald's great," Phil indicates with more meaning than simple friendship.

"He sure is."

"He said you need something. I'm all ears," he moves the conversation along.

I take out the memo and slide it over to him.

"What is that?" Taylor curiously asks. He hasn't seen it up close yet. I only explained the gist on the drive over.

"The memo," I inform him. I pull out another copy and hand it to him. "I have the original tucked away safely on a flash drive. I made some extra copies." They both closely look the memo over and read. "A man gave me this. I didn't see his face and I don't know who he is. But he has my cell number and said he would contact me," I explain. "The smoking gun in my case," I conclude.

They look at me with ominous expressions on their faces. The gravity of the memo could be worth hundreds of millions, and more importantly, could be worth killing over.

"This is big," Phil points out, with a concerned tone.

"This is special. It's an interoffice hand-delivered courier memo, Nick," Taylor states with an equally tenuous tone.

"I know. It's big." I agree with them both, knowing full well what I have in my possession.

"You need me to find the guy?" Phil asks, trying to figure out what I need all on his own.

"I need to know who R.D. is," I state, and both men's eyes flash to the bottom of the page.

"He's not the President or VP?" Phil logically asks.

"Not on my roster. And I checked—no changes have been made for years to the executive branch." I pull out another piece of paper and slide it over to Phil. It's the list of Beltran Food Corp's execs. "I want the name of the man who wrote this order." I am serious and focused in my tone.

"All right. You pay up front?" he asks.

"Tell me your retainer and it's paid," I say without flinching.

"Just five hundred for you, counselor. Normally it would be two-thousand, but you are a friend of Ronald's which makes you a friend of mine."

"Thank you."

I pull out my personal check book, write out the fee, and hand it over. I feel Taylor's eyes looking over my shoulder. I'm sure he's wondering why I'm writing a personal check.

"Watch your backs," Phil relays his concern. We all rise up to our feet and exchange handshakes.

"You don't want to know my name?" Taylor asks Phil as they shake hands.

"If I need to know—I'll find out." Phil closes the discussion and Taylor nods. "Can you please close the door behind you?"

"Thanks again," I repeat and we exit Phil's office, closing the door behind us. We walk back to the front and head toward the exit.

"See yas later, beautiful," Teresa states as she flips through files, continuing to look busy at her desk. I smirk at Taylor knowing the good-bye is just for him, and we leave Detective Phil's office.

Nineteen

Nineteen

I take the keys to the car and drive. "Where are we going?" Taylor asks with curiosity.

"It's a surprise," I state with devilish grin.

"Then a surprise we shall have," he happily gives in.

The first thing I do is drive to an In N' Out Burger. "You ever eat here?"

"Can't say I have," Taylor replies.

"That, in itself, is a crime. I am going to treat you this time." I have decided to randomly take control of the afternoon. For one thing, I'm starving. It's nearly one o'clock and I haven't exactly been eating well of late. Secondly, I don't like being the mouse chasing the cheese. It's not that I'm a girl that doesn't appreciate a man taking care of me or opening the door every now and then. It's just that Taylor's chivalry is something I'm not used to. Thus far, there hasn't been a door he has tried to open or a kind word he hasn't tossed in my direction. I'm not used to being taken care of. Even when I played housewife for a few years, I made sure to take care of everything. No maid. No nanny. Just me, cleaning the house, doing the laundry, taking care of the girls, and doing all the shopping. I became a self-made, gourmet mommy-chef. Now Taylor is a man who buys me dinner and opens up doors. I didn't ask for either, but now I'm going to treat him to something special: two burgers, fries and two milkshakes. It's not the kind of meal either of us normally eats. But, it's freakin' In N' Out Burger and I'm in the mood for something special.

"Can I text my friend?" he asks.

"The detective?"

"Yes. Let me do this. Let me make sure your family is safe." Taylor always speaks with conviction when referring to family. It is something that is so *real* and important to him. I appreciate that about him. It makes me trust him.

"You can contact him."

Taylor nods and texts him.

After picking up our beautifully wonderful, unhealthy lunch, I drive us to a special location. He showed me Fossil Falls, a beautiful natural landscape. Taylor did a lot of thinking at those ancient falls. When I have to think I go somewhere beautiful as well. 'Til this day, I have never taken anyone else to *my* special place. One secret deserves to be shared with another.

I drive to Pacific Palisades, a wonderful community distantly overlooking the Pacific Ocean. There is this place I love to go for my moments of introspection. The Getty Villa is a beautifully constructed house of art. It is a sight to behold. Normally quiet, uncrowded, and surrounded by near-perfect weather, the location is ideal in every way. I carefully place our food in an oversized canvas bag I have in the car. I take the milkshakes and do the same.

"You're going to ruin that bag," Taylor jokes.

"It's worth it. Besides, I keep this in here for just a purpose like this." I put an emphatic point together. Our visit here has many layers. It's time I orchestrate some of what I'm being wrapped up into.

Taylor smiles as he looks at the beautiful architectural achievement. I watch him for his expressions. I want the confirmation of enjoyment. Seeing him happy makes me happy. I want to share this with him and *only* him.

"The Getty Villa. I've seen pictures," Taylor sights.

"You will do better than the internet. You're going to touch history," I poetically state to him.

We walk through the Entry Pavilion, an open-aired walkway lined with meticulously manicured shrubbery. Our stroll is marked by handholding, a romantic jaunt through a vision of beauty. We move on and enter the villa. The villa itself was recreated off an ancient Roman country house found in Herculaneum, Italy. We gaze upon the ceilings containing bronze lanterns, reminiscent of those carried in the streets of Pompeii long ago.

"Come." I pull Taylor along. His eyes seem mesmerized by the architectural detail. But inside is not where I bask in thought. I lead him outside to the breathtaking beauty that brings me back again and again.

Stepping outside, you see the incredibly, long fountain, which looks more like an Olympic sized swimming pool in length, only much thinner. It is the centerpiece, bookmarked perfectly by gardens and shrubs. Flowers are everywhere, and I always wonder how they keep them looking so perfect, so tranquil. Our stroll through and around the villa is special. We find a bench and have a seat. I look around; we are safely alone on this weekday afternoon. I pull out the hamburgers and shakes and we dive in.

"I can see why you come here," he says as his eyes take in more of our surroundings.

"It is something, isn't it?" I say in awe, as I look around, so appreciative to have this to enjoy.

"What do you normally think about when you come here?" he queries me, the last question he will probably sneak in before I ask him a few of my own.

"I think about anything. I don't just come here when I'm sad or emotional. Sometimes I come here to *be*. I'm just drawn here. I can't help it. It's so nice. And it's not far off my route to and from work. So, when I want to come, I come."

Taylor nods. I like his questions. He shows so much interest and I don't get to talk about *me* and things having to do with myself. In fact, except for some fleeting moment recently with Jessica and Angela, I haven't delved into myself much at all, lately. I have been an afterthought in my own life. Maybe that's why I finally feel alive. I don't want those feelings to end, but I want some answers from Taylor.

"Why haven't you gotten an assistant yet?" I ask.

"It's funny you should ask that. I had a few interviews set up for today."

"You did? I didn't know! You should have gone up there," I scold Taylor a little, but really, I'm happy he made the journey with me.

"You needed me." He stares dead center into my eyes and my knees weaken. His answer is definitive and enthralling. I can wrap myself up on a cold night with that answer and it would keep me warm forever.

"I did. But, I have more questions."

"Fire away," he opens himself up.

"Your family? You had so much money, but you went into law and helped those in need battle for their rights?" I ask based on some interviews and a bad bio I found online.

"I have helped a lot of people. As many as I could, for as long as I could. But there are things I've been asked to do. Things my family needed me to do after my father died. It's been an interesting journey, I guess. I wasn't the best person in the world. I had trouble; many issues for a long time. And something happened. I changed. So, I went the other way. I wanted to make amends, I guess. I had so much handed to me when many had so little. So…I guess that's it. I did what I could. But when my father passed away, things changed. A lot changed for my family. So, that's that." Taylor is clearly a little uncomfortable sitting on the hot seat. His answers are so perfectly constructed, most of the time, but now he is searching for words and not nearly as smooth. I like that choppiness of truth. I'll take it. And, I want more.

"These burgers are *for real*," he says with vigor as he enjoys his hamburger.

"I know. They're somethin'," I agree.

"What else do you want to know?" Taylor stares at me

"Where and who are these clients you have? It's like you're here one moment and gone the next."

"Mmm. Good question. This is a tough one because some of my clients are powerful and stay off the grid. And sometimes they require me with little or no notice. These are men of power . . . men of action. Some I'm related to and some are my father's friends."

Taylor doesn't exactly clear things up but at least I get the backdrop. Not enough details yet. I want more.

"Fair enough. You ever been married?"

"No." He follows with a chuckle, a telling sign he never even considered it. "Whatever the opposite is, that was me for a long time. I was a caricature of a wealthy young man—a spoiled, young man."

"And now?"

"Now I am a man. Just a man."

"A very pretty one, I might add," I joke, following up Phil's secretary, Teresa's, comment from earlier.

"Yes. I've heard that about me." He smiles, playing along.

"You close with your family?"

"Ah, that's tough. I'm not and I am. Definitely a rough subject. Lots of money. Lots of problems. I don't have a conventional family. Not in normal terms. I rarely spend a holiday in a house, especially not a house belonging to a relative of mine. Maybe I attend a party or go to a bar. Money has seemingly been my family's number one friend, and that has dominated my life."

I nod at his honesty. "How long have you lived out here?"

"I got the beach house a few years back but only started staying there six months ago. I have a place I mainly live at in the desert, by the border, on Nevada's side. I lived there a lot throughout my childhood. As an adult, when I wasn't traveling or working out of state, I'd head there. It's pretty great and extremely relaxing."

That explains Taylor's visits to Fossil Falls. "How do you know the LA detective?"

"Ah, Detective Craig Howard. That's an interesting story. We were both in Texas when I met him at a bar, of all places. I happened to be with a small group of people and he was with a woman. Unfortunately, one of the people I was friends with, at the time, was Hanz Glitzman, a wealthy German kid; a lot like me. He happened to also be a racist pig.

Craig Howard was on a date with a girl in Houston at our bar. Clancy's, I believe was the name of the place. Hanz had an issue because the bartender helped Craig before him. He had been waiting, but was too busy fondling one of the ladies we were frequenting with. Hanz blurted out, *you're serving this nigger before me?* It was dark and loud in the bar, so only Craig and a few other patrons heard the insult. Clearly, that didn't sit well with Craig. He was a young man who was about to graduate, with honors, from the University of Houston and go to the police academy in LA. Getting into it with Hanz Glitzman, a third generation billionaire with diplomatic immunity, was not the greatest idea. But, a fight broke did break out and a few other *good ol' boys* jumped in once they saw a black kid fighting a white kid. It was a big brawl that came to a quick end. I sat in a holding cell beside Craig, after. Hanz was quickly rushed away curtesy of a call from the German consulate. Alone, Craig and I talked for a long time. He impressed me. He was a great young man; far greater than me. It took a while, but he told me what happened . . . what Hanz said. When the police came to question me further, I took responsibility for the fight. I told them I was drunk and joking around and other people jumped in. It would be expected for me to cause a commotion. I wasn't a great young man, like Craig. Nobody would know Hanz from me in the dark, so the story took. I told them Craig was innocent and did nothing but order a drink. Craig was released without charges. I took the bullet, and my father cleaned up my mess, as he always had. His opinion of me couldn't have gotten lower, so I did something selfless, for once in my life. I didn't want Craig's life ruined over Hanz Gliztman. I made sure it wouldn't. We've stayed in touch and have been friends ever since. Now, he's a detective with the L.A.P.D."

"Wow. What happened to Hanz?" I curiously ask.

"There was a boating accident. He died, along with three others," Taylor states with emotionally charged sentiment. I nod, not wanting any more elaboration on the incident. We sit in silence for a few moments, giving our lunch more attention.

Taylor wipes his mouth with his napkin and clears his throat. "And how many others have you brought here? How many potential suitors?" he asks with a twinkle in his eyes.

"Just you. Only you." I grin at him, knowing he's busting my chops a little. We quietly finish our burgers and enjoy the shakes. Together, we share in the beauty surrounding us. I put to rest my inquiry and, for now, am satisfied with the answers.

———————

Taylor and I park back at the offices. We give a simple smile and *goodbye* with a longing look. We have a business trip in the morning, so we will be seeing each other shortly. That knowledge makes it much easier to separate. There is an expert we want to depose who lives just outside of Lincoln, Nebraska. He is a scientist that teaches part-time at the University there. Albert Penn used him in every major case he has fought for nearly two decades. That is, every single case, except this one. I want to know why, and hire him for our side. But for now, it's Halloween and I have to get home early for my girls.

I'm always excited about getting them in their costumes. However, this year, some of that luster is gone. It's not them. It's Aiden and I. As our cold war continues, we both have failed to make concessions of any kind. We have been relegated to roommates sharing a bed and two children. But now, we will be forced to work our neighborhood streets together. I've invited Jessica in hopes that walking around with her can help keep the peace and make the evening with Aiden palatable. Aiden invited his best friend, Eddie, and his wife, Bernice. It appears we both have wingmen for this night.

I get home and rush through a shower, so that I'm ready and waiting when Aiden comes home with my babies. He knows I have, yet another, business trip on the way. This one is two overnights in Lincoln, Nebraska. It could be anywhere. The fact that I'm leaving adds more fuel to our fire. So, his silence could be a demonstration for that. It could be over money or it could just be that we are beyond the rut we've been entrenched in, becoming damaged beyond repair. I feel like he's a kid that needs the coddling, some affirmation that he is doing a noble thing by being a good father. I push my negative thoughts down and travel to higher ground. This is for my girls.

They are angels in their costumes; innocent, excited angels, bursting at the seams to carry their little orange pumpkins around for the holiday.

One thing is clear, as we get ready to head out for the early evening event Aiden is not going to crack so I break the ice. "How's work going in the city?" I start light.

"Coming along," the man, of few words, states. I used to love his simplicity. Now his lack of elaboration is like pins piercing my eyeballs.

The doorbell rings. "Could be Jess," I surmise.

"I'll get it," he offers up. He heads to the door as I provide the finishing touches on my two rug rats.

"Nick!" Aiden calls out with a somewhat annoyed tone. I can't figure out what I've done now. *Could it be Taylor at the door?* The thought is a blip in my mind, but a terrifying proposition. He couldn't—he wouldn't.

I walk through the dining room to the entranceway, cringing every step of the way. I get there and see a black man in a suit. On his belt is a badge.

"Can I help you?" I ask, confused.

"The detective has questions for you," Aiden stares at me. His face looks confused but his eyes have daggers for me.

"I'm Detective Craig Howard, ma'am."

Then it becomes clear. This is Taylor's friend, sent to help. I wasn't expecting a three hour turn around on this.

"Do you have a moment to talk?" Detective Howard politely asks.

"Of course. Please come in. I'm Nicki and this is my husband, Aiden."

"Pleasure." He respectfully nods to both of us.

"I'm confused." Aiden is way behind on this one.

"A call was put in because there's been some suspicious activity." Detective Howard conceals Taylor's name in the explanation.

"Here in the dining room." I lead Detective Howard to the table and we sit.

"Aiden, can you just finish getting the girls in their coats and ready to go?" My orders aren't harsh but Aiden does not seem to like them and with a huff and a puff he also seems to be annoyed by Detective Howard's presence in the house. It's not the detective he's upset at; it's me and the unknown. He exits the room as I speak. "It's nothing big," I begin.

"A man followed you?" The Detective asks.

"I'm not sure," I reply. The question is a difficult one to surmise.

"I'd like you to come to the station. We can make a sketch. You *should* come to the station," Detective Howard urges me to emphasize the importance of the situation.

"There are two men, but only one I've seen up close. He was tall, had silver hair, a gritty face, like ex-military, and about forty-five to fifty years old."

"Okay, that's a start. Anything else I should know?"

"They drive a dark sedan. Not a Cadillac but something like it."

"Okay." He continues to take scrupulous notes.

"I haven't told Aiden yet," I confess.

"He's your husband?"

"Yes." My answer conceals much of my displeasure. It's not an enthusiastic *yes.* It's just a confirmation of fact.

"I'll be in touch. Here's my card and please, come to the station," he reiterates. "After my business trip, I'll come by," I promise.

"Okay. Now, I gotta get home to my little ones also. Enjoy your Halloween, Mrs. Connolly."

"Thank you, detective."

He leaves and I let out a breath of air, relieved. I'm glad I got to speak to him and I'm also happy things weren't worse with Aiden present to hear snippets of what's going on.

Soon after, Jessica arrives, and then Eddie and Bernice. Aiden and Eddie have been close ever since high school, when they played football together. And despite

Eddie's dark, black skin, they are as close as brothers could be. Bernice, on the other hand, is a *pill*. She is Korean and can be, how can I say this kindly?—high-maintenance, at times. They live in Westlake Village, one town over from us.

Jessica, Bernice, and I start off together as Eddie and Aiden peel off for their *man moment.* The kids hit the houses as we walk in two distinct social clumps—girls and boys.

"So, how are you, Bernice? I haven't seen you in a while," I try to make conversation, but in reality, it is very uncomfortable. Bernice is a brutal conversationalist.

"I heard you opened up your own Korean Restaurant!" Jessica adds to the conversation. I had no idea Bernice owned her own business. Good for her.

"Great. And we have been very busy. I'm working a lot, but it's good. Eddie helps at the restaurant, now that there aren't any more jobs going on." Bernice's comment could be a stab at me or a thankful assist. I'm not certain. It's because of me that Eddie isn't working as much. He is Aiden's right-hand-man on his crew. I take it in stride and assume the glass is half-full. Bernice is a difficult read, but I'll roll with it.

"At least they have the city job right now," I point out the positive.

Bernice stares at me confused and shakes her head. "Eddie said that job was delayed," Bernice states with a hint of bitterness.

Jessica's eyes blaze open; she too seems to be sensing something is very wrong. Things just don't add up.

"I thought they were just behind," I try to clarify with no real knowledge of what is going on.

"Behind? I don't think they are on the job at all, right now. Eddie sits at home every day or has been with me in the restaurant for the last month."

I turn to Jessica who shrugs in stunned silence of these new facts being presented. Bernice's admission sets me back even further with Aiden. I'm fuming inside and frustrated. Maybe that's why Aiden is so bonkers over money right now. But what is going on? He speaks with Angela more than me. He's lying about his job. I have no idea which way is up and which way is down with us. There is one thing I do know—Aiden and I are destined for a very hard conversation; our World War III. But, it's going to have to wait until I come back from Lincoln, Nebraska. I'm due to leave early in the morning and a late night war is not on the menu for me. I refuse to do that to him, the girls, or myself.

We continue trick-or-treating, conversations remaining light. All of us women have been silenced for the most part. I silently stew as the kids have a great time, and that is all that matters.

Twenty

I wake up early in the morning to see my babies off to school. I won't see them for two days and that kills me. It's a hard goodbye. I also avoid any landmines with Aiden. We exchange a friendly kiss on the cheek. He wishes me luck and I tell him *I'll call*. And that is that.

I head to the office, where Taylor and I are meeting. I figure we'll be taking my car to the airport. This was a single ticket not too long ago and I was planning on taking a taxi to LAX. I arrive in the garage and see a limo parked by the underground entrance. I curiously look at it as I park. Then, Taylor's head pops out.

"A limo? That's not in the budget," I joke.

"I made room for it. The cost is ten bucks more than leaving your car for two days at the airport, the gas, and whatever other numbers I made up to make it virtually the same." He smiles. And suddenly, my mind has shifted. I am excited about our deposition. I'm excited about being alone with him and talking some more. After a short, drama-induced, Aiden break, my butterflies have returned.

I get into the limousine after the driver loads my two bags into the trunk and we are on our way to the airport in style. "I feel like this is prom," I joke. The last and only time I ever sat in the back of a limo was for that event. Ironically, it wasn't with Aiden. We had broken up just before prom, our soft landing prior to the college separation. I always thought he was bitter that I was going away to school even though Santa Barbara wasn't that far away. Made no difference, though; it was the end of our relationship, for a period of time, and I went with Jake Tarnoff. Jake was a silly kid and a forced last-minute replacement to my long-term boyfriend of the day. But, he was a gentleman and allowed me to have a great time with my bestie, Jess.

"So, did Craig get in touch?" Taylor asks me.

Craig? I think to myself. "Oh, Detective Howard!" I blurt out.

"Yes.""He came to my home! That's a pretty fast turnaround," I state, impressed.

"Yeah. He is like that; great guy, good family man." Taylor compliments his friend with envy. I enjoy the moment of humility. Normally, I have no idea Taylor has money. It's an interesting contrast to the *playboy,* spoiled kid he made himself out to be, when he visited memory lane with me at the Getty Villa.

"I am supposed to come down to the police station when I get back," I alert Taylor to the update on the situation.

"Definitely. Let him know what's going on. He will take care of everything."

There's a moment of silence as we both gather our thoughts. It's not an awkward silence, but I just don't know what direction to head in on this business trip. Taylor has become a lightning rod of energy in my life and I always find it necessary to pace myself and not be too needy when speaking with him. I'm not a clingy, needy person at all. In fact, all the men I've seemed to attract have been of that variety. They've all needed those pats on the back to let them know they were good. I don't do pats on the back. I do self-confidence. I do self-reliance. I don't want needy people. I hope my girls turn out strong and independent. I have always wanted that for them. I feel like I've made choices in life and I want them to have choices.

"Have you ever been to Nebraska?" Taylor asks out of the clear blue, breaking my train of thought.

"No. Never been to the heartland. You?"

"Yes and no. I had a buddy of mine, Christian Blackstone. Chris was a funny guy. After high school, we drove his cherry-red, convertible corvette across the country. We passed through many places, a lot of which I couldn't tell one from the other. The heartland is special. It's like another world."

"I'm sure you and Chris met a few women along the way," I gest.

"Perhaps. And a few bars. A lot of drinks. And, we had an amazing view of the world. It was a good trip."

"Is there a place in this world you haven't seen?" I tease.

"The world is small and big all in one. You can see it all, but never really see any of it," Taylor smiles with a profound bit a wisdom.

"That is very true," I agree.

"Why this man? Why Lincoln, Nebraska?" he asks.

"This scientist has supported Albert Penn and their law firm for decades. He is their *go-to* scientist. But, not this time. He didn't sign on for some reason and I want to know why."

"Maybe he just couldn't commit for this journey? Or maybe he retired from legal cases; the strain too much for an old man?" Taylor queries a couple of questions, all of which are legitimate. And although there is no guarantee we will be able to hire the good scientist, I, at least, want to look him in the eye when we get there. I want him to tell us there is nothing to our case.

"He will give us answers, one way or another," I state.

"You haven't called him?"

"He is teaching. He is there. That much, I know," I confirm Taylor's obvious suspicions that I'm flying by the seat of my pants on this one.

"You haven't spoken to him or asked him these questions! Ha. That's classic. The balls on you; I love it!" he states with invigoration. I am spending the firm's money, on a trip, to see a man I have no confirmation will help our case. I need a stranger to give me answers, something that, I'm sure, will be very difficult.

"I haven't. But *we* will. We will get some answers from this scientist." I am determined in my resolve. I will not be deterred. This is just another piece of the puzzle I am hoping will bring this case to a close.

"Does Charles or Bob know?" he asks with a grin.

"They know what they need to," I let him in on my rouse.

He claps, laughing, and enjoying every bit of it. "You're fantastic." he cheers.

"It's game time. There is no *playing it by the book.* I am all in and hell-bent on getting this case wrapped up. If one-hundred million didn't move the needle with Ramsey, I need to get two-hundred million. Money may not buy back the damage done to them, but a lot of money could help them to turn the page on their lives and move on. Court is never a guarantee and circumstantial evidence without corroboration can sink even the best of cases. Right now, it is a battle of experts. Right now, we have a pretty good case. We are in the driver's seat. But, going up against big money, when you are a little guy, can be exhausting. I have three experts to testify. They have twenty. I have one smoking gun that disappeared, but is supposed to call me, and a secret office memo. But, my greatest evidence is the people of Ramsey and their many issues. It is clear the factory is to blame. Now, it's just showing fault. It's all so simple yet complex. *It's exhausting.* This scientist could go a long way toward me being able to squeeze Albert Penn and his cronies into a small, dark corner. I don't want them making an offer inside their office in a glass box. I want them in our conference room with Charles and Bob standing behind me, big grins intact, making an offer from their knees. It's dramatic and extreme, but they have done damage and they are playing dirty," I finish my rant.

"I think there's more to you than people realize, Nicki. There's *a lot* more to you." Taylor smiles and nods, enjoying some of my layers of depth, for once. It's not often I get recognition for much. It's nice. I don't ask for it. I'm not one of *those.* But, it is nice to share my calculated plays with someone. To show someone *that* side of me. To be appreciated for being smart. Taylor sees that and he acknowledges it.

"I think this is going to be an interesting trip," I state with a smile.

"Nicki Connolly, I tend to agree with you." He smiles back.

We arrive at the airport and I am about to get the tickets when Taylor stops me. "I have them. I had them changed into my name."

I relent and he gets our tickets. We make our way through the airport. There is the normal hustle and bustle at LAX.

We take turns sending one another glances; quick smiles. We enjoy walking to tightrope of freedom together. It may be a short trip, but we are giddy for the mini-vacation. We walk side-by-side, like a couple, and it truly feels that way. It feels comfortable. Our energy together is so positive; I can see people smiling at us as we pass by. I may be making more out of it than I need to, but it feels nice. Far too often, I am surrounded by stress and doubt. Right now, I'm floating on a cloud, mini-oasis amidst the stress of the daily grind. I'll definitely take the good company and the mini-trip.

We sit and wait patiently at our terminal. I am alone at the moment. Taylor has gone off to get us some coffee. As I sit in the terminal, I find it funny where I am in my life. Just two weeks ago I was reading a romance novel, desperate to find an ounce of that emotional energy . . . an ounce of some passion. Good old Veronica Palsey. She once was my oasis. A book series about a businesswoman who traveled the country. And, in the midst of her travels, had an affair. And then, she had another. Her random meetings infused her with enough energy to survive her daily grind, find her own inner freedom. It wasn't a romantic fairy tale. It was a passionate outlet of volcanic magnitude. She didn't care about being called a slut or a whore. She had decided to live life on her own terms. She played by the books all her life, and now she went off the deep end. I think that is way too extreme. But, at the same time, living the duel life, as she does in her stories, it is empowering to think how you can make choices. It is empowering to know you control your own destiny. You can be the whore or you can be the good wife. You can live in a cage or you can break free. You have the choice. But sometimes, the choices aren't easy. And being good and being bad become very blurry. Veronica Palsey became bad. I enjoyed reading the bad. I liked being a part of her naughty excursions. But, as I sit in the airport with Taylor, headed to the center of nowhere, I wonder what choices I will make next.

"Here you are," Taylor brings me my Starbucks. *Ah, I love my Starbucks.* I take a sip and relax.

"Where do you see yourself in five years?" I ask.

"That's a good one." He laughs, drinking his coffee. "I'd have to say, I'd like to be happy. I know that sounds corny. But I think in five years, I would want more for myself; to grow. I'm not sure what that could mean. Maybe a family? Maybe marriage? I don't know where life is going to take me. But, at some point, I may want to celebrate a Thanksgiving or a Christmas in a conventional manner. As much as I like Chinese food and random countries, during the holiday season, I think I'm beginning to feel my age. Once you break into the mid-thirties, I guess it's time to grow up a little. I've been working my way toward that for a few years now."

I nod, enjoying his answer. Who doesn't want to hear from an incredibly hot guy that his days of roaming the world for various conquests are getting old? I like Taylor. It's wrong to say. It's wrong to think. I have a husband. I have kids. It's a broken record of repetitive facts rolling around in my head. But, realities be what they are, I like hearing he is a man with greater goals than spending money and living as a playboy all his life. With his looks, the cars, and the homes, he could live however he wanted in this world. Not many people can choose their life's path. I feel as though Taylor could, whether that is fair or not. He has opportunities others just don't.

"You?" Taylor coyly asks back.

"Me?" I guess I walked into this one. It is a difficult question to digest and answer. For me, I honestly have trouble figuring it out. There is a politically correct answer: I hope Aiden and I, somehow, find love again and rekindle our romance. But, in many ways, I feel like I settled. It is terrible to say. But in life, you feel like you're supposed to *do* something or *be* something. I came from an old way of thinking: marriage and kids. It wasn't all about a woman having a career and certainly not as an attorney. Very few women from where I grew up have big careers. They are waitresses, secretaries, assistants; women of value, who have more to offer but lack the opportunity to fulfill their greater selves. So many people are placed in that box . . . that isolated box, where they fail to ever climb out of. It is imposing. I got caught in that box despite getting a law degree. I thought it was what I was supposed to do. Be a mom. Be a great mom. And I am. I love my girls. I just couldn't sit by and not show the world what I have to offer. I have dreams too. I should be able to be a mom and reach for the stars. I am doing both, and I refuse to apologize to Aiden for wanting that. Every day his resentment grows, my disappointment with him grows. Has it all gone too far? The answer to my own question posed will speak volumes to that. "I would say I want to see my girls grow up, share in their lives, and just maybe open a law firm of my own. Maybe I'll have a good partner." I smile and open the door to the future. Do I see Aiden in that future? It is an ever-changing stance that, right now, is in the down-cycle.

"Good goals." Taylor smiles.

The voice of the flight personnel comes over the speaker, announcing the boarding of first-class passengers on our flight. I don't move a muscle, but Taylor gets up.

"We have time," I tell him.

"They called us," he states. I look at him with a smile laced in confusion.

"Yeah. I upgraded us," Taylor fesses.

"First-class. You upgraded our coach tickets to first-class?" I ask.

"Yup. If there's one place I like to be spoiled, it's in a plane. I get a little claustrophobic in the back.

"Okay. I can deal with that." I try to not celebrate the move to first-class because I don't want to appear as if I like being spoiled. But I have never been in first-class and, inside, I'm doing cartwheels at the prospect of being one of those special few that get better treatment. I know it's silly. But, I'm excited nonetheless.

We get into the plane and sit in the premiere section. First-class is not Disneyland, but wow, the big leather seats and the space feels the equivalent of sitting in a large sofa chair at home. As the rest of the passengers file in and pass me, I see their faces glancing over at us. Are they thinking what I usually think? *Who are those people? Are they actors, producers in Hollywood? Are they wealthy businessmen?* I always have been a little jealous of those people fortunate enough to blow $1500 for a single air ticket. I don't have that kind of money and have never been so fortunate—until now that is. And now, I'm the one people think is special. It's pretty damn cool. In reality, it's just a seat on a plane. But it's a really *awesome* seat. I even have my own private LCD TV screen. I'm like a kid in a candy shop. I'm excited about how this trip is starting. A limo and now first-class; if I didn't know better, I'd say Taylor is trying to impress me. He makes me feel special and that feeling is what I can't get enough of. It's pretty amazing.

We sit side by side, watching movies, eating, drinking champagne, smiling at each other, all the while, holding hands like a couple. No work. Almost no talking. Just enjoying the silence together, like two comfortable shoes.

We land safely at the Lincoln Municipal Airport quite a difference from LAX. There isn't the same noise, the same hustle and bustle. There is a calm as we step off the plane. There aren't as many people as the scale of the airport is smaller. Despite being smaller, the inside is spacious and clean. And, surprisingly, there is incredible artwork, including an amazing mural. A photo montage of the history of Lincoln hangs on the wall. Naturally, there is a red tractor display and an amazing classic-red plane, hanging in the lobby. Truly awesome stuff for an airport. Definitely not what I expected. Everywhere I look, I see either sparkling clean stuff or something cool to see. Much better than looking at the droves of people packed together in LAX, like sardines. How refreshing.

We head out and hail a cab to the Carriage Inn, right in the heart of downtown Lincoln. The fall foliage is gorgeous. Rows and rows of yellow, red, and orange leaved trees provide great scenery as I stare out the window of the taxi. So rarely have I seen seasons up close. I've traveled a little, especially for this case. But I've lived mainly in the desert and Thousand Oaks. The trees do change color a little but not in a vibrant way. This truly is Fall, and it's breathtaking. I'm glad to be here.

We arrive at the Carriage Inn and head inside. The hotel is very nice. It's probably not the kind of five star hotels Taylor is used to, but I like it. It's clean, matching the environment all around the town. Everything is so nice.

We head up to the tenth floor. We have two rooms that are adjoined. *This is going to be interesting.* We stand outside of them and stop, looking at one another. Where do we go from here?

Twenty One

A small grin breaks through his lips, and I return a smile of my own. It's a smile that speaks a thousand words. *Yes,* I say with my eyes. Another silent moment only Taylor and I share together.

"Dr. Schecter is teaching in an hour. I'm going to call the cab company. Meet you downstairs in thirty?" I keep things innocent. *Work,* I remind myself. I'm not a teenager in heat. I'm an attorney and, right now, I have a job to do. I have thirty-six hours to convince Dr. Schecter to join my team.

"Okay. Sounds good," he agrees without hesitation. I would have liked an *aw-shucks* look or some disappointment from him. I would love for him to pick me up, off my feet, kick my door in, and have his way with me all over my hotel room. I think and speak business, but the devilish girl inside me wants him to want me. I take my time as my fickle brain battles ration versus urge. I pretend to struggle with the door lock. Taylor opens his door and gives me one last pause. "I'll see you down there," he says.

My door clicks open, giving up my silly helpless girl routine. "See you soon," I say with a smirk. He enters his room and I follow into mine. I close the door behind me and lean against it, letting out a deep breath. The emotional war breaks out inside me. I argue with myself, my mind torn. *You swore before God. You are a mother. You are married.* My righteous self, hurls grenade after grenade.

But, you have sacrificed. You are being overtaken by misery. Aiden hates who you are. You deserve passion. You deserve happiness. You don't have to be a marital martyr. The rebels strike back with equal force.

I take another breath and decide it's a perfect time to check on my little ones. I toss my things on the king size bed in my nice room and take a seat just as Aiden answers.

"How was your flight?" he asks. And that's it from Aiden, the bare minimum. That's how I feel. All we're doing is the bare minimum. I speak to my two angels, my two lights. They are so adorable, firing off a million questions.

Lacy is insistent I should be surrounded by corn. And Ariel is asking about Superman. I smile and, as usual, they remind me of what is most special about my life— *them.* They are my greatest creations. I wrap up my conversation with my two beauties and Lacy asks me if I want to talk to her dad.

"No," I reply. "Just tell him 'good-bye.'" It's a cold end to a beautiful conversation, one that has the rebels, inside me, cheering victory.

"I love you, Lacy-girl,"

"Love you too, Mommy."

We hang up and I smile. *My babies.*

I change my clothes, fix myself up, and head downstairs to the lobby. Taylor is there waiting with that damn smile. A hotel bar is nearby and I can't help but long for a few drinks right now. First things first.

"Let's do it," he says and we head outside to the waiting taxi. We ride over to the college in Lincoln. It's a short drive and I'm anxious to meet the good doctor.

On the Lincoln campus, we find the same beautiful, lush fall foliage I enjoyed on the way to the hotel. It's certainly magical here. I wish I would have visited the heartland sooner. We stroll along, finding the science building. I check the class list I printed off my home computer and we head to Dr. Schecter's class. The, mostly full, class is close to beginning. Taylor and I stick out like sore thumbs with our professional attire in a sea of casually dressed students. We take seats in the back of the class which looks more like a small theater. The half-circle theater seating wraps around the front small stage. A single podium resides in front of a pulled down projector screen.

Dr. Schecter strolls up to the front of the class and begins his lecture, immediately. The scientist has a distinct German accent. Not too thick that you can't understand, but it's there. He kicks into his lesson and uses slides shown on the projector to further his point, storming away at the material. I can see why he would be an effective witness in court. He sounds smart. With his glasses and a salt n' pepper beard, he looks distinguished. But the material isn't for me, and I sneak my cell phone out in the dark. It's a long fifty minutes before the class is wrapped up.

Taylor and I wait as a few students rush the professor to ask questions while everyone else exists. The lights remain dark by us as we walk down to the front, and the last of the students leave.

"You are not in this class nor did I give you permission to sit in on my lecture," the professor states.

"No, doctor, we're not," I respectfully reply.

"I do not believe we have an appointment." Dr. Schecter collects his things, apparently not wanting to speak with strangers.

"No, sir. But I do have one question for you," I manage, as Dr. Schecter makes his way toward an exit by the stage he just thundered away on for an hour. He doesn't respond, so I take my shot. "Ramsey, California. Beltan Food Corp. They hurt people and you know it," I keep it simple and direct. He pauses. I sense an opportunity and go for it. "People are hurting. They're sick and I know you have an idea why. I know that's why you won't testify for Albert Penn. I just want to talk," I urge the good doctor to lend me his ears for a moment or two.

"If you just wanted to talk, you would have called. But, you flew all the way here. You didn't come *just to talk.* You want more." He is right. I do. I want him to sign on with us and testify. I want him to do the right thing.

"Why don't we just meet? Give us twenty minutes. We'll buy you dinner." I try to work an angle.

"I have given you two more than I want to. Good day." He walks away. I let out a frustrated breath in defeat. Then Taylor lunges forward and gently grabs his arm.

"There are kids involved. Just ten minutes. No strings. Tonight or tomorrow. Then we're gone for good." Taylor's appeal catches Schecter's attention and we wait for his delayed response.

"There are always kids," the jaded man states.

"But you know the truth. Ten minutes. Text me. We're at the Carriage Inn downtown." Taylor extends his card.

"Three o'clock tomorrow, at the bar. Maybe I'll be there. Maybe I won't. Save your card." He then turns and walks away, giving us a small ounce of hope. Taylor and I share a look of subtle optimism.

"It's something," I say.

"Yup. We'll take it!" Taylor celebrates our muted victory.

We head out and catch a cab downtown to the steakhouse a block away from our hotel. It's dinner time and I'm starving from a long day of travel. Sitting in Monty's Steakhouse, in the heart of downtown Lincoln, Taylor and I have a nice booth in the corner of the restaurant. We are sitting by candlelight as is everyone else. We are each sipping from glasses of Chardonnay with a half-full bottle on the table.

"What are we?" I ask as I nibble on a freshly-baked warm buttered roll.

"What do you want us to be?" Taylor plays this game all too well.

"You're good." I smile.

"I'm not good at defining. Definitions equate to commitment. I've always been terrible at that. So, I guess I'm like a ship in the night. And I wonder if you're going to pass by. I wonder if our lights will catch one another. Maybe they will and then we'll sail on. Maybe we'll guide one another to the shore. I don't know." Taylor's short speech is layered and so interesting.

"Okay. I'll take that."

"You think the Professor will come?" he asks.

"Ah, the good doctor. I'm hopeful, but I don't know."

The waiter drops off two salads and we start eating. "Where do you go?" Taylor's cryptic question has me piqued.

"What do you mean?"

"When you're lost. In your mind, where are you traveling? What do you think about? I see you fade away at times. A lot to think about these days?" Taylor's question is poignant. It is a quandary for me. It would require *real* answers. It requires me to tell him that I am struggling with *this*—whatever *this* is. He is right. We are two ships in the dark waters of the night. We are angling somewhere for something. But, just because we pass by one another doesn't mean we are bound to share our darkness. It has to be right—it has to be certain. *I must* be certain where I sail and why. And right now, I'm scared and clueless.

"You ever see Indiana Jones . . . the one with Sean Connery?" I ask him.

"*The Last Crusade*. Of course. Great movie," he answers with a hint of excitement in his voice.

"You know when Indy navigates through the challenges to reach the knight and the cup of Christ? He has to avoid all the booby traps. One false step, one bad move, and he's dead?"

"Yes."

"At the end, he has a chance to choose the cup of Christ. He has to look inside and choose the right cup to drink from in order to save his father who's dying," I continue.

"Harrison Ford and Sean Connery—two of my favorites. Han solo and James Bond! What's not to love?"

"I'm not sure if I'm trying to avoid those traps or if I'm choosing the cup right now. I know I'm somewhere, but I'm not certain where. So, I always second-guess myself. Because if you don't know where you are, how do you know where you will go?" my profound explanation hides a lot of real feelings while still sharing a hefty amount. More importantly, it seems to satisfy Taylor's curiosity.

We continue with our *date*, making small talk as our entrées arrive. We look into one another's eyes as we dine, enjoying each other's company wholly and completely. It's so comfortable, oddly. Taylor is a man who draws looks from almost every woman who passes by. He is beautiful and presents an adorable authenticity to himself. He always smiles and allows strangers to momentarily share in a single glance that he acknowledges their existence, that they are real people to him. He never looks down at anyone; always eye-to-eye. Such an endearing quality as we talk favorite colors and favorite movies.

A great steak, a few laughs, a few too many drinks, and we head back to the hotel. We stroll down the streets. The town is quiet on this weeknight. Nebraska Cornhusker sweatshirts and signs are everywhere. This world is all about them.

We arrive at the hotel, holding hands. We don't talk much as we head through the lobby and wait for the elevator. Just grins of anticipation of what *might be*. We are both happily tipsy. We share glows and sparkles in our eyes. We are clearly on the same page as we enter the elevator, the night smoothly progressing like an unencumbered Hemingway passage. We separate hands and I move to the opposite end of the elevator, waiting for the doors to close and head up to the 10th floor. Taylor takes a small step as they close, sensing our moment, until a hand just keeps the doors at bay.

"Oh, sorry!" An older man enters the elevator, struggling to carry a large travel bag followed by his wife. They look as though they're in their seventies. Taylor helps the struggling man inside.

"The wheel is broke," the man complains, as Taylor helps him.

"Well, it wouldn't be so hard if you just bought a new set like I told you!" his wife barks back at him, continuing an argument that clearly has spanned a great deal of time. The wife appears feisty with her comments.

"I'll just rob the nearest bank and you can go on a shopping spree," he sarcastically stabs.

"Then that's a two-for-one. I'll by new luggage and have some peace and quiet when you go to the big house!" the old woman snaps back.

The older couple playfully bickers between Taylor and me. We stare over their conversation and smile, once again displaying our silent secrets. It's sweet to think of a future where two people together have enough passion to wage a playful, verbal battle.

The elevator *dings* and the couple start to make their way out.

"Let me help you with that." Taylor helps the guy with his luggage, momentarily disappearing out of the elevator.

The woman pops her head back inside. "Are you two married?" she asks.

"Oh, no. Us? No."

"Well, you will be some day. I know when two people are in love. And the way you two look at one another, I can tell. I know these things."

"You do?" I amusingly smile at the older woman, playing along.

"Yes. Don't worry. Your time will come. He'll pop the question soon enough when it's right," she finishes sharing her infinite wisdom. Taylor pops back in the elevator and she gives us one last encouraging smile. "You guys are a wonderful couple. You'll do great." The woman pats Taylor on the shoulder and disappears, the doors closing. Taylor looks at me and I shrug with a confused smile, playing dumb. The elevator *dings*. We arrive at the tenth floor, *our floor.*

Twenty Two

The elevator bell is like a ding at a boxing match. We are thrust into each other's arms in uncontrollable passion; surges of energy neither of us can any longer contain. Our mouths taste each other hungrily. Our embrace—timeless—just as it was on the beach.

As the doors open, we remain entrenched in passionate warfare. We are about to be enclosed by the impatient doors when Taylor's arm swings out and his hand stops it from closing. Breaking away from one another, we clasp hands, taking a breath to step out of the small box.

We walk toward our rooms, silly grins on our faces. We are transplanted back in time as if we are giddy kids, enjoying every second of being released from our chains of responsibility.

I take my card out and our hands break apart for just a moment. I swipe with ease and the door opens. I push the door open and wait with a smile.

"After you, Mr. Diamond."

Taylor smiles and steps up to me, the two of us looking at one another as if we are about to explode again. He leans in slowly, containing the passion inside. He runs his hand along my face and his lips caress mine. They slide back and forth so slowly, teasing. I remain controlled, just as he is. Our breaths are both inconsistent, held in the moment, wanting to achieve so much more. My arms slide around his neck and our lips come together in a slow, gentle kiss. We make our way into my room and the door closes behind us.

More kisses, gentle, soft. His hands now drop, searching my sexy blouse for their buttons. One at a time, he unhinges them, my shirt bending open at every inch of freedom. With our bodies separated for a moment, I start to unbuckle and remove his belt, wasting little time. Then, my hands shoot up to his collared shirt. I follow suit, mechanically and slowly undoing one button at a time, starting at the top and working my way down.

We look at each other with passion, but the moments are slow and drawn out. Neither of us is rushing as our hands reach to one another's face. Another kiss and we connect once again, an art we are beginning to perfect. The kiss is as good as I could hope for. We fit like an old glove. It's just right. Our arms move around one another, mine to his neck and his dropping down to the small of my back. We continue to kiss. I want so much more, but I can't decide if I'm ready for it. I want to take him right to my bed, but it's not an easy task. I've crossed a line but I haven't crossed *the* line. Once I make that move, I feel as though I could lose myself completely. I have always been morally sound and I want justification. I want to know that I am right. But, there are no easy answers here and no one will give me the confirmation I want. No one, that is, except Taylor and me.

I'm so easily lost in his eyes, in his kisses . . . in his embrace. I am perfectly happy and amazingly energized with him. I want him more than anything. I just don't know if I can take *that* step.

Suddenly, he pulls back. It's as if the man is reading my mind. We are so good at that; reading each other's thoughts. I do get confused with his cryptic replies and grins at times. He is beautiful and that, in itself, can be distracting. But, we do a great job of unwritten communication. It is something I wanted to have my entire life. To look across a room, at a man, and he knows exactly what I'm thinking.

"We need to stop," I helplessly whisper. I can read his mind too. His eyes are pulling away from me, not

because he wants to, but for me. I can see that. He knows I have an internal struggle.

"There's nothing I want more right now," he starts.

"Me too," I breathlessly agree.

"But, it's a big step. It means a lot. It would mean a lot to me. It's not just casual, not how we are," Taylor shares his feelings, ones that align perfectly with mine. There is a mountain of dilemma surrounding *us*. The step is gigantic and the repercussions potentially enormous. "I have no doubts," he insists. "And there is nowhere I'd rather be," he hammers home his feelings toward me.

"I am so happy with you." Tears well up in my eyes. I should take this man and hurl him onto my bed. I am about to. My mind is telling me to. I reach out, but look down; my hands still at my side. I'm as stiff as a board, my mind and soul constantly contradicting one another.

"I am going to take a *very* cold shower. I'll be right here." Taylor looks at our connecting door. "I'm not going anywhere." He smiles and gathers himself, leaning forward to give me one last perfect kiss on the lips.

"I'm sorry," I apologize for being a coward. I feel like one. He sensed it. This perfect man sensed it and pulled back. It couldn't have been easy. He knows I want him so badly. But, he wants me to smile in the morning. He wants more than just a fruitless night. So, he took an extremely trying high road. I am so happy to be with him right now.

"Don't you dare." He grins. "You have nothing to be sorry about. These have been the best kisses of my life," he thanks me with grace. Taylor heads into his room and gently closes our adjoined door.

I fall to the bed and look up at the ceiling, running my hands over my body. "Holy shit," I say out loud to myself. I lie there for a moment, upset. I'm disappointed in me until I think of Taylor. I think of his reaction, what he had to say. He is stealing my heart one beat at a time. A smile overcomes my face. *This is amazing*, I tell myself. *This is so damn amazing!*

———————

I'm in bed after a very hot shower. I toss and turn for hours, staring at the adjoining door. I can't help it. I want it to open. I want to open it. It's tough. 1AM. Then, 2AM. I can't sleep. I check the clock every thirty minutes and it doesn't help my self-driven insomnia. I shake my head and give up. I walk out to the small balcony attached to my room. There is a patio chair set; two plastic seats and one small table. I sit down, my bathrobe wrapped around my body for warmth. I look out at the view of Lincoln, Nebraska at night. It's amazing.

"It's so beautiful," Taylor speaks up.

I look over and see him, sitting on his balcony.

"Yeah. It's something," I agree. I see in Taylor's hand a half-full glass of red wine and a dark bottle nearby on his table. "Is that wine?" I ask with a wink to my tone.

"Why, yes it is. Not Chardonnay, though. But a very good Cabernet Sauvignon." Taylor takes a sip.

"I'm coming over." I invite myself.

"There's plenty," Taylor happily accepts my self-invite to his balcony.

I make my way to the door separating our two hotel rooms. It is more than just a door separating our two rooms, it's a metaphorical divide. I hesitate for a moment, my hand reaching for the doorknob. I reach and open the door, watching it swing by my eyes. I pause as if some great catastrophic occurrence will happen to prevent my feet from crossing the threshold. But nothing will, and I feel as though my next steps forward are exactly the steps I should be taking. I take the plunge.

I arrive at Taylor's balcony and we sit like two honeymooners, drinking wine, enjoying the night air on a balcony. Again, it's all too perfect . . . too easy. It is as if this moment was somehow written in the stars; fate brought us to this moment. I am not a spiritual person per se. But, I may be becoming one.

"How did you get these glasses?" I ask Taylor. I sip the wine and my face lights up.

"They threw them in with the bottle."

"Holy cow! This wine is great! What did you say about the glasses?"

"I said they came with the bottle. When you buy a bottle of wine worth $1,800, they generally throw the glasses in," Taylor casually states.

I choke on a sip of wine, coughing for a moment. "$1800! Holy crap."

"That's how you get free glasses." Taylor smirks as he furthers his point, amused by my reaction.

"I think I'd have to stick to my $17.99 Chardonnay," I joke. I keep sipping though, the taste is amazing.

"It's made by Screaming Eagle Cabernet. It's a Napa Valley vineyard. You should visit it someday," he suggests. It seems everywhere we travel is beautiful, but I know for a fact that Napa is amazing.

"That would be great," I agree.

We drink and laugh in the moonlight as we continue to share our lives. He knows many of my stories but I share more. My father was a drinker. He sometimes got angry. He never hit anyone, but my mother and my father also never seemed to have that passion in their lives. They failed to be each other's soulmates. They too were high school sweethearts. And when they got married, my mother was seven months pregnant with me. Taylor never truly got along with his father. They were both so different. His mother was in and out of his life. But, he doesn't elaborate any more about her. Our eyes are hanging low, both exhausted; the talking and the wine taking their toll. "Let's go to bed," I offer up. "Can I sleep with you? I want to fall asleep in your arms." My question comes from the heart. I am not drunk, although I am a good ways there. I am tired and want to feel safe. Taylor makes me feel safe. Happiness and passion are the two ultimate bonuses to how I feel when I'm with him.

"Of course," he happily agrees.

I move over to the bed and drop my robe, exposing everything not hidden by my panties. I don't look at him, knowing this is an opportunity to check each other's bodies out for the first time. But rather, I slide right under the covers. He removes his robe, only his boxers remaining. I lift up the covers for him and he slides into the bed beside me. I move close and lie in his arms. He holds me tight, our two bodies mostly naked. I have on only silk panties on, my breasts pressed against his chest. Taylor gently runs his hands through my hair, further relaxing me. I fall asleep, my body relenting to the early morning hour.

———————

I awake and stretch. I hear the water running in the shower. I look at the clock, which reads 10AM. I can't even remember the last time I slept this late. I rise up out of bed with just my silk panties on. I look over at the dividing door between the rooms. I smile again. I am exactly where I want to be. My mind, heart, and soul, all together with one singular focus and I leap forward across the metaphorical threshold. I have sailed through the depths and found my way.

I walk over to the closed bathroom door with the light creeping out below. I open it to a fresh cloud of steam. I confidently close the door and walk over to the glass shower one. It's fogged up but Taylor can see me through the fog. I notice him reaching up to shampoo his hair.

"I'll get that for you," I seductively offer.

Taylor happily slides the glass door open and I pull my panties down. I am naked before him; never more confident, never more determined, and never more certain. I step inside the shower and close the glass behind me. I move in front of Taylor and we stare at one another for a moment. I smile at him, a seductive girlish smile and he grins back. I turn him around and gently pull his head back. I massage the shampoo into his scalp. I look down his muscular toned back. My eyes gaze down to his perfect bottom. He is a great looking man and he is in the palm of my hands, inside a hot steamy shower. I'm nowhere and everywhere, all at once.

I pull the cheap showerhead off the shower wall and rinse his hair. Once I'm done, I turn him toward me. His manhood is erect. I felt it by my leg last night, as I fell asleep. It would be a mistake I will not repeat again. I lean in and kiss him while my right hand plunges down, grasping him, and I begin to stroke the head of his manhood. His breaths quicken and his head dips back. I've seen this before in my numerous dreams. But, now it's really happening.

Our mouths find each other as my hand continues its sweet torture. I pull back reluctantly, and then slowly, I dip down and drop to my knees. I take Taylor's impressive size into my mouth, filling it. The anticipation of feeling him inside of me, quickly builds up.

His hands spread out onto the walls, unable to hold himself up straight, giving into his vulnerability. My tongue surveys the tip, rolling under and around. I try to draw him in deeper and deeper into my mouth, slowly increasing the speed of my tongue. I begin to suck harder, my head going back and forth, grabbing his nicely shaped, tight ass with my hands. His left hand drops to the back of my head, aiding the motion to just the perfect pace for him. "Oh!" a breathy yelp escapes his mouth. His breathing is so rapid, it's nearly out of control and I move faster, bringing my hand forward to join in the effort. I can feel him grow even harder as he slips through my lips, thrusting deep, nearly hitting the back of my throat. "Ah!" he groans, the warm fluid firing into my mouth, filling it up. I drain every single ounce out of him. His breaths are deeper and start to slow as he completes his orgasm. I finish and gently pull off. I swallow and before I can even decide to stand up, Taylor is lifting me to my feet. He takes the soap; his face red from the heat and the intense orgasm. He lathers up his hands then runs them all over my body, probing every inch of me. He turns me and his hands work their magic again. His fingers gently spread my legs. He runs them around my inner thighs to tease me, slowly caressing up towards my spot. He continues to survey the area around my spot, my body yearning for him to go at me and take me, while my mind loves the slow tease. His index finger takes the lead and makes its way towards my clit. It gently moves across it, and then back, and then across it again, and back. He has quickly located my ultimate sensory and my knees quiver as his finger perfectly rolls back and forth over it; again and again. "Oh," I gasp. He gently presses with the perfect pressure and rubs. I almost can't take it anymore and he delivers what my body is yearning for; penetration. His index finger slips into my spot and I let out a gasp. It's a short-lived tease as he continues and soaps up my body. He takes the shower head and sprays the soap off of me, dipping the head down to my spot. The stream hits my clit with just the right pressure, exciting me further. After he has removed the soap, Taylor drops down to his knees. He kisses my inner thighs and now it is my turn for my head to dip back. I close my eyes as he takes my right leg and guides it over his left shoulder. The warm water and steam only making me yearn more. His tongue hits me just right, sending electric currents deep into my core. It's sensational, his tongue working me up and over, making my knees weak further. He slowly circles around the outside, lapping up my taste; a clear signal of a patient man, working up gradually toward a frenetic finish. He circles around my clit as two of his fingers slide deep inside me, working this angle, as well. It causes my knees to nearly buckle. Taylor pulls me closer and lets his fingers slide out so his tongue can take liberty with me. It plunges in, hitting just the right spot, working me quickly into a heart-racing whirl of sexual build.

"Oh my God!" the words slip through my mouth in a high-pitch tone. I'm unable to control the noises as I breathe and shriek in ecstasy. His tongue is relentless. So much is building and I gasp again, "Oh, God!"

He squeezes my ass hard and pulls me closer. With one hand gripping the sliding glass door and the other finding the back of Taylor's head, I clench his hair and pull him harder into me. We create a perfect rhythm, and I scream. I can't help it. "Yes! Yes! Yes!" I yell again and again. Taylor hits my spot continuously. My legs begin to shake uncontrollably. "Yes! Oh my God! *Yes!*" I explode inside, holding my breath as the warmth spreads, sending tingles throughout my entire body. I nearly stop breathing, and just gasp for phenomenally beautiful bits of air. My breaths return and I release the back of Taylor's head. We slowly return to each other, our faces glued to one another. We both crack a smile. Then I lean in and hold Taylor, our bodies wrapped together in the steam and hot water.

After a few moments, I feel him hardening again. I look up and he looks down. We begin to kiss. The passion in our kisses hasn't failed to diminish despite both of us achieving amazing orgasms. I reach and turn the hot water off. We move slowly together, connected, out of the shower and to the bathroom door. Taylor opens it and we seem to have the same thought—*head over to the bed.* We passionately explore each other's mouths without relenting. Our hands survey each other's bodies. We are a sexual epicenter for passion and can't stop.

We make it to the bed and Taylor sets me down softly, our lips separating for a rare moment. I open up the rest of the sheets, making room for us. He climbs between my legs, lying on top of me.

"It's cold in here," I smile, feeling the chilly air of our room as opposed to the hot steamy shower.

"Yes. Damn." He shivers slightly. He pulls the sheets around his backside, giving us both some extra warmth. We continue to kiss, but I don't want to wait anymore. I can't wait. I slowly tilt my hips up, grinding into him, letting him know I'm ready for him. He moves with me, his excitement sliding up and down my slick folds. Not wasting another minute, I reach down and take him in my hand, guiding him to my entrance.

"Oh, yes," leaks out of my mouth as I feel myself stretch to accommodate his size. He fills me completely, and then slowly pulls back before thrusting forward again. He reaches up with his hands, grabbing mine and pushing them back above our heads, interlocking them as he finds his groove. I am his now. He is taking control and I am vulnerable. He pushes deep inside of me with each thrust, the feeling perfectly building upon my last orgasm. The momentum of a new build begins from deep within me; another volcano, begging to erupt. As his thrusts get harder and deeper, I can't leave my hands out of it anymore. I pull away and reach around to his back. My fingers dig into his skin and he picks up speed, somehow penetrating me even deeper. I feel him hitting my cervix, a combination of a little pain and a lot of pleasure. I love it. I like it hard and he is going for it. I feel myself build up and quickly flip Taylor over, so that I'm on top, once again seizing the upper hand. I pause for just a moment and then begin. I slowly grind, my hips shifting back and forth. Taylor is perfectly plunged deep inside of me and his hands run up my body to my breasts. One of his hands stops there, playing with my breast, gently teasing my nipple with his fingertip. *Oh, fuck that feels good.* And his other hand makes its way up my neck, gently pressing my head back. He slips a finger into my mouth and I suck on it diligently as I ride.

I start to gasp again, losing control of my voice. My pitch gets higher as I go faster. I feel Taylor's hands reach to my ass and squeeze tight, his body rhythmically moving in perfect concert with mine. The bed is rocking as I ride the shit out of his body, every second, every moment, feeling perfectly orgasmic. And I can feel my rise getting more intense. "I'm getting close!" I yelp uncontrollably, my body is a giant hub of sexual energy. Taylor slides his hand around front; his thumb applies pressure to my clit. I start to yell again, unable to control it. I don't give a shit who hears me. Taylor is filling my entire sex up and I am about to explode. "Oh, my God!" I cry in ecstasy.

"Yes!" Taylor lets out. "Oh, yes!" He squeezes my ass harder and applies more pressure. I have never ridden anyone so hard and felt so good. And then it happens, my climax hits; full steam ahead. *Oh, my God. Again?! I can't believe it!* It surges through me and deep inside my core, making my body move more frantically.

"Oh my God! Oh, yes! *Fuck yes!*" I yell. Taylor's grunting matches my sentiments. His body thrusts up, pushing as far into me as he can go. I again hold my breath, slowing down, both of our bodies enjoying massive, mutual orgasms. I roll backwards and forwards slowly, my orgasm cresting and going as if I am being sexually purged from within. Taylor's body is a giant rock, driving up inside me and then we simultaneously relent.

Both breathless, we are glazed over in sweat and smiles. We try to catch our breaths, both our bodies completely satisfied beyond anything I could have ever hoped feeling.

"I think we need another shower," Taylor jokes with sincerity.

"Why don't we have another together? I'll wash you, if you wash me," I offer.

Taylor smiles and I smile back. We once again agree silently; both on the same page.

Twenty Three

After a second shower, in which we slowly washed one another and exchanged numerous passionate kisses, we get dressed and head out for lunch. It's past noon, and Taylor and I have worked up quite an appetite. We find a small diner nearby and sit, enjoying more of Nebraska's personality. The waitress has pigtails and looks no older than twenty. Her energy is great and her smile could light up a room anywhere. She reminds me of a beautiful farmer's daughter.

"Howdy, y'all! Can I start y'all off with some coffee?" she asks with a full wave of hospitable energy.

"Please. Two." Taylor says as we review the menu. The waitress scurries off and I gaze up at Taylor's beautiful face. He can't help but break a smile back at me.

"You didn't go running home this morning," I joke.

"I figured I'd stick it out," he gives it back.

"Oh, yeah?" I reply in a playfully challenging way.

"And you have the plane tickets, so I sorta have to stick it out," he stabs back, and I shake my head.

The waitress hurries back with the coffees. "So, need a sec?" she asks.

"We both want breakfast. What would you recommend?" Taylor asks. I love his way. He is respectful and smooth all in one. His debonair personality is infectious too.

"Oh, I'd say that flap jacks are amazing. Get a good plate of 'em with some eggs and bacon," the bubbly waitress leans forward with excitement, lowering her voice as if she were telling us a secret she only wants us to know.

Taylor looks to me and I nod, still with a grin on my face. The one downside to Taylor is going to be the wrinkle lines I'm going to get from smiling so damn much. But, I can't help myself.

"We'll take two," he informs her. I gather our menus and hand them to her.

"Thank you," I tell the kind girl.

"Yes, ma'am. Thank y'all." The young waitress rushes off.

We sip our coffee as I look around. The town is quaint and just as beautiful today as yesterday. The difference is I'm completely bonded with Lincoln. I am so relaxed, so fulfilled. Is this what happiness is? Is this the start of love? I don't know, but I love how I feel. When you've been drowning for so long, you start to forget how to swim.

"You've obviously traveled a lot," I spark up a new conversation.

"I have, yes."

"Where was your favorite place? Where did you go when you said to yourself 'There's no other place like this?'"

"I once went on a science expedition to Antarctica. It was on a vessel that my father owned. I saw things others would only dream of; Georgian Bay Islands—amazing. The islands are just off the coast of Antarctica. The colors were glorious. A distant wall of ice rises up above the mountains as if it were a tsunami coming toward us; penguins, birds, peace, and beauty are everywhere. There were so many massive glaciers, like perfectly sculpted giants. Pieces of ice would fall off into the frigid waters and you just look and think, *wow, this is life. This is REAL life.* It's invigorating. I saw similar things in Alaska too. You just can't say enough great things about untapped nature. It's something else." Taylor describes the trips as if he could smell the clear, uncongested air. I can almost touch his memory and I'm momentarily mesmerized.

"I think I'd like that."

"I'd like to take you some day," he confesses. And he's done it. I wasn't certain about tomorrow; I was just living today. And today was *freakin'* great. But, he made the leap to the future and I'm excited there could be more days with Taylor Diamond.

"We had quite a morning," I bring the subject back to us.

"Yeah, we did," Taylor agrees. "A double-header," he adds. "I do want to say that usually a few more minutes are required in between," he attempts to explain his uncanny ability to *recharge* his penial battery so quickly this morning.

"Oh, yeah?" I smile at him wanting this perfect man to squirm just a bit more.

His cheeks flush a bit, "Yes . . . well. I don't much . . . umm . . . how can I say this?"

"Brag?" I finish his thought, continuing to enjoy the Taylor show.

"Yes. I don't. It's more about who you're with more than some God-given attributes."

"I'd say your attributes are *very* God-given," I quip.

"Let's just say you bring out the best in me."

I burst into laughter, enjoying seeing a more innocent version of the dynamic confident man. We are sharing everything now. I don't think much can stop us.

"And, here's those flapjacks!" The waitress sets down two massive plates of gorgeous, unhealthy food.

We walk the downtown area, getting in some exercise after our carb-charged meal. The pancakes were as advertised—amazing. But, I feel like a million pounds trying to digest them.

"What made you become a lawyer?" I ask.

"Ah. The *origin*. Always a good get-to-know-you query," Taylor states, momentarily stalling.

"Yes it is."

"Well, I wish it was exciting. I wish I could tell you it was my dream, my calling. But, it wasn't. I love it, but it was my father that made me go to law school. In fact, he pulled every string to ensure I was there and I'd graduate. He made sure of that." Taylor's voice trails into a dramatic memory.

"Why? Why did he push you?"

"Maybe he did it to save me from myself . . . to save me from the money. Maybe he did it to get rid of me. He sent me to boarding school when I was ten. Maybe college and law school were an extension of what he wanted. My father was a complicated man. He was someone I never could figure out." Taylor finishes his speech and turns to me. He raises his eyebrows and smiles, like he's waiting for my turn to begin.

"Okay. I'll give. I wasn't exactly a *pretty girl* growing up. And I had a big mouth—biggest in my family. So, I studied a lot, and I argued a lot. I became a pretty darn good debater. And I love the law. I liked the idea of fighting for people who couldn't fight for themselves."

"Like your cousin," Taylor chimes in.

"Like my cousin. Like my parents. Like everyone I grew up with. Nobody could fight for themselves. They didn't know what to do or how to do it. I wanted to be able to show people a way . . . to show them where to go. Just like you have over the last few years," I share some of my Google information search with Taylor.

"You did your research." He smirks.

"Not really. Just a basic Internet search," I confess.

"Yes. Far too much out there. No secrets," Taylor digresses.

"We have one," I quickly chime in.

Taylor smiles and nods. "We sure do." He pulls me close and I rest my head on his shoulder. His arm naturally wraps around me and we stay close, continuing our afternoon stroll.

We sit in the bar at the Carriage Inn. No crazy bottles of wine. This time I order Taylor and me two Bud Lights. Why not? I'm not much of a beer drinker but at 2:45PM, it hardly seems right to drink Chardonnay or wine. So, a little light beer it is.

"What do you think?" I ask. We are sitting at a high-top table just off the bar, a perfect spot to see the two entranceways. We don't see anything but a couple of afternoon regulars and a few traveling salesmen, drinking their mid-afternoons away.

"I don't know. It could go either way." Taylor looks around, sipping his beer. We both are hoping the good doctor makes an appearance. We traveled all this way. I feel like I've gotten so much out of this trip just by spending time with Taylor. But this is for Ramsey. It's for the little people. It's for Rebecca and Casey. I know we have a good case, but I want to bring Belton Food Corp to their knees. They deserve to pay dearly for what they have done, for what they, knowingly, did to save a few bucks.

We wait, sipping our beers. I'm nervous and anxious. I feel as though it's going to be a lost cause. "Here he is!" Taylor loudly whispers, as surprised as I am to see the good doctor.

Dr. Schecter arrives in a plaid coat with a matching bowler's hat. He looks both ways as he enters the bar, as if he's trying to make sure he has adequately concealed his identity. Taylor and I look at one another, recognizing the doctor's insistence on privacy. He moves over to our table.

"You have a room?" he asks under his breath, looking over his shoulder, seemingly paranoid.

"Yes. We're staying upstairs," Taylor replies.

"Then upstairs we go," he insists.

We nod and head up to the room. It is a quiet elevator ride with Dr. Schecter, carrying his brown leather-bound satchel and holding his tongue. Neither Taylor nor I want to spook him, so we remain silent. Once in the room, Dr. Schecter removes his hat and coat, shaking his head.

"It is madness, me being here," he proclaims.

"Doctor, tell us what is happening in Ramsey. Tell us what we already know," I beg of him. We have others. We have people who analyzed and came to conclusions. But, the amount of money that Beltan Food Corp could spend on scientists, doing far more extensive digging and analysis would yield more definitive results. We have hypothesis. We have *possibilities*. But, my scientists conducted their research after Beltan already adjusted their processes. Therefore, to definitely find results, I need the smoking guns. The mysterious man may have something. But, he is a ghost right now. Dr. Schecter is here. And, he knows something. I can feel it.

"It is complicated."

"It's always complicated, doctor," Taylor throws back words that the German scientist used as an excuse, the day prior.

"You two, you think you can survive this? These people?" Dr. Schecter lays out the undeniable threat. We are now treading in deeper waters as I am becoming increasingly concerned with but fully aware of the gravity of the situation. As the case gets closer to its culmination, I feel the heat is being turned up at every turn. And the brilliant doctor is asking a good question.

"My cousin, her young daughter—they're sick, Doc. They're hurting as well as others. What the heck happened?" I reach and pull out my tape recorder.

"No. No recordings. I have family too."

I nod and put the recording device away and settle to hear what the doctor has to say off-the-record.

"It was many factors. It was many things. These decisions, they can be dark and confusing." He lets out a big sigh before taking a seat. "I was part of the team that evaluated the area. We measured for health concerns. We made sure things would be all right. But, we did not take in consideration other factors. They changed the processing. The winds shifted dramatically, more than we thought. A bad storm, combined with the increased carcinogens, made everything worse. It made things more complicated." He shakes his head, holding a world of secrets inside him. There is a moment of pause, as if he is uncertain if he wants to go too far.

"Uncomplicate things for us, Doc." Taylor is poignant in his question. He wants answers just as badly as I do.

"They had approval." He reaches into his satchel and pulls out multiple files, tossing them on the bed.

My eyes meet with Taylor. Our entire case could, potentially, be victorious with the documents Schecter just took out. There are pages upon pages of studies. These are the answers to the many questions we have. These are the answers that the scientists today can't find from the actions of yesterday. This *could* be everything, and Taylor and I both know it. Our eyes flash back to the doctor, both intent on getting more information, getting to the bottom of things.

"Start from the beginning, Dr. Schecter, please. Take us through it all," I ask.

He subtly nods, starting to give us the grand tour of Beltan Food Corporation and how they possibly poisoned the residents of Ramsey. Everything is a fact that must be digested and logically lead to a conclusion. It would be all too easy if there was direct contact. But, that's not how this works. Poisons can be leaked into the ground water. Poisons can end up in the air. But nobody directly poisons someone. It can be intentional, but unlike when the trigger of a gun is pulled and someone dies from that bullet, this is far more complicated. The trigger could be an old memo, an initiative to cut costs and use substandard processes. These processes could lead to leaks and additional poisons ending up in the air and the water. Poor testing and poor restrictions could easily end up polluting people. And for what? For money. To save a few cents per item made which equates to hundreds of millions of dollars over a short time. The cost is a small desert town just in its wake. An unwitting group of poor people, that happen to live in the wrong spot when the winds shift for a few months a year. That is the case. That is what we have to prove beyond a reasonable doubt.

The doctor goes on and on. The information is scientific. It's inconclusive to the point where you wonder how anyone could make an educated choice based on such thin reasoning.

We finish with the doctor after three hours of back and forth. He is worn down and tired. "I have told you everything I know, now. I have a clear conscious. I have nothing to hide, but hide I feel I must."

"You won't testify?" I ask.

"I cannot, dear. But I will send you a statement . . . a sworn document and certain facts. And, then, I will be gone."

"I won't be able to use it in court," I state.

"But we can use it out of court," Taylor sites.

"Yes, you can. Quite effectively, at that," the doctor surmises.

Nodding, I tend to agree with the two men. A kind of document like this would increase the offer from Beltan to the point where they would be inclined to settle at all costs. The mere presence and possibility it could be leaked to the public would be devastating *PR*. It could double or triple their current offer. This would give me more juice to close the case with Ramsey.

"Good day to you both. And good luck. I hope safety shines upon your souls." Dr. Schecter nods and places his coat and hat back on.

"Thank you, doctor." Taylor shakes Schecter's hand.

"Thank you, sir." I respectfully shake his hand as well.

"To you both." He tips his hat to us. Grabbing his satchel, he exits our hotel room.

I turn to Taylor with a big grin. "Holy shit—we got them!" I walk forward and jump into his arms, the two of us hugging. It is a big win for us. It is the start of something that could close the case for good.

"Let's celebrate. The night is ours."

"Definitely." I couldn't agree more. I'm charged up with positive energy. Taylor runs his hand across the side of my face, moving my hair off my eye. We both sparkle at each other, our smiles interconnected. We lean in and kiss.

Twenty Four

I call my girls and have a good long conversation about school. I am having the time of my life in Lincoln, but there is a hole in my heart being away from them; it's incredibly difficult. Taylor helps the time pass, that's for sure. But nothing can replace the love for a child. I get my fill, even though they are resistant to stay on the phone too long with me. They want to play before they have to eat dinner and the night comes to a close for them. I know, in my mind, that as they sleep Taylor and I will be enjoying the evening somewhere, doing something. I blow kisses from many miles away and they blow them back. I feel their love and they feel mine. Aiden is out, having the babysitter watch the girls for the evening. I have no idea where he is, although the girls insist he had to go to work. They are sure of it. I don't press them and am satisfied I spoke to the only two people I wanted to. We say our goodbyes and hang up and smile at the picture of them on my phone that flashes up.

The connecting door opens and Taylor appears completely naked holding a bottle of the expensive wine. "I just had a great idea," he says.

"Oh, yeah!" I smile at his completely naked body and can't help but be interested in what he has to say next.

"Why don't we tailgate a bit before we go out," he offers.

"I'm not sure what it is we are going to do, but you can count me in."

"I got the shower running. Ever do body shots with wine?"

"I thought it was two-thousand."

"I bought the best one they had for this. The idea just came to me," Taylor smiles in anticipation for some early evening fun.

"I've never done body shots, but I'm pretty damn excited to start." We might as well write our names on the wall of Taylor's bathroom.

"Tell me what you want me to do to you," I stand naked in the shower before Taylor.

He holds the open bottle of wine and smiles. "Ladies first." He hands the bottle to me.

"But, I don't know what to do," I reply.

"I'll help you," he says with a devious smile. Oh, that damn smile of his.

"Okay," I happily accept his guidance.

He begins to kiss me all over my neck, navigating slowly down my body. "Pour," his whisper in my ear is so seductive. "Pour just a little." It is then I realize what he wants and I slowly pour the wine down my neck, the cabernet sauvignon, trickling down my body. Taylor's tongue attacks the wine running down my wet, naked body and licks it up, leading all the way from my naval up to my breasts, and finally, to my neck. He sucks every last ounce of the wine off of me. And then, he continues to kiss me again, slowly moving down.

The water striking my back, combined with Taylor's probing tongue, is relaxing and exciting all-in-one. Whereas I was a pile of pent up energy this morning, I feel as though Taylor and I have graduated to seasoned *newlywed* status. I find myself enjoying his tongue more, every feeling . . . every sweet, erotic feeling. His tongue laps all over my sweet spot, the coolness from the wine and the heat of the water on my back an extraordinary contradiction.

I pour more wine, this time it runs down to my waiting sweet spot. He starts there this time. I feel the cold wine sneak just inside me and chills run down my spine. Taylor's warm tongue penetrates me, lapping it up.

My breaths explode out, one gasp after another. I haven't had oral sex performed on me in nearly eight years (*not that I've been counting*). I get back in the game and a pro is going down on me, caressing every possible inch of my inside. A little more wine; the contrast of cold and hot is insanely turning me on.

"Ahh!" Sounds explode from deep inside me as I struggle to hold the bottle . . . to remain balanced.

This is the Holy Grail of sex. I am in heaven as Taylor drinks the wine and sucks on my special spot. He sucks and licks the energy building inside once again.

My moans graduate to wails, a high-pitched, amazingly wonderful wail.

Taylor grabs the bottle of wine from me. A little more wine—this time he pours right above the mouth of my spot, Taylor drinking, licking, and sucking, all at once. *Oh, God!* I can't get enough of it so he pours more.

I get a quick glimpse of the bottle getting set down just outside the tub. Taylor needs it no more.

"More! Yes! Right there!" I start to yell as if we are the only people in the world and my screams would fall on deaf ears. Then he slips two fingers in, his tongue moving to work solely on my clit. "Shit!" I am on another level of wonderment.

"Oh, Taylor. Yes! Right there! Fuck, yeah!" I am uncontrollably blurting out words, no longer nervous, no longer chained. I hold nothing back, feeling free. "Ah, yes! Oh, yes!" My knees are buckling. My legs—shaking, as I feel a sweet tightening and a massive tingling sensation building up deep in my core. I yell, grabbing the back of his head with authority, my other hand clenching the bottle tightly. I use Taylor's head and direct him right into me, adjusting his speed to just the right tempo, grinding him slower and deeper into me. I would scream, but I have no breath left; all my sexual energy, bursting in one perfect spot between my legs. The release is the greatest of my life. I grind him inside me over and over again, working the last quake out. I guide him perfectly, and his sweet tongue and amazing fingers do it all.

"Oh, God," my breathless voice finally leaks out, crying in perfect agony. It doesn't stop. He doesn't stop. I can't stop. The warmth fires through and out of me uncontrollably. Every pressure—every concern—is released from inside my body. I can't count time, but my orgasm, as it finally finishes and I can breathe once again, is a world record for me, and I finally gasp, pulling in large amounts of warm, steamy air. My breathing begins to slow and I pull my weak knees in underneath me.

"Oh, shit. That was incredible. I love this fuckin wine," I joke, still catching my breath, my face as flush as I have ever felt. I stand up straight and Taylor rises, a champion.

"Shit." I reach outside the shower and grab the bottle of wine. I pour the last drop into my mouth, the wine bottle inexplicably empty.

"That was some pretty damn good wine," Taylor gests without a care in the world.

"It sure was," I agreeably joke. "I'm sorry, though." I wince for using the whole thing on my body.

"I have a good idea," Taylor begins, stepping forward toward me, wrapping his arms around me as the hot water continues to shower upon the two of us.

"What's that?""Let's get some food. We'll order in."

"Sounds perfect."

Our two perfectly content souls order Chardonnay, a nice bottle, better than anything I could afford. We order four varied meals and four desserts to go with them. Taylor and I sit in just our bathrobes and enjoy a private victory party. We don't eat a lot, both of us knowing we aren't nearly done with one another's bodies. It's refueling; a short break. It feels like halftime at a football game and we recharge with the best Chardonnay I've ever had and the best tastes the Carriage Inn at Lincoln, Nebraska has to offer. Our personalized buffet is a perfect complement to the evening as we pick at and try it all. What a joyous time. Reality stops for me in his presence. I am swept up into a world where I'm not stressing about every penny spent. I am free of bitter resentment and constant judging. It's just endless fun and laughter. And with most of the wine finished, and satisfied we've eaten enough food for one night, Taylor proudly presents the desserts to me as if he were an Italian waiter. I smile and focus on the warm apple pie topped with a huge mound of whipped cream. I have a naughty thought brewing.

Without a word, I stop Taylor's presentation, a new goal set forth in my mind. I push him back onto the bed and undo his robe. I follow suit and both of us are once again completely naked before one another, something I can't remember doing with another human being, nearly this much. I take two large, cloth dinner napkins and use them to tie each one of Taylor's wrists to the small bedposts stationed atop the small headboard. *He is all mine.* He lies there, waiting . . . vulnerable. I can have my way with him, however I please.

I take the apple pie and seductively lick the sides of it. It's warm and the whipped cream has started to melt. I take the remaining whipped cream and strategically place it on and around his thick, hard member. Taylor's breaths quickens slightly in anticipation of what I may do to him next.

First, I slide my tongue around the base, licking off the whipped cream. Then, taking my time, I run my tongue up and down the sides of his shaft. I roll to the tip and gently suck the whipped cream off. Taylor's chest rises and falls rapidly as his excited breaths pop from his mouth. Oh,

I take my time. This will *not* end quickly. Tomorrow morning ends our world as we've shared it and all that is left is the unknown. We make the silent covenant to enjoy each other tonight. He began with pleasing me and I now take some hot apple pie in my mouth and wrap my dessert-filled mouth around his cock, the extra warmth and creaminess drawing more moans from him. I continue slowly, and with his body writing and moans coming from his mouth, I know it's driving him mad. I'm doing some of my best work and he feels every tongue lap I offer . . . every slow suck. I now position myself between him, preparing to go in for the kill. I start to go to work, my intensity slowly picking up as my mouth and tongue are perfectly synched. Taylor's body writhes helplessly up and down, his breaths quickening. He seems as if he is swirling inside, like the build is occurring. I love that he is so vulnerable.

"Yes," he gasps to confirm my suspicions. He is well on his way, and I work harder to please him.

The bed creaks from his muscular and toned arms, pulling on the posts, their small bodies being stretched to the limits.

I tighten my mouth slightly before popping off. My right joins in my efforts, working him from the base as I swirl my tongue around his tip before taking him in again. I apply the perfect pressure, causing him to writhe and moan, his breath uncontrollable.

It's too much for Taylor and like the Hulk, he rips both bed posts off. I jump and he sits up, both of us laughing for just a moment at his incredible surge of energy. He quickly wiggles his hands free of the ties and wastes little time mounting me, plunging himself deep inside. *Oh, it's so big.* He goes swiftly, thrusting forward like he wants to rage hard and find a release point quickly. I can sense that he is already built up and his dam is full. But, he does his best to bring me along and I enjoy the ride—his body pounding away hard—having his way with me.

We simultaneously breathe; the heat and friction we're creating causing us to begin to sweat, a light glistening on both of our bodies. My head bends back and my hands grip the sheets as he continues to thrust into me.

Then, Taylor abruptly pulls back and rolls my left leg over so that he is now straddling my right leg, never breaking contact. And he pushes in hard.

"Oh shit!" I blurt out. This position is an absolute winner. I've never been had like this and Taylor is going for it. He increases his speed. I gasp for air and grip whatever I can find. I bury my face and shriek through the sheets as he goes at me again and again. This feels utterly sensational.

His momentum: unstoppable. The fullness I feel: unbelievable. He penetrates harder and faster. Oh, it feels *so* good! And then, he starts to peak, his exertion seemingly reaching the pinnacle. He charges ahead with a primal groan, exploding thrust after thrust. "Oh!" we both scream. He is so deep inside me, as he grinds through his orgasm, my body completely overcome by his larger frame. He goes and goes, slowing down every second as his whole, perfectly-sculpted body tenses up. He finally grinds to a halt, our mutual, perfect, orgasmic agony coming to a close and we breathe. I didn't have an orgasm, just amazing sex. I've had three orgasms already . . . in less than sixteen hours. *This has been banner day for me.*

Taylor slowly rolls off me and we catch our breaths, our bodies slowly calming down. We lie beside one another for a moment of silence . . . a moment of calm.

"Is it weird if I want to try the apple pie now?" Taylor jokes and I burst into laughter, smacking his shoulder. It's so easy . . . so perfect.

"We're pretty good at this," I confide to Taylor.

"No. We're definitely *great* at this," he one-ups me, and I like his version more.

We grab cold glasses of water and lie naked in the dark, watching a movie and eating some apple pie. *It will never be better than this.* At this rate, Veronica Palsey is gonna start reading my autobiography to get off. She's got nothing on Taylor and I and I have no need for her. I'm living my fantasy and that's a heck of a lot better than dreaming it.

We fall asleep, naked, in each other's arms, happily fulfilled, with apple pie in our bellies and sexually satisfied beyond both of our wildest imaginations. Good night, world.

Twenty Five

Awake, we head to the bathroom for a quick shower together. No time to play; we have a plane to catch. We do wash each other, smiling ear-to-ear at one another. What a two days we shared together at the Carriage Inn.

We pack our things and step out of the room, a look of fondness on both of our faces. We are reminiscing in the moment. The two of us don't want our private party to end but it has to, at least for now.

Just before Taylor and I can move on, a man sneaks up from behind us. "Hey," he whispers to us. Taylor and I turn around, not sure what to make of the man. "I don't want to bother you both. But, I just wanted to say thank you," the man says to us.

Taylor and I both have dopey smiles on our faces, each confused as to what this stranger is talking about. "Okay. Thanks," Taylor speaks for both of us. Neither of us knows what this man is talking about.

"The wife and I hadn't been doing well. It's been rough. But, then, we heard you guys . . . ya know . . . *doing* it a lot and she couldn't take it anymore. She was so turned on, she jumped my bones and we had the best sex ever. This is strange, I know. But, thank you. You made my trip!"

"You're welcome. It was our pleasure," Taylor responds with a big smile.

"Safe travels," the man says.

"Howard, come on. Hurry up," a woman from inside the man's room begs.

"See?!" The man asks excitedly before rushing back into the hotel room, shutting the door behind him. Taylor and I look at one another and burst into laughter.

"Oh, my God! Was I that loud?" I ask and hide my face in Taylor's shoulder.

"I guess we're inspirational," he jokes.

Taylor and I laugh and walk together as the couple we have become. From the elevator, to the lobby, to the taxi, to the airport; we are bonded with hand holding and silent smiles.

As the plane soars through the sky, we are comfortably seated in first class, once again. With a glass of champagne in our hands and movies playing on the screens before us, I close my eyes. I'm so tired. I want to sleep. I could sleep. But, there is no way I'd want to not share every last moment I can with Taylor. So I open my eyes and I share lunch, a movie, and cheap champagne with my new beau.

I start to become nervous about how Taylor and I are going to navigate the next steps of our relationship, if that's what we can call this. Aiden and I have a long overdue verbal war planned upon my return. I'm quite certain things are going to continue to go south between us. And I start to remember all the concerns and worries I was able to leave behind just hours before. I spent two days forgetting about my problems and my concerns. But now, I'm going to be face-to-face with my many issues. I decide to face the most pressing one head on.

"How are we gonna do this?" I ask.

Taylor nods, as if he was wondering the same thing—how to exactly define *what* we are.

"I mean, I understand if I'm...well, if you wanted this to just be what it was—I get it. I really had an amazing time, probably the best of my life. But, I . . . I don't know—"

"—Nicki," Taylor sighs, leaning in and taking my hand in his own. He stares into my eyes with the kind of smile a girl only dreams of man giving her. "It wasn't just a couple days for me. I don't tell people about me. I never have. I've told you more than I've told anyone in a long, long time."

I smile and nod. I know Taylor likes me but I wanted to hear him say he wants more than just the amazing two days we had. I *needed* to hear those words. I'm heading into uncharted, choppy waters and I don't want any question marks in my head. Taylor steadies me. He is my peace right now. I don't want to lose that, but I also can't be fooling myself.

"Good. Good," I state. We each take a sip of champagne.

"Texting's not good though," he says.

"True," I agree. As I think about it, the less texting—the better. Just in case one of my girls sees my phone or, God forbid, Aiden. That would definitely make things much more difficult than they need to be. As is, life changes are on the way for me. It's just a matter of time. But, expediting those changes, when I'm in the middle of this case, without communicating and swiftly navigating the end of my marriage is a colossal undertaking. I'm not ending my marriage because of Taylor. It's going to end because it should . . . for the Aiden *and* me. And, it goes without saying; I have my job to worry about. If Charles and Bob find out about Taylor and me, I'm fairly certain I'd be in deep crap. As is, I feel as though I walk on eggshells, being a woman in *their* world. Fair or not, I don't want this to be my lasting legacy. Every law firm will know and I'll be a pariah.

"Obviously, we can text about work," Taylor adds. "I just shouldn't be sexting you too much." He smiles at me. I chuckle and look down, blushing for just a moment.

"Okay. By phone, when possible. Agreed. Oh, and Angie just sent me an itinerary for tomorrow. We are meeting with the President of Beltan Food Corp at Albert Penn's offices again."

"We can swing by the beach house after?" he quickly throws out.

"Definitely," I agree without hesitation. It seems we will be piggybacking our work dates with our personal dates.

"And we can just play it a little by ear at first. We have a lot of work to do with the case. Beltan may have a surprise for us." Taylor seems confident in our case. I like his confidence. He gives me some and reduces my stress. I'd rather Taylor be sitting beside me than Bob Myers, who was going to attend some of the big meetings.

"That sounds good."

"I know this is going to sound strange and probably corny, but remember when we were sitting on the balcony, the first night at the hotel?"

"Of course." I smile and reminisce with Taylor, excited to hear what he has to say next.

"Well, I think of that moment, when we were both looking up at the sky. I remember thinking to myself how beautiful it looked, how many stars there were. I mean, we seemed so much closer to the sky there than we are at home, ya know?"

"Yeah, I remember. It was incredible. The stars were popping in the sky, millions of them," I add to his thought.

"So, we look to the sky, when we want to think of each other. We look up at the stars and we connect through something greater than a cell phone or an email. We connect through the stars and that can bring us home to one another." Taylor lays out his plan to deal with the uncertain longing we both will be experiencing upon returning to Los Angeles. We spoiled ourselves twenty-four seven with one another. Now things will be different—segregated. His idealistic ideas are very *Disney*-like. Sure, it could be seen as hokey to some, but I think every girl could use a little *Disney* in their lives. Everyone can use a fairytale every now and then. And if looking to the stars gets us by this difficult time, then looking up we shall do.

We arrive back at the terminal and another limousine driver is waiting with the name Taylor and Nicki written on a card. I feel as though I want that name card as a memento. But that is silly and only a fleeting thought.

The limousine ride is quiet. Taylor and I are both tired, and the moment is hitting us that we are about to part. He reminds me of Jay Gatsby. Am I his Daisy? It is a strange, complicated tale we have weaved? We are as intricately patterned as the dilemmas and drama surrounding that great F. Scott Fitzgerald novel. The scenery has greatly changed and the challenges are completely different, but I feel that allure. I feel that want and that desire, which is so perfectly crafted in that epic tale. He seems to be methodically wooing me; a limousine ride, first class travel, incredible wine selections, and his beach house. Journey after journey leads to another perfectly orchestrated moment—the kiss on the beach in the pouring rain with lightning striking around us and thunder raging above—sitting on the balcony of the Carriage Inn drinking extraordinary red wine—the intense passion that exploded multiple times in the shower—the amazing feast of sexual pleasure we exposed to one another. It's like I'm riding Jay Gatsby's magic carpet ride through Taylor Diamond's heart. I hope it never ends. I hope tragedy eludes us. I don't want this feeling to go away. But, for now, we must part.

In the parking garage, we step out of the limo and separate. No kiss. No hug. Just a longing stare into each other's eyes, a silent promise of a return to the magical state we both find ourselves in. We make that vow through our silence, and then we walk away.

I take a deep breath upon getting into my car. The most amazing two nights of my life have come to a close and now, I am getting set to do battle with Aiden in what is sure to be an awful time. My only salvation is that I'm taking the girls to their soccer games tonight, which are on adjacent fields. Aiden is working on something today. It's a good thing for me anyway. I miss driving my girls to their events; we sing songs together and laugh together. I honestly can't wait for this case to be over, and if I walked away from the legal profession, I don't think I'd bat an eye. The Ramsey Suit has taken quite a bit out of me.

I drive home and practice speaking with Aiden. I'm not sure if I should talk about Taylor. It's too soon to address outside influences. I convince myself that discussing our own issues and our future is the better way to go. Certainly, it's a lot easier than fessing up to an affair I've begun. It's crazy to think that I am an adulteress. Always the *good girl*. I was never a one-night stand. I was never a *cheater*. I always played by the rules. But now, I feel like I never really lived. It's sad to look in the mirror and realize you made the wrong choices. You did what you were supposed to do, but it didn't get you where you wanted to be. You fooled yourself into thinking life was right when, all along, it was dead wrong. I feel like I took a test and scored a *C*. I could have had an *A* but I settled. I can beat myself up all I want, but the fact remains—I need to start to move forward. My ship has sailed away from Aiden and no matter what happens with Taylor, my excursion into the dark side has exposed the poor decision-making of my past. Aiden and I were good friends—we were *great* friends. But, we weren't great lovers, and now I see, we have never had a great marriage. It is a fact I feel I cannot argue with. I am happy I have my two beautiful girls and I will take that to the bank as a huge success for us. But, I think everything else is lacking and if I have to be the strong one, then so be it.

My dizzying complex conversation with myself comes to an end as I pull into our driveway. Aiden is home, which is good. We can discuss things.

I enter the house and it's quiet downstairs. I set my things down on the kitchen counter and take a deep breath. I hear noises coming from upstairs. It sounds like it's coming from our bedroom. I am two hours early. I expected to go to the office for a bit today but instead, came straight home. Now my mind wanders as the strange noises from upstairs continues. I can't make it out. There are no voices, just creaking and moving. It doesn't sound right. It also doesn't sound like just one person is up there.

I curiously and quietly move away from my things and creep up the staircase.

Who's up there? Clearly, Aiden's here because I saw his truck. But who else is here? Who else is in my bedroom? I mean, I can't be angry or upset if Aiden's eyes have started to wander. I would be, but I'd be a complete hypocrite for holding his feet to the fire. But if someone is doing something, upstairs in my bedroom, with my husband, there will be hell to pay. That is just disrespectful.

I carefully make my way up, just tiny creaks giving away my location. I slowly walk down the hallway to maintain a thief-like approach. I see nothing out of the ordinary. I can't tell that there is anything wrong, but *something* isn't right.

I approach the closed bedroom door and take a deep breath. *How do I enter?* I'm not sure what I should do. Should I scream *"Ah-ha!"*? Should I casually stroll in? What sort of entry do I make? I don't want to give away any suspicion even though I feel inside there may be something to be suspicious about. But I'm almost numb to feelings when it comes to Aiden. It's plummeting that fast.

I take a deep breath and go for casual.

"Hey, Aiden." I enter the bedroom and find him on a step stool, changing a lightbulb in a pair of jeans and no shirt on. He looks a little sweaty and haggard, but it's just from doing handiwork around the house.

"Hey. You're back early," he says with a casual look. He wipes some sweat from his brow. I take a quick glance around but don't want to appear to be casing the room.

"Yeah. I'm exhausted. Good trip, though. The doctor is gonna come through."

"Who?" Aiden asks, completely clueless as to what is going on with me. For a second, I had forgotten we don't share much anymore and he has no idea what I'm talking about.

"You said you work tonight?" I ask.

"Yup. Down at the site again."

"Is Eddie going because his wife didn't seem to think he was working with you anymore?" I come right at Aiden. It's a soft casual attack, but I strike him right between the eyes with this one. I want to see if he will bury himself in a ditch or come clean.

"He is. He's picking me up today. I haven't been able to afford as many crew members and I hate to say it, but I went around Eddie for a bit. I brought in a couple of migrants at a lower wage to catch up." Aiden doesn't even bat an eyelash as he finishes changing the ceiling bulb. Maybe everything is made up in my own mind to justify what's happening with me. Maybe Aiden still is that reliable middle-of-the-road guy that you can count on and I'm the one that isn't faithful. I nod and look around, unsure of what to do next. "Where's your stuff?" he asks.

I realize I don't have my things because I was trying to be quiet and snoop. I quickly search for a response. "Oh, my arm was killing me. I set them down in the kitchen and completely forgot to bring them up. This whole case is just too much."

"Yeah, tell me about it. We agree on something." Aiden's jab showcases some of that hidden bitterness I know resides inside him. I want to hear his resentment as opposed to feel it. Two years of a spiraling marriage that is finally hitting the wall and this is the first comment he has made about not being happy with my job. I nod and just let it lie. He doesn't want to engage me and I feel as though my thunder was lost by failing to catch him in some carnal act in our bedroom. I choose instead to shower and get ready to pick the girls up. We have soccer games to get to!

━━━━━━━

I grab the girls from school and we have a snack at home. They are giggling, arguing, and complaining. It's amazing. I've missed being a mommy so much. The good and the bad, it doesn't matter. It feels good to be *Mom* again. Aiden greets the girls and, just as he told me, Eddie Hart arrives dressed in his knock-around work clothes.

"Hey, Nicki!" Eddie greets.

"Hey, Eddie. Don't let Aiden keep you too late!" I joke.

"Work is work. Late is sometimes a good thing." He smiles. Eddie is the cream of the crop. A nice man who would probably lend you the shirt right off his back if you needed. Aiden is lucky to have a friend like him.

The two *hard hats* disappear to go work on some site I have no idea about. Aiden has referenced the city. And normally, I would be far more diligent in making sure my husband was all right or keeping tabs on his whereabouts in case of an emergency. But, I'm distant. And he hasn't elaborated, so he's equally distant. We're both removed and, since it's mutual, no one is complaining about it.

Time for soccer! With the girls dressed in their uniforms, we head back in the car and I shuttle them to their games.

"You guys excited?" I try to build up some energy in the car on the way to our big soccer event. Of course, it's just a regular game to them, but to me, I get to see my girls in action for the first time since I caught a game late last spring. I made nearly half of their games last spring despite dealing with my promotion and the attention it required to Rapture and Myers. The girls are nearly done with this season and I haven't seen a game. Where does all the time go?

"Yeah!" Lacy is the first to get excited.

"I'm gonna kill 'em!" Ariel bellows out, an angry scowl on her face. The scowl gives quickly to a smile though, as she can only hold that face so long, and the girls giggle together. I follow suit.

"I'm so excited to see you both play today. And I'm glad your games are side-by-side."

"Yeah, it usually doesn't work out that way," Lacy thinks out loud.

"I'm just happy to be with you both." I glance at the girls in the rear view mirror and smile. I truly miss this.

We arrive at the field and the girls take off to their teams. I immediately see Jessica. Haley and Ariel play on the same team, so it is always fun to see Jessica at the field when the girls have games. Jessica looks surprised to see me.

"Wow. I wasn't expecting you." Jessica walks up and gives me a hug and a kiss.

"Yeah. I get to be mom again . . . at least for a day. Aiden had work and I got home early."

"Yeah. I'm used to *Mr. Mom* being out here," she jokes about Aiden.

"How is he when he's out here?" I ask Jessica, seeking a second opinion on the mental state of Aiden.

"He's fine. He's been on his phone a lot about work. But, he's pretty normal. I haven't seen much of a difference from him."

"I told you I felt like we're growing apart. You know how that was. It makes you feel sick." I open to Jessica once again because she's been there. She is literally days away from finalizing her divorce. She moved on long ago and she is in the best position to give me life advice at this point.

"It's hard, Nick. It's really hard. Honestly, I feel like everyone deserves a second go-around. The first shot doesn't always hit the bulls-eye. Sometimes it takes a second chance to discover what was *meant to be.* Or maybe we're all full of shit and we just get older and realize to start to compromise—to be more attentive and listen. But really, it comes down to you two. I can't tell you which way to go. Maybe try marriage counseling." Jessica adds her two cents, not really moving me in either direction. But the marriage counseling is an interesting idea. If we vent our grievances and see that things aren't meant to be, then we can both go our separate ways. At least then, I don't have to disclose my big secret to Aiden. I'd rather us move on as friends than break-up in a giant blaze of destruction and pain.

"Counseling is a good idea," I agree.

"Oh, look! There goes Ariel!"

I stand on the tips of my toes and see Ariel dribble past the last defender and strike a perfect ball past the goalie. Her arms erupt into the air and she starts to jump around, getting mobbed by her teammates. I am injected with a massive smile of pride and jump up and down clapping.

On the field next to us I hear Lacy scream for Ariel. "Nice job, A Ram!" Lacy shouts from her field, waiting around as players are being substituted on and off the field in her game. My heart melts as my girls are both jumping for joy. So much pride in one singular moment.

"That's Ariel's first goal!" Jessica shouts to me. It is a fact I am not aware of. I know she came close last season to scoring but played a lot of defense.

Ariel comes running back, points right at me, and rushes over.

"That was for you, Mom!" She lunges forward and leaps into my arms and gives me a quick kiss before rushing back onto the field.

Perfection. I have tears in my eyes. Just absolutely perfect.

———————

After their games, we celebrate with pizza and a girls' night. It's wonderful. I want more of these. I've missed them so much.

Twenty Six

I'm in a great mood as I wake up in the morning. It was a magical night with my girls. I've come to the conclusion that they are more important than killing myself in a law office. I'd love to have my cake and eat it too, but to be a great lawyer requires many, many hours of work. I can't work eighty hours a week and be a great mom at the same time. I can love my children and be there as often as possible, but I can't be the mother I want to be. And spending an entire afternoon and evening with my girls, by myself, spoke volumes to me about my future.

I got Aiden's text that he was staying over on the site with Eddie. Both of them had their phones on them, in case of an emergency. I let him know I'd take the girls to school. He will have pick-up today because Taylor and I have a big meeting with the President of Beltan Food Corp. It will be the first time we get to speak with him directly, albeit, with Albert Penn and his obnoxious legal team, sitting by his side.

I drop the girls off at school, completing our sixteen hours of *girl time*. I shoot over to the offices. I have reports to pull and files to review prior to meeting with Beltan. Taylor is also heading in, so he can help me with preparation and strategizing what we do and don't want to say. With the addition of more documentation on its way from Dr. Schecter and the mysterious memo we received from the whistle-blower, we need to discuss how, and if, we want to unveil certain new bombshells of information. We may want to hold some back. We may want to go full-frontal with them and pour it on, overwhelming them and forcing another, bigger, offer. I know what Ramsey wants, but I'm thinking Rapture and Myers are right to want a settlement. As long as it takes care of the people well beyond what they need, I can live with pushing hard for that. I think it's best for everyone. We're all tired and we all want a victorious end. Defining *victory* is all that will stand between us and a settlement. Beltan Food wants this to go away. I think today, Taylor and I can find out if we can get Ramsey what they need. It also could be a bonus for them. They are pushing for a settlement before the end of the year. They may have motivation to turf any settlement in quarter four of this year. Rolling it over to next year could only weigh them down. But, stuffing it into the backend of a profitable year could limit the damage. I can see their motivation and I'm game to use it against them.

I arrive at the office and immediately after parking, in my usual spot, I see changes. A new security booth has been erected. It stands by the entrance of the parking garage. We've always had a guard upstairs by the street level entrance, but nothing by the garage. The officers' uniforms have changed, as well. They all read *Crane Security*, matching the trucks that were here the day we left for Nebraska. As I approach the front, I'm met by the new officer, asking me to swipe my badge into a small kiosk to enter.

"I haven't gotten one yet." I show him my old badge.

"No problem, Miss…," The guard looks over my badge, "… Connolly. Just allow me to call upstairs and confirm."

I nod. I don't mind the extra security. It can only be a plus.

The guard gets off the phone and returns back to me. "They have a new badge for you upstairs. You can enter." The guard steps aside and I head up to the office.

In the elevator I notice something new: a small camera, up in the corner of the cube. *Interesting.* I guess

Taylor and I won't be sneaking kisses in the elevator anytime soon. I smile at the mere thought. When the elevator opens, I walk through a. far more, quiet office. People are working but there isn't the usual hustle and bustle. I first go and seek out Ronald at his desk. He is not there. I immediately become concerned because all of his stuff is gone. It's as if Ronald was never an employee at Rapture and Myers. I look around searching for answers, but our quiet office gives me none. I make my way through the office and I see Angela at her desk. Her face is ominous as she is packing a box with two Crane security officers standing by her side.

"What is this?" I ask.

"They're letting me go," she says in a sad tone.

"Who? You're my assistant. They can't fire you!" I belt out.

The two security officers look at me and barely bat an eye. They have a job to do and, like soldiers in the field, they pay me no mind. They stand over Angela as if they were escorting her to prison.

"She doesn't go anywhere or it's both your jobs!" I use an angry wag of my finger to get my point across.

"Ma'am, no offense, but we don't answer to you." The first security guard speaks. The second looks just the same, the two almost indistinguishable. They are both relatively tall, with dark hair, broad shoulders, and clean shaven.

"You can take it up with Mr. Crane. We answer to him and him alone," the second guard confirms.

"Where is he?" I ask, my patience thin.

"Don't know, ma'am," the first officer replies. And both men return to their job, ensuring Angela gets all of her things and leaves.

I march right over to Charles Rapture's office. I arrive in a blaze of fury and walk right past his assistant, Julie.

"Ms. Connolly!" she shouts and rises to her feet, attempting to get me before I enter Charles's office.

"I'm gonna need a moment, Jules," I state, without a care for her opinion.

"He's in a meeting!" she shouts as I push his door right open.

I burst in and see Charles at his desk talking to a man seated in the high-backed, leather chair before him. I could care less about the meeting and only see his dress pants and black, shiny dress shoes. I focus only on Charles Rapture and am in no mood to play games.

"What is going on, Charles?" I bark with no fear.

"I had a feeling you would come by the office today," Charles's tone is strange.

"I'm sorry, sir. I tried," Julie conveys her apologies, unable to stop me.

"It's okay, Jules." Charles holds up his hand. "Give us a minute." He relieves Julie of being in the office. She nods and backs out of the office, closing the door behind her.

"What is going on? Ronald, who does nearly all of my research, is gone. Angela, my assistant, is being escorted out of the office! What the heck is going on?" I am furious and want to throw and hit things, but I attempt to quell my anger the best I can.

"We have a new security company and they discovered we had some leaks. This is Michael Crane, owner of Crane Security."

The man, who had been cloaked in the chair, facing Charles Rapture's desk, rises.My eyes must deceive me. The first thing I see is the finely trimmed, silver hair. The man's stare is unforgettable. His broad shoulders and tall frame cause me to take a step back. I am breathless, looking at my stalker dead in the eyes. The silver-haired man is here. I don't know what to say.

"Hello, Ms. Connolly. I'm Michael Crane." The man approaches me and extends his hand.

I want to slap him, but I can't bring myself to do so. I have no "out" plan for this situation, and am completely stunned. I reluctantly shake the man's hand, his eyes piercing my face. I feel as though I'm staring down my arch enemy and he has somehow made home inside my house.

"He is top-of-the-line. Mr. Crane did an analysis of our employees and decided some changes needed to be made. He brought them to my attention and I concurred. I think we are heading in a bold, new direction and as your case wraps up, we can look at additional options. For now, I feel as though Mr. Crane, here, has our best interests at heart," Charles finishes his introductions and the speech.

Unlike Charles, I have nothing to say. If I call Crane out, I look crazy. If I don't, I lose Angela and Ronald. I have no idea what to do at this moment.

"I want my people back," I say under my breath.

"What was that?" Charles asks.

"I want Angela and Ronald back. They are invaluable to me."

"I'll tell you what. We finish the Ramsey Case and we'll talk about it." Charles uses the case as leverage for me to get what I want. It's a dangerous game we are playing and with the presence of Michael Crane, it appears I am losing the internal struggle inside my four walls. I am on an island and I have no one—no one *except* Taylor Diamond—to count on.

"Why don't I see you out?" Crane offers.

"No, no. I got it." I am clear and concise in not wanting the silver-haired creep anywhere near me.

I stare him down, an angry bitter glare. He returns my glare with a victorious smile. He knows far more than I do, and I am playing a losing hand. It's time to fold this one and start over. I nod and quickly exit the office, closing the door behind me.

I march through the hall and when I arrive back at my office, Angela is already gone. I throw my head back in frustration. I feel like crying, but that's not what I do. I want to get angry, but I'm confused where that anger should head. And before I can think of my next move, a hand is placed on my shoulder. I jump and turn around.

Taylor is standing in front of me with a confused look on his face. I let out a relieved breath of air. He sees immediately that I'm distressed and I wave him into my office. I close the door behind him and run my hands over my face in frustration.

"What is going on? Where's Angie?" Taylor's questions are filled with confusion and I'm not far away from where he's at. I am equally confused and have no idea what to do.

"They fired them—Angie, Ronald—they fired them!" I loudly whisper to him, infuriated and growing increasingly paranoid.

"What?" Taylor looks completely confused, looking around the office.

"What's even worse is that man . . . that silver-haired man," I declare with great frustration in my tone.

"The one following you?" Taylor asks.

"Yes. I know his name. It's Michael Crane. Of *Crane Security*." I establish the colossal issue facing us.

"Crane Security. The new company here?"

"One in the same. And that man is here. That son of a bitch is here!"

"Where is he?" Taylor looks incensed.

"In Charles's office. All the new equipment, security cameras, all of it—it's him. Why would he be following me? What's happening?"

"I don't know," Taylor paces, thinking to himself. I wait and let him think. I am exasperated at this point. I can barely tell up from down and desperately need his opinion.

"What have you told Charles? What do they know?"

"They don't know about the memo on the flash drive or about Dr. Schecter. They know about the mystery man because the silver-haired—Michael Crane, and his little crony were there." A thought strikes me. "Oh, shit, I pepper sprayed the new head of security. What the fuck is happening, Taylor?"

Taylor is calm but seems deep in thought. I think he may be attempting to hatch a plan. I wish I knew his thoughts.

"I have to hide the documents," I say to Taylor.

His eyes flash quickly around the room in a paranoid manner. He walks up to me with a strange look on his face. He seems confident and concerned all in one, as if he has figured something out.

"Let's just head to our meeting," he says, with a strange look on his face, his eyes trying to tell me to leave.

"We need to game plan," I say. "I have my files here."

"Let's just get out of this building." Taylor reiterates.

"Okay." I grab my things and we exit my office.

In the elevator we both glance up and see the newly installed camera. *Big Brother* is watching and we feel *his* eyes upon us. We snap a quick look at one another and I can sense that we are thinking the same paranoid thoughts. We say nothing and only share that one glance. No secrets will be given away in front of this tiny camera, inside this small box.

We head to the parking garage and, as we move through the parking lot lobby, the peculiar, short, balding man is entering. He glides through security, the staff knowing and respecting him. I haven't seen him much, but enough to know what he looks like. I remember his squinty eyes. And as he passes, he gives me the most covert smirk and I can't help but open up my mouth.

"You can't stop me!" I shout at him. Taylor turns around upon hearing me shout at the man. The man slowly turns, as well, that same cocky smirk on his face. He waits for me as if to see what I'll say next. I stare him down, not relenting for a moment. I take a step forward. I'm in no mood to play around. "I know it was you." My statement is a direct accusation and I don't mince words. "You and the silver-haired man; you're just henchmen." My declaration is a direct accusation against their character. I reduce him to some low-level thug, a lackey for somebody else. He just looks at me—the tension palpable.

Taylor takes a step past me toward the man, looking at my face and then back at him.

"And what do you know?" The man has the same cocksure grin as his partner, Michael Crane, had when he stared into my eyes at the restaurant. They are above rules, above law. At least, that's how they perceive themselves.

"I know you are evil," I say without regard for any reaction. I am daring him to lose his temper because I have lost mine.

"It's him? He's one of them?" Taylor, agitated, begs for me to say *yes*. He looks as though he is about to be fired out of a cannon.

"This isn't your fight, young Diamond. We have never met." The short thug tosses an insult Taylor's way. Taylor's eyes squint and fire rages behind them. He charges the man, giving in to his anger.

The security guard rushes past me. It all happens so quickly. The lower parking garage lobby suddenly gets far too exciting.

Taylor grabs the shorter man by his shirt and runs him up against the wall, lifting him off the ground. "Now we've met! *Now*—this is *our* problem!" Taylor is trying to push him harder into the wall as the man uses his forearm to defend himself. He is not trying to hit Taylor or fight back, merely attempting to hold his ground.

"You'll regret this," the strained words slip out of the balding man's mouth as Taylor has his hands tightened, like a noose, around his neck.

More security guards empty into the hall and I join in helping Taylor. The security force seems torn, not wanting to touch or harm Taylor. At the same time, their priority, for some inexplicable reason, is to protect the short, balding man.

"Come on, Taylor," I say, pulling my angry man away from the fray. Taylor steps back and gives the man an angry glare.

"I'll be seein' you—*both* of you." The man uses a challenging tone to cast a veiled threat. He licks his lip, blood tricking from a small cut on the side of his mouth.

Taylor and I are, all of a sudden, the outsiders; the security force and the man, glaring at us, using their eyes to see us out of the building. We oblige and move on.

We get into our cars and drive to Taylor's beach house. It is close to our meeting at the firm of Harper and Penn. It's a logical choice to hide away and game plan. Right now, it's the only place where I don't feel under-the-gun and judged. It's the only place, in the world, I feel safe.

Clouds are again rolling in and it seems every time I head to the beach, it rains. No rain yet, but the skies are growing darker, despite it being late morning. The water is matching much of what is happening in my life. What's more frustrating is that I haven't heard from Ronald or Angie.

Charlie greets us at the door; the excitable lab is full of energy.

"Hey, girl," Taylor welcomes her.

The house is spotless and I see Estella for the first time. She swings by to introduce herself with purse in hand and a jacket around her shoulder, clearly on her way out. The short Venezuelan woman has chunky, raised, smiling cheeks, thick, black, curly hair and a thick, stout frame.

"Hola, senorita," Estella greets me.

"Hola. I'm Nicki."

"Estella," she says. And the two of us exchange smiles and a handshake.

"Adios, jefe," she says to Taylor and kisses him on the cheek. "Be good," she says in a motherly tone with a pointed finger. Taylor nods and Estella leaves.

"She seems very nice," I compliment.

"She practically raised me. Truth be told—she did," he releases another fact about his life.

"What do we do?" I ask.

"For the meeting?"

"Yeah. Should we show our hand? No better time than with the President of Beltan coming to the table," I sight.

"I think we should shove our feet up their asses and let them see how it feels," Taylor states with conviction.

"Alright, let's kick some ass, then." I concur with Taylor and we set out minds for an afternoon dogfight with Albert Penn and the President of Beltan Food Corp.

Twenty Seven

We enter the Harper and Dunn offices not as strangers—not as gawkers, enthralled by the art and décor—but as legal mercenaries, ready to do battle. I'm focused and angry. I start to evolve ideas in the back of my mind, trying to figure out who and what Crane Security is. The thoughts of the mysteries, whirling around me, haunt my focus, but *that* is it. I sidebar them in my mind, ignoring them like a well-adapted schizophrenic. I hone in my focus and my thoughts. We march through the office and are escorted to the glass box. Nothing is intimidating me on this trip.

Of course Albert Penn is already seated and flanked by his army of Ivy League attorneys. A new group of people have joined the fray. It is headed by Victor Harris, CEO of Beltan Food Corporation. Victor is a wealthy, heavy-set, Texan whose donned in a cowboy hat to accent his casual attire. His executives wrap around the table and we are left with our two seats and about four feet of space on either side. It is them versus us. A single stenographer is seated in the corner of the room, preparing to record our conversation.

"Well, welcome back." Albert Penn's smug smirk and glow is alive and well.

Victor Harris rises and tips his hat before sitting back down.

After pleasantries, we begin. Simple questions; we want to make the most of this visit and start by lulling the crowd to sleep. After twenty minutes of asking about structure, communication methods, and confirming names and people, I start in on the good stuff.

"When did you know you were poisoning people?"

The room stops. The Beltan executives uncomfortably shift in their chairs.

"What was that?" Victor Harris asks with his thick, profound Texas accent.

"Excuse me?" Albert Penn follows up, annoyed by the question as if I just insulted his mother.

"Oh, sorry. I'll be more specific. What was the exact date you became aware you were poisoning the people in Ramsey, California?"

"Why you little—"

"Victor!" Albert Penn shouts from across the table. Victor holds his tongue. "This is a courtesy, *Mrs. Connolly*," Albert Penn says with contriteness and anger. "We don't *need* to do this."

"But you should answer the questions. On record, as we are, it will look terribly evasive for you to end this meeting or avoid answering the questions," I sight.

"What is this side show? And him too?" Victor lashes out and looks as Taylor as if he isn't supposed to be there. "I thought you had this under control, Penn," Victor speaks as if he expected us to have drinks instead of him being grilled about secret company information.

"I'll help y'all out," I do my best southern accent to drive the spike home and distribute the memos I received in convert fashion. "Take a gander. I made some copies."

They look the memo over and Victor Harris shoots Albert Penn an angered and annoyed look. It's clear we've outmaneuvered the big powers this time. And . . . we have more up our sleeve.

"Where did you get this?" Albert Penn fires with a serious and annoyed tone. "Stop typing!" he orders the stenographer. The tension in the room is quickly escalating.

"She types. That's not how this works," I play hardball.

"Who gave you this, pixie?" Victor Harris attempts to show his displeasure using a condescending tone and a weak insult.

"Watch your mouth, old-timer," Taylor fires back in my honor. Victor Harris stares at Taylor angrily and he returns the favor. The two men are like cowboys in the old west. It's interesting how Victor seems content to not challenge Taylor despite clearly showing a temper. "Who gave it to me isn't important. Who sent this memo, Mr. Harris?" I ask. My P.I. has yet to discover his identity, but I'm sure Victor Harris knows who wrote it. "Who is R.D.?"

Victor Harris smiles. He starts to chuckle and shakes his head.

"If this is a fact-finding mission, Ms. Connolly, I can assure you these proceedings are finished."

Victor looks at me and opens his arms. "Anything else?" "We also spoke with Dr. Schecter," I pile on relentlessly.

"Who?" Victor blurts out.

"You know him well, Mr. Penn," Taylor pops in and puts their whole team on the defensive. Their faces look uneasy with scowls forming.

"Can you excuse us?" Albert Penn asks of Taylor and me. "We'd like to discuss some things in private."

We both nod and grab our things. We exit the glass box and sit outside in the massive research library area, surrounding the conference room. One of their well-grounded, young paralegals brings us coffee. Then water. And then, a tray of muffins. We wait for nearly two hours as heated exchanges and discussions take place before our very eyes in the soundproof glass box. Suddenly, Victor Harris and the Beltan Team exit the box and leave without a word to us. Albert Penn steps out. "You can rejoin us now. Mr. Harris has other business to attend to."

"I wasn't done with my inquiries," I fire back at Albert Penn from a position of strength.

"You are for today, young lady. But we have an offer for you."

Taylor and I enter the glass box, once again. *Another offer*. It appears we have stumbled upon secrets Beltan prefers to keep quiet.

"Now, all of the information you think you have— these supposed *smoking guns* you whipped out today—they aren't relevant in court. My guess is you don't have sworn testimony or witnesses lined up to testify. These are alleged *whistle-blowers* who are ghosts. They don't exist. And I don't see a sworn statement from Professor Schecter but I prefer not to discuss that because he signed a NDA with us and non-disclosures with us won't permit any of his testimony. So, what you two have is a show here today. Smoke and mirrors; not admissible in court." Penn is correct for the most part but it doesn't change the facts. We got to information they never expected our eyes to see. We ruffled their feathers and we did it inside *their* house.

"Maybe. But you're still going to up your offer," I poignantly retort.

"Yes, Ms. Connolly. Yes, we are."

Taylor and I go to sit down. "Not necessary. Normal rules apply. Sign this NDA. We're going to put this in writing." Penn gives us an offer sheet to work off of. Taylor reads the NDA as I look the offer over.

"You will find that the offer raises our last offer by fifty-percent; a hundred and fifty million dollars, Ms. Connolly. There won't be another offer from me and my clients. This is the end of the line, before court in the spring."

"I'll take it to my clients," I state with simplicity. I give no reaction to the increased offer. It's a lot of money, but right now, Penn is on the run and I enjoy keeping him there.

"You do that," he replies bitterly.

Taylor and I leave, getting back in his car. We both are exhilarated, dropping bombs on Beltan Food Corp and forcing Albert Penn into a rare position of weakness has left us feeling victorious on this day. It's rainy out as we drive back to his Malibu beach house. It's just 4pm but the dark skies make it feel like early evening.

Once again, we enter the beach house wet. We are but a few steps into his home when he whirls me in his arms and starts kissing me. Our wet faces and lips slide smoothly against one another and we connect like lost lovers being reunited for the very first time. "I missed you," he moans as we kiss repeatedly. He pulls back and then slowly dives into my neck, gently kissing it. We start to remove wet clothing and walk toward his living room, keeping our lips locked as much as possible, leaving a trail along the way. We are both in the mood to celebrate, why not do what we are best at?

I back up near the large glass windows leading to the deck. The dark skies and rain give us perfect cover from Taylor's private beachfront property. With just our underwear remaining, we each remove what is left. We both want it; a symbiotic urge neither of us will deny.

Standing by the glass, I seductively turn around and give Taylor my best sexual glare. I give him my backside as a target and silently ask for him to take me from behind. He smiles and runs his hands along the sides of my breasts down to my hips. His hands slide forward and tease the outside of my spot. They then ride up my body, caressing my breasts as he pushes himself up against me from behind. I can feel his hard length pressed up against me, and I feel as though I'm moments from being taken.

He runs his right hand up along my neck toward my face, and I take one of his fingers into my mouth, sucking on it. Suddenly, I feel myself expand around him. "Oh," escapes my mouth as my teeth start to gnaw on his finger. He pushes up against me, slowly thrusting deep inside me.

My body goes forward and I'm pressed up against the glass, the coolness sending shivers down my spine. My breasts feel amazing as they press firmly onto the cold window. It is the perfect sensation as Taylor does some fine work pushing deeper and deeper into me. The angle we are in, the way his dick is sliding up, it's hitting the sweet spot inside me. It's a wonderful feeling. My head turns sideways as it presses further up against the window.

Taylor starts to go harder and I bend slightly, releasing my grip on his finger. I want him to go as deep inside me as possible—I want it hard. I bend over at the waist and tip my backside up. Taylor gets maximum penetration, thrusting inside me again and again. I peek up and see lightning strikes above the ocean again, our passion erupting inside the beach house and outside all around us.

His pace quickens. Taylor's breaths are loud and is grunting follows suit, starting to strain as both our breaths increase tenfold. We are vocally breathing in ecstasy, writhing in perfect harmony together. It's constant and building as Taylor holds my hips firmly and is thrusting with all his might. He appears as if he is about to peak. I quickly pull forward, ejecting him out of me. He catches his breath as I turn around and look deep into his eyes.

"I'm not done with you yet," I announce.

Taylor smiles, enjoying my game. I push him back and lead him to the couch. A slight shove from me and he ends up on his couch. I mount him there and straddle his firm legs. My hips begin rocking back and forth, riding my beautiful, strong man. I grab his hands and press them back, pinning him down. I lean forward and kiss him as I ride, taking him deeper. I go slowly at first, getting the feel. I want him to rub against me just the right way. I want to feel the build-up begin. And as I ride Taylor, it starts. I lean back, the energy focused down to my spot. I thrust over and over again, his hands finding my breasts. He rubs my nipples and squeezes my breasts as I ride. I start to pick up speed.

"Yes!" I let slip out of my mouth, the momentum of our sexual energy starting to build to that amazing point. We are both into it and just as I'm about to go harder and make my run to the finish line, Taylor abruptly uses his power and raises us both up off the couch, keeping us attached where it counts most.

"I'm not through with you yet." He smiles.

I smile back as he carries me to the stairs and sets me down. He kisses my body all over, and then his mouth caresses my inner thighs as they travel. His tongue flattens, licking up my center. It's a perfect progression, the passion infusing all kinds of sexual energies inside me. His tongue presses up against my clit, licking and gently tugging away.

"Oh, God," I mutter. It appears we are going to have a sexual buffet all over the house. It is the middle of an amazing session.

Taylor goes to task writing the alphabet with his tongue, the varying swirls, digs causing an array of pleasure that brings *moan* after *moan* out of my mouth. I can barely take it as I near orgasm, his tongue guiding the way. Then, I pull his head back. I'm out of breath and smile at him. "We're going to finish this one together."

We get up and make our way into his bedroom. I haven't seen it yet and I allow him to lead the way. Taylor keeps the lights off as we enter a large bedroom with white, fluffy carpet. His bed has large, erected posts and a white, sheer canopy bed curtains hanging around the top of the bed. The plush, white, down bedding is complimented by white, down, puffy pillows. Taylor pulls the bedding back and lies on his back. I climb on top and settle him back inside of me. It doesn't take long for me to find the right spot. I rock back and forth, running my hands up to my hair. I lift it above my head and around my eyes. I breathe heavily, every movement providing me with the perfect friction against my sweet spot. I squeeze around him as I slide up his shaft, bringing us both closer to climax. I pick up the pace.

Taylor reaches up and runs his hands along my breasts and then around to my backside. He squeezes and pulls on my ass, gripping his fingers harder into me. I grind harder, my hips working overtime. Now I've found my groove. Taylor's own hips rise up, getting maximum penetration inside me. We are once again in rhythm, two sexual beings soaring toward orgasm.

Harder and harder.

"Yes!" I yell. "Oh, Taylor! Yes!"

"Harder!" Taylor calls to me. "Leave nothing left," he orders. The two of us rock and rock, his bed shaking so violently, the posts are swaying like flagpoles bending in a hurricane. Except, there is no wind in the room, just the force of our bodies intertwined in sexual harmony. I go for it. I feel as if I'm going to explode. I grind down harder onto Taylor's pelvis, his penis rocking my insides. I feel him pulsating, as big as ever, inside me.

"Oh, YES!" I am about to finish. I go hard and then I feel Taylor's hips fully thrust up.

"Oh!" Taylor moans.

"Yes!" I scream, my own explosion taking place. Our two bodies are tense as I grind us to a smooth finish. Both of us are exploding at the same time, our perfect orgasms creating another perfect end to a memorable sex session between us.

We slow our breathing as I finish working out every last bit of the sex each of us have inside us. I slowly roll off Taylor and we just stare up at his perfectly painted, white bedroom ceiling.

"We are *really* good at this." Taylor smiles and looks at me.

"You won't hear a complaint out of me. Shit," I joke in return. We both continue to stare up at the ceiling.

"Over there is a balcony," he begins, "I sat out there and looked up at the stars last night, thinking of you." Taylor subjects me to more romanticism in our perfect afterglow.

"I did too. After the girls went to sleep, I snuck outside with a glass of wine, sat in the backyard, and stared up at the stars. I made a wish."

"What was it?" Taylor asks.

"Normally I'd say, *I can't tell you. It's a secret.* But being that it just came true, right now, at this moment, I guess I can say this was it. This was my wish."

Taylor and I continue to catch our breath, and our hands slide over together on the bed, our fingers interlocking. We just lie quietly in each other's company, relishing our final moments of the day together. The rain continues to fall outside, beautiful melodic noise, storming around us.

Twenty Eight

As I drive home in the rain, I can't help but smile, thinking about Taylor. It's hard not to fall right into the daydream of us together, for more than just an afternoon rendezvous.

The case seems like it's wrapping up. This offer should persuade the Ramsey folks a little. It is a lot of money, and despite not having their day in court, they may be able to live with this.

I feel good. I'm hoping things are coming together. What was hard and difficult seems to now be turning a corner. I feel like my life is turning a corner.

I arrive at home and see no cars in the driveway. No surprise though. As the rain continues to fall lightly from the dark skies of early evening, I remind myself how much Aiden hates his pick-up being out in the rain. It's likely in the garage, where he usually stashes it when the weather is like this.

I enter though the front door into darkness. The lights are on upstairs and I hear scurrying up there again. I'm quite certain Aiden can't be changing more light bulbs, but I'm sure it's just the girls rattling around. I take a deep breath and head into the kitchen to grab a glass of juice. I should be hungry but with all the excitement today, I'm actually feeling queasy. My stomach is definitely churning due to the impending deal with Beltan Food Corp in sight and the excitement of my relationship with Taylor. I have a million butterflies dancing inside of me and they have sapped my hunger.

I sip my juice and take a moment for myself. I don't have enough of these moments. There is something about the silence of a dark room. My mind slowly moves to thinking of Taylor's smile. It is hard walking away from him each time we are together. The difficulty is in knowing we can't communicate when we are apart. And with dark skies tonight, the clouds won't even yield us the wonderment of looking up to silently communicate and comfort one another. No stars tonight. Despite my optimism, I know there still remain numerous moving parts that can greatly adjust my future and cause it to swing one way or another.

I drink the juice and hear the rustling. I walk toward the staircase and something catches my eye in the dining room. The pillows are disheveled and many of them are cut open. Suddenly, the rustling upstairs becomes concerning. I quietly walk into my office and it is completely tossed. Someone is going through my things searching for something. All that has been taken is the terminal to my desktop. I have other things of value in the room that are untouched. I'm frozen for a moment, unsure of what to do. I take out my phone and call 911. It is clear someone has been in this house with bad intentions and they *could* still be inside.

"There's somebody here," I whisper. I listen as the 911 operator asks for my address and then the movement upstairs stops. I stop, lifting my head away from the phone. I listen as a creak sounds behind me and—

———————

I awake in the hospital with a bandage on my head. Aiden is sitting by my bedside. He has an annoyed look on his face. I'm fine except for a headache and being a little woozy.

"When were you going to tell me a police detective was checking on our family's safety?" Aiden is upset. There is no: *how are you? How are you feeling?* He dives right into being angry and frustrated, an old shoe we fit perfectly in together. How is it possible that there are men stalking you and you don't even tell me about it? You put yourself, our kids, and me in danger by not telling me.

"What would you do? I told the police, Aiden. I took care of it, just like I take care of everything else." I fire back, not much in the mood for a lecture. We may have fallen out of love with one another, but I would think he'd at least ask how I was before diving into an argument in the hospital.

"Right, Nick, it's all you. It's always all about you." Aiden's resentment shines center stage as he spews angry venom from his bitter-toned tongue.

"There *you* are. Finally. There you are." I am satisfied to hear my husband finally speak from the heart. "You have been angry I went back to work and finally you admit it. Finally, you speak from the inside. Finally—,"

"—Get off the soapbox, Nick. I don't want to hear it. I don't need the rhetoric. Yes, I know big words too." Aiden has come to play. This is all long overdue.

"I'll take this over silence any day," I fire back, preferring he speak his mind than suffer in silence.

"So this is what you want? This is what you want, right before Thanksgiving? Right before Christmas? You want the war? You want the all-out war?!" Aiden thunders away like never before.

"Where are we, Aiden? Where are we both?" I ask a fair question and see if Aiden's honesty persists.

"We are nowhere right now. We are lost," Aiden eloquently speaks.

A subtle knock on the open door grabs our attention. Detective Craig Howard is standing at the doorway. "Ms. Connolly, excuse me if I'm interrupting." Detective Howard, as usual, is very courteous.

"No. It's all right. Come in," I welcome him into the room.

Aiden turns, exasperated. He, seemingly, has had enough of it all. He takes a seat in a chair in the corner of the room and waits to hear what is coming next.

"I spoke with your husband a few minutes ago. There doesn't seem to be much missing from your house except the computer from your office. Papers are everywhere and there's no real way to know if some of them are missing unless you tell us. But any other valuable in the home such as TVs, jewelry, any real valuables that would be easy to grab, weren't even touched. I guess what we're trying to figure out is, what could be so valuable on that computer and in your office that they would want to steal it?" he inquires. Unfortunately, his inquiry is in front of Aiden and will only stoke his angry fires if I tell the truth. The Ramsey Case is heating up and clearly I have put myself and, potentially, my family in danger. I see that now, but there was nothing at home that would be worth stealing. One mystery after another unfolds before me, and only after we got an increased offer from Albert Penn.

"Are there any prints?" I go straight for answers. I'm not interested in answering questions. This only angers me further. I want to know who did this. Are there leads? I want to nail Beltan to the wall.

"You're obsessed," Aiden decrees. He rarely would ever speak his mind and it is even rarer for him to do it before a group of onlookers. He clearly is fed up with me and has no more patience.

"I want answers," I declare.

"I don't know yet. We canvased the house but there doesn't look like any easy leads. My guess is they wore gloves and left nothing behind. This doesn't look like the work of rogue criminals." Detective Howard is right on. It's not random criminals. They were after me and whatever I have inside the house. But, they didn't find it. They didn't find anything. The original flash drive is hidden safely in a false drawer in my desk at work. Nobody knows but me.

"This is about the case, isn't it?" Aiden asks. He has no idea how intense things are getting. If he even knew there was the first hundred million dollar offer and it was rejected, he'd probably lose his mind. This case has consumed us . . . it's consumed our marriage. But, in reality, our marriage clearly wasn't strong enough to begin with. We should be able to conquer all. I may live in a fantasy world, but these challenges we're facing?—we should walk hand-in-hand and face together. But we haven't. We aren't holding hands. We are two individual boats, sailing far away from one another in the cloak of night.

"So, you think it might be those men?" Detective Howard asks.

"What men?" Aiden is again faced with new information.

"There are some people who may have been following me."

"Jesus, Nick!" Aiden erupts again, this time getting up. He seems beside himself.

"Where are the kids?" I ask Aiden. I don't want them standing outside the hospital room listening to any of this.

"The girls are with your friend, Jessica. We were at Tara's, on a play date together, when I got the call. The police said you had called 911 and were accosted. I didn't want the kids to see, so I left them behind. But, we're going to be going to my parents tonight." Aiden's declaration is a definitive decision. He has no interest in my input, but in this case, I agree.

"All right."

"Listen. I'm . . . I need to get going. The kids have to get showered and to bed." Aiden returns back to silence, retracting back into his former self. He has no interest in fighting any more. His only interest is to get away from me, I guess.

"All right." I, too, have no more interest in fighting.

Aiden turns to Detective Howard. "Here's my card. Please call me and let me know what's going on with my family. My wife has failed miserably at doing so." Aiden hands him the card. He pauses and looks back at me. "I really do hope you feel better." And with that, Aiden exits.

Detective Howard turns back to me with his eyes wide open, probably a little uncomfortable by the marital exchange.

"I'm sorry about that," my apology is paper thin. I could care less about the argument, but I feel like it should not have happened in front of Craig Howard. He had no business having to listen to that.

"It's all right. I'm married. I've been there," he says with a smile.

"You're kind. But, you haven't been here."

"You're right. Thankfully, I have not." Detective Howard gathers himself and reviews his notes.

"The man who had been following me is now working in my law office. I don't know who did this because they hit me from behind. I never heard or saw a thing." I let the detective know everything I know.

"He now works in your office?" He seems as confused as I am.

"Yeah. I can't really explain it either. Something is wrong. But, when you're dealing with a multi-billion dollar company, that has the reach of this one, and there's this much at stake, I guess I was naïve to think it would be easier. I was naïve to think I could handle this all on my own."

"You're not on your own," Taylor states, standing at the doorway. My eyes light up upon seeing him enter the room. Then, I realize Aiden just left. I throw a nervous look. "It's all right. Aiden's gone. I made certain." Taylor and I can't stop staring at one another. Our eyes are fully engaged.

"Okay. If you think of anything else, let me know," Detective Howard grasps our attention back. "In the meantime, we'll have a car outside your home until this case concludes.

"Thank you."

Detective Howard walks by Taylor. "You be good," he warns his close friend.

"Aren't I always?" Taylor says with his trademark grin, showing off his pearly whites.

"That's what concerns me," Detective Howard jokes and pats Taylor on the shoulder on his way out of the hospital room. Taylor walks over to the bed.

"I think visiting hours are over," I alert him.

"It's a funny thing. My father donated a lot of money to this hospital in his day and if you'd believe it, he was a board member to the day he died. So…"

"So, you get to do what you want." I smile and shake my head at the charmed man.

"Well. I can't do MRI's for fun. But, I can break curfew here and there."

"Of course you can."

Taylor sits by my side and runs his hands along the side of my face. "Are you all right?"

"I'm fine. I just have to be here one night for observation." I relay the doctor's message.

I am exhausted and fall asleep with Taylor sleeping by my side, in an uncomfortable chair. When I awake, in the middle of the night, he is on the bed with me, side by side. I smile and turn, resting my head on his chest. One of the scariest nights that have ever happened to me has turned into something different now. My hero came to sleep by my side. *What a day.*

I wake up in the morning and I see a glass of orange juice, a freshly made spinach and cheese omelet with fresh cut avocado on top, sliced oranges, wheat toast, and a single red rose. A small hand written note reads:

To a wonderful start to the day, partner. I had to head out, but I will check in later.

Feel better! If you have any doubts, just look to the stars.

Taylor-

Taylor keeps the note simple, perfect, and just vague enough in case someone else looked at it. I am definitely falling in love with him. I will not deny it. I am not going to pretend the feelings aren't strong just to protect myself. It is crazy. He is a little younger than me and the odds are stacked super-heavy against us. The fact that I'm married to Aiden is a big hurdle. I have two kids. The list goes on for reasons why we probably won't work. But, I don't give a crap any more. I've never just *gone for it* in life. I've never put all my chips in. So, if this is where I take my stand, if there is where I look life in the eyes and say, *I deserve more,* then so be it.

I look over at my phone and see two texts. Ronald and Angie. Oh, thank God they're still talking to me. I have far too few friends in this world to lose them. I make an appointment for lunch with them. I'm bringing them both together. I have a plan and I won't be stopped.

Once I'm released from the hospital and dressed, I step downstairs and Angie is waiting with Ronald in the passenger seat in her old BMW. "Oh, my God! Are you okay?" Angie rushes out of her car, concerned.

"Why didn't you tell us, honey?" Ronald steps out of the car, as well, to greet me. They both are overly concerned but I can't say getting some attention isn't nice.

"I was sorta unconscious," I joke with Ronald. "But I'm fine. I'm good."

"Who did it?" Angie asks.

"It's this case, isn't it?" Ronald is far too smart to think otherwise.

"Let's just go to lunch. It's on me," I tell my two best allies.

"It better be on you! We're both out of work!" Ronald jokes.

We get into the car and head to California Pizza Kitchen. We stare at a gorgeous pie Ronald hand-picked out. As we start to eat, I tell them exactly why they are here with me.

"I'm hiring you both," I start, getting right to the point.

"What are you talking about? Rapture and Myers canned us." I can tell Angie still feels the sting from getting terminated.

"Yeah. And what makes you think I'm available? Ronny is in demand, honey," Ronald jokes.

"You get another job yet, Ron?" I ask with a smile.

"No. I don't even know how to make resumes!" Ronald laughs.

"You guys are mine. You're *my* team. We've always been a team at work and you're the best two people I could have by my side." I make my pitch.

"But, how?" Angie still has an issue figuring this out.

"I'm going to get you paid. I'm not positive how. But I'm going to figure that out."

"Honey, you had us at *hello*," Ronald jokes.

We have a nice moment together—a great lunch. Now I have to figure out how to pay my good friends. As we smile and eat a text comes over my phone.

Be in Laughlin, Nevada tomorrow. More details to follow.

The text is from my whistle-blower. Game on.

Twenty Nine

I have to go back into my house. Taylor is driving me this time. We aren't waiting until tomorrow to head to the desert, we are heading there today. Taylor's desert oasis is in Nevada, between Las Vegas and Laughlin, providing us the perfect hold-up as we wait to contact the strange man.

I texted Aiden, but he was less than thrilled about me heading to Nevada. All he replied with was: *Be safe. We have to talk when you get back.*

With my car still in the driveway, Taylor parks behind me and I enter my house. I'm not traumatized. It's just weird to think people were in here. I never saw a face, so getting smacked over the head and being knocked out for a little while is better than being attacked head-on. I guess it's splitting hairs, but I feel like I shouldn't feel scared. I just don't feel right.

Taylor follows me inside, just as I finish being sick and head upstairs. The house is still a mess. Neither Aiden nor I have been home to clean up. I feel guilty leaving things this way, but I have to go. I have to finish this once and for all. I can't say I even want to practice law tomorrow, but today . . . I have to finish this. There are too many desperate people counting on me.

I get my clothes and Taylor drives us by the girls' school. He remains in the car as I make my way inside. I refuse to leave town without giving both Lacy and Ariel kisses and hugs. I pull them out of class for a moment.

"Are you okay, mom?" Lacy asks. She is always sensitive to things.

"I am. I'm good, honey," I genuinely reply.

"I love you. I'm proud of you for what you're doing for all those people. I like that you help people that can't help themselves. I know it takes you away from us, but you're doing a good thing. I'm proud of you." Lacy nearly brings me to tears. No person on this earth could have said those words and made me feel that way. My daughters are so important, and for my oldest to understand, even in the littlest bit, what I'm doing, is huge to me. It brings great relief to my psyche and is a burden removed off my shoulders.

"I couldn't be prouder of you, girls, darling. I love you, guys." I give her a big hug, a couple tears sneaking down my face. It doesn't happen often, but they are worth if for what Lacy just gave me.

I grab my little Ariel and squeeze her tight, giving her a big hug and kiss. These little ones are too much. They melt my heart.

After I say my goodbyes, it's off to Nevada. The drive is nice. Taylor keeps the car top on, so there won't be too much light. It's a beautiful, sunny afternoon with puffy clouds in the sky. The weather is absolutely perfect—a crisp sixty degrees. I keep my sunglasses on just in case my eyes get too sensitive to light. The doctors didn't think that would be a problem either, but I don't feel like having another headache today.

I am exhausted from everything and find myself happily falling in and out of sleep. I feel safe, and I need the rest. I feel spent. It's all so much. Hopefully this trip will yield even better news for Ramsey and take care of the case. I can only hope. I'm anxious to find out what the mystery man will say this time.

Within no time, we crossed the Nevada border and now, two hours later, arrive at Taylor's childhood home. It is an epic estate, to say the least. The nearly six hour drive was worth the wait. The estate looks huge and spacious, like a compound of many buildings surrounded by wrought iron fences with sharp points at the top. This truly is a massive oasis in the middle of the desert. The Mexican-style villa is meticulously built, every trim and piece of architecture; a compliment to the grand portrait. The house is edged with finely cut, adobe tiled roofing. The white exterior is marked and highlighted by flashes of red clay with the window sills and shutters matching the roof top. The grounds themselves are finely groomed; green plants and vibrant flowers, marking the edges of the cobblestone leading to the front entrance of the home. The land is surrounded by desert and cacti. The Diamond Estate: etchings of DE are marked on the front gate as well as the front door, to personify where exactly a visitor has landed. The crest on the door with the DE logo is truly remarkable, handmade white gold plated lettering attached to castle-like double door entrance. The wood doors are huge, standing nearly nine feet in height. They appear thick, with steel fixtures and bolts holding the giant entryway together. I feel as though I am entering a magnificent castle. It is almost surreal.

"Holy shit. You grew up here?" I ask in envy of what I'm seeing.

"Yeah. Now it's used as a vacation home, for the most part. There's staff that live here year-round though. They have to take care of the grounds and the animals," Taylor nonchalantly states.

"The animals?" I ask in a curious fashion.

"Oh, yes. My father loved exotic animals. There are a few here. It's all a little too much for me . . . this place. It's like living in a different realm of reality from the world. It's magnificent, yes, but also displaces you from everyone else." Taylor's words are introspective. Being rich isn't a crime. He needs no apologies to me. I'm just happy to have made the trip and see this amazing estate. The fascinating part is I've only looked at the outside.

We stand by the front door and wait a moment. "What are we waiting for?" I ask as Taylor carries both his and my bag.

"It's what we do. They know we're here," he confidently states. And no sooner does he say it, a loud unlocking sound occur, the kind of sound when someone unhinges a twenty pound lock. It truly is a set of castle doors.

The two massive doors slowly open inward. Now their true thickness is visible. Each door is over six inches thick of solid wood, making me think the doors themselves weigh a ton a piece. "Wow." Just looking at the doors awe me.

"You haven't seen anything yet. My father, he built this for my mother . . . for us. He thought if he built a dream house, no one would ever leave—we'd never get tired of it. We'd deal with him never being there." Taylor gives some insight to his childhood and just a few of his family's issues.

"Welcome to Diamond Estates," the voice of a small man bellows out from inside the estate's hallowed walls. The small, old, man steps forward in a white tuxedo. He has dark skin, a thick Chilean accent, and tremendous pride for his job as showcased by his ear to ear smile.

"Thank you," I kindly respond.

"Hello, Benjamin," Taylor says endearingly. "It's wonderful to see you, sir. Welcome home," he returns with the same emotional tone as Taylor. Benjamin is clearly a professional, but you can tell he is part of Taylor's family. Taylor and I step forward, Benjamin taking the bags from Taylor without a word.

"Ben," Taylor tries to stop him.

"Not a chance, sir. You know the rules." Benjamin races away with the bags, leaving a smile on Taylor's face.

Taylor turns to me. "He's family. He also takes his job seriously. Benjamin takes care of the house. It's his home as much as mine." Taylor is so giving and kind. He's nothing like the, self-professed, *bad boy* and *playboy* he claimed to be at one time.

We enter the vestibule, a beautiful naturally lit area (due to the glass ceiling), connecting the front door to the rest of the house. Two cast iron cocktail tables sit on either side, between sets of chairs. *What an entrance.*

Entering the house requires stepping through the French doors that Benjamin left open for us. As I step through them, I enter an entirely different world. It's darker in the main entranceway to the house. I am struck by solid oak flooring that spreads throughout the first floor as far as I can see. A massive crystal chandelier hangs from the center of the room. The structure hangs down from the vaulted ceiling with a spiral staircase curling up around it, leading to a second story. There are doors, openings to hallways and of course the grand staircase.

I am simply awestruck by the works of art on the walls and gorgeous vases on nice antique tables, set along the walls. I am limited in my knowledge of art, but I can see genius and beauty and recognize the paintings from somewhere. "Those are amazing," I share my awe out loud.

"They are originals. My father donated a lot of artwork to various museums, but he kept his favorites. He liked Monet and van Gogh the most. We have a few of those. Also, he loved unknown artists. He would buy paintings from contemporary artists who nobody knew, but their skills were unmatched. Tragic, when you think about it."

"What's that?" I ask.

"They are only appreciated once they are dead. A terrible irony to greatness don't you think?"

I nod in agreement. I see a strikingly beautiful, black grand piano off in the distance.

"A piano? I had a smaller one when I was younger." I point out.

"Yes. Do you play?"

"A long time ago. My grandmother used to play. It was hers, and she lived with us for a while until she passed away. She used to make me play all the time. The 'Moonlight Sonata'," I share. "It was always my favorite."

"Ah . . . Beethoven." Do you want to play now?" he offers.

"No, no. I haven't. Not in a long time. I—not right now." I shake my head adamantly.

"Okay." Taylor gives me a little understanding wink.

"What about you? Do you play?"

"Just for fun." He shrugs. I nod and we both have a silent moment. Then, we move on.

Taylor takes me down a hall that has glass encased artifacts and treasures from all over the world. This is like a museum in itself. The walls are covered with more artwork and each room seems to have its own décor. The finely crafted wood floors run throughout the house but burnt bronze fixtures mark the long hall. Taylor refers to it the *Untouchable Room.* It is a train car-like room, filled with the artifacts, wall-to-wall paintings and expensive brass craftsmanship highlighting the ceiling and creating designs, flowing freely through and in between the art. Then there is the dining room. A massive table with sconces lit on the wall. The room has no windows, so its enclosed nature leaves it quaint, dark, and quiet. A small brass chandelier hangs above the long table and more artwork decorates the wall, including a Jackson Pollock. I can tell because I'd know that splatter paint anywhere.

The kitchen is a massive cookery with multiple ovens and a huge island. There is a nook as well as a white table with chairs. Large glass doors lead to a deck, which then leads to a huge pool with its own small waterfall. The deck has outdoor seating and a perfect view of desert; the sun and mountains in the near distance. I can't believe my eyes with the pool. It is surrounded by actual rock and more gardens, which not only decorate around the pool, but some have become part of the pool. This is a work of art itself.

One room after another seems grander, more impressive. Then we head downstairs, through the kitchen, which leads to an underground cave. The cave too has torches to light its way. Nearby is an adjoining wine cellar, its door guarded and a high-tech air control system keeps everything just right. You can see all the rows of wine through the glass walls. And the cave, itself, is something special. A Jacuzzi sits above the pool, the water gently overflowing into the twenty foot, indoor swimming structure. It is smaller than the pool upstairs, but far more private.

"I can't believe all of this," I again sound like an awestruck child.

"I want to show you one more thing. My favorite."

I nod and follow him. We go back upstairs and exit out to the backyard. We exit through a lavish dining room, more art with perfectly twined, authentic Asian rugs donning the floor, and crossed samurai swords donning the walls. Painted glass paned doors lead to the backyard where large enclosures stand erected. It's as if I walked out of the house and entered the San Diego Zoo. A lion. Then I see a Siberian Tiger. And over there, a panther. Extraordinary, deadly animals, lying and basking in the sun. It rains over the lion's cage, built-in water systems provide relief in the heat and help to water the terrain.

"Holy shit," I utter.

"Yeah. It's something else. We had more, but we thought it best to get them to a zoo. Not many people around here anymore."

"Yeah. That would make sense," I mutter. "Weren't you scared as a child?"

"No need. Doug here!" The African tone draws my eyes behind us and I see a dark-skinned man in a tan suit. His wide-brimmed, round, tan hat matches his outfit.

"Doug!" Taylor and Doug share a hug.

"I have missed you, boy."

"I missed you too, Doug. Sorry I've been so busy." Taylor makes an excuse for not visiting but I feel as though his childhood could have more to do with not being here than his business.

"Do you pet them?" I ask. I have no idea what to think of the massive, intimidating creatures.

"No, no." Doug chuckles at me. "Ever since Mr. Diamond, God rest his soul, brought these animals home, we have provided sanctuary. They are not domesticated, but can no longer survive in the wild. So, we spoil them rotten. I sometimes will play, but it isn't child's play; very, very dangerous creatures." Doug makes it sound all so easy while, at the same time, reminding me how deadly the animals are. I nod. It is all a great deal to take in, and I haven't even visited the second story. I do look up and see that there are numerous balconies on the second story that overlook the animal sanctuaries. What a sight it must be to live along the side of such creatures.

"Are you hungry?" Taylor asks.

"I can go for a swim." I smile.

"Okay. Swimming it is."

"I don't have a bathing suit, however."

"Then we can just go skinny dipping," he says nonchalantly.

"This is where I break off. I will see you both again." Doug walks away, leaving us to our decision of swimming naked or not.

"You embarrassed Doug," I tease Taylor, but, also, I'm a little embarrassed too.

"No. If we go to the pool, Ben will leave us drinks and towels and disappear. They are ghosts when we are here. It's what they do."

I nod. This world is so foreign to me. I let Taylor guide me through.

───────────

Taylor dives into the pool as I sit with a towel around me. I look around, not completely trusting we'll be alone. The sun is dipping behind the desert; a beautiful seventy-five degrees here. It's warmer than where we came from. I watch Taylor as he swims laps, sticking my feet into the perfectly heated water. I look around. We are alone, although, I know there are others who live here. It's an odd feeling.

Lights come on and provide illumination all around the compound, including the pool area. Taylor swims up to me, darkness gaining more and more on what's left of the light of day.

"Nobody is watching," he reiterates.

"This place is crazy."

"I know. It's another world. I told you."

"I don't even know where my bag is. It took thirty minutes just to walk through the downstairs and see the zoo. I mean—a freakin' zoo!" I shake my head at all the amazing things I've seen.

"Let's go down to the cave."

"Okay."

I get up to walk away and glance back, seeing Taylor's naked body emerge from the warm water as he moves over to his towel. His body wet is too good to resist, too much not to stare at. All of a sudden, I'm brought back home. Surrounded by the magnificent desert palace, seeing Taylor and the water running down his toned, perfect body brings me back to my reality. I take a deep breath—an excited deep breath. And we head down to the cave. We go straight for the Jacuzzi. I have no problem taking my towel off for this. I sit in the Jacuzzi—naked—enjoying every bit of the freedom of it all. By the pool on the surface, I didn't feel relaxed. Now, down here in the cave with Taylor, this is perfect. He exits the wine cellar, the glass door closing behind him and locking.

"It's cold in there. So, you can't look when I get in the water," Taylor jokes. He comes over with the bottle of wine already opened.

"I promise I'll only peek a little," I reply with a devilish grin. Taylor pops in and steam starts to rise off of us. He hands me the wine.

"No fine Carriage glasses?" I ask with a smile.

"This time we go old school—straight from the bottle," he jokes back.

"Why did you leave?" I ask, my voice echoing inside the cave.

"Here?"

"Yeah. Why did you leave this place?—really. I want to know more. I want to understand more about him.

"Not an easy question."

"It's a cave question," I jest with a smirk on my face as we pass the bottle of wine back and forth, each taking small sips, savoring it.

"Yes. I guess it is." He takes a moment, thinking to himself. "When you're born into a life—a life with many expectations—you have little wiggle room I stood tall on the shoulders of a powerful man and had nowhere to go but down. His expectations were high. I don't even recall a moment when he said the words, '*I'm proud of you, son*'. There were never pats on the backs or hugs. It was tough love . . . silent love. He wasn't a man who kissed me goodnight. He wasn't a man that made apologies for his shortcomings. He was a hard man. And I barely knew him. He traveled a lot, always away on business. He left us on this island. He built this castle for us and then never came back—at least not emotionally. He was a complicated man, and this place used to make me angry. It used to make me think of him . . . of his isolation. So, I ran. I ran as fast as I could, doing as many stupid things as possible. I lived a life many would dream about; no cares, no concerns for money. I just lived casually and irresponsibly. That's what this place and my father did . . . or, so I thought. Then I came to the realization that I am my own man. I can create my own legacy. I don't need to live in his shadow. I just didn't realize that while he was alive. I often wonder how he would have reacted." Taylor's look into his past is invigorating to me. It's a bird's-eye view of how he became the man he is versus the boy he was.

We drink more wine and enjoy the heat.

"What about you?" he breaks the silence after a few minutes.

"Me?"

"Any sad stories?" Taylor asks, half making fun of his own revelations to me.

"Ah. Growing up? None. No sad stories to speak of. Nothing like yours."

"It's ironic, isn't it?"

"What's that?" I ask.

"It's ironic that my family has had all the money in the world and it took a long while for me to grow up and be a man. And you, your family's from the desert, poor, and yet you fought and scrapped your way to a partnership in a world where women struggle to thrive. You are my hero, Nicki."

I look down, Taylor humbling me. It's nice to be appreciated and it's something Taylor has been very good at. Suddenly, a red light flashes twice in the corner of the room. It's a light I did not know existed, buried into the cave and hidden. "What is that?"

"It's Benjamin. He's just letting us know dinner is ready, if we want."

"I could eat a little." I admit.

"You must be starving. You slept through my Del Taco run in Barstow and haven't eaten all day."

"I haven't been hungry lately. But I'm excited to see what Benjamin has made."

"Oh, not Benjamin. Rosetta does the cooking," he corrects me.

"Rosetta?"

"Yes. She is the housekeeper here. When Estella moved to California with me to be closer to her children, Rosetta, her cousin, moved in to the estate here."

We dry off and bring the bottle of wine with us to the dining room. Candles are lit on the table and the atmosphere is romantic. A roasted duck with many fixings is set on the table. A dozen red roses provide a splash of romance and elegance. Fine china and gold plated silverware are set up for us. The table is set with the two place settings on either side of the long table, each of us expected to sit at either head. Taylor and I sit down and stare at one another from across the table. We are nearly twenty feet part in the massively long table.

"Do you need anything?" Taylor asks, half-shouting from across the room to ensure I can hear him.

"This is easily the longest table I've ever seen." I smile at the enormity of the table.

Taylor nods and grabs his things, moving closer to me.

"How about we eat together," Taylor says as he sets himself next to me.

"Did your parents eat this far apart?"

"When my father was here, they did. My mother at one end and my father at the other. A huge divide between them. It's tradition."

"This is really good!" I say as I nibble at my food.

"Rosetta can cook. She and Estella are the best," Taylor boasts.

"Where do you think we'll be in a couple of years?" It's a question I like to pose to Taylor. I guess it's the young girl in me.

"I can tell you where I want to be. I want to be with you." Taylor smiles and we continue to eat, finishing our nice dinner.

After dinner we make our way upstairs to *our* room. It is the size of two master bedrooms combined. It has an attached sitting room with another classic chandelier, hanging from the ceiling. Everywhere I look, I see art, chandeliers, and precious antiques. It isn't exactly the kind of home you would expect a child to grow up in. It is the home of an exquisite man who had exquisite tastes.

Taylor sits on the bed and looks fondly at me. He is displaying a glowing smile. "What?" I ask.

"I wasn't sure we'd get another night together. I didn't think we'd have this chance again," he states with relief. He has a serene happiness to him. And as I stare at him, I realize that even though I've been tired all day, I am now infused with the same kind of romantic energy brewing in Taylor. And in my mind, I establish a new sex playbook—a new level of excitement for me to work from.

THE PLAYBOOK TO NICKI'S BIG**GER**-O

Step 1: Begin with a hot couples shower. Oral pleasure is a must, and each participant should wash one another. (note: If hair needs to be washed, wash hair prior to oral stimulation for relaxing pleasure.)

Step 1A: If participants wish to not shower, sexual stimulation in other areas of the house, via oral or penetration, are encouraged. Such areas include: the stairs, kitchen, living room, bathrooms, couches; anywhere you can stand, sit, or lie down.

Step 2: After oral stimulation in the shower (may or may not result in orgasm number one), proceed to the bed for sexual penetration. (note: If additional oral pleasure is engaged, that works too—the more the merrier.) Feel free to use alcohol for body shots and food for . . . well . . . everything.

Step 3: Dealer's Choice: The sexual positions will not begin the same way every time. The way we engage in sex will be facilitated by our mood. The starting position can be from behind, flat stomach position, missionary, side-ways, upside down, etc.

Step 4: Kissing is a MUST! To ensure that maximum stimulation and build is complete, ensure a great deal of kissing and passion before and during all facets of intercourse,

Step 5: Vary the positions during sex. Go hog-wild moving from position to position. Make it fun and random. Let the sex be your guide. Don't hold back, but don't go too fast. Make it last.

Step 6: I move to on top to ride (If I didn't already finish). I'll start slow and gradually increase my pace. I'll find my sweet spot and allow him to be as creative as he would like with his hands. Maybe I'll have him tied up in a vulnerable state. Maybe I can blindfold him. I have no bounds.

Step 7: HFO: Huge Fuckin Orgasm.

Step 8: Lie next to Taylor Diamond and enjoy every bit of the sex we have. Hopefully it never ends.

End of Playbook.

Taylor leaves the bedroom and I think about my new playbook and how I would love to engage Taylor in it this evening. I'm feeling frisky after a day of doing very little and having some wine tonight. I reach into my bag and pull out the sexy, expensive, purple lingerie Jessica had bought me. I love the way it looks and I walk over to the balcony and stare out into the clear night, taking hold of the silk curtains to wrap cover myself, just in case. There is nothing around to disturb us. I see the animal sanctuaries down below. Most of them are asleep, except for the lion. I watch the lion, feeling sexier as the silk caresses my body.

"Wow," Taylor says from behind me. I turn my head and find him staring at me from just inside the bedroom door he just closed. The moonlight is shining into the room from behind me creating a picturesque view for Taylor to feast on. The lace, purple lingerie is a nice touch, and I see his mouth hang open.

"Thanks," I reply in kind. There doesn't need to be too many words. He moves over to me slowly as I remain wrapped in the see-through silk curtains. I make Taylor slowly unwrap them as if I were his present. He unravels it all and pulls my, mostly naked, body closer to his. His eyes can't communicate how badly he wants me anymore than they are. I can see he is looking to take me. And with the game plan, that I formed, all set for the night, we begin.

After going through the first two steps, our hot showers together becoming a favorite past time of ours, I move straight to *Step 6*. But instead of me getting on top of Taylor, I have something else in store for him. I roll his naked body over and say, "Get on your stomach."

Taylor looks a bit nervous at first, my suggestion frightening him just a little. "You'll be nice?" he asks with a smirk on his face.

"No promises," I reply with a devilish grin. He lies on his stomach and I grab the scarf I had in my bag. I gently tie it around Taylor's eyes, making him blind. I take out the massage oil I had brought, warm, exotic oil I found one time in my limited travels. I apply the oil to his back and break up our evening of sexual conquest with a relaxing back massage. He moans and groans as I relieve his stresses, working his body over. From his back, I move to his thighs, making sure to press just right on his perfectly round butt, working it out as well (*that being more for me.*). I run my hands down his hamstrings, to his calves, and all the way to his toes. I make sure I oil him up good as I work on him. Then back up to his neck for the finish. I make sure he enjoys his neck rub and he is perfectly, blissfully relaxed. Some may think it's not smart to relax a man; their urge to have sexual intercourse could dwindle. But as I roll Taylor onto his back, I have plans of my own. I work on his chest and shoulders. As I rub, his subtle sounds of pleasure make me excited. Our oral exchange in the shower already got me going. So, this is cherry on the cake. I move south right past his member to his thighs. I rub his thighs and move down to his feet once again, making sure I didn't miss any part of his body. Then, my hand slides up to his penis. The key is to not apply oil, this way his penis won't be too slippery when I mount him . . . which is coming shortly—*as will I.* I rub up and down, switching between the use of one hand and two. I make sure the rolling motion of my hands brings him to maximum excitement. But not too excited! I don't want him finishing yet. He is going to finish in me, after I finish riding him. My plan is perfect, and just before I can mount him, his fingers slip inside my pussy. It delays me just a moment.

"Oh, yes," I moan. I wasn't expecting his fingers to probe me again. It delays my plans, but only momentarily. I'm the captain of this ship tonight and I break away from his fingers and get on top of my fully erect mate. I start to ride him, his blind hands searching my body for my breasts. I love that he can't see me. It's empowering and I always worry about my *sex face*. I lean forward just a bit, kissing his neck and face. I drop my breast down near his lips, begging him to lick. And he obliges. He licks my nipple and then starts to suck on it. He is so gentle—so perfect with his lips. I want to go slow, but I'm worked up too much and I take off, pulling back, riding him hard.

I'm relentless. I can't imagine this ever getting routine, us ever getting boring. I ride and ride, my body already built up from the shower and the massage. I'm a sensual being, bursting at the seams. His body is oily, and I love it. I love my hands running against him, my body rubbing upon him.

We are one perfect, sexual object, moving in unison together until our inevitable end arrives. I start to explode; the release is something I really needed. I start to grind Taylor out, the amazing feeling causing me to slow. As I clamp down on him and roll slowly, he bows up just a bit, he, too, is finishing. I feel his body strain, the moans increasing from his mouth. His release is just after mine, and as I slow, we both happily breathe. I remove the scarf from his face, allowing him to once again see.

"I love you," the words trickle out of his mouth so smoothly. I dive down upon him, my lips going right after his. I am speechless and can only kiss him over and over again.

Thirty

I awake in Taylor's arms. His body is wrapped around me, just as we fell asleep. I turn toward him, seeing his eyes already open. I bring my hand over my mouth, well aware I have morning breath.

"You're awake."

Taylor smiles at me covering my mouth and mimics my oral safety measures. "You were so peaceful."

"I love you, too," I say with all my heart. I never thought those words would mean so much. Each time you fall for someone, each time you have those butterflies, you want it to be this way—you want it to be the fantasy, to be perfect. Taylor smiles as if he already knew. "So, what now?" I ask a question Taylor and I seem to be faced with at every turn.

"Now? Now, we eat breakfast," he states with simplicity. I smile and nod in agreement. I finally have an appetite and am looking forward to a freshly made breakfast.

We get ourselves together and head down to the kitchen. We are going to eat out on the deck, just outside the kitchen itself. A fruit plate, omelets, a few crepes, bacon, wheat toast, milk, and orange juice are spread about the table. It's a regular buffet for us. We start to eat, enjoying the morning and the view. "I can live like this," I admit.

Taylor and I look at one another and burst into laughter. Clearly, anyone *could* live like this. It is a dream house—a whole other world, as Taylor pointed out. As we eat, I receive a text.

Be at this address in two hours. 24 Landmark Ave. Fairworth. Await my next word. You may be waiting a while.

I show the text to Taylor. He maps it out. "It will take us about an hour to get there."

"Let's finish up and hit the road."

Taylor nods. We finish eating and get dressed. When we head downstairs Taylor and I part ways. I am heading to the front where his car is parked.

"No, no, Nicki. We're going to be driven there."

"By whom?"

"Pong," Taylor says with one definitive word.

"What's a Pong?"

We head out to a garage I didn't know existed. There are at least half a dozen cars parked in here. Waiting in a chauffer's uniform is Pong. He is a very fit Asian man.

"This is Pong."

Pong bows to me. I do a half-bow back, unsure of what the customary greeting is for this man. "I'm betting you're more than a driver," I deduct. It doesn't take me long to recognize that Pong is simply a wheel-man.

"You are correct," he says with a thick Asian accent.

"Pong is a specialist in many ways. He is a fourth generation samurai. He is a great driver and also tells some great jokes." Taylor smiles as he looks at Pong.

Pong gives Taylor a subtle nod back. "Good to see you again, Mr. Diamond." The Japanese man is in excellent shape.

"Which car are we taking, Pong?"

"I was thinking the Cadillac, sir—just in case."

"Okay," Taylor agrees.

I am a passenger in this decision and have no real idea what's going on. But it all sounds good to me. Pong heads over to the car and stands by the doors. I turn to Taylor, looking for an explanation.

"He is a good man to have on our side. Seeing what has already happened to you—"

"Tay," I place my hand on the side of his face, caressing it, and stopping him from talking. "I am all for it." We definitely could use a little extra cover as we walk into the unknown. Having some experienced muscle can't hurt.

And we go. The Cadillac is quite luxurious and completely stocked. "Why the Cadillac?" I ask out of curiosity.

"Ah. Pong likes it. It's steel reinforced. The windows are bullet proof. The car is a tank."

Wow, the whole situation seems far scarier now. I wasn't really thinking about safety issues when I started this. I didn't see things getting dangerous in any way. But when I think about all that has happened—all that is happening—danger does seem like a concern at this point. I have been blind, but Taylor is well-aware. He is a confident man who knows his plays before he makes them. He is smart, and protecting the two of us. Pong and the Cadillac are big insurance policies for us.

We arrive in the middle of nowhere. Fairworth is terribly desolate, and the address we are parked at is a beat-up pool hall. The place looks closed but is actually open. It's just so rundown, and the town looks like something out of the old west. We sit and wait. I'm growing anxious, but there is really nothing more we can do. At first, we just sit in the car. Almost no one goes in or out of the pool hall. Maybe it's another bathroom meet?

After an hour of window shopping from the car I grow antsy. "Let's go inside and wait," I implore.

Taylor nods. He knocks on the glass divide. It's not a normal feature in Cadillac's. I can only assume the senior Diamond had it put in, so he'd have complete privacy in all matters. The glass rolls down. "We're going to wait inside," Taylor relays to Pong.

Pong nods.

We head inside the old pool hall. There's a bar attached and as we enter, you can smell the stench of beer and hear the cool rhythm of 1970s rock music blasting out of a jukebox. It sets the entire mood in the hall, making me feel like I'm back in the movie *The Color of Money*. I love pool halls; they were part of my teenage years, and I am a deadly shot.

The mood wouldn't be set if not for a smattering of rift-raft; locals here to shoot and drink.

"Do you recognize anyone?" Taylor asks as we scan around the hall.

"I don't think I would even know if he was here." I try to look without being too obvious. No one looks familiar to me. It is difficult to pick the mystery man out of a line-up, when I barely got a glimpse of the side of his face.

We sit on two stools at a high bar table and wait. We wait so long, the waitress grows annoyed with our presence; we haven't ordered a single drink during her multiple trips to us. 3pm passes and nothing. Taylor grows tired of doing nothing and finally orders a drink—honey whiskey on the rocks. I just get water. The waitress nods as if thinking to herself, *finally*, and heads off to get our drinks.

The door jingles every fifteen minutes or so as a person exits or enters. Regulars, bikers, people who are looking to disappear for a few minutes and have a good time. After receiving our drinks, I down mine. Within moments, the water runs through me and I need to pee. "I have to go to the bathroom."

Taylor nods and I wander off. I stroll into the ladies room and as I enter, I wonder, *is he in here waiting for me again?* There are three stalls and I bend down, looking to see if anyone's feet are hanging. I slowly push open one stall, then another, and finally the last. Nothing. No one. I look up and see a small barred window that no human could fit through even if there weren't iron bars on it. He is not here.

After I go to the bathroom, I wash my hands. The beat-up bathroom hardly fazes me on this covert mission. I take a deep breath and turn into a waiting body. I jump slightly, caught off guard. It's a tattooed biker chick. I am uncertain what will happen next.

"Excuse me," she says. That was it. And she disappears into a stall. I nod and smile, the tension of the situation getting the best of me.

I walk back out and Taylor has a rack of balls and couple of pool sticks. *Why not,* I think. He gives me the same look with a smirk on his face. "Nine ball," I proclaim.

"What's that?" he asks.

"Nine ball. That's my game," I say with pride.

Taylor smiles and stares at me as if not believing a word out of my mouth. "Nine ball? That's your game?" he mocks me a little with his tone.

"That's right." I proudly stick out my chest.

"Okay. We'll see."

"I'm no ordinary bar bunny, Mr. Diamond," I joke with my hand on my side.

Taylor smiles, seemingly amused. "No, you're definitely not." He gives me *that* look. He grins and smiles at me lovingly, as if I am the only girl in the world. I love that look.

"I'll break," I volunteer.

"Ladies first." He happily steps aside for me.

I chalk my stick and line up the break. "What are we playing for?" I casually ask as I close one eye and focus hard on the cue ball.

"What do you want?" Taylor asks with a hint of sensuality, opening the door up to anything.

"Let's start with the winner of game one gets choice of dinner," I offer up.

"Okay. Sounds good."

"I rear back and execute my first break shot, sending them scattering about. The balls chaotically bounce off walls, the nine ball slowly moving toward the back corner pocket. I get two other balls to fall first, then the nine takes her sweet time, but rolls just hard enough to get to the hole and ekes to the edge. After a tense moment, the nine drops inside. Game over.

"Shit," Taylor utters in awe of my skills.

"Le Fritz in Paris, France," I ramble off without hesitation. I read it was an amazing restaurant in some magazine and who wouldn't want to go to Paris? Sure, it's extreme, but why not. "What are we betting next?" I ask. His eyes are opened wide and his mouth is hanging open, in shock over it all.

"So you've played this game a few times before?" Taylor has a big smile on his face, impressed with my stick abilities.

"I know my way around pool halls, yes."

"I better think hard about the next bet," he surmises.

As Taylor starts to rerack the balls again I feel my phone vibrate and I check. A text message: *Head east on Highway 12 to Storage Depot just off Dust Hill Road. When you arrive, text me.*

"What is it?" Taylor asks.

"We gotta go."

We have Pong drive us and arrive at Storage Depot. It's nearly 5pm now and the sun has dipped. Darkness is riding in, but lights around aren't taking effect. Maybe this is what he wanted—darkness with limited lighting; the prefect time of day to hide in plain sight. We arrive at the gate, which is locked. We wait a moment and all of the sudden, the gate starts to open for us. Before Pong moves forward, I see him reach into the glove compartment and pull out a gun. I am again reminded of the seriousness of our situation. He pulls ahead slowly. The storage units are mainly one level with two larger buildings, providing a second story for indoor access. It is deadly silent at Storage Depot with few people in the area. Pong weaves through the facility without any direction.

Another text: *Who is with you?*

Just my partner and our driver, I send back honestly. I don't want to have the contact question me in any way. I don't want to spook him off.

Just you. Second level of containment building 2.

"He says to go to building 2, the second level," I tell Taylor. Pong drives to our destination. I know Taylor won't let me leave the car alone. He will shadow me, so I wait until we get there to try and argue with him.

A Volkswagen is parked a few feet away with a container gate open. We can't see who is inside. But I have to take the stairs to the indoor second level. "Watch that one," Taylor instructs Pong. Pong nods, keeping his eyes ahead on the Volkswagen.

"He wants me to go in alone," I break the bad news to him.

"I can't let you." Taylor is adamant.

"It will be okay. I've met with him before." I try to put his concerns at ease.

"You don't know who *him* is."

"He'll leave if he sees you," I express my concern.

"Then I'll follow behind you—right behind you."

"Okay," I agree to the compromise. Taylor has my best interests at heart, so I'm not going to deny being protected.

I am nervous—very nervous. I feel like puking. I exit the car slowly; dusk quickly turning to darkness. The lights at the center fire on causing me to jump. Taylor waits for me to start walking. I go through the door and disappear into a mostly dark stairway. The light is barely working as I make my way up the cold cement steps. I only hear my own footsteps echoing and the light wind, whistling through the large metal building. My breaths have quickened, my nerves taking hold. I feel as though I'm a lab rat, walking through the metal box. I reach the top of the stairs and carefully look both ways. Nothing.

Storage unit 8, is texted by the mystery man.

I walk around looking at the numbers. I feel a cool breeze and hear a soft click behind me. Sounds like Taylor trailing behind, just entering the building. I continue walking slow, cautious steps. I still see nothing as I walk. I arrive at unit eight and curiously look around. The gate flies open, scaring me half to death. The man is standing before me, wearing a hood and a scarf around his mouth. "You are going the distance," his raspy voice says.

"I am."

"The passcode: CHERRI, with an *I,* all caps, will open the files you want." The man speaks cautiously as if we were spies. The gravity still hasn't gotten to me completely, but I'm getting there.

"Another flash drive?" I ask.

"No. It's already on the one you have. You've had it all along. A small Trojan horse is in the top right corner. It blends into the background. Click it and enter the passcode. You will see everything you want. Go the distance, Nicki," the man urges me.

"Who are you?" I ask.

"Nobody; just a cog in the machine."

There are two doors that slam on our floor, each from opposite ends of the second floor. The man snaps his head around, sensing danger. "They're here," he states with a paranoid tongue.

"Who?" I ask, looking around nervously.

"Listen to me. The man you're with—I know him. He is *not* to be trusted. Keep this secret. Trust NO ONE."

The man runs away, sprinting to a door that reads: *Roof Access.* He rushes through the door and is gone, just like that. A hand grabs my arm. I jump and see it's Taylor. "He just ran away," I say.

"I saw the tail end. We're not alone. We need to hide in here." Taylor backs me in quickly. He reaches up and slowly closes the door, trying to make as little noise as possible. We wait in the darkness. At first, we hear nothing. Then, there are footsteps, two distinctive sets of footsteps. They echo in the metal halls. They also start to get closer and closer, ever-so-slowly. We hear them check storage doors—one at a time, as they move from opposite ends, closing in on our location.

"We have no lock," I whisper, stating the obvious with great concern.

"If they open it, I'm going to charge whoever is there. You run." Taylor urges me in a strained whisper. He quickly gets on his phone and is sending a text.

"No. I won't leave you," I insist.

"You run." Taylor says again, an order he is insistent upon.

"Did you text Pong?"

"Yes," he confirms.

"He won't get here." I am negative, but realistic.

"I know," Taylor ominously agrees. The footsteps get closer and closer and we hold our breath, the moment of truth about to arise. They are almost at our container. The door-to-door search arrives at us. "Get ready," Taylor quietly whispers. He readies himself to charge out and take whoever on. A set of feet arrive at our unit and pause. It's dead silent. Here we go.

Pop! Pop! Two gun shots from outside the building. The feet, near our door, scatter and take off in the opposite direction, their footsteps growing distant as they head outside. I let out a relieved breath of air.

"Come on," Taylor urges me to leave and he slowly opens the door. He steps out first, looking around. We see no one.

"Was that a gun shot?" I ask with concern.

"Sounded like it."

We head toward the door we came through, when it opens and shuts. We pause, not knowing who may be there. Taylor takes no chances. He rushes me away in the opposite direction and we sprint to the far end of the storage floor hoping to exit out one of the far stairwells.

"I got two!" The man shouts from behind us. We don't know who he is and I glance, but only see a man charging toward us with a gun drawn. Taylor yanks me along and we head down the stairs. He leads me to the doors outside. A woman is lying on the ground near the Volkswagen. She looks unconscious—possibly dead—but it is difficult to tell. Pong and the Cadillac are gone.

"Come on," Taylor pulls me along and we wrap around the side of the building, attempting to disappear into the maze of storage unit rows. We run as fast as we can, darkness setting in. I feel as though we are in way over our heads.

Pop! Pop! Again, gun shots sound, causing Taylor and me to hurry against the wall. They came from above our heads, by the rooftops.

"They're behind us and above us." Taylor takes out his phone and presses something.

"Where is Pong?" I whisper with great urgency.

"He is coming," Taylor confidently states. "Just stay calm and be quiet." We slowly move along the wall and enter another corridor. There is a doorway leading to building one and the other indoor set of second story storage units. Taylor opens the door and listens. He doesn't hear anything. "Come on," he urges me. We sneak inside as I hear the man from behind us starting to close in. Taylor makes sure the door gently closes, and we quietly head up the stairs. We reach the top and Taylor walks into the open space first. "We're clear."

I follow behind him and we hear some noise from outside, men shouting, but I can't make out what they are saying. We seem to be temporarily safe. We walk quickly with our eyes scanning all around, readying for anything. The walk turns into a jog and we reach the mid-point of the unit and another exit. There's also a stairway access door, leading up to the roof. We wait and listen, Taylor trying to figure the safest route.

"Stay against the wall. I'm going to check the stairs and outside first." Taylor stares dead into my eyes, not an ounce of fear, only intense focus. I nod, nearly crapping myself. I can't fathom how I got here. But, I am very thankful Taylor is by my side to help protect us. He makes his way down the stairs. I stand still when I hear the door on the other side, the one to the stairway roof access, slowly open. The mystery man slithers out—shot.

"Oh," I quietly gasp and move across the floor to him, getting down by his side. "Oh, no. I'll call an ambulance."

The man grabs me, his bloodied hands gripping my shirt with all the life he has left in him. He pulls me closer with great might. I'm frightened but am unable to pull away. "He is not who you think," he struggles to speak. I stare at him, confused. Who is he talking about? *What* is he talking about?

"Who? Taylor?" I ask with great confusion, not knowing what this dying mystery man is telling me. The man nods, blood coming out of his mouth and pooling around his body.

"Don't tell anyone. Trust no one. Make them pay. Make them all pay." The man's grip on me releases and he slumps back down to the ground, lifeless.

My mouth hangs open as I'm grabbed from behind. "Are you all right?" Taylor asks with great concern.

"He's dead. This is him. Oh, my God, he's dead," I utter in shock.

A door at the opposite end of the building is opened and clicks shut. "We have to go," Taylor urges with great concern.

I am frozen, in shock. I don't know what to say or do. I can't move a muscle.

"Nick, we have to go. Please," he reiterates and drags me away from the dead man. I have never seen a man die. I certainly never heard anyone's final words. His blood is stained on my clothes, my hands, as Taylor quickly drags me across the center of the floor, back to the middle set of stairs to exit the building.

"He's down! Over here!" A man screams.

We get to the bottom of the stairs and the Cadillac pulls up with Pong driving. He gets out with a gun drawn and helps us inside. He is taking no chances with our safety.

"Is she okay?" Pong sees the blood and is concerned for me.

"It's not hers. There's a man inside. He's shot. We need to get out of here," Taylor informs him. Pong nods and quickly heads back into the car. I look out the window and the door opens to storage building one, the same door we just came from. As Pong hits the gas hard, I see the short bald man glaring at the car as if he can see me. We speed off and I'm left breathless.

Thirty One

I can't get the image of that man out of my head; his bloodied hands, his intense eyes. He stared into my soul with the very last ounce of his breath. I am still speechless. "It will be all right." Taylor assures me, running his hands through my hair with great concern. *The man you're with— I know him. He is not to be trusted.* The words keep replaying over and over again in my head. I can't fathom what is happening or what it means.

Taylor and I return to his estate. He leaves my side to make some calls. I call my girls. I need to hear their voices. This day has taken a toll and their little voices are all I can ask for—it's all I can trust. I run a warm bath in the master bathroom's whirlpool tub. With a glass of wine, probably an extremely expensive brand of red something or other, I sip slowly and savor. I try to relax, the day an absolute blur. *Don't trust anyone*, he said to me. And the flash drive; it's in the office. I have to walk into the offices of Rapture and Myers and escape with the flash drive. As I ponder things further, I feel I have nowhere to go. Suddenly, the Diamond Estate isn't the greatest place on earth. Suddenly, I don't have a home to go to. And I can't go to work, where a potential psychopath could reside. Between the short bald man and the silver-haired freak, I can't seem to get away from drama or danger. I need to relax. I wish I could relax, but I can't. What did that man mean? What is wrong with Taylor? How could anything be wrong with him?

As I ponder more and more, I receive a text message. It's from Detective Phil.

I need to speak with you as soon as possible. I got something.

I let out a deep breath of air, unsure if I can step back into the case so quickly. My head is spinning round and round so much, I feel dizzy.

I get out of the tub and rush to the toilet and throw up. After I'm done, I do feel a little better. I am unsure of where Taylor is, but I head out back to call Detective Phil on my cell. I walk by the animal sanctuaries, the deadly creatures mostly sleeping. I dial. "Phil?"

"Nicki Connolly?"

"You found something? You found out who RD is?" I ask.

"No. I'm still working on RD. But, I found out something else. I went through paperwork and found something strange. The man you work with, his name is Taylor Diamond, correct?"

"Yes." As I walk and pace, I become increasingly alarmed by what he may say next. I pace and pace, looking around to make sure I am alone—to make sure Taylor is not around.

"There is something strange I uncovered, Nicki," Phil begins. "Taylor is listed as President of a shell company. You know anything about that?"

"No," I am confused by this line of inquiry from Phil.

"Well, the strange thing is, this shell company has an outside affiliation with a company called The McGregor Group. And the McGregor Group is a hedge fund that has close ties with Beltan Food Corp." The information sinks in quickly. I'm not a Wall Street executive, but it doesn't take a lot to realize there is some sort of connection.

"No," I utter under my breath.

"There's more, but I don't know how deep you want to go into this guy." He leaves the decision to me. But, seeing my first dead body—falling in love with a man who I may not even know—I feel as though I have no choice but to get to the bottom of things.

"All the way, Phil. I'm going all the way," I proclaim, not interested in sticking my head in the sand. If something isn't right—and there's a whole lot of that around me right now—I'm getting to the bottom of it.

"Okay. He also has a listed address in South Dakota. I thought that was strange, so I looked further. The address belongs to a Martha Scott."

"Who is Martha Scott?" I quietly ask and look around to again ensure that I'm alone. *Is he married? Does he have an entire family?* Negative thoughts are hurled in my mind, like grenades on a battlefield. I am now cloaked in a lot of darkness and uncertain of what to think.

"That's his mother—at least, according to a birth certificate I dug up. Not easy to find either. I thought you might want to ask her some questions. She may be able to shed some light on what's going on. There are a lot of rotten vegetables in your garden, Ms. Connolly."

"Can you send that address to my email, Phil?" I ask, my voice trailing off as if someone close to me just died.

"You got it."

"And let me know about RD on that memo. I still want to know who made the order," I tell Phil with urgency. I want to get to the bottom of it all.

"Still working on it. Hey, Nicki, you all right?" he asks.

"I don't know," I honestly reply.

"All right. I'll stay on it."

I hang up the phone. I look behind me and see the massive lion standing just a few feet away by the fence's edge. "You came out just for me?" I ask of the mighty beast. He does a small roar, like he is trying to communicate with me rather than howl in anger. The lion slowly collapses to the ground and plays innocent behind his fence. He turns his body and rolls over, making his skin available to touch. With his mouth slumping to the ground,

I move even closer. I am compelled to pet the lion. I'm shaky and nervous, but the beast has his back to me on purpose and with his head on the ground, his body on its side, it gives me the opportunity to lay my hands upon him. And I do. I bend down, reach through the fence, and carefully pet him. What an exhilarating feeling. I pet him again and again. *Wow.* This is a definitely a rush.

"I like your coat, Mr. Lion," I state as if he can hear me.

"You can just call him Leo." Taylor's voice normally brings butterflies. But, now I feel something different: paranoia, fear, the unknown. I finish petting Leo the lion and rise back up to my feet.

"Leo. Why Leo?" I ask.

"I don't know. It's what my father named him." Taylor has a smirk on his face. He normally would smile, but after the day's activities, he too is shaken and can only muster a subtle grin.

"You always follow your father's ways?" My question is a direct assault on Taylor. I am seeking answers to what is happening around me. I am convinced he knows more than he is letting on. And that to me, constitutes lying.

"You've wandered into the lion's den and survived," Taylor poignantly states. "Not many people can say that. You touched an actual African lion."

"I feel as though he poses far less danger to me than many I know in my life." I walk by him without another word and head back into the house. I want my statement to marinate. I want him to feel some of my trust wilting away. I want to see if he will preemptively lie or will he open up and be honest with me. Is this the man I truly love or a wolf in sheep's clothing?

I awake in the morning and hear the shower. Taylor is getting ready for the day. No sex last night, just silence. I fell asleep before Taylor got to bed and have no idea if we even slept together. My exhaustion kept me asleep all night long.

I head downstairs for breakfast and everything is already set up as it was the previous morning. I start to eat and try not to think too much. I have a trip to South Dakota to plan. I text Ronald to see if he'll join me. I need a traveling partner and Taylor is out, for the time being. It's time I find out who I'm in bed with—*literally.*

As I enjoy picking at breakfast, an empowering thought strikes me. I decide it's time to take control. With everything around me falling apart, I'm going to start fighting back. I'm not going to lie down and let everyone dictate to me. I'm a fighter and it's time for me to throw a few punches and get ahead, instead of chasing from behind. I've fired a gun in my life—many, in fact. I don't have an obsession, it's just something my father taught me when I was young. And I'd lie if I didn't say I've been to the gun ranges a few times, in my adult life, to blow off steam. I don't own a gun, but now would be a good time to carry one. I also took karate as a kid and self-defense classes as an adult. I *can* take care of myself and although I've felt helpless of late, I think I need to kick some ass.

Taylor arrives and sits down to eat with me. "I know what you saw was bad—," Taylor starts. "—How many dead bodies have you seen?" I cut him off. "You hardly flinched." I am determined to nail down points with Taylor. No more beating around the bush.

"I saw a few from an accident long ago. Friends of mine. It was terrible. Still haunts me to this day."

"Ah." I nod and my noise is casual, as if only half-believing him. I've mentally detached from him. Angry and frustrated, I don't know or comprehend everything that's happening. He's not going to get warm hugs and kisses from me right now.

"Are you all right?" Taylor poses. What a loaded question. I have a thousand different ways to answer. But, I want control. I *really* want answers. Taylor's mystery trips when he disappears for days on end is only the start of my concern; the lies, my house ransacked, the Ramsey case, and the evil men haunting my days, Mr. silver-haired man and the balding, short jerk. It's all too coincidental not to be tied together. *How,* is the real question.

"I'm tired. I need to get back to LA. A lot to do." I am bland and leave little wiggle room for Taylor. I can see by his raised eye brows that he senses something is up. He knows I feel something wrong.

"Okay." Taylor agreeably nods.

After breakfast we hit the road. I pretend to be tired and sleep on and off. I actually do pass out for a bit on the long drive, but it's more about mental solitude. The pieces of the puzzle aren't fitting and I need to figure out how to make them fit. When Taylor stops for a bite to eat and a bathroom break in Barstow, California, the half-way point, I text Angie.

Book two tickets to Dakota Dunes, SD, on my business card, for Ronald and me. We land at the Sioux Gateway Airport. Check my client list and push back anyone I was going to see this week and tell them next week we'll be meeting at my house, for the time being. If they ask why, tell them I'm working from home.

I have no interest in meeting with people at my firm of Rapture and Myers. The silver-haired man—for one—and, Charles Rapture. I can't figure how any of them come into play with all of this, but it isn't safe there for me. I do have to figure out how to get my flash drive out of there safely, but I will get to it after South Dakota.

We get back home and it's a huge and quick kiss good-bye. I don't mix many words and I leave Taylor pondering what is happening. "You're upset," he points out the obvious.

"We'll talk later. I have some business to take care of." I am the cryptic one now. I start to walk away, leaving Taylor looking like a sad puppy in my wake.

"I do love you, Nicki." His words cause me to stop in my tracks. "No matter what is happening around us, at least know that." He knows he is wrong, he just doesn't know what I know at this point.

I slowly turn back around, his words providing me with some solace, but I will not cave. "You can tell me what's happening. You can tell me more. If you do love me, trust me with the truth," I put it to Taylor. He takes a deep breath, as if he's unsure of how to respond to me putting him on the spot. "This isn't over. It's just goodbye for now." I leave Taylor with a lot to think about and take control of whom and what I am. If I'm being played, I'm going to walk the path on my terms, not be lead around like a trained monkey.

I drive home to my house. I get there to find Aiden's truck in the driveway. After the long drive, the day is gone. It's nearly dark. I have to take the hundred and fifty million dollar offer to Ramsey, but not before I see the flash drive. I need to figure out what the circumstances of everything are. In order to take care of these people, I have to know everything. I have to figure out these mysteries to guarantee Ramsey is protected and gets the best deal possible. So, I begin with my travel plans to South Dakota, and we'll see where we head next.

I enter the house and see Aiden has cleaned up the downstairs. Piles of trash bags are lined up near the front door; the remnants of the break-in. I take a deep breath preparing for the worst. Aiden and I have unsettled business—serious unsettled business. It's the worst kind. I hear him moving around upstairs, and make the long walk to the bedroom. He is putting things away and taking things out all at the same time. He has a half-filled suitcase ready to go. Everything makes you think twice. Every decision you make is objectionable and your conscious does you no favors. *Have I made the right decisions? Did I go the wrong way?* I look at the suitcase he is packing—this husband of mine—this good, honest man and I wonder if I went the right direction. So many times, we reach crossroads in life and every decision can be scrutinized. It's a road of difficult decisions and self-reflection. And every mistake can be magnified.

"Hey," I say to Aiden.

"You're back," he points out the obvious, barely looking me in the eyes.

"Yup. So . . . we gonna talk about this?"

"I'm moving in with my parents for now, Nick." Aiden gets right to the point.

"Okay." I feel the words come out of his mouth deep in my gut. A cacophony of mixed emotions complicate my mind and overwhelm my senses. It is hard to see the trees through the forest right now. I am in a fog of emotional question marks.

"What did you expect?" he follows up in a challenging fashion.

"I don't know," I answer honestly, blithely. Everything is blurry.

"Yeah, I didn't think so." He continues to pack, annoyed.

"I'm going to quit my job soon," I let him know. I have no idea why I'm bothering, but I don't want my girls to be taken away from me because I work too much. And all of a sudden, I feel it necessary to protect my interests as a mother.

"Of course you are. *Why not?*" he says in a massive negative tone.

"It doesn't have to end this way."

"There is no good way to end things, Nick. I don't even know what we are, co-parents? Friends? Acquaintances? You don't tell me anything. What do you want from me?" Aiden is exasperated with our relationship issues far more than he ever let on.

"Nothing. I don't know." I have no answers for his negative challenges. I am not looking to apologize for our combined issues. I do feel bad, but not as if I have destroyed my own marriage. You can't break what has already been broken.

"When you figure it out, get back to me." Aiden closes up his suit case. "Like I said, I'll be at my mom's. You want the girls tonight?" What a question. And so it begins. Two homes; two lives for my girls. Aiden hasn't even officially left and I feel divorced already. It's inevitable, it just doesn't feel good.

"I can't take them tonight. I'm flying to South Dakota on business in the morning," I explain.

"Of course you are," Aiden flings back with a serpent tongue.

"I can see the girls now though—tonight. I'll take them to dinner." It's a strange mediation that's happening. I don't know whether I'm asking permission or telling Aiden, at this point.

"Yeah, whatever you want, Nick." Aiden expresses frustration through his short sentences. He wants no part of me. It definitely is over. He leaves. I sit on my bed—alone—full of questions. Where did it all go wrong? How did I get here? Officially separated from my husband—two kids, inevitably, caught in the complicated web of divorce. How does someone get here? When you're happy, the bad seems so far away. You are covered with a huge comforter of bliss that acts as a shield, keeping away all the dark clouds. And when things go bad, the good seems so far away. You can't even see it anymore. I am a pendulum of conflicting emotions, swelling over into a sand trap of chaos. I may be lost, but I will find my center. My home is my girls. I take them out to eat, leaving my self-wallowing for another day. *Take it slow Nicki,* I remind myself.

I have a wonderful evening with my kids. We laugh and have a great time at Chuck E Cheese's. I'm normally not a big fan of all the noise, but I need the distraction and want to treat them to a lot of fun. I drop them back off at Aiden's parent's house. I kiss the girls goodbye and Aiden hardly says a word to me.

"See ya," is all I get from him.

I call Ronald and ask him to sleep over. We have an early flight, but really, I don't want to be in the house alone. I break out a bottle of Chardonnay for us to sip over and Ronald arrives at my house with his trademark grin. "Hey, doll," he greets me with open arms and we exchanges kisses on the cheek.

"You want a drink?"

"Girl, you never have to ask Ronny twice."

"I need to talk. I need to tell you what's been happening." I am serious in tone but have a smile plastered on my face, super happy to see a close ally.

Ronald and I sit in the living room together and slowly but surely work our way through the bottle of wine as I share it all with him—everything.

"Oh. My. God!" Ronald belts out in a squeaky, high-pitched, shocked voice, his hand over his mouth. "You and Taylor?"

"I just got finished telling you I saw a man die and you go straight to Taylor and the sex?"

"Twenty-four karat, honey—you bagged a thoroughbred! The dead guy is terrible. But, I can't get the thought of Taylor out of my head!" Ronald's face of shock has a glimmer of grin mixed in. He is such a character.

"But, I don't know if I can trust him." I return to one of the many problems at hand.

"You have no proof. And as an attorney, you know better." Ronald gives me a brief short expose on the law.

"Well, let's see if we find some in South Dakota."

"And you and Aiden are…?" Ronald makes a breaking visual with his two hands.

"Beyond repair. I can't prove anything but I swear he's been having an affair. He has been gone for a long time now, ya know?"

"Ronny knows, honey."

"What should I do? Am I being paranoid? Is this trip to South Dakota worth the time? What am I doing?"

"Do you love him?" Ronald asks a stirring question. I take a deep breath and pause. I know what my feelings are but they are currently marred by self-doubt. "I know you *like* him. We all know that. And, he likes you. We could see the way you both stole smiles. It was something special." Ronald lets me in on the secret that everyone suspected.

"I do, but I feel played. Something's not right." There is a dark cloud over us and I can't figure out what it is. I can't put my finger on it, but I know it's there.

"Some things may not be kosher, honey, but you can't fake that look he gave you. In the bar, when you would look elsewhere, he looked at you—not a *Ronny's checkin' you out* sorta way, but he *looked* at you. He was trying to see your soul. I don't know what's happened or what's going on, but I can tell you that boy has got it for you, for real. And we'll go on this trip and figure things out," he says. I let out a deep, relieved breath of air, thankful to have Ronald on my side. I lean over and lie on his shoulder. He rubs my head. "I can't believe you got on that. He so damn hot, girl," he jokes. I shake my head, the two of us giggling together.

———————

Morning arrives and we hit the airport. I reacquaint myself with the passengers in coach. *First class was so much better than this,* I silently and sadly reminisce. We arrive at Sioux Gateway Airport in Iowa. It's strange flying to Sioux City to go to South Dakota, but that's where Dakota Dunes lie. Union County, home to Dakota Dunes, hugs the very South East corner and tip of the Mount Rushmore State. It also kisses the Missouri River, a fact that has Ronald very excited. He hasn't traveled much. The researcher in him has probably studied nearly every place in the world. But he has not been to many outside of *Google Earth.*

I'm all business and barely realize we have transported into another beautiful scenic Midwest state. Ronald talks and talks, sighting all the fall foliage, the animals, the beauty, the seasons, and the life, moving around us. His voice is white noise for me. I'm focused and anxious to speak with Martha Scott. Right now, that's everything to me. It may be selfish. It isn't exactly like I'm just doing this for Ramsey. I know I'm doing this for myself. We arrive at the Holland Brook Suites Assisted Living Community. The community is beautiful—the entire area; the brainchild of land developers to create gorgeous golf courses and beautiful estates, nuzzled against the Missouri River. The views are spectacular and the nature surrounding you is unescapable. We approach the front desk at Holland Brook.

"What do we say?" he whispers to me nervously.

"I have this," I tell him.

"Welcome to the Holland Brook Suites," the woman at the front desk welcomes me as if I am entering a luxury hotel in Maui.

"I'm here to speak with Martha Scott."

"Okay." The woman shuffles through some papers. "What is your name?"

"Charlie." Ronald gives me a strange look and then glances back at the woman.

"I don't see you on the guest list."

"I wasn't going to her room. I'm a friend of Taylor's—her son." I add the perfect context to my convert operation. It is an effective cloak that could help me find my way in.

"Yes. Mr. Diamond. Of course!" The woman up front clearly knows who Taylor is.

"I just need to speak with her on the patio. It's family business," I share.

The woman nods. "Well, wait on the patio, and I'll see where she is," she responds. We start to walk away when the woman calls to me. "I'm sorry. And who are you to Taylor?" she asks.

"I'm his partner," I state. The woman nods and picks up a phone to make a call.

Ronald and I head outside to the patio area and wait. The chairs and tables are set up on a covered, expansive patio, featuring a large stone deck. The view off the patio is beautiful. I let out a breath of nervous air, just happy to get to this point, unsure of what I'll say next.

"Impressive," Ronald compliments.

"What's that?" I ask.

"I like this new, aggressive you. That must have been some bad ass sex you two had," he jokes.

"The baddest." I smirk in return, giving him a little nugget to chew on.

"Girl, you're my hero." Ronald and I chuckle and look around at the beautiful green surrounding us. A couple of deer visit the grounds on the outskirts, picking at the grass.

"Who are you two?" a raspy voice sounds from behind us. Ronald and I snap our heads around to Martha. She is accompanied by an orderly and the woman from the front desk.

"Just a few minutes," the woman, from the front desk, states. I nod and she walks away. The orderly remains, standing silent, a few feet away.

"I'm a friend of Taylor's," I attempt to establish a rapport with her.

"Taylor has no friends. Are you the whore?" Martha is nothing if not blunt and borderline vicious in her tone.

"I'm Nicki," I confess.

"Nicki," Martha thinks and shakes her head. She takes out a cigarette. The orderly steps forward and snatches it out of her hand, then goes back to the corner without a word.

"You son of a—," Martha grumbles under her breath. She takes out an e-cigarette. "Is this acceptable in the patio area, you ape?" Martha sarcastically barks. She starts to inhale her nicotine and blow out the vapor. She savors it, as if missing an old friend, and continues on.

"This isn't the same—but it's something; designated areas for everything in this prison." Martha pauses and then returns back to me. "I'm sorry, dear, I have a touch of the Alzheimer's, they tell me. What was that question of yours…what's your name again?"

"Nicki," I kindly remind the old woman.

"Nicki, you say? I'm bad with names. But a name doesn't mean a thing to me anymore. I've heard of you. I've heard him speak your name—utter it through his lips. I can't place you, though."

Ronald and I are confused over Martha's strange way of communicating. "Yes. I am a friend—," I start to explain.

"And who is he, your driver or something?"

"This is Ronald. He is a friend and works with Taylor and me." I try to clear everything up for Martha but she looks through us—past us. I can't tell if she understands me or is spacing out.

"Conspirators. I hate what you do. All of you. You're terrible," she slings some venom at us.

"What does Taylor do, Mrs. Scott?" I ask a testing question to gauge where this confused woman stands.

"Ms.!" She corrects me, clearly insulted by the insinuation of being considered a Mrs.

"I'm sorry, Ms. Scott. What does Taylor do?" Ronald looks at me with interest, as if he's wondering what I'm doing. It's a prompt. I want to see where she heads with this line of simple questioning.

"You know. You both know." Martha begins, pointing both myself and Ronald out with a wagging finger. "Let me tell you something about Taylor Diamond, little lady. You both think you know him. No. You don't know him. Nobody truly knows him. He is evil inside. He is the worst of the worst. He'll woo you in, bring you close, then, he will stab your soul and watch you emotionally bleed out, and he'll enjoy every minute of it. That is Taylor Diamond. That is your *friend*."

Ronald and I share a concerned look, not knowing what to think. I can't tell if this woman is a mother or a mortal enemy of Taylor's. Either way, this is frightening to say the least.

"Is he plotting something?" Ronald can't resist and joins the Q&A session.

"He's rich. He's powerful. He's never *not* plotting something. You are the two patsies. You're errand boys for the evil slayer. Your eyes are open. If you choose to dance with the devil, then so be it. I did once and I pay for it every day. Who do you think put me here—here in my prison?" Martha snaps, an annoyed look over at the orderly. "That's who your Mr. Diamond is. Run away from him. Get as far away as possible. If you're lucky, he won't take you down with him."

The woman from the front desk charges back out to the patio with a cell phone by her ear. She looks annoyed and hangs up the phone. "Get Ms. Scott back to activities," she tells the orderly.

He nods and walks over to her. "Come on, dear. Let me help you up."

"Activity time, activity time! All right, all right," Martha concedes. She smacks away his hands. "I can get up on my own. Waste your energy on that Brenda Fillmore. She is the one that plays helpless every day," Martha angrily mutters.

The woman from the front desk has an angered look on her face and aims it right at Ronald and me. I know the words before she speaks them. "You will both need to leave. You are not family and I've been told not to allow you to speak with Ms. Scott—whoever you both really are. Now, before I call the police, why don't you get going, right quick."

Martha stops at the doorway and turns back to us. "Just when you think you know someone, they pull the rug out. Open your eyes before you both hit the ground . . . before you hit it hard." Martha is pulled away and disappears. "Okay, okay, Brutus!" We hear her grumble from inside the building.

Ronald turns to me with a perplexed look on his face. "Well, that cleared things up," he sarcastically states. I shake my head. *I need to get to that flash drive.*

"Now!" the receptionist orders. We both oblige and leave.

Thirty Two

We fly back. It is dusk, and my phone is blowing up upon landing. I wait until all the messages seize loading. My worst fears are realized. I read the first text from Jessica.

There was an accident. Aiden and the girls are in the hospital.

My heart drops. I go on autopilot. Everything around me seizes to exist. I sit down, breathless.

"Are you all right?" Ronald asks.

I shake my head *no* and listen to my voice mails. I'm shaking, hoping for the best news possible, but fearing the absolute worst. I have messages from Jessica, Angie, and Aiden's mother, Helen. They all say the same thing: *The kids and Aiden are recovering. They all look like they will be okay.* "There was an accident," I mumble in shock. "They're all in the hospital," I tell Ronald.

"Come on, honey, I'll drive. Which hospital are we heading to?" Ronald attempts to calm me. I'm a blank stare—shock has taken over—unsure of what is happening around me. "Which hospital?" he asks again.

"Westlake Hospital," I mutter. Ronald nods and we head off.

The car ride is equally a blur. I'm catatonic. My shock and anxiety are through the roof. I have to get to them and be by their side. My poor girls. With my hands shaking, I call Jessica, hoping she answers and is still at the hospital. I prefer not to speak to Aiden's mother. I can't speak to Helen, not right now—not in this climate. She can be brutal on good days . . . on happy days.

The travel up through the hospital is excruciating. The lobby. The damn elevator.

"Angie said they were okay. Just breathe." Ronald tries to calm me down in a quiet voice, rubbing my back.

The doors to the elevator open and I explode out like I was shot out of a cannon. I rush through the halls and approach a locked door. The sign reads: Pediatric Unit. I hit the buzzer and wait.

"Yes?" The voice sounds through the speaker.

"I'm here to see Lacy and Ariel Connolly. I'm their mother, Nicki," I say in desperation. The door buzzes and I yank it open and head inside, followed by Ronald. I rush to the front desk. "Where are they, please?" I beg, exhibiting some uncharacteristic hysterics.

"They're right—," The nurse begins.

"Over here, Nick!" Jessica calls.

"Thank you," I say to the nurse and jog over to Jessica.

The girls are sharing a room with beds side by side. Lacy has a bandage on her head and Ariel a cast on her little arm. "Oh, my God." I start to cry. It is a rare moment that I shed tears and even rarer that I sob. But my emotions get the best of me as I hug and kiss each of my girls.

"It's okay, Mommy," Lacy says, my eldest always the cool, calm one.

"We get video games, Mommy!" Ariel cheers over the little things. After a few moments of me sitting with the girls I let Ronald, Jessica's daughter, Haley, and the girls play video games. I step out of the room with Jessica.

"What the hell happened?" I ask her in confusion, hoping to get some insight.

"They said it was a hit-and-run. They were at a red light, I think. Aiden never saw it coming. A black SUV, of some kind, came out of nowhere and rammed the side of the car. It was early morning, near Helen's house. There was almost no one around. The girls are good, although Ariel had a slight fracture from awkwardly hitting the side of the car. Lacy bumped her head. They said she didn't sustain a concussion but both a just being observed right now. Aiden is one floor upstairs. He's okay. He had a concussion, sprained wrist and cuts and bruises to his face. But, he'll be okay too."

"Did they catch the guy?" I ask.

"I don't think anyone knows who or what did it," Jessica hypothesizes.

"Okay. Thanks, Jess. Thanks for being here." We hug.

"Of course. I'll always be here for you—no matter what."

I let out a breath of air filled with a million emotions: nervous, angry, and upset, just to name a few. I want to blame someone. But who is there to blame? Is it just a case of being in the wrong place at the wrong time? It happens to thousands of people a year, across the world. I'm emotionally spent and spend a few more moments with the girls before heading upstairs to speak with Aiden.

I make my way up the elevator. I am unsure of what the discussion will be between us. I have no idea if he will blame me for this incident, as well. Are we going to war again or making a truce? I am clueless as to what to expect. I'm just thankful my girls are all right.

I get to Aiden's room and he is watching TV. A basketball game is on. He sees me and turns it off.

I just stare at him from the doorway. My eyes well. He stares back, his eyes welling also. His arm is splinted and his face cut and battered. He is a beaten man. I feel the swell of emotion I have for him, inside of me, come out. He is a man I've spent many years with—a man I've loved—a man, in some ways, I still love. I walk over to his side and his arms open wide as he sits up. We embrace. I feel as though all of our anger is emptying into this one glorious, loving hug between two people who have shared everything in life. It's long and fruitful, each of us squeezing the other tight. I pull back and bring the chair beside his bed closer, so I can take a needed seat. I set myself down beside his bed and wipe my tears clear.

"Didn't see this one coming," Aiden jokes.

"Nope. I definitely didn't." I chuckle. We both have a smile over the extreme circumstances we are both now juggling.

"Jessica told me what happened," I inform him.

"I was at a red light. I didn't even see the car coming. It came over someone's lawn or the crosswalk. I saw the car at the last possible second and it rammed us. It hit us hard, but I heard screeching. The car stopped. I told the police. I just saw two men in sunglasses. Nothing else."

I nod, just thankful all is well. We sit quietly next to one another. We are emotional but we are both realistic. "You know, I still love you," I say. "No matter what, I'll always love you."

"I'll always love you too, Nick." Aiden grabs my hand. We hold each other's hand and I take a deep breath.

"So . . . when are you getting your bachelor pad?" I ask with a smile.

"Ha. A bachelor pad. Right. With two rug rats, crawling all over me? I'll pass."

"We'll be okay, right? We can do this, can't we?" I ask. It's as important as us getting engaged. Getting divorced is the same thing in reverse. We know we aren't meant to be. We know the love we share is something different than we both want, something different than we both deserve. We both know, and that's all that matter. We agree.

"Of course we will. We're friends first, Nick. Always friends first," Aiden confirms.

"Thank you for that."

"How are the girls feeling?" he asks.

"Good spirits. Playing video games. Eating chocolate pudding. I'm going to go sleep next to them tonight."

"Good." Aiden smiles, happy to hear his daughters are good.

I spend a few more minutes beside Aiden and head out. The moment I leave the room, I'm met face-to-face with Helen Connolly—a difficult woman—one I have never got along with. She is a strong woman, a homemaker who took care of a difficult husband for many years until Aiden's father passed away. She remarried and now has ten years with her second husband.

"Nicki," Helen looks up at me but, at the same time, down. She has this way. As mother-in-laws go, she fits the bill on the nasty side.

"Hello, Helen." I nod respectfully.

"I heard some of that," Helen refers to my conversation with Aiden.

"Eavesdropping?" I make the accusation with a smile, but there is sincerity behind it. I was talking with Aiden, not his mother. And our thoughts and difficulties are private.

"Nicki, dear. I know I've always been hard on you. You might even think I'm a bitch. And, I have been. I've been a hard woman. But I've been hard on you because I respect you, Nicki. You took a stand and lived your life. You are so smart. You are a strong woman. I was proud of you when you went back to work. I knew Aiden would have a problem with that. He is like his father. His father was stubborn and quiet like Aiden; kept things inside. And when he passed, I did lose a man I had loved. But I found another man—one that I loved even more. My marriage to Martin has been an awakening for me. It made me a resurgent woman. I found myself again. If Aiden's father had lived as long to this day, I'm not certain we'd still be together. People say how hard it is to fall in love. I think it's easy to love, but far more difficult to be *in love*. There is a difference. I know that. And now, you may have an idea of that, as well. Aiden is my baby boy. I've always been protective of him. So . . . I was hard. You are a good woman, Nicki. You have given me two wonderful grandchildren. If this is the end for you and Aiden, then you will start a new beginning. I hope that new beginning gives you what I have found with Martin. And you will always been welcome in my home." Helen leans in and kisses me on the cheek. She heads back into Aiden's room and leaves me standing in sheer shock. She has said but a handful of kind words to me over my lifetime and I feel as though she packed in a thousand compliments in a single conversation. I'm stunned. And, in a weird way, relieved. I go and sleep up in the girl's room on a cot.

I go downstairs to grab some coffee and a sandwich. *I can't remember when I ate last.* I exit the elevator to the lobby and am met, almost immediately, by Lincoln who is carrying two bouquets of flowers. "Lincoln?" I curiously ask with a smile.

"I just heard about your family. I called Angie. Nobody knew where you were." He expresses concern and also lets on that the office is searching for me. "Are you all right?" Despite what's happening at Rapture and Myers, Lincoln is still all right in my book. He is a good man.

"I am. Thanks, Lincoln."

"You headed somewhere? I wanted to see if we could talk." Lincoln's face is long and his wide eyes draw me in. He has something important to tell me.

"Yeah, come on. I'm just heading to the cafeteria." We walk to the cafeteria and I get a sandwich.

We sit down and Lincoln hands me the two bouquets of flowers. "These are for the girls. I'm glad to hear they are all right."

"Yeah. It's just crazy. One minute everything's all right, the next—you know."

He nods. "I want you to hear it from me first, Nicki. I'm leaving Rapture and Myers as soon as the New Year arrives."

"Why?" I curiously ask. I can relate for numerous reasons, but I am curious why Lincoln has tired of Charles Rapture and Bob Myers.

"Why? I can't count the ways this place has gone crazy. We used to be a simple firm. Now, we are getting into bed with pure evil. The place is bugged. Cameras are everywhere. I'm worried when I take a leak in the bathroom that someone is watching. I'm too old for this." Lincoln expresses his many concerns with Rapture and Myers.

"Everywhere?" I ask. "They have cameras everywhere?"

"The phones are tapped. The place is bugged. I saw one. I've seen cameras all over. This Crane Security is no ordinary security force. And I think they're at the firm because of you and this case. It's all too intense for me, dear."

As Lincoln expresses his concerns I have a flashback of my own. I remember when Taylor and I were in the office and he looked around my office all funny. I couldn't figure out what he was looking for. We were going to discuss the Ramsey Case strategy prior to going to our meeting with Albert Penn when he pushed us to leave. He knew the room was probably bugged—cameras hidden—eyes upon us. That makes him guilty for lying to me but, at the same time, he tried to protect me and the case. *What the hell is going on?*

"You're a good friend, Lincoln. You're so much better than *them*—you've always been so much better than them."

"Charles is furious with you. James Bonner has asked for you to be removed from the Ramsey Case and terminated. And that Crane man is strangely powerful. I don't know what's happening, but watch yourself. You should get away from here, too." Lincoln gets up and kisses me on the cheek. "Good luck, Nicki. I'm glad the family is all right."

"Thanks, Lincoln." And with that, he leaves.

I finish eating and thinking about Lincoln's words, when I realize I left my cell phone in my car. I head outside to get some fresh air and check my messages. I head to my Excursion parked in the multi-level garage. I open my car door and immediately see my phone. It's flashing from numerous messages. As I sit on my driver's seat I see an envelope strategically placed under my windshield wiper. I stare at it and then look around, seeing if anyone is watching me. I check other cars to make certain there aren't flyers or some weird messages on their cars. There aren't. I step out of my car and grab the envelope, sitting back down in the seat to open it. I reach inside, inspecting the contents. I keep my eyes open and my head on a swivel, checking to see if anyone is around. Satisfied I'm alone and not being spied upon, I pull out a white piece of paper. There is very little on the paper except strange letters looking more like a ransom note. The letters have been cut from magazine articles and spell out one word: **SETTLE**. I look inside and there is one more item. It's a newspaper article. The paper is the Lincoln Times, from Nebraska. The headline reads: **FAMED GERMAN SCIENTIST FOUND DEAD**. My heart sinks and my brain scrambles for answers. I take pictures of the ransom-like note and the newspaper article and send them to Taylor. I have no idea whose team he's on, but I need confirmation of what's happening. I look through my phone contacts and dial Detective Howard. He is the only man I can truly trust to help me at the moment. He isn't there, so I leave him a message and ask him to call me as soon as he can.

The girls are released from the hospital and we head home. Aiden has to stay one night but is heading back to his mother's house when he's released. I bring the girls home. They are excited to finally sleep in their beds again. I get them showered up and we play Jenga—a family favorite. I make mac and cheese and peanut butter and jelly sandwiches, the girl's favorite food. I shower attention and love over them. Then I put on the movie *Frozen* and they eat buttered popcorn and M&Ms. They fall asleep, watching the movie and, one by one, I carry them up to bed. I did my best to make sure they have pleasant dreams.

The doorbell rings and I grab my mace as I head to the front door. I look through the peep hole and see Detective Howard standing at my door. I'm relieved and open it up. "Detective. You are a sight for sore eyes," I greet him.

"Ms. Connolly. I heard about the accident. Is your family all right?" he asks me.

"They are. Thank you, detective. But, this was no accident, which is why I called you. Look at this." I give the detective the note, which had since been put in a baggie in case finger prints are available. I am no crime expert, but that much I know from the legal world. I show him the newspaper article, also in a plastic baggie. "This isn't all coincidence," I assure the detective as he closely reviews all the documents. Detective Howard paces as he thinks to himself.

"And this was found where?"

"On my car, at the hospital."

He nods. "These people . . . they're behind all of this? They're dangerous? You think they went after your family?" he drills me with questions.

"A rogue, black SUV with two males, in sunglasses, rams my family's car, at a red light, in a quiet small neighborhood. This letter and article are placed on my car at the hospital. I've already been followed and Taylor and I saw a man murdered in Nevada. And one of the men who followed me appeared to be at the murder scene. Pretty extraordinary if all these things didn't connect to the class action lawsuit, worth hundreds of millions of dollars, I'm involved in." My rant is complete.

"Taylor never told me you saw a man murdered." He looks annoyed that his friend hadn't confided in him.

"Maybe Taylor isn't telling you everything, detective."

"I'm going to have a car here day and night, on this street, for the next week. We'll go from there. I'll have our crime lab check for prints, but I doubt we'll find any. And, in the meantime, you stay out of trouble."

"Okay. Thank you."

Detective Howard leaves and I pace. I am not satisfied being the hunted, being a sitting duck. I am determined to go on the attack. I refuse to be vulnerable and will not let them win out of fear.

I call Angie and Ronald over to house sit. They know the kids, and if they wake up, they'll feel safe. I'm going to Rapture and Myers in the cover of dark. I'm going there to get my secret flash drive, hidden in the false drawer in my desk. I'm sure they haven't found it and it's killing them. But, I have to go there when they are unsuspecting. And right after my family got injured is the time to attack.

With my informant murdered and Dr. Schecter dead, *probably murdered*, I need that flash drive more than ever. I have to get into my office. If they want a fight—they got one. It's my turn now.

Thirty Three

"Are you sure? Do you want me to go with you?" Angie offers after I tell them my game plan.

"I'm glad *you* offered. That place scares me," Ronald jokes.

"I got this. Just watch the girls. Text me if they wake up. But I shouldn't be gone too long." I don't want to dilly-dally at Rapture and Myers. This is an *in-and-out* operation.

They each give me kiss and well wishes.

"Good luck," they both say as if I were heading off to war.

I go to my car and look around. Doesn't appear as if a squad car has arrived just yet. I also don't see any suspicious people. I don't waste a lot of time looking though. I'm a sitting duck, out in the open, in the dark of night. I get in my car and start it. The engine hums and for a moment, I think about movies when cars explode. *Could that happen to me? Would they do that to me?* I am a victim of my own cinematic paranoia, but I don't want to take any more chances. I want this all to be over. And the only way it ends is if I get that flash drive.

I pull out of the driveway and head down the street. I'm nervous, thinking about going into the building. I really have no plan. My plan is to show up and get inside with few people noticing. I'm no cat burglar so this is going to take some creativity, if I'm put on the spot. The good news is, as attorneys, we've always had twenty-four hour access to the building, despite it being closed.

As I'm driving I notice someone following me. At least it appears that way. I'm still in my *cloak and dagger* paranoia mode, but it does appear a set of headlights is following just far enough back to be inconspicuous, but close enough that I notice. It's nearly eleven o'clock at night and that car has been behind me for a good mile now. As I turn, they turn. As I slow down, they slow down. They remain behind me, this smaller black Mercedes. I sit at a red light, trying to see who is inside by glancing casually into my mirrors. I don't want them to know I'm on to them. I wait at the red light and it turns green. I wait again. The car doesn't go around me or honk. I put my hazards on as if I have a problem. I wait through the green light and see a few cars in the other direction, waiting for their green. My light turns yellow and then red. I go. I step on the gas, my wheels squealing. I just get through the intersection as the cars going across stop and hesitate. They hit their horns and then continue on. The car behind me is forced to stop as the other cars continue by them. The steel barriers allow me to successfully get a big head start. I make an immediate turn at the first street. Then, another turn. "Follow this asshole," I angrily challenge to the faceless man or men following behind me. I make another turn and speed safely away.

I arrive at Rapture and Myers but park on the street. I usually park in the underground parking garage, but I feel like it's too risky. I would feel trapped, and stepping through the downstairs lobby by the parking garage seems like a bad spot for me.

I walk right up to the main entrance on the street level. I swipe my card and the door doesn't open. The light on the security swipe sensor remains red. I swipe again and it still remains locked, the red light flashing once again. The Crane Security officer at the front desk lumbers over. The man with his mustache and beer belly looks annoyed as he takes the steps over to the glass entranceway. "The offices are closed, ma'am!" he shouts.

I press my badge up against the window. "I work at Charles and Rapture!"

He looks at my photo id and matches it up to my face, focusing and making sure I am who I say I am. "You should be entering from the underground garage after hours, ma'am!" The security guard insists.

"I know, but I need to just drop this off with Michael Crane. He asked for it personally." I show the man a random envelope I have in my purse. The man shakes his head, annoyed. "I don't have time. I really have to go!" I shout.

The security guard opens the door just a crack. "Lady, you have to go—,"

Before the security guard can get another word out of his mouth, I whip out my mace and spray him in the face. I push the door open and kick him in the balls. He falls to his knees, blinded and in pain. I move inside quickly and kick him in the face, rendering him unconscious. He falls to the ground. There's that karate and self-defense classes, coming back in spades!

I step over the guard and rush to the stairs. I stay away from the elevator, just in case they cut the power. I don't know if they can do that, but there's a camera in there and if they didn't see me just kick the lobby security guard's ass, they will definitely see my face on the elevator cam.

One flight at a time I head up the stairs. I go slow, nervous I'm about to be found out. Fortunately, I don't hear anyone coming and I continue up. I reach the Rapture and Myers floor and peek my head out. I don't see anyone and it's mostly dark on the floor with only the hallway lights on. I look around and take a deep breath. My office isn't far way. But I'm worried about taking a step onto the floor and exposing myself to the cameras. I don't think there are cameras in the stairwell, but I can't be certain. I take a deep breath and casually begin to walk. Running would be obvious. If I walk casually, perhaps no one will think anything of it. There isn't a soul around as I take nervous step after nervous step, attempting to get to my office.

The elevator distantly *dings.* Somebody is on their way up. Are they coming for me? Are they coming to this floor? I don't have time to find out and rush to my office. I race to my desk and open the door. I pull out the false bottom exposing my safe. I enter the password, Lacy's birthday. The safe opens and I take out the flash drive. *Thank God they didn't find it.* I quickly stash it in my pocket when a small lamp on the far side of the room is turned on. I'm frozen, breathless. I look over and see the small balding man. He is in a suit, as always. He stares at me with bad intentions but shows a cocky smile. He is the fox who was waiting for the hen and I walked right into his trap.

"I knew you'd come here. I've been waiting, night after night for you. Just a matter of time, really." He is so full of himself as if he perfectly planned this moment all along.

"Did you hurt my family?" I ask with anger.

"You don't get to ask questions. What did you put in your pocket? I need what you put in your pocket." The man remains seated but I see a gun in one of his hands. He's gently tapping it on his leg. Now I can see why he is so cocky. He has me, dead to rights.

"You killed him, didn't you?"

"Again. Ms. Connolly, you're going to have to stop being a counselor for a moment and realize that you are in great danger. You are moments from a nightmare—one that you will never wake up from. Do you want this to be the end? Your daughters will never see their mother again." He rises to his feet, growing impatient.

"How do you know I didn't make copies?" I ask.

"We watch everyone, Ms. Connolly. We don't miss a thing. And you wouldn't be here if you did have copies."

339

A fist flies through the dark and strikes the small balding man across the jaw, knocking him down and temporarily out. "You missed that." Taylor is standing over him, more than happy to deliver the blow. I look up at Taylor confused. "I was following you tonight. I drove a different car and I was going to watch over you and your family all night. I wasn't going to let these animals harm you." Taylor's declaration is nice, but is it all a show?

"I don't know what to believe any more." I am honest with him and confused over my next move.

"I will get you out of here, Nicki. But, you're going to have to trust me." He extends his hand. I don't have a lot of time as we hear the elevator *ding* again.

"Okay," I whisper. I take the plunge and once again place myself in Taylor Diamond's hands. I follow him as we hear men and footsteps. They are fanning out through the floor. We sneak around and reach conference room B. "In here," I whisper.

Taylor hesitates, seeing the all-glass conference room. "Here?" he whispers back. I think he is confused as to why I'd choose such an open location to hide.

"Trust me," I tell him.

He nods. We rush inside the room and I quickly lead Taylor over to the long hanging curtains, which are ruffled to the side of the large windows. I get behind a curtain which stretches from floor to ceiling. Taylor does the same and we are ghosts along the wall. The darkness of the room, combined with the sheer openness of its layout, is the perfect hiding spot no one would suspect. I hear footsteps down the hall, near the room. A flashlight shines all around. I hold my breath. I can't see Taylor and just wait, agonizing second after agonizing second. The door to the conference room is opened and a slow, uncertain stride enters. Then, there is a long endless pause of silence. I can hear a man's breath. It is subtle as his eyes are probably scanning the room, looking for anything he may have missed. We are just a few feet from being found, our lives potentially at risk. After a few anxious moments, the door is closed and the footsteps lead away. I let out a relieved breath of air. A hand abruptly is placed on my shoulder and I jump ready to strike the man in the face. It's Taylor.

"Let's go," he whispers with urgency. I am relieved and follow him. We make our way to the door, staying low.

"There is an access door to the stairs just around that corner." I point. We are a few feet away from a potential exit strategy. Taylor nods, agreeing with the plan. He cracks the door and stays low, looking both ways. With the coast clear, he stealthy moves softly on the floor to the corner. I follow behind him and look back, forgetting to close the door behind me. It's cracked. I go to close it when footsteps appear to be headed right at us.

"Leave it," Taylor urges me. He goes to crawl forward and footsteps sound in front of us, headed right toward the stairway access door. We are trapped. With footsteps coming from both directions, we are looking as though we are about to get squeezed.

"What now?" I nervously state.

Taylor whips out his cell phone. He looks through and presses a button. A telephone rings on the other side of the floor by Taylor's office. The men heading toward the stairway stop, probably hearing the phone ring. There are two men and they take a few steps back around the corner giving us clearance. The men behind us are about to clear the corner and we'll be visible. "Now!" Taylor urges me and we rush to the stairway access. We quickly sneak inside the door and gently let it close, narrowly escaping. Taylor goes to drag me down the stairs and I pull on him.

"Up. Not down," I tell him.

"We have to get out of here," Taylor states.

"We are. Follow me." I turn and head up the stairs with or without him. I hear him grunt but he follows behind me as we quietly start up the stairs. The access door below opens from where we just were and Taylor and I stop, pressing our bodies up against the wall. We are not visible in the stone, blocked off staircase, but a single sound could draw their attention toward us. We wait. Multiple set of footsteps head downstairs, dissipating with every step they take. I smile and wink at Taylor. He rolls his eyes with a smile and we again head up to the roof. We step out onto the roof of the building and have an amazing view of the city around us.

"What now?"

"Now, we head to the rear stairs. There's a cargo elevator and it's on the backside of the building, where maintenance workers travel."

"How do you know about that?"

"Because Angie, Ronald and I, a long time ago, smoked a joint up here and we got lost heading back to the office." I tell the story and smile.

Taylor nods and laughs. "Yup, that will do it."

"Come on." I urge him.

We head down the back set of stairs. We seem to be in the clear, although heading down the many sets of stairs is exhausting. We are finally almost at the bottom, when we hear an access door open from above us. We stop moving for a moment, waiting. The door closes maybe two or three floors above us. It's hard to tell. We wait for a moment. Then footsteps quickly start downstairs in our direction.

"Fuck it. Let's go." Taylor whispers loudly and we give up our position and rush down the stairs. We can hear the men above us shout into a walkie-talkie. The jig is up, but we reach the lobby floor and rush out of the stairway. We see the glass doors to the exit up ahead with the security officer I had knocked out earlier, still on the floor, unconscious. We run, smiling, hand-in-hand. We are a team once again, if not just for this last time.

"Let's go for the glass doors!" I urge.

"Parking garage is more cover though!" Taylor shouts.

"The security guy is still out on the floor. I think we've got this."

Taylor agrees on the spot and we make the decision to bypass the stairway leading to the parking garage and race past the elevators toward the mouth of the large, glass, enclosed lobby on the street level.

The elevators ding, two of them reaching the bottom floor any second. We pick up the pace, hoping to beat them to the lobby doors. We rush out into the open lobby area. "Freeze!" We hear a man shout. We stop and look to the side, the silver-haired man, sitting behind the security desk. Beside him are two security officers with guns. He was staring at the various cameras in the building, just waiting for us.

"It's over," he says with a cocky smile.

Taylor turns to me. "You run and don't look back," he whispers.

"Not again. No way," I tell him, his self-sacrifice not necessary.

"You can make it," he mutters under his breath.

"Enough chit-chat! I want the drive! We know you have it. Where is it?!" Crane shows little patience. The short balding man and additional security emerge from the elevators. His face is bloodied from where Taylor broke his nose.

"I have the drive," Taylor states as he steps forward. He reaches into his pocket and clinches something in his hand. "It's right here." He glances back at me, wanting me to run. He gives me a subtle nod. The world slows down. I feel as though I'm in slow motion as I run for the door. I can't hear anything as I pray to make it.

"STOP!" Crane shouts.

"Run, Nicki!" Taylor shouts back.

I race to the door and look behind me, men chasing after me. Taylor's hands are up as he surrenders to them. Two gun shots are fired, my heart dropping to the ground. I have no idea if they are at Taylor or meant for me. I hold my breath as I reach the door and police cars come zooming up to the curb. I open the door and rush out. I sprint to the first door opening up. Detective Howard steps out of one of the cars, and I lunge into his arms for protection.

"Get in there!" he orders the policemen, wasting no time. Uniformed officers rush inside. I look back, unsure of what happened. I have no idea if Taylor was shot . . . if he is alive. I am in utter panic and shaking. I wait.

Thirty Four

I wait outside as things are being sorted out. Detective Howard is inside, along with everyone else. I don't see any major problems—no stress over ambulances—no arrests. Taylor emerges and is pointing and angrily yelling, his lip bleeding. I can't make out his words, my panic level still way too high to focus on much of anything.

Detective Howard and the police all start to file out of the building. Taylor approaches me. "Are you all right?" I ask him.

"I'm good. You got it?" Taylor asks. I reach in my pocket and pull out the flash drive. It looks cracked from the fray. Maybe when we were crawling on the ground, I don't know.

"Oh no," I mutter.

"Put it away. It doesn't matter. They think you have it and that's all that matters. Let's get you home," Taylor states.

"What about them?" I ask about Crane and his security team. Detective Howard comes out and steps up to us.

"Are you going to arrest them?" I ask.

"They aren't pressing charges. That was the best I could do." Detective Howard explains.

"Pressing charges? Pressing charges!" I am beside myself. "For what, trying to kill us?"

"They said you jumped a security officer, spraying mace in his face, and basically kicked his ass. And you didn't follow after hours protocol on entry. Is that true?"

I look down and shake my head, annoyed. "Sort of," I respond like a teenager caught with no way out.

"Well, they're not going to press charges being that you work here and whatever is going on with you two. I have no idea what's happening, but I can tell you need to stay away. Don't tempt these people," he warns me again.

"What about the guns they fired? They tried to shoot us."

"Tried? I got hit!" Taylor proclaims. He pulls his shirt to the side and has the bruise to prove it.

"Rubber bullets," Detective Howard explains. So, it's a push apparently. They can't get arrested and they won't get on my case for kicking their guard's butt. "Nice job on the guard, though," he adds jokingly.

"Thanks." I let out a smirk at the compliment.

"Come on, Nick. Let's get you home." Taylor ushers me away.

I drive home with Taylor following behind. We get there and find both Ronald and Angie on the couches fast asleep. I throw blankets on the two of them and let them sleep.

Taylor and I move to the kitchen and sit on the barstools at the island counter and stare at one another. We are at an impasse, a point of decision-making. We know how the other feels, but there are too many unanswered questions. And how can I trust someone who clearly didn't have good intentions going in? It's time for answers and I want all of them.

"I need to ask you questions. If you can't or won't answer them, I can't do this. We can't be anything to each other. I'll never be able to trust you." I begin.

"I owe you many explanations. *Many.* I'm sorry. I wasn't supposed to fall in love with you, but I have."

"What do you mean, *wasn't supposed to?*"

"There's a lot you don't know. There's a lot happening you don't understand." Taylor is too cryptic for my liking again.

"So, tell me." I come right at him, wanting answers—demanding them.

"I will tell you that a powerful man wanted to make the Ramsey Case go away. He tried to use me for that. He used his power to manipulate Rapture and Myers. And as long as that man thought he had things under control, I could help the people of Ramsey the best I could. Beyond that, I can't tell you much more. You have to trust in me that I did what was right, that my intentions are not evil." Taylor puts it to me. But why should I? If we are to start a relationship beyond what we have, honesty should be first and foremost at the forefront. And right now, I don't feel as though he is telling me enough and I know, for a fact, he isn't telling me everything. That, in itself, bothers me.

"It's not enough," I tell him.

"It has to be. For now…it has to be…" he trails off.

"I want more," I quietly demand.

"I know. And I'll be able to tell you more, just not yet. It's to protect you. I have to make sure this all ends. And right now, I'm going to have to go. There may be people looking for me." He stands up. I've never seen this look on his face. He is facing a mountain of trouble that I cannot begin to comprehend. I wish I knew more about what was going on with him. But for now, I am going to let him leave until I gain the knowledge I need. No more diving head first into a pool blindly. I want to know where I am heading. I can control that and, after feeling out of control for so long, I value that feeling so much more.

Taylor walks up to me and leans in, kissing me on the cheek. His lips are so soft and so perfect. The kiss is gentle and long. I close my eyes, savoring it. I've never loved so passionately in my life and now I have to let him go. I must have faith that I'm doing the right thing for myself and my children. I will not trust him without him giving me full disclosure. For now, it's a kiss I will hang on to. "I will always love you," he whispers into my ear.

Tears flow down the sides of my face and as he walks out of my kitchen, and possibly, my life. I can't move. I am frozen as I stand just thinking about the possibility of never seeing this heroic, beautiful stranger, that so recently came into my life, again. I don't know what to say or do. And with the soft closing of the front door, he is gone. My heart immediately aches and I wipe the tears from my eyes.

"That must have been hard," Angie comments empathetically.

I sniffle and wipe my eyes clean. "Yeah. A little bit." I agree in no uncertain terms. She comes and sits down beside me at the island. "Did you get what you needed?" she asks.

"Oh, my God. I forgot to check."

Angie and I head into my office and I grab my laptop bag. With my desktop terminal gone, my laptop is all I have left. I insert the flash drive carefully, the damaged piece of equipment needing some maneuvering to even connect but finally get it in. I wait for it to load and click on the flash drive to access it. A message pops up: *External Drive Damaged.*

"Fuck me," I mutter in anger and frustration.

"What is it?" Angie asks.

"The damn thing won't work. I did all this and the damn thing is broken now!" I pace and plop myself down on a chair.

"I'm sure a tech wizard can go in there and extract the information somehow."

"Maybe. Maybe not." I let out a breath filled with annoyance. "It's all right. Let's just go to sleep. You guys have done enough for today. Go home."

"We'll stay over, Nick." Angie's offer is so sweet, but I feel terrible.

"Go get some sleep. I don't want you two to have to—"

Angie places her hands on my shoulders, stopping me. "We're a team, girl. The three of us, we are a team. And we're going to stay by your side. Besides, Ronald promised he'd make the girls chocolate chip pancakes when they were in the hospital, so he's excited. We're staying. Even with that cop car sitting out front."

"Detective Howard. He sent one."

"Okay?" Angie is a sweetheart—a true friend. We hug one another and I start to sob hysterically. I can't stop crying. She squeezes me tighter.

"I'm so tired," the words barely leak out through my tears.

"It's okay. You've been strong for a long time. Let it out." Angie just holds me as a lot of pent up emotion sheds off of me in one beautiful release.

———————

I wake up to the smell of amazing cooking and a lot of giggling. I head downstairs and see the girls, Angie, and Ronald, eating pancakes.

"There's the sleepyhead!" Ronald shouts. He is wearing a *Kiss the Cook* apron he brought from home and a puffy white hat.

"What is that from?" I ask, completely amused.

"I bring out the *uni* when it's game time, honey! And right now, I'm making Ronny's award-winning flapjacks!" Ronald proudly boasts.

"Mom. These are sooo good!" Lacy says with a mouth full of pancake.

"Yeah, Mom. You gotta have some!" Ariel concurs.

There are cheesy eggs and chocolate chip pancakes *for days*. I've definitely worked up an appetite and have no problem digging in. "I'm definitely eating some of these! Bring it on!" The hell with eating healthy this morning. I'm going *ham* on this awesome looking breakfast.

Breakfast is amazing and we all enjoy it together.

It's Saturday and I drop the girls off at Helen's. Aiden is home and I know he would love to see the girls. I have a great task in figuring out how to get this flash drive to work. Ronald, Angie, I, and our makeshift mobile law firm, make our way toward a tech wizard Angie knows. But, before I even drive a mile away from Helen's, I get a call. Private Investigator Phil is calling me. He tells me we have to meet immediately.

"We have to meet with Phil," I let Ronald and Angie know.

"My boy has something?" Ronald asks with excitement.

"Maybe." I'm hopeful but don't want to get my hopes too far up. This journey has been long, with many twists and turns. Everything has come to a head now as court proceedings have gotten closer. I want there to be more information. I want this all to end.

We head over to a park in Sherman Oaks, in the heart of the San Fernando Valley. It's on the way to Angie's friend, who lives in Studio City. Both spots are within a few miles of one another, so this all works out. We get to the park look around, not knowing where Phil is.

"Where is he?" Angie asks.

"I can't see anything," Ronald says. We look around and only see an old man walking a small bull dog. We stand there with confused looks on our faces.

"Over here," he mumbles. Now it is clear. The old man isn't an old man. We curiously make our way over to him.

"Phil?" Ronald asks, unsure if that is him.

"Yeah. Keep it down."

"I love when you wear disguises," Ronald excitedly whispers.

"Over by the bench; just Nicki. You two walk around like a couple." Phil lays out the game plan for us.

I walk over to the bench and hear Ronald mumble to Angie, "I love being part of undercover operations!"

Ronald and Angie walk arm-in-arm around the park. Phil sits down on the bench holding the leash to the bull dog. Upon sitting down, the lazy, fat bull dog happily does the same.

"Damn dog loves to sleep." Phil shakes his head.

"You have something?" I ask.

"I have a lot," Phil confirms, getting me excited about the prospect of what he is about to tell me. I take a deep breath, readying myself for what he may say. Is there bad news about Taylor? Does he have the information on who R.D. is? Will Phil put everything together for me? "First off, I told you Taylor Diamond was head of some shell corporation called The McGregor Group." Phil pulls out a file and hands it to me. His research is inside the file. Numerous documents are inside.

"Okay," I look through the papers and the pieces of the puzzle I've been trying to put together are now at my fingertips.

"This is where things get weird. You met with his mother in South Dakota—Martha Scott."

"Yes."

"Did you happen to see his younger sister there?" Phil's question throws me for a little bit of loop.

"A sister?" I ask in shock.

"In South Dakota, a woman by the name of Mary Scott Williams resides. Mary is the daughter of Martha Scott. But her father is unknown—at least there's no birth record or document that confirms such a child's existence." Phil's information sends me for a loop. That certainly helps explain why Martha lives in South Dakota. But if Mary is Taylor's younger sister, then who is the father? What is that family secret? Did the mother cheat on his mercurial father at some point? "What's also interesting is that Taylor flies out there almost twice a month, according to flight manifest records.

Mary also has a husband, Dennis Williams, and a son, Julius Taylor Williams." I nod, digesting all the information. Taylor visits his mother and sister all the time. But how could his mother say such bad things about him? It doesn't make sense. Why would she ever believe he was evil?

"There's more," Phil alerts me. I know there's a big kicker coming.

"Go ahead."

"R.D., the man whose name is at the bottom of that document you had." Phil begins, drawing my attention right in. I want to know exactly who that is. I want that man's head on a silver platter. As I lean in closer, my eyes glaze open with intensity. "Those initials stand for one Randolph Diamond. Randolph sits silently as the single largest shareholder of a company named Dynico Corp. Dynico technically owns the McGregor Group. Dynico also owns a large share interest in Beltan Food Corp. And by large, I mean they own nearly the whole damn thing. However, Randolph isn't listed as President of Dynico. He is listed as Private Consultant. That's why it's been difficult to figure out who he is. And as far as R.D. goes, that's who I believe it stands for. It's Taylor's uncle."

"But you're not certain?" I ask, playing devil's advocate.

"Certainties can be a difficult thing, Ms. Connolly. But, I can tell you that, although I'm not a hundred percent sure, I can say that I'm pretty certain this is the man you are looking for. And on the paper, just below your fingers, is his home address. He lives in Laguna Nigel, just a couple hours away."

I let out a deep breath. "His uncle? No shit?" I am faced with too many truths I'm frightened to deal with.

"That's it. A secret sister, a mother with Alzheimer's in an upscale care home and an uncle pulling all the strings. Do you know that Dynico and some of its business partners just recently changed law firms? Guess who they changed to?" Phil poses to me as the ultimate kicker to this secret saga.

I know the answer before I say the words. "Rapture and Myers," leaks out of my lips. It's a reluctant guess, but one I know is right.

"Exactly. Looks like someone struck a backroom deal, but why?" Phil puts it to me.

And I know why. I know what *may* be happening. Everything is about control—control of information. Everything is about money—stock prices. They want a settlement. *Everyone* wants a quiet settlement. Taylor was placed by his uncle to deliver that. When he started to fail, Crane applied additional pressure by the direction of Randolph Diamond. The puzzle is becoming complete; the picture is clear. I am the patsy and Taylor was supposed to be the insurance policy that guaranteed the result. Charles Rapture and Bob Myers pushed hard for settlement because Randolph Diamond told them to. And in return, they gained powerful business allies and a multi-billion dollar roster of clients. Everything is happening because of money. And I was in the middle of it all. "I think I know why, Phil. It's all about sick people—sick, poor, innocent people in the desert. They want their silence. That's what this is about."

"Whatever it is, be careful, Ms. Connolly. These are very powerful people. They won't hesitate to stop at anything to get what they want. I've seen these kinds of people in action. Just. Be. Careful," Phil's warning is well-received.

What now?

Thirty Five

Phil walks away with his bull dog, inconspicuously moving through the park. Ronald and Angie walk over to me. "What's the next play?" Ronald asks me.

"We are going to need what's on this flash drive."

"I just talked to my friend, Goose. He can come by your house. He's in Oxnard, running late."

"Goose is his name?" I ask with concern and surprise.

"He's totally good with everything software related. If he can't do it, no one can."

"Okay. Goose it is," I agree.

"This is so exciting! I love adventures," Ronald cheers us on. We start the car and head back to my house. Upon arrival, I see a limousine in the driveway. My first thought is Taylor. Some butterflies start in my belly. "A limo?" Ronald questions with a smile.

"What's going on?" Angie asks.

"I'm not sure," I comment. We step out of the car and Michael Crane gets out of the passenger's side of the limo. The short, balding man, with his nose bandaged and blackened eyes, gets out of the driver's side. "Shit," I mumble to Ronald and Angie.

"Are those the bad guys?" Ronald asks with great concern.

"Yeah, those are the bad guys," I confirm. We all step out of my car. "See that car right there," I point to the squad car across the street. "They will shoot you both—trust me—they will," I threaten without hesitation.

"Nicki," Angie says, as if surprised I'd be so blunt and make such a threat.

"I don't think I like adventures anymore," Ronald nervously states.

Crane whistles at the short, bald man and nods his head to the side. The short, bald man approaches me. I nervously swallow and hold my head up high, attempting to present a brave front. He stops a few feet away from me, my hand reaching in my purse for mace. "I'm sorry," the man grumbles out of his mouth. His battered face is a display I quiet enjoy. His humility is something unexpected. He has done his duty and turns with his tail between his legs, heading back to the limousine. He disappears into the driver's side.

"You think that makes it all better?" I direct at Crane.

"It's a peace offering. A negotiation, Ms. Connolly. Everything in this world is negotiable." Crane is a man who speaks with confidence and wisdom, but I don't like him very much at all. And, he is always a threat to me, peace offering or not.

"I thought you wanted me dead. I thought you were after us," I challenge Crane. Both Ronald and Angie are nervously looking on. "If we wanted you dead, you'd be dead, Ms. Connolly. Be that as it may, situations change. Circumstances change. All of you are invited to meet with R.D.," Crane speaks as if I don't know what those initials stand for.

"You mean Randolph Diamond, Taylor's uncle?" I showcase my knowledge.

Angie looks at me in shock. I hadn't shared all of Phil's information with Ronald and Angie yet. So her expression of shock is expected. "His uncle?" she says with surprise.

"Well, it appears you've almost caught up, Ms. Connolly." Crane's sarcasm doesn't go unnoticed, but he is right. I have *almost* caught up.

"Why should we come with you?" I challenge Crane.

"Because Randolph Diamond doesn't meet with people just to *shoot the shit,* pardon the expression. He will answer your questions. Mr. Penn has headed down there and is awaiting you with a notary. They have an offer they feel you can't refuse. They will meet your terms, Ms. Connolly. All it will take is a drive. Just a drive to get what you want."

"I'm bringing my team," I demand. I want to bring Angie and Ronald along.

"We have a member in the car already," Crane replies.

"Team. Is that me?" Ronald nervously asks.

"Deal. Just one thing. Bring the flash drive with you. And any copies of the documents you have."

"*Deal.*" I smile with a deadpan glare, using Crane's exact wording. Crane nods. He steps to the back of the limousine and opens up the door, waiting for us. "Well, what are we waiting for?" I walk forward into the unknown, gladly going into the limousine. Ronald and Angie are more hesitant, but they follow along. We get into the limo and I see a strange young man.

"Hey! What's up?" The excited boy says.

I sit down adjacent to him and when Angie enters she calls to him. "Goose? What are you doing in here?"

"Ang! What's up?" Goose excitedly states.

"This is Goose? He looks like he's twelve." I point out Goose's youthful baby face and frail body. He is dressed in a hoodie and sweat pants along with flip flops and white socks—a big fashion no no. The young Silicon Valley-wannabe is full of youthful spirit.

"I'm nineteen, thank you very much," he proudly boasts. I shake my head and the door is closed after Ronald gets inside. Goose, Angie, and Ronald look around, seemingly unsure of what to do. This isn't my first rodeo in a limo anymore.

"Just relax and enjoy the journey kids. Bust open the mini fridge. This ride is on them." I sit back and enjoy the ride, now preparing my mind for a verbal confrontation with a powerful man and a powerful attorney. I should alert Taylor—send him a message. But this is his uncle, so I don't trust the situation. I don't understand the situation. So, I will go into the lion's den with my eyes wide open and alone. I will have three others by my side, but it is going to come down to me and Randolph Diamond—I know it.

We arrive in Laguna Nigel. We are taken to a country club, Seaside Cliffs. The exclusive club looks gorgeous as does the view by the ocean. It rests atop a large cliff looking down upon the Pacific. It is a priceless view. Homes, in the area, range anywhere from five million, on the cheap side, to upwards of fifteen to twenty million. This is truly an exclusive neighborhood of the rich.

We are escorted into a dining room. It is cleared. Only Randolph Diamond and Albert Penn are seated at a table, eating lunch. We are escorted in by Mr. Crane. I don't even believe Crane is his real name.

Upon hearing us, Randolph looks up. He is dressed in an expensive suit with a silk handkerchief hanging out of the pocket. I can see his shoes shining all the way from where we stand. "Ms. Connolly and others, welcome," Randolph greets us and rises to his feet. He is a pompous man full of hubris. I can feel that right away.

"Randolph Diamond," I say with a certain amount of bitterness.

"In the flesh."

"Are we eating lunch?" I ask.

"If you would like."

"I want answers." I am direct.

"Yes. I'm sure you do. Let's have everyone clear the room." Randolph wants this to be a private conversation. Crane holds his arm out for everyone to go to an adjacent room. "There's a buffet next door. Feel free to enjoy whatever you like, on me," Randolph, graciously, offers.

"Nice! I love buffets!" Goose excitedly shouts.

"I'm getting nice champagne. That's all I know," Ronald mumbles. Angie pats me on the shoulder and follows everyone out of the room.

Randolph doesn't look back, but tilts his head just to the side. "You too, Albert."

Albert Penn looks annoyed but won't say boo to Randolph Diamond. It's clear Randolph is a powerful man, who wields a big stick. He doesn't even look at Penn as the big time attorney gets up and steps out of the room.

"So it's just you and me," I say to Randolph, wanting him to know I am ready for any challenge he poses.

"Please, have a seat, Ms. Connolly."

Randolph moves back to his table and sits down. I take a chair across from him and have a seat. I look to my right and the view through all the glass windows is an amazing ocean scene. People dream of this view. It's a peaceful scene of beauty and grace. The power of the ocean's crashing waves upon the sandy beaches of Laguna brings a bout of a mixed bag of emotions for me. I'm reminded of Taylor and his beach house. But, I'm not there. I'm very far away from Taylor and those moments. Now, it is the showdown; Randolph Diamond and me—mono-a-mono.

"Is this all about money? Is that all this is about?" I ask of Randolph.

"Speak not of my debts, Ms. Connolly, unless you mean to pay them." Randolph smugly jokes.

"I made it here. I went all the way," I proudly proclaim to Randolph.

"I didn't think you would, Ms. Connolly. You've got guile, I'll give you that."

"I've always lived my life cautiously. I've always been the safe one. But I learned the brave may not live forever, but the cautious never really live at all." I give life lessons to a man who has lived far more than I have. But I am on his level. I will not be subjected to being below Randolph Diamond and all his power.

"I must say—you are classy, attractive, and full of piss and vinegar. Darling, you are the unencumbered vision of elegance and beauty. I can see what Taylor saw in you. You are the perfect bait for him. It's too bad we didn't have a different play in mind."

"So you admit he was paired with me as bait?" I wag a metaphorical finger at him

"Let's not mince words, counselor. Let's not be simple people. We are both educated. Let's bring our big boy pants to the table." Randolph has a way of speaking. His deep voice bellows out, an excellent speaker. He drives his words home with flare and the utmost confidence. He fears nothing and knows everything. He is a tough opponent to joust with. But I'm game. I have nothing to lose in this meeting.

"If we are so *above* it all, why the goons? Why the murders?"

"We live in a violent paradise, dear. Now, we can dance around the elephant in the room for days. But more words do not feed the friars. And Ramsey is very hungry. Are you ready for this game of chess we are playing here? Are you ready to risk your king to win?" Randolph again attacks as if he is in a position of strength. It's time to bring it back at him.

"You think you are in control?" I ask the powerful man.

"I know I am old, Ms. Connolly. I know I do not have a lot of time left on this earth and I choose to spend my days in enjoyment. The truth can be a terrible habit, but I'm tired now and willing to open up this discussion and close this case for good."

"Never complain about getting old, Mr. Diamond. So many people never get that chance." I fire back.

The wealthy, old man laughs and takes a drink of what looks like scotch on the rocks. He takes his time, savoring the alcohol. "Do you consider Taylor a friend, Ms. Connolly?" he steers his question away from business and I have no idea where he is going. It is a verbal sparring session that sees no end. But I have time. I made the trip. I plan to put this all to an end today—now.

"Why do you ask? Do you care? It seems you are using Taylor as an instrument for evil more than caring for him as a nephew." I throw a blind dart at the board. I have no idea if what I said is true, but I'm looking for information—insight into Taylor and Randolph Diamond's world.

"I don't see him here. I expected him to come. I expected him to be sitting by your side. Your hero. Your savior." Randolph seems bitter in his description of my relationship with Taylor.

"He doesn't know I'm here." I enlighten the old man.

"Doesn't know? Hmm. I doubt that. This was inevitable in this game. It was always going to come down to us. I remember a man, a very smart man, once told me that a friend is someone who dances with you in the daylight, and walks with you in the shadows. The shadow is cast wide upon you now, Ms. Connolly. Where is Taylor?"

"I don't know," I honestly reply.

"You don't know?" Randolph asks as if he doesn't know either and has been looking for him.

"No."

"It's a gift of his," Randolph starts.

"What's that?" I ask with curiosity.

"Disappearing. It's a special gift he has. When you need Taylor Diamond most, he has a way of vanishing. Poof. Just like that and he's gone. The young playboy—the *boy king,*" Randolph's words flare with sarcasm and pent up anger.

"With all due respect, Mr. Diamond, he didn't get sick in Ramsey, California. Taylor didn't live in the hot desert sun, poor, desolate and slowly being poisoned by a greedy corporation. He isn't sick, Mr. Diamond. Let's talk about the people who *are* sick." I put it to him.

He smirks at me. He stares with cockiness and confidence, but his glare is a defense mechanism. He is projecting strength while, at the same time, knowing he is wounded. "You're sacred. I can see you're scared, dear. Do you have the courage to go all the way with this? Do you think you can finish it all?"

"Mr. Diamond, there can be no courage without fear. And you, Randolph Diamond, are full of fear. That much, *I* know."

"Scared? Of you?" he attempts to scoff and play surprised. But I have him right where I want him and decide to go in for the kill.

"What's your offer?" I ask for the goods. No more playing around.

"Two hundred fifty million," he offers.

"Four hundred," I fire back without hesitation.

"Four hundred million? Have you gone mad, child?" he asks.

"Four hundred, not a penny less." I stick to my guns.

"You can't get that much in court. Not even close. Not with your evidence. I'll give you three hundred and consider it a gift."

I lean forward, staring directly at Randolph's eyes, making sure he feels my glare, feels my serious stare. "The evidence I have would bring the world down upon you, Mr. Diamond. It will break you." I am a fireball of intensity.

Randolph takes out a box of cigars. "I got these from Fidel Castro a long time ago. They are authentic Cuban cigars. The Cubans make a fine cigar, Ms. Connolly. You want to try one of these?"

"I'll take one." I am agreeable to light a victory cigar as I sense my teeth sinking into Randolph's neck and finishing off the class action lawsuit for good.

Randolph hands me a cigar and strikes a match on the table. I confidently lean forward with the same glare he displayed to me and allow him to light my cigar. I hold it like a confident man would, my cock in my hand, blowing smoke up into the air, like I owned the air around me. "I can see why Taylor likes you." Randolph points his cigar-holding-hand at me.

"You said that," I remind Randolph with cool arrogance.

"I thought it was important enough to say twice."

We both blow smoke into the air. "Four hundred million. The entire case is turfed. Sealed with non-disclosures attached. Anyone speaks a word, and we'll sue for all four hundred million and any broken down pick-up trucks and tumbleweeds they have." Randolph is brought to his knees, but he doesn't go quietly. He still carries his verbal pistol of threats, making sure I fully understand he is still powerful and still very dangerous.

"You killed two men to get here. How does that feel?"

"Dr. Schecter died of a heart attack. I know you read the papers. And I don't know who that second man was. He never existed." Randolph plays dumb.

"Taylor does. And I don't believe for a second Dr. Schecter had a heart attack on his own."

"Do you want your four hundred million or are we going to court?" Randolph challenges in the only way he knows how.

"Bring in Penn and the notary. I'm ready to sign this deal on my client's behalf." I make a bold move to close the Ramsey Case. They *could* be angry. Some may hold their reservations on principle, but with lifetime health coverage and every person receiving a healthy seven figure sum, it's hard to argue with this deal. It's hard to make a case against settling for this much.

Randolph picks up his cell phone and makes a call. "Come on in." He hangs up. Everyone files back into the room. They all look around, as if wondering what the two cigar-smoking people have been discussing. "We're going to sign a deal, Albert. Right here, right now," Randolph makes his declaration.

"You don't want to discuss anything in private first?" Albert Penn is a passenger on this ride, a position he has not often been in.

"Four hundred million, signed and sealed," Randolph blows smoke into the air as if he just signed a check for twenty dollars. The amount of money means nothing to him.

"Four hundred?" Penn's mouth hangs open.

I look to Angie and Ronald who both have smiles on their faces, excited we landed such a big deal. "And health insurance—lifetime," Angie chimes in.

"That's right," I point out. Randolph looks annoyed. "Albert and I had that one in writing," I point out.

"All right." Randolph extends his open hand. "I'll just need one thing before we put this in writing."

I reach into my pocket and pull out the flash drive. "All this fuss over this little thing," I comment.

"If this isn't the only copy or we see private corporate information leaked, we'll sue everyone," Albert Penn chimes in.

"I'm quite certain of it." I smile at Albert Penn and blow of thick cloud of smoke in his general direction that quickly encompasses his face. *My victory dance.* Randolph's hand remains extended, waiting for me to place the flash drive in it. I reach forward and place my palm atop his and enclose my hand upon his own. I look him dead in the eye, "Checkmate."

Randolph subtly nods, showing a great deal of respect for me. I release my grip on his hand and the flash drive, sitting back in my chair. It's over as Albert Penn draws up the draft of the agreed upon terms for us to sign, prior to creating a greater agreement for the court. The deal, in principle, will stick.

"It's damaged, ya know?" I mock Randolph Diamond. He peers over at me with a smirk. "The flash drive; it's damaged. I don't even know if it will work," I say. Angie and Ronald look shocked that I'm disclosing this information to Randolph.

"What flash drive, dear?" He blows smoke into the air. And that is that. The mere fact it exists is more damaging than what potentially is on it. Taylor was right. The game is over. We won. Now I have to share the spoils of war with Ramsey. I'm certain the town will rejoice even if my cousin, Rebecca, is a little disappointed. They are all set for life and hopefully, with the right health care, they can all live a long time.

Thirty Six

It takes a few days, but I get the full agreement in writing. And, within a week's time, I'm heading out to Ramsey. I enjoyed my week off of work. I didn't do a thing, except hang with my girls and catch up on Veronica Palsey. It's a funny thing . . . having time—time to think, time to enjoy yourself. Sitting outside on a cool day with a nice breeze, staring up at puffy clouds, and drinking hot chocolate, there's nothing quite like it. I felt free— unchained. My rat race came to a complete halt and the mountain of stress, I had been under, dissipated almost completely.

With the girls well on their way to recovery and Aiden improving, everything is coming together. Aiden and I still have a lot to talk about, but at least we know where each other stands. Life is moving forward—finally.

I drive out to Ramsey alone. I wanted to speak with Rebecca first, just the two of us. I arrive and we greet each other with hugs and kisses as always. And then, we sit. I tell her what she needs to know. I don't include the murder mystery plots or the struggle to get to this point. I simply keep to the facts that are vital to her case—vital to the settlement.

"No court?" Rebecca's first words.

"No court," I confirm.

"And nobody will know?" She is grappling with the facts. I knew she would. She wants a public hanging. She wants to drag a body in the streets. She wants revenge.

"Ramsey will know. And that's all that matters, Beck."

"The world won't know. The news won't know," she continues.

"No, honey, they won't know. But you will and all the families. You are all going to have a lot of money to live wherever you want. You're going to have health care for your entire lives—great health care. It's the best deal you can get—in or out of court."

"I want them to pay, Nick."

"I know you do. And they are. Listen, this may not help and it may not mean much, but Beltan didn't know they were poisoning people. They did it. They cut corners. They are responsible. But they didn't pull the trigger knowingly. They broke rules and they are going to pay for it. In court, we should win. *Should,* but not definite. And the amount of money won't be anywhere near this amount of money. And the time it will take, through appeals, will cost all of you dearly. You would sacrifice everyone's health, your health, Casey's health, over revenge?" I put it plainly to my cousin. There is no way around it. She must accept the deal.

"You're right."

"This started with you and the people here look up to you. You have to help me convince them this is the best and only deal they should accept." I add Rebecca to my team and we are nearly at the goal line. Once the documents I carry with me are signed, it's over. It's all over. And Rebecca and I meet each and every person in Ramsey personally to see if they will sign.

———

I stroll into Rapture and Myers with a big smile on my face. My self-confidence is beaming. I cannot help but take a victory lap through the halls and enjoy my moment in the sun. I go straight to the conference room, where a partners meeting is already in progress. Lincoln Thomas, James Bonner, Bob Myers, and of course, Charles Rapture, all sit. I had gotten an email and a phone message about the meeting. It was mandatory. I am showing up late without a care in the world. Conference room B again—one last time.

"So nice of you to join us, Ms. Connolly," Charles angrily grumbles. "Where the hell have you been?"

"It's funny; this room. This glass encased room. Why glass? Why transparent glass? We can't hear what's happening in here? Is it the esthetic? Why do so many people like these kinds of rooms?" I hypothesize for no reason as I wander around the room.

"I sure as hell hope you have something on the Ramsey Case?" Bob demands. Bob's tone is demeaning and if I gave a shit, I'd care about being spoken down to.

"Oh, Bob, I think you boys are barking up the wrong tree here. I have a few demands to make that need your approval."

"Demands? Is she kidding?" James Bonner crows.

I toss the Ramsey Case signatures all around the table like I'm tossing hundred dollar chips in at Bally's Casino. It's a confident *I don't give a fuck* flip. And all the men stop, looking over the signed documents, their mouths hanging in shock. I see Lincoln's eyes flash up at me with a big smile on his face. He has his reading glasses on as he looks the documents over and gives me a proud nod. I smile momentarily and then go back into my *bitch* mode. I need to be a bully for effect. It is my moment in the sun. And I'm going to fuck with them all I can.

"Four hundred million!" Charles and Bob erupt in excitement.

"So, I'm glad you let me into your boy's club for a little while, but consider this my resignation."

"Resignation? Why?" Charles plays confused.

"And here are some of my invoices for the case. As well as a severance package I've personally signed off on for myself, Angie, and Ronald." I make my demands continuing to own the room.

"Severance? What are you talking about?" James again cries over spending money on others.

"Non-negotiable," I declare. "And here are my invoices. I want them paid in full to me and my private investigator no later than next week." I toss more papers on the desk.

"This is absurd!" Charles joins in with James in the crowing session.

"No. it's not. What's absurd are the backchannel deals you constructed to interfere with my case. You jeopardized everything I had worked for and didn't have nearly enough faith in me. On top of that, I think many of you are just plain assholes and I don't want to deal with your smug, egotistical asses any more. I sat and broke bread with Randolph Diamond. We smoked some Cubans and found some equal footing."

James Bonner erupts in anger at the table, not much liking the taste of a woman talking down to him for once.

"This is ludicrous! Call Crane and have her thrown—"

"Enough, James." Charles holds up his hand. The mere name dropping of Randolph Diamond put the conversation on another level. Now that the jig is up, it's time to deal. A wily veteran, like Charles Rapture and Bob Myers, knows that. They know when it's time to fold and move on.

"Lincoln, James, can you both step out of the room?" Bob asks. Lincoln smiles and gets up, giving me a wink as he exits the conference room.

"Please, sit down, Nicki," Charles offers. The conversation has entered a new level. Charles and Bob want only the three of us to know what truly has been going on. "So, you know a lot. You are a smart woman, Nicki. A very smart woman." Charles says after Lincoln leaves the room.

"We always supported you," Bob starts.

I smile and shake my head. "Listen, it's a hell of a thing, ya know. All of it. I did my job—not for you, for my clients. I did my job and landed you a lot of money. Now, you're going to pay me what I'm asking for. You're going to pay Angie and Ronald for trying to severe them from me as innocent casualties. So many innocent casualties. It's just money, gentlemen. You're both old and already have so much. So, what is it?"

"You think this is about money, Nicki? We know you're smarter than that," Charles balks at my insinuations.

"Then what? Tell me." I ask.

"You wouldn't understand. You're too young," Charles placates me.

"Try me," I dare him.

"Infamy!" Bob barks out. "The name Rapture and Myers will continue on forever, long beyond our days. That means something to us. Infamy is forever, dear."

I smirk and nod. Once again, the hubris of men. I shake my head and rise from the table. "Your brilliant lies have got you nowhere. But I do agree on one thing, you are infamous. I will never forget you both." I turn to walk away.

"What if we don't agree?" Charles asks.

I stop at the door and turn back. "Oh, don't do that, Charles. Don't tempt me. The truth is a terrible habit. A terrible, terrible habit. I'll allow you to have your legacy. But you will sign those papers and send out those severance packages by next Monday. If you don't follow through, I will bring these walls down upon your heads. Your legacy will be covered in the ash from the blaze of righteousness I reign down upon you. Are we clear?" I bring out my *boom* stick as a parting shot.

"My girl, you are everything we hoped you would be. It's truly a pleasure to *finally* meet you, Nicki Connolly. And yes, you will have the paperwork in hand by the beginning of next week. Well done, child," Charles compliments me as if he enjoyed me barking at him.

"Good luck, Nicki. I'm sure you will do well for yourself," Bob also wishes me well.

I guess whipping it out on the table and hurling your ego around like a wild animal is the way to garner respect from these old school souls. They have difficulty respecting much. They, themselves, are dinosaurs in a young man's world. They may not be women, but they are endangered nonetheless.

I pack my things up and leave Rapture and Myers with my head held high. Things were getting rough, but I closed the Ramsey Case and we settled for a heck of a lot of money. I made the firm wealthy and more importantly, landed nice payoffs for my two close friends.

———————

I enjoy my self-imposed sabbatical. Rapture and Myers do pay up on time. I check in with Rebecca and she and Casey already are receiving treatments to help with their lungs and the damage that affected their bodies over the last few years. Their prognosis is fair. There is no guarantee they will ever be one hundred percent. But with Casey's spirit, there is hope she will once again run and kick a soccer ball.

It's been over a week and I head to Taylor's beach house. We haven't spoken or said a word. No texts. Nothing. I pull up to the driveway and the gate is already opened. That isn't ordinary and I become concerned. I also don't see his car in the driveway, but I do see a Prius. I get out of my car and head to the front door. I ring the doorbell and a woman appears at the door. I haven't seen Taylor in nearly two weeks but I can't believe he moves *this* fast. The woman is pretty with auburn hair. She has blue eyes. Her skin is pale, definitely not someone that hangs around the beach.

"Um. Is Taylor here?" I am frightened to even ask.

"No. I'm sorry. He's not," she tells me. We just stare at one another for a moment.

"Okay. Thanks." The conversation is awkward and I quickly yield, giving up, turning to walk away.

"Are you Nicki?"

I stop and slowly turn around. "Yes. Who are you?" I ask.

"I'm Mary—Mary Scott Williams," she says.

Mary Scott Williams? That name...

"You recognize that name, don't you?" she asks me.

"Martha Scott. You're Taylor's sister," I guess.

"Why don't you come inside?"

I enter Taylor's beach house. It looks like just as I remember. In fact, the only thing missing is Taylor and Charlie.

"You know this place well," she surmises.

"I do," I don't bother to hide the fact. Mary can clearly see that, I'm sure.

"I saw your face when I answered the door. Did you think I was another one of his women? Perhaps he had moved on from you?" she asks.

"I did." I smile. We both have a chuckle. "And you live in South Dakota," I make the guess based on Detective Phil's information.

"Yes, near our mother. She has Alzheimer's, so Taylor put her in a place where he knew she would be safe. My husband and I live in the same town, so we see her quite often. But, you know where we live, don't you?" Mary knows I was there. No need to deny it.

"Yes. I was worried. There was a lot going on."

"The case. The class action lawsuit," Mary guesses. She guesses as if she knows.

"Yes. It's over now. Thank God. But there were so many issues. What do you know about it?" I ask her. Why not? She seems to know quite a bit.

"As you can tell, my brother and I don't have many secrets. You have two beautiful daughters and a man you are still married to. But that doesn't change the fact that my brother loves you and you love him. Am I close?"

"So far, so good. But, love is complicated," I say what I want to feel. I hurt not being with Taylor but he hurt me more by lying and deceiving me.

"My brother isn't that complicated. But there's something you have to understand. I am his half-sister. We have the same mother but his father is not my father. And Taylor's father was a terrible man. He was a cruel, mean man. He was relentless and it caused my mother a lot of pain. Taylor was always under his thumb, but fought to be the opposite. And it made his father furious. Now, his uncle Randolph controls everything. It was all left to Taylor to inherit when he was thirty-five; the age his father believed he needed to wait until to claim his place. Taylor never wanted that. However, there's a clause in the will. If Randolph and the board of directors, that manages the inheritance and Diamond interests, decide Taylor is unfit, then Randolph retains power and Taylor gets nothing."

"Then, why not walk away?" I ask as if it were so easy to disappear from all that they have.

"Because then Taylor, our mother, and myself would get nothing. Taylor is the best of all souls. He is a good man. He was crazy and wild at one point, but now he has grown into the kind of man his father would only have dreamt of—a much better version of the Diamonds before him. But he has to play ball with his uncle. He has to *appear* to be on their team—at least in theory. If Taylor is defiant and refuses to partake in the family business, he's cut off, and so are we. Taylor would never let that happen. He would never sacrifice us over his own pride. He'd rather eat his uncle's shit and take care of us. I've told him to walk away. We don't need all the money. We can go on without it and find our mother a less expensive home. But he refuses. He wants the best for all of us. And you must understand we've never known anything else. This is the world we've always been a part of."

"Who is your father?" I ask. I know I may be overstepping my bounds, but I ask anyway.

"I don't know. My mother had already started to lose herself. Only Taylor was around to see it."

"Why does she blame Taylor? She spoke so ill of him when I saw her."

Mary laughs and composes herself. "The most bitter irony of all. She looks at Taylor and sees *him*, the man who left her to rot in the desert alone. She doesn't see her son anymore. She sees her husband—if we can even call him that. Once in a while, she recognizes Taylor, but often he endures terrible words from her. Still, he comes. He sees us twice a month. And now, Nicki, he is gone. He hasn't visited. He hasn't called. It's been nearly a month. He's vanished. And it seems you were the last person he saw. Estella doesn't know. She took Charlie home with her for the time being. She's worried and called me. It's not like my brother to disappear. Maybe the old playboy would have, but not Taylor now. Not my big brother."

"I wish I knew where he was," I sadly respond. My concern grows but I don't know what to say. "Excuse me." I rush to the bathroom and have to throw-up. This news is terrible.

───────────

After parting with Mary, I head to the doctor for a check-up. I'm upset in so many ways. Taylor. Everything he did was for me. Everything he did was to protect me and protect his mother and sister. Everything he did was to protect everyone else but himself. And now I want him more than ever. I have completely misjudged everything. I had no idea he was so heroic in all this. He didn't try to use me. He was there to save me. And he did. He saved me from everything. And now he's gone and no one knows where he is. And the fact that I am not feeling a hundred percent healthy myself isn't helping things much either. I haven't felt well in a while. I feel good some days and other bad.

Doctor Schwartz, my primary physician, runs some basic bloodwork and tests. Before ordering a CT scan, he brings me into his office to talk.

"Is everything all right?" I ask, concerned. He looks over my chart and has a sneaky smile on his face. "What is it, Doctor Schwartz?" I ask. His smile is confusing to me. Doctor Schwartz often has a strange sense of humor.

"I looked over your charts from the hospital—from the accident. I reviewed the blood work. And I'm happy to tell you that I think your head is going to be all right."

"Good. Geez, you had me concerned."

"No concern. But it's time for celebration, Ms. Connolly."

"Celebration?" I ask, confused.

"You're pregnant," he says with a big smile. He slides over the bloodwork to prove it.

"What?" I shout in shock.

"It says it right there. We checked it twice."

"Check it three times! I have the implants," I declare.

"I told you those ran out last year. And you said Aiden was going to get fixed. Well, now you have another little one on the way. Congratulations, dear."

A nurse pops in. "Doctor Schwartz, Mrs. York has one more question."

"Okay. Yes. Ms. Connolly, I'll be right back." He pops up and exits the office.

I'm left in shock, unsure of what to say. And then the thought hits me straight on. *Who's baby is this? How long have I been pregnant for?*

BOOK 2
THE CONNOLLY AFFAIR
PROLOGUE

What is a man to do? You marry a woman, you love her, you vow to stand by her side—you grow tired and bored. You feel as though you are shrinking and being blanketed by darkness, by her dark shadow cast long above you. Do you seek counseling? Do you try couple's counseling for intimate issues only the two of you live through and are aware of? They are mediators, trained to mediate problems and challenge minds and hearts. But they are temporary fixes. They don't solve your problems. They create a mirage to make you think you've solved issues by talking about them. They attempt to highlight the greater demons in the closet—nothing more, nothing less.

I know Nicki loves me. She's been a good wife in the past. Up until recently, she was loyal. Up until recently, she was supportive. Up until recently, we were *in love.* But now I know it's faded away. We still care for one another, but we aren't in love like we were. I've felt stronger love in the past for another. Nicki doesn't know that. How could I explain that? It's complicated. And I was hurt badly— worse than I ever thought possible. I loved madly once before. But it wasn't with Nicki. And as things go bad between us—as the flame dies out, I feel compelled to look back to my past and compare the raging inferno, which still burns deep inside me, against the withering flame that is my marriage. As my marriage dies in a cool, soft breeze the raging inferno isn't far away from my memory. I can still feel the heat and long for that kind of flame again. I am not brilliant, but I'm not stupid. And I know when things aren't working. I know when I'm being betrayed.

What is a man to think when his wife seems to stray? Do you follow her new lover? Do you seek him out and follow him to his Malibu Beach house? Do you not let on to your wife so you can carry out a devious plan—a plan no one would suspect of you? Do you wait outside his rich, beachfront home and watch as she goes inside his house. Do you imagine what is happening inside—your wife doing unspeakable things with an intruder—a man performing thievery on your marriage. There is pride to think of. There is pain to consider. There is anger that brews and evil thoughts that once seemed only plausible for criminals and maniacs are introduced to your mind. What is a kind man to do, when driven to madness?

Now, I am no saint. I am no innocent, and my eyes are wide open. I know where I stand and who I am. But she strayed. She sinned with a stranger. And I know that man's face. I know that man's scent. So I have options.

I am an excellent construction worker. Owning my own company, I have the ability to bury things people would never find. Take for instance a work site in which we are laying cement. It is not easy, but with a few construction cones and wet cement, a body can be laid to rest in the cement and can be buried forever without a trace. Hardened cement is something that would be difficult to unearth, and no one would suspect a body would be buried there. It is the perfect way to *bury* my problems.

What about in the desert? A hunter friend of mine once taught me something about burying animals. I can dig a five foot hole and toss the body inside—his dead body. Then I can put some dirt on top of him. Next, a bag of lemons. The lemons will help with the scent and if a dog comes looking for a body, they will never find it. Toss some dirt on the lemons. Then, a dead deer. Toss the deer atop the lemons and your three-tier burial is complete. Cover with dirt and you are in the clear. The deer is insurance just in case a good bloodhound discovers the body. But after the deer is found, they'll move on.

There are so many ways. There is so much anger. I can go many different directions. The first step is following him—taking him. I don't know what I'm going to do, but I'm going to do something. Something *must* be done.

Brett Scott Ermilio

Award winning writer Brett Scott Ermilio currently resides on the Jersey Shore with his eight colorful roommates: his loving wife, four beautifully chaotic children, two small yapping dogs and one moody fish.

www.ingramcontent.com/pod-product-compliance
Lightning Source LLC
Chambersburg PA
CBHW061306170626
46817CB00001B/70